VESPERS

Historical Mysteries Collection

Barbara Gaskell Denvil

Copyright © **2021** by Barbara Gaskell Denvil
All Rights Reserved, no part of this book may be
Reproduced without prior permission of the author
except in the case of brief quotations and reviews

Cover design by
It' A Wrap

Also by Barbara Gaskell Denvil

<u>Historical Mysteries Collection</u>

Blessop's Wife

The Summer of Discontent

Vespers

The Flame Eater

Satin Cinnabar

Sumerford's Autumn

The Western Gate

The Deception of Consequences

<u>Cornucopia</u>

(*An Historical Fantasy series*)

The Corn

The Mill

The Dunes

<u>Stars And A Wind Trilogy</u>

A White Horizon

The Wind From The North

The Singing Star

The Omnibus Edition

<u>Mysteries of another sort</u>

Between

<u>The Games People Play</u>
(*A serial Killer Trilogy*)
If When
Ashes From Ashes
Daisy Chains

<u>Time Travel Mysteries</u>
Future Tense
<u>The Barometer Sequence</u>
Fair Weather
Dark Weather

Notes from the author

Just a few words to anyone reading this book.

The background to the plot, the events of England in 1485, are correct within the boundaries of known and accepted history. The same events have been interpreted differently by other authors, but since there is no poof in either direction, I have kept with my own judgement, all of which is entirely possible, probable and logical.

I have used modern language throughout, including words unknown in that period, and a manner of speech which most people of that time would not even have understood. I consider this also logical. Their own fashions of language at that time would be barely understandable to us now, and I have no wish to drive my readers crazy with medieval wordage.

Therefore, I hope you will forgive any colloquial conversations which may seem out of context. I assure you, you could hardly enjoy any accurate medieval manner of speaking, unless you are an academic historian.

Another issue may be in English and American spelling. We share the same language more or less but have chosen to spell so many words differently. I am English and this novel is set in the English medieval period, so I have kept to the English spelling. I hope this doesn't cause any problems.

I simply hope you enjoy my book.

Chapter One

The smaller body lay flat within the little wooden boat, her face to the damp seat and her arms spread out over the gunwales. Yet the boat had obviously been caught in the current, since the slush in the bilges lapped around her bare feet.

Partially covered by a threadbare blanket, only a long curl of her hair lay over her back, wet, and grimed with the river's pollution. A faint trace of dawn's pastel pink spangled both hair and hood.

The wherry boat bumped gently against the bank, the slap and splash almost silent where it was tethered as the water followed its course downstream. The sun's first rays slid across the river's water and the waving tips of protruding green weed.

The other body was much larger and lay flat on its back under the willow tree. Where the shimmer of leaf blew in tiny wet twists across the grass below, a muscular and naked arm protruded. The unmoving fingers were clawed into blood-soaked threats.

As Rustin lifted the waving branches, he jerked back. The rest of the body lay in blood, the throat ripped.

He yelled at once, then clamped his mouth shut and raced into the great house, ready with the dreadful news for his master. The bodies were very different and neither together nor close, but Rustin had never seen one dead body before, two on the same morning seemed to be a step too far.

His lordship leaned back, legs stretched, half dozing as he broke the night's fast.

Then the candle blew out.

Dark shadows swallowed the table, the perfumes of new baked bread, fresh cut ham and sliced onion, mellowed into the darkness. The morning's light had not yet discovered the windows.

"Damnation," sighed the man, mug of ale halfway to his mouth. "What do you want now, Rustin?"

"My lord, I'm sorry." The older man carried the smoking candle to the small fire on the hearth, and relit it, cradling his hand to keep out the draughts. "But there's two bodies, my lord. I don't know how that's possible?"

"There are two what?" demanded his lordship, cold eyed.

"Dead, my lord. Proper dead. There's one I don't know, that's in the water. That other is a worse shock, sir, it's Fillip Pike."

The pink dawn was mellowing into a warm morning, but the young boy who was following Rustin shivered.

"It's urgent. Will you come, my lord?" Now both grooms were trembling. "Two dead bodies, as if one wouldn't be bad enough. Right by the banks."

The river was not visible from the windows, but the early morning sunshine was reflected in his lordship's breakfast ale. Lord Stark turned, raising one eyebrow. "Rustin, it seems that my brain must still be sleeping off the hangover. What the devil are you saying?"

"Two dead bodies, my lord. Dead as the winter's snowdrops. Not only the one I don't know, but the other one I do. For under the old willow tree, it's Fillip the farrier lying dead."

VESPERS

He paused, waiting for Lord Stark's reaction, but his lordship had already left the room, the door swinging behind him as he marched from the house and followed the cobbled pathway to the river. Across the abandoned table the pewter mug of ale sat basking in the sunshine, but the platter of bread, cheese and bacon was splattered beneath the linen napkin. Once again, the candle had snuffed.

The man sprawled beneath the low spread of the yew tree, was blood stained from neck to waist, head back against the tree trunk, arms loose at his side, legs straight out in the damp grass. Dominic knew his farrier had always been more popular with the horses than he had with the other servants, but murder had never taken place on these premises before, and now – two.

Unless they had killed each other.

The farrier's two sons worked as grooms at the stables. They would know by now.

Dominic walked to the riverbank and stared down. A small rowing boat was tied to the tree roots, hardly moving in the placid waters, but there was a slow leakage and a grubby ooze collecting around the body's already sodden skirts.

Having certainly recognised the remains of his own farrier, his lordship now stared down at the girl, surprised to see someone he had certainly never seen before. Reaching down, careful and precise, he gently rolled the body over onto its back. And then, looking so closely, he was able to see the rise of her breasts within the part sodden tunic, and the faint drift of condensation from between her lips.

Turning back to the men behind him, he stepped upwards onto firmer ground once more, and pointed. "This girl is alive. Both of you, pull the boat up onto the bank, wake her and ask what the devil she's doing here."

As he strode back to the house, he heard the noises. The bang of wood on mud, the slap of the water and the girl yelling. But he was far more interested in returning to his breakfast and called for his steward.

"Benson, have you heard our morning news? Spring brings more than dew on the crocuses, it seems. Go and find out exactly what the devil is happening."

"Immediately, my lord."

His lordship relit the candle, pulling it towards him across the tablecloth as he drained the pewter mug of ale. When he looked up, someone else was watching him. He watched the frown unfold, carefully swallowed by the usual politeness of servant to lord.

"Are you hurt?" He asked, watching her reaction. Apparently, she had none. Her eyes were half shut but glinted green behind heavy lids and thick lashes. Her cheekbones were sharp and her cheeks hollow. "You look hungry."

"Not at all, my lord." Abruptly he saw the anger glint behind her lashes. "If you allow me to leave, sir, I'll leave and not return."

Pausing, Dominic regarded the girl standing before him. Rustin held both her arms behind her – entirely unnecessary – but his lordship did not order her release. He thought her twenty or less, obviously poor and half starved. Her neck disappeared into a stained tunic of drab hessian, her feet were bare and as filthy as a mole in its tunnel. Her arms were twigs and there seemed only a tiny rise of breasts across her chest.

He said, "You suspect the food I offer being poisoned? Or perhaps you believe I might take you captive for the theft of the city wherry in which you arrived."

She hid the sudden glare and looked down at her mud-covered toes. "I borrowed the wherry."

"Does the owner know that?"

The girl did not answer.

It was Rustin who broke the silence. "My lord, the wench tried to run off and kicked me, when I grabbed her. I reckon she's run from the sheriff or from some master she don't like. But I got to say, my lord, I be more worried about the farrier. Has this wench done it? Maybe Fillip tried to grab the wench."

Looking up, the girl shook her head. Her hood tipped back, and grubby water fell from her hair. "I know nothing of it. I slept, that's all. I was exhausted and slept deep. If there was noise, I didn't hear it."

Ignoring her answer, Dominic spoke to his gardener. "Had she committed murder, I doubt she'd have tethered the boat so close and cheerfully slept next to her victim."

"True enough, my lord." Rustin sniffed. "But who was it then done such a terrible thing?"

"Somebody else," Dominic was speaking softly and more to himself. "Is Fillip disliked?"

"My lord," the girl interrupted. "May I leave"

"You've an urgent appointment upriver, perhaps?" Dominic turned to stare again, unblinking.

She remained silent, pink cheeked and unmoving. Then said, "My lord, I ask nothing from you except my freedom. I do not run from any sheriff, but I hope to travel north. As far as possible north. You don't know me. Why keep me here?"

It was her desire to leave which created his to keep her. "Tell me what is so urgent and what you are trying to escape." He pointed. "There's food on that platter beneath the napkin. Help yourself, but you'll not be leaving yet. What's your name?" His eyes were ice cold. "Sit there." Rustin pushed her down onto a wooden stool. "Now first, your name?"

She sat, her hands in her lap. "Jetta, my lord. And – thank you – for the food."

Then she gazed at the ham, manchet, smoked bacon and wedges of stilton. At first, she tried to resist, and then could no longer do so. With a small gulp, she quickly bent her head and started to eat.

Nodding, his lordship stood, turned, and without another word he left the room. Rustin called. "Do I stay here, my lord, to watch the girl?"

"Come with me, and lock the door behind you," Dominic spoke from the passage. Rustin did as he was told.

Barely moving, Jetta sat and ate. She had never eaten Manchet before, since wheat bread was never offered to servants. Nor had she ever eaten so much at one sitting. In fact, she had barely eaten anything at all for five days since rowing upstream. Tethering to the bank each evening had been simple but offered no supper. Sleep at night and speed during the days had been more important. Now the platter was crumb-less and clean as the knife she had not used, but the small blade lay temptingly on the tablecloth. Looking around and impressed, Jetta rubbed one careful finger across the bleached linen cloth, stared around at the walls, one painted with a mural of forests, the others wooden panelled. The windows seemed huge, metal framed and bright with genuine glass. Although she had seen grand houses before, this seemed almost too beautiful.

She tested the one doorway, and found it locked as expected. Returning to the table, she took the small knife by its metal handle, and hid its blade as far as possible within her clenched palm. The food she had eaten gave her strength, but so much after so long was beginning to threaten the peaceful acquiescence of her digestion.

Half dozing in the high-backed chair beside the empty hearth, Jetta was jerked awake as Dominic returned. He had left her for a considerable time, and she had been dreaming, almost forgetting where she was, until she heard the grating click as the door was unlocked and swung open. Jetta sat upright like a thief caught in the act.

Striding in, his lordship regarded her, then turned to the man behind him. This was neither Rustin nor one of the grooms she had seen before.

"Benson, take the girl to one of the stables, or a storage shed. I want her kept here until we solve the problem of the farrier."

"But my lord," said the tall man, "in any of those quarters, it will be impossible to lock her safely. She will escape unless someone is set to guard her day and night."

Dominic shrugged. "True. Then put her up in one of the bedchambers. Make sure there are blankets. She appeared half frozen. Then lock the door."

The steward was amazed. "In one of the spare guest bed chambers, my lord?"

"What else would you suggest, Benson?" His lordship seemed barely interested.

"The wine cellar perhaps, sir." The steward appeared confused. "The pantry, even. Anywhere with a lock, I imagine."

The steward was a tall man, but Lord Stark was taller, and looked down on him. "Shocked at my lack of propriety, Benson? But a runaway kitchen maid in a locked bedchamber is easy kept and convenient for questioning. Do as I've asked, Benson."

She had listened to the irrelevant conversation, waiting for one of the men to come close. Jetta still held the knife, expecting to attack the steward as he came to grab her. But it was Lord Stark who passed her first as he strode from the great hall.

The distance between them was slight but he neither touched her nor walked close enough to touch. Yet Jetta spun around and jabbed out one foot to trip, and the knife to cut.

His lordship, more accustomed to battle than any woman, kicked her ankle away from his legs, but at the same moment, since utterly unexpected, the blade sliced both his wrist and the back of his hand. Rushing forwards, Benson struck out with one fist to Jetta's face, but as she fell, crying out from the force of the punch, Dominic caught her and twisted her beneath his arm.

The pressure of his upper arm squeezed around her chest until she could hardly breathe. Then he tossed her against the wall.

Jetta crumpled, sliding down to the rug beside the hearth. The back of her head trickled blood as her eyes closed. She appeared unconscious. His lordship, narrow eyed, shook his head at his steward.

"Follow up on Fillip Pike, Benson. His sons will be back in the stables by now." And Dominic turned again to the girl at his feet. Reaching down, he gripped her arm and shook her awake. "So, it seems you might be a murderer after all. You'll come with me," he told her.

Jetta felt the pain at the back of her head, and of the growing bruises. In a guttural whisper she croaked, "I can't breathe."

And he replied, "If you couldn't breathe, then nor could you speak."

Dominic hauled her up the stairs. Her feet barely brushed the steps, though flakes of dried mud scattered. Now, with one fist on her arm and the other around her neck, he kicked open a door along the first passageway from the stairs and threw Jetta to the bed. She rolled over and gasped for breath. The hem of her smock had creased up around her thighs and she rolled back, trying to pull it down.

His lordship regarded her with ice cold eyes as he advanced.

Jetta scrambled back within the bed, holding onto the headboard. "No," she yelled in his face. "Don't you touch me."

Dominic stood in the deepening shadows. "I have a woman who pleasures me when I want her," he said jaw clamped, "and I'll never take a filthy servant brat between my sheets. You are not here for my pleasure, and I am most certainly not here for yours. But you will make no attempt to escape until I have fully understood the mystery of my farrier's death."

Striding from the room, Lord Stark did not look back. He left and locked the door behind him. Jetta heard his footsteps down the stairs.

Chapter Two

For long moments, Jetta did nothing but gaze at the closed door. Then she began to peer at everything else.

Her thoughts remained on the past that she had been so determined to escape, and on the future in which she was determined to remain free, to belong only to herself, and never again experience fear. Terror was once more threatening, but there seemed to be one small pleasure keeping the threat at bay.

This was a room unlike any other bedchamber she had ever seen. The bed where she lay was sumptuous and deliciously soft, the huge window, as those downstairs, was real glass and facing the bed there was a hearth with a chimney rising into the wall.

It was late morning and she had dozed, she had eaten, and she had been surrounded by the most unexpected comfort and amazing warmth. Yet although the room now swaddled her and the bed promised a better sleep than she'd had since she left her mother's arms, she needed to get away. The man who had captured her seemed similar enough to the master she'd escaped before, and she could, she was sure, expect the same treatment. The belt across her bare back, the horse whip across the back of her legs, and perhaps worse.

Jetta examined the window. Impressed by real glass, she rubbed her thumb along its leaden frames. The casement had a handle, amazingly easy to open with a quick push and jerk. She was able to stick her head out into the spring breeze. Looking down, she made her decision.

Her cloak would certainly flap in her way, so she tied it around her waist and climbed from the open window. This entailed pushing into a strange position with both legs out and her head to her knees. With one partially cracked rib squashed over her thighs, this was painful, but Jetta was accustomed to pain. Once free of the casement, she felt for the ivy twists which covered some of the brick, snatched at its thicker branches, and risked her weight to its strength.

Climbing downwards, though sliding was probably a better description, equivalent to only one flight of stairs, her bare feet quickly touched soil, and Jetta snatched up her hems and turned to run.

Immediately she found herself in a tight embrace and stared up at his lordship's interested gaze.

"You don't like my guest bedchamber?"

His grip was neither gentle nor affectionate and she felt the suffering rib crack once more.

She accused, "You're hurting me."

"Really?" he said without loosening his grasp. "It's of little consequence. Had I wished to hurt you I would have done something quite different."

She was struggling, but his lordship's grip seemed impossible to break. She was pressed so close that she felt the pulse of his muscles, the width of his chest and of his upper arms. But he felt only the skeleton width of a starving sparrow, the tiny twigs of bones and the protruding joints of her spine. He could, however, feel her heartbeat fast and furious against him. Looking down with faint amusement, he saw only the damp grit stuck within the curls of her hair and smelled the faint aroma of a polluted and muddy river.

Her words were muffled against his shoulder. "I didn't hurt anyone. Let me go. You'll never have to see me again."

"Tempting as that may be," he replied, "your appearance in my grounds at the same moment as my farrier lay brutally murdered, is far too disturbing and I do not believe in coincidences. Nor did you show any disinclination with the breakfast knife. You will therefore remain here until I am quite sure that you were not in any way involved. Your only reason for escape would be your own guilt."

Still within the crush of his grip, Lord Stark had once more taken the girl into his home, up the stairs and into the same dark bedchamber. The key remained in the lock, and he left it there while dragging Jetta to the bed, then he pushed her back onto the sumptuous eiderdown. Two tassels on silken cords held back the bed curtains, and he untied one, winding it around the bed's upper post and then to Jetta's wrist. It was not such a clasp as would hold her prisoner for much time, but for the moment it kept her still.

He then strode to the window, and with the tiny metal key he locked each window frame, holding its square of little glass panes, took the key with him, left the room without saying another word, and finally locked the door behind him.

Jetta waited until his footsteps faded. Then she kicked herself into a sitting position and began with difficulty, to untie the clasp of cord at her wrist. Able to use both her other hand and her teeth, it was not too long before she was free again.

Lying back, she calmed her breathing and the tension in her shoulders. She closed her eyes. What little stomach she had fell flat, and she allowed the panic to leave her body, banishing the sense of frantic nerves. She knew that would not serve her. It was more likely to cause mistakes.

So, with a careful stretch, she unwrapped her cloak from her waist and found in its folds the knife she had stolen from the dining table downstairs. It was metal handled, the metal only pewter but crafted into the swirls of an intricate pattern. One tiny smear of blood remained on the blade. His lordship's blood. But, she realised, it had been a shallow and harmless wound. This time she hoped the knife would be more useful.

Crossing to the door, she inserted the knife's point into the keyhole and began to grind it in the opposite direction to that she had seen his lordship use when he had opened it. Pushing further, she heard the click. The door opened.

Wrapping the knife again into the thick twist of her cloak, Jetta tip toed downstairs. The doorway into the vast hall was shut, and she hoped his lordship would be inside and therefore unable to see her. Barefoot, however grubby, she made no sound. She kept within the deeper shadows and hurried to the outer door. It opened when she turned the handle and immediately scurried into the oblivion of the bushes, the wall of drooping willow trees and the archway of briar roses.

Now running, she passed the stable block and quickly shrank back into the shadowed bushes. Three horses, sweating and kicking, were being led in, unsaddled, and scrubbed down. Jetta realised what it meant. The sheriff had arrived.

Slipping further into shadows, she crept from tree to tree until she glimpsed the dark blue of the river between the leaves. Then, horrified, she realised two things. First, her wherry had gone.

Secondly, she was standing under the falling branches of the willow tree where the dead body of the farrier had been found, and she was standing directly in the dark sticky patches which had been puddles of blood.

And then, once again surrounded, she was facing his lordship and looking directly up into the cold glare of those black eyes.

The grip around her was as hard and close as before and she felt her lungs losing air. She gasped the same old story. "I – can't – breathe."

And the same reply. "You speak, so you breathe. And you continuously manage to escape, therefore you confess your guilt."

Jetta spluttered something which Dominic presumed was a denial. He had no idea how she had discovered any escape route this time, but he did not bother to ask. He beckoned the sheriff.

"Sheriff Kettering, this is the young female I mentioned. I cannot remember her name, but I thought her imprisoned in one of the unused chambers. Yet, it seems she is better at escaping than I had supposed."

"I'll question her, my lord." The sheriff was a very short man and since his lordship was exceedingly tall, they made a badly matched pair. "May I use one of your antechambers?"

"I'll have someone take you there and stand guard."

The sheriff looked up with a smile. "I shall be more than content to question the wench alone, my lord."

Dominic's smile appeared more ambiguous. "Perhaps in that case, I shall be present myself, sir. I'm not convinced of the girl's guilt, and do not want her harmed."

"I *am* harmed already," Jetta gasped out, trying to break free. She managed an elbow to Dominic's waist. "I'm hurting. Badly."

The sheriff was shocked. "That alone is worth a whipping, my lord," he said, "proof of the wench's temper."

"Follow me, Kettering," his lordship informed the sheriff, "and remember, we are investigating the murder of my farrier, and not the manners of this young woman."

"Humph," said the sheriff.

The antechamber was small, dark, windowless, and led from the back of the great hall. Dominic dumped Jetta on one of the stools, and took a small wooden chair positioned between her and the door. He indicated another chair for the sheriff. Dominic stretched his legs. The sheriff hovered, then sat with a thump. Jetta sat quietly and kept her head down.

"Well now," the sheriff began. "We'll start with who you are, strumpet. Give me your name and where you come from."

Jetta sat straight and glared back. "All my life I've been taught to be polite, to do as I'm told, and to respect the nobility and anyone in authority." She bit her lip and suddenly looked away. "But," she continued, twisting her fingers as she stared at her toes just peeping beneath her hems, "you can't just accuse me of things I didn't do. And, it's obvious I didn't do it. Why would I kill a man I've never met? He'd have been five times stronger than me. I was on the river. I didn't get out of the boat. And I wasn't rude, but you are. I'm no harlot. You know nothing of me."

The sheriff leaned over towards her. "Speak to me that way again, miss, and I'll take you into custody. I've two assistants waiting outside. They'll have you in chains if you're not careful. Now – your name and position."

Avoiding his scowl, Jetta sighed. She reverted to diplomacy, but she imagined a dragon swooping down through the window, stretched claws in the sheriff's pudgy neck while carrying him off with a screech. Instead, she spoke quietly. "I'm Jetta Lawson and I've rowed upstream from the city. I was – working – in London."

"As a whore? Or as a kitchen slut? So you broke your agreement, deserted your master and ran away?"

"I didn't have any agreement," Jetta's voice had shrunk into a whisper. "I left – yes alright, I ran away - because – I had to."

"Stole a wherry, rowed up the Thames, and attacked the man who saw you and would have given you away no doubt." The sheriff flexed his chest with self-importance.

Jetta felt the same helplessness she had known most of her life. "How dare you jump to conclusions? I never met that man. I never saw him. He couldn't have seen me either. I didn't even hear anything. I just needed to sleep. I was so exhausted."

Scraping back his chair, the sheriff jumped to his feet and leaned directly over her, his chin almost to her forehead. She felt the cold spit of his words in her eyes. "With what a sweet innocent young maiden you say you are," and here the spit was hot, "why then are you carrying a knife?"

"I – I took it from the dining table."

Dominic laughed at her expression of guilt. "I might have

guessed. Not much of a weapon though, I admit. Barely cuts the meat."

"Still – a knife, my lord. What innocent wench carries a knife?"

"The one who wants to pick a lock," Dominic said, still grinning. He did not mention the cuts on his wrists, now hidden beneath his sleeves.

She glared again. "Don't say you'll arrest me for that?"

"You're coming with me, troublemaker," the sheriff boomed, grabbing at Jetta's shoulder. "A slut steals a knife, threatens a lord of the land, and has murdered his farrier. You'll spend the night in gaol, and that's for sure."

Jetta stood, pushing off his hand. She scowled at him. "If you do that, then you'll be the criminal. I've committed no crime." She turned without much hope, staring at Dominic. "Yes, it was your knife, but I didn't steal it. I never saw your farrier. If that coward takes me, I'll rot in Newgate for life. They'll prove nothing against me, but they'll keep me there anyway."

Lord Stark recognised the gulp in her voice as her attempt to stop herself crying. He paused a moment and shrugged. Indeed, his concentration had lapsed and instead of following the sheriff's business and the girl's possible guilt, he had been distracted by other, although pertinent, matters. Jetta's ankles, for instance, were sweetly curved, the skin very white but with a faint trace of the blue vein, which seemed somehow particularly beautiful. Her rough-cut tunic was without shape but as she moved, sometimes the sudden twist of her hips was outlined.

Now called to concentrate elsewhere, he looked up, smiling without explanation. "Tell me, for instance Miss Lawson, why you felt the need to escape with such desperate risk from your previous master? What were you? A kitchen girl?"

"Aha," roared the sheriff, once again bending over her, so closely that she smelled the garlic on his breath. "So you killed someone before? What else would make you run into the night?"

Her voice dropped again. "I attacked nobody. But somebody did attack me."

"Where did you work? Quick, girl, quick. Your master's name and title?"

Jetta shook her head. "I'm not going back there."

His lordship stood slowly and ambled to the door behind him, flinging it open. "I think that's enough." He nodded to the sheriff. "I appreciate your coming to my call, and I apologise. But I believe I shall take over now. I'll call for your services if I need you again. But in the meantime, I shall keep the girl here, and set up my own investigation."

The sheriff blustered. "But my lord, there's been a murder – perhaps two. I'm obliged to stay and come to my own conclusions. I need to arrest the wench."

Shaking his head, Dominic indicated the door. "I make the decisions here, Kettering. The girl stays." His voice was a little less cordial and somewhat more decisive.

The sheriff bowed. "Indeed, my lord. I understand. But I've had long practise, sir, and I know a slattern and a criminal when I see one and this female is a liar and a murderer."

"Indeed?" Still smiling, his lordship showed the sheriff from his home. "I shall call you Kettering, if and when I need you." And he turned away, closed the door and returned to the small dark annex.

Regarding the girl, who scowled back, he continued to smile.

She asked, "So can I leave now? Where's my boat?"

"It is not your boat," said his lordship. "You cannot possibly own a London wherry. And while questions remain unanswered, you will stay here. You will be comfortable and well fed, but you will not leave. Your remarkable talent at picking locks and climbing from closed windows has been noted. You will therefore be kept in greater restraint. But," and his smile tucked up at the corners of his mouth, "at least you are not at the mercy of the sheriff. Nor will you be arrested or taken to Newgate until I am completely convinced of your guilt in something so seriously troubling. Now – I wonder where I shall put you this time. I am running out of secure havens."

Chapter Three

Sir Dominic, Lord Stark, Earl of Desford, called for his steward.

"Benson, take Mistress Lawson, to one of the larger bedchambers on the eastern side, second floor. Make sure she has a jug of clean water for drinking, then ensure the windows and doors are locked. Leave her in peace, but arrange for one of the servants to sit in the corridor outside the door. Let me know only if there are any problems. I shall be busy."

"At once, my lord." Benson gripped Jetta's upper arm and marched her upstairs. He then thrust her into one of the unlit rooms, checked the windows and locked the door behind him.

Without the knife which had been taken from her, Jetta knew she'd have less chance of seeing a way out. She explored the room, finding it so richly comfortable, she was tempted simply to settle on the bed, accept her fate, and sleep.

Ignoring anything that even hinted of temptation, Jetta first examined the windows. The centre square was firmly locked, and the other casements had no method for opening. Looking down, Jetta realised too, that no vines grew on this side of the manor house. Long brick walls fell some distance without interruption, and at their base was a paved pathway leading to the stable block, so no soft landing to cushion a fall.

The large wooden door was shut, its metal handle did not turn, and the keyhole did not respond to any pointed item she could find in the room. Jetta even crawled into the large open hearth and peered up into the narrow blackness. She saw no way of escape within the soot covered tunnel stretching above her and would have been too scared to attempt it.

Sinking back onto the bed, she was at least relieved not to be tied, and so far, not to be whipped. The sheriff, on the point of arresting her, had been sent off. Jetta felt no liking for the arrogant and cold-eyed lord, but she did feel a sense of relief. As a prisoner, unjust though that was, she had been well treated.

It seemed so long since she had been well treated. Rowing up the Thames had been hard work, yet the enormous relief and delight in escape had brought the strength she'd needed. Even the cold nights hadn't bothered her.

It was the young Lord Maddock's face she kept seeing, his sneer, the claws of his fingers and the slime of his voice. "I'll tell my father. Then I'll hold you down for him before he holds you down for me."

"It's common enough, my girl," had said Mistress Chilling, in charge of the laundries. "Common enough indeed. Just close your eyes and put up with it."

"They say you can beat a servant if she steals or curses or breaks what she was meant to clean. But no law says a master can rape her." Still crying, Jetta was also furious.

"Might make him like you," had suggested another cleaning woman.

"It's not right," Jetta muttered, and had run from the kitchen.

Now she wondered if it would all happen again. She was unable to escape the room, but anyone could unlock it to enter.

There was nothing she wanted to remember yet forgetting was difficult. Sleeping had those moments when the imagination wandered, and Jetta had always been careful to take herself into a world of water where she could float and watch the stars flicker in the great nothingness above. She did whatever would help her imagine safety and shut out the memories of reality.

But the memories came creeping back. Creeping, then rushing. The footsteps in the night, the leather straps around her wrists, the lash against her naked back, and the snarl of the man who had ordered the punishment.

Without climbing beneath sheets or eiderdown, Jetta clamped her mind shut and within moments, she was dozing again.

She woke to the face looking across at her. With neither scowl nor smile, his lordship simply regarded her in silence.

It was, perhaps, the first time she had really looked at him as he carried a small lit candle that smelled of honeycomb. Jetta did not like the eyes that stared. They were intrusive, very dark and cold beneath heavy lids and thick black lashes. His nose was extremely straight, cheekbones high ridged, and his jaw line too rigid. Nor did she like his mouth, being wide but thin lipped.

Turning her head away, she muttered, "What do you want of me now?" There was one thing that seemed very frightening. She had only just managed to escape her employer. Two floors up, how would she escape this time? Her anger and fear mounted, and her heartbeat quickened.

But Dominic said only, "It is supper time. Food will be brought to you shortly." He then left and Jetta had no idea if he had been smiling or not.

Rolling over, she sat ready for the food to arrive. Having eaten rarely on many occasions during her life, she was hungry without being frantic. She had missed the midday meal, so was ready for supper. Though she would have adored more readily to be served at a real table, there was a small topped chest beside the bed, and she could use that. It was still considerably better than eating from the floor or her lap as she often had.

When the food was brought, she was surprised that it arrived on three large platters all placed on a wooden tray. One platter held stewed lamb beneath a thick pie crust. Another held a small bundle of lettuce and parsnips, while the third held soft pieces of fish in burgundy. Even more surprising to her, there was a jug of rich burgundy wine and a cup of pewter. She ate and drank the lot.

The same servant arrived later to collect the tray and empty platters. But Jetta kept the knife and the man said nothing.

The evening drifted slowly. She watched the sunset from the window, half hidden by trees and the stable roof. A blackbird was fluting its claim to the territory, and she saw a heron glide high over the river. The water was visible only in dark threads, but Jetta wished she might be back there. Rowing upstream had been a struggle, exhausting and even frightening at times. But it had been freeing and the deep yearning desire for freedom had come to mean more than anything.

She didn't even know what she could do with it once she got it. Neither marry – that was once again the loss of freedom – nor slump back into servitude for some other rich or noble family. That was more frightening, at least until you knew fully what your master might wish to do.

Long ago she'd learned to cook. She might open an Ordinary, making pies, fresh baked manchet and other food she might sell. But first she would need the money to buy a shop, buy an oven, and then the ingredients she could turn into whatever she might then sell. Without even a farthing to start such a business, true freedom might seem a long way off.

Or she could sell herself. Walk the streets while saving enough pennies to start the business. But she would sooner throw herself in the river. The Thames was deep enough to carry her. Drowning, they said, was sweet enough after the first panic for lost breath. Perhaps that was the only real freedom after all.

VESPERS

Down two flights of stairs in the principal hall, a small fire had been lit across the wide stone hearth, for the evening had brought a chill.

"You've found yourself another woman?" smiled Avery, "isn't one enough?"

"You're keeping count?"

"Well, even I can count to two," objected Sir Avery Peasop from the deep cushioned chair by the flaming hearth.

Dominic sat opposite, his chair high backed, and his feet stretched out towards the flames. "I haven't seen Teresa for some time, as it happens," he said. "But I assure you, my crackpot friend, this female stashed upstairs is not one I'm courting. She's an interesting character, but not in the usual way."

"Keeping your secrets close as always," Avery nodded. "I won't snoop. Or at least – not in your hearing."

"Drink your wine," Dominic told him, "and stop imagining the dramatic impossibilities of my boring life. You know my farrier was murdered in my own grounds. That's hardly something I intend to ignore. This girl may be involved. If not, I'll release her, and she can go where she pleases."

"In a stolen London wherry with a stolen knife?"

Dominic sighed. "Go and talk to my grandmother," he said. "She makes as much sense as you do. No doubt now the entire tale will be spread over the entire city by tomorrow – but the story will be twisted beyond recognition. I told my grandmother nothing, but the sheriff spoke with her personal maid when he left here, and now a very strange version of the truth is presumably creeping beneath every door in the house."

"The truth," Avery told him, "is always so damned dull compared to the spreading far-fetched stories. Let's have a little drama before we die of boredom. Why should we have to wait until Christmas for the Mummings."

Dominic yawned. "When someone attempts to poison my entire

household, I shall inform you, Avery. In the meantime, I'm afraid nothing so interesting has occurred." The fire was crackling, and the disintegrating logs spat. He leaned forwards, kicking one log back deeper into the hearth. "Or we could set fire to the house, my friend. Would that be sufficient excitement for you?"

Sniggering, Avery simply pointed upwards. "Just tell me about your killer."

"There's little to tell."

"You have a beautiful young female locked in your bedchamber, and you want to convince me there's nothing to say about her?"

"She's not beautiful," Dominic said, "and she's most certainly not in my bedchamber. The poor child is thin as a bed post, desperately needs a bath, and I imagine she's escaping from some kind of past abuse. Clever though – with an aptitude for finding different ways of escape."

"And committing murder."

"I doubt it. But I'll find out what I can tomorrow."

Once his friend Avery had left, Dominic sank further down into the comfort of his chair. It was too early for his own bed, so he mentally retraced the events of the day, the attitude of the sheriff and whether he believed in the girl's guilt.

Yet before any decision wielded direction, Dominic realised he was simply thinking of the girl herself. He had denied her beauty, but now he visualised her again, dressed her in his mind in the clothes of society, watched her smile at the improvement, and then, almost without intention, found he was undressing her entirely

His lordship stopped his meandering thoughts, abruptly turning to other matters. He decided, however, that since the mental stripping of a girl who remained a scruffy stranger had absurdly absorbed him, it must be high time he visited his mistress again. And then it was Jetta's eyes he saw gazing down at him, the flash of golden green beneath black lashes.

Once again, he stamped at the fire, this time extinguishing both flame and spark. He marched from the hall, called his steward, demanded his coat, hat and horse, and within a few moments he had mounted and was riding along the cobbled road leading from his manor house towards the flattened pathway following the banks of the Thames to the small village of Hammersmith.

A spacious cottage sat beside the village green, and here he stopped, dismounted, and tethered his horse to the small stone manger by the front entrance. There was no lock on the door. Dominic pushed it open and immediately a pretty, large-breasted woman virtually leapt into his arms, throwing her own arms around his neck.

His lordship kissed the woman's piled curls, and then released her, moving backwards from the exaggerated affection. "You'll crush my silks, my dear."

The woman pulled away, pouting. "You always say something mean, my lord. Just teasing I know, but I don't like it. And you know I don't like it." She fluttered her eyelashes and turned pout to smile. "It's been such an age. I've not seen you for a month or more."

Dominic found himself vaguely irritated. "For almost two weeks, Teresa. And I leave you in comfort, I believe."

"Well, let's not argue, my lord, since you're here at last. Yet I see you've brought no gift. When we first – united – sir, each time you were sweet enough to bring me some gesture of appreciation."

"My decision was a last-minute choice," Dominic told the woman, his gaze now expressionless. "But if you choose to sulk, I shall leave. Few men relish a woman whose mouth droops at each corner. Can you manage a smile, little one? Or shall I leave?"

This worried her. Teresa smiled obediently. "Of course, sir. I'm only too delighted to see you again. Our bed is waiting, I'll bring the wine."

It was well gone midnight by the time his lordship returned home. He left the horse at the stables and marched indoors. Throwing hat, coat and gloves to the balustrade, he climbed the two flights of stairs to check on the girl held there. The groomsman left to guard the door was asleep in the corridor, his back to the fast locked door.

Pleased, Dominic nodded to himself and retired to his own bedchamber on the other side of the passageway.

Chapter Four

The sunshine was bright through the long windows, rising into the beams of the huge, vaulted ceiling. It was late April, and though the evenings could be bitterly cold, most days were bathed in golden warmth.

"I've begun the initial negotiations," sighed his highness, leaning over the small table beside one of the windows. The entering sun flooded his quill, ink pot and paper. "Being still officially in mourning, the passage ahead is neither straight nor well lit."

"I'm surprised, your highness. Easier to get it scribed by someone else." Frances Lovell looked out at the brilliance, then back at his royal friend. "You've had enough loss lately. Bitter loss, one after the other."

"Easy isn't my interest or my aim, Frances." The king turned to look at his companions. "Anything easy would be a fatuous solution under the circumstances."

The man sitting on the opposite side of his king laughed. "Your grace accepted the crown. What could be more complicated, time consuming and tiresome? You accepted the hardest position in England. Not that you had much choice, sire."

His highness, King Richard, the third of that name, pushed back his chair and regarded his friends. "Thank you, Andrew. There's no hiding it at present. I am, as kings must, arranging for a new wife to replace the one I still miss." He nodded towards the three young men sitting close. "I trust your advice, but I've not called you here for advice today. It's discussion I'm wanting."

"Well, let's get the advice over first," Andrew said. "I know a good relationship with Portugal could be helpful, but the Lady Joanna is well past child-bearing age. No doubt you can get rid of the Lady Elizabeth to the Portuguese duke although he might complain that in spite of being the late king's eldest daughter, she's considered illegitimate. You, on the other hand, need Spain on your side, not Portugal."

Dominic interrupted. "I've met neither of your prospective wives, sir, but Lady Joanna is thought to be religious to the point of fanaticism, utterly chaste, far too old for children, and a rigorous prude."

Richard managed a faint smile. "I could call you a fanatic yourself, Dom, although in a different direction. Remember all these negotiations are a matter of diplomacy. Overlooking Portugal and writing directly to Spain would be extremely unwise. Portugal first. Once discussion breaks down – than I'm free to prod wherever I wish."

"So, it'll be Spain eventually?"

"Spain, Belgium, even Bremen or Saxony." The smile had faded. Now the frown sank deep into Richard's forehead. "But I can't return Elizabeth's legitimacy, it's been far too deeply disproved. Spain would insist on legitimacy, whatever they do behind closed doors. Yet I need to marry for an heir and diplomacy. Meanwhile Elizabeth sends me letters of hope. She wants a life and deserves one. I aim for a Spanish wife, but for my niece to be chosen by Portugal."

"I pity your niece." Andrew shook his head. "The wretched girl was practically brought up as a nun. Her unpleasant mother wasn't risking any scandal. And now I imagine the poor girl's desperate for courtship and children of her own."

"And that reminds me," said Dominic, now grinning at Andrew. "Your lovely Tyballis, my lord. Has the great deed been done?"

Andrew laughed, but it was his highness who answered. "You are behind the times, Dom. Lady Tyballis was presented with a son a month back. Andrew is now lucky enough to show off his heir, unlike myself. Although I am to be the Godfather."

Lovell raised his cup and drank slowly. "Congratulations to you, my friend. My little wife won't be a mother any time soon, since she's closeted by her own. We were both tiny brats when we married, and I was barely allowed to see her. Not that it ever bothered me."

"Don't you want children?" Andrew asked.

"No. They die, and then you're left distraught."

Richard looked away, rolling up some of the papers on his desk. "True enough," he murmured. "For more than a year I've missed my son. And now Anne. I admit I married her out of conscience and sympathy. Marriage was my only way of rescuing her. Anne had been through utter misery, and almost imprisoned by my dear brother George."

"I knew Clarence well at one time," Dominic sighed. "But we were never friends."

"He made the excuse that Anne was his sister-in-law and took her forcibly under the pretence of protection. But his reasons were political and financial." The king turned back to his friends and drained his own cup of wine. "We may not have married for love," he said softly, "but we soon learned to love each other. I miss Anne deeply. Now I'm arranging another marriage but it's obligatory and not for pleasure."

"We all miss Anne," Dominic said softly. "Our sweet queen was kindness personified. Elizabeth too. The only time your niece," he smiled at Richard, "was allowed to enjoy herself was when Anne stepped in to support her. The dance, for instance, where they both wore similar clothes and pretended to dance together."

Lovell leaned back again. "But our queen had lost her beloved son and died of the same terrible illness. You've been extremely unlucky Dickon."

"Enough, or you'll have me weeping, my friend." Richard stretched his legs out over the thick Turkish rug and shook his head. He was long legged and might have been a tall man like his brothers. Yet bad luck had slowed his birth, and his mother had thought he might die while caught for hours in the womb. He had been born with the proof of it in a twisted spine. Richard frowned again and the crease in his forehead became deeper etched. "To become King of England? Most would call me lucky enough. Of five sons born, I am the youngest, but inherited the crown."

"And you so love to sit on the throne?" Andrew was smiling. "Admit you preferred your life at Middleham surrounded by friends, your wife and your son in health, and as far as possible from court and your brothers."

"I'll be satisfied if I manage to return this country to peace and justice."

Nodding, Andrew's smile faded slightly. "You've managed a good deal of that already, and you've not sat the throne for two years yet. You're already loved by the people."

"Except for -," Richard paused, clapped his hands and called for more wine. The page who waited just outside the door, peeped in and bowed, then rushed to obey as the king turned back, "my sister-in-law's treasonous family and Margaret Beaufort's lying son."

The large jug of rich red Burgundy was brought in as the four men were laughing. The page poured from the jug with great care, partially filling each cup before leaving the jug on the table and hurrying from the room.

"Henry Tudor," Andrew said, "is an uneducated dolt. I've met him a few times on my espionage trips to Brittany. Even under Lancastrian hereditary, he's only about twentieth in line to the throne."

"That won't stop him," Lovell said. "He's attempted to invade already."

"It was a poor show," Andrew said. "But I'd not be surprised if he tried again."

"Especially now he has French support. Before he only had a handful of Woodville's and a couple of Bretons."

"Not unexpected," Richard said. "They will back anyone who fights against us. The French have hated England for five hundred years."

Lord Stark, Earl of Desford rode home from Westminster Palace as night finally masked the drifting sunbeams. With his retinue at some distance behind, Dominic kept to the riverbanks once more, seeing the sheen of stars reflection on the silent water. As though painted, a swirl of milky white moved with the ripples.

He rode slowly, but it was not the stars he was thinking of, nor his king and those matters of state.

When he rode into the great pathway within his own grounds towards the stables, it was a very different woman he saw.

Dominic's grandmother was invariably in bed well before midnight, but now she stood at the open doorway, her hair tousled, her expression wrinkled in fury. The aged countess was wrapped in two eiderdowns and each of them dragged across the cobbles at the back, but caught up her nightdress around her knees at the front. Her bowed and wrinkled legs, white skinned but bulging with the veins long broken, showed her age even more than the wrinkles across her face. She shivered in the night air.

Dismounting immediately, Dominic put both arms around her, leading her inside as he spoke softly. One of the grooms ran to grab the reins and lead the horse away, watching as Dominic disappeared, careful not to trap the dragging train of eiderdowns as the door closed.

"My love," he told her, "I'm here. What the devil has happened?"

His grandmother's bedchamber covered almost half of the first floor, with three rooms and a separate privy, with long windows looking east where she might watch the dawn rise like a torch over the river. Dominic almost carried her there now, wrapping the coverings more safely around her. Setting her on the bed, where she sank back against the pillows, he sat on the mattress edge and smiled.

"Your odd new female," his grandmother gulped, her face thickly tear stained, "she jumped on me. Jumped, I'm telling you! Smashed my little bowl of rose petals, and then ran. Dominic, you must not leave me alone with such danger. I screamed, but nobody came. I might have died."

He paused, his frown deepening. "You were attacked?" It was impossible, the house was as safe as any palace, although his grandmother frequently saw interesting creatures which did not exist. Dominic leaned over and gently kissed her cheek. "I am here to protect you, my lady. Now, tell me what happened."

The countess closed her eyes. "I've told you already Dominic. Don't be vague. You weren't here to protect me at all."

Creeping shadows without candlelight brought their own threat. Dominic reached behind him to the bedside chest, finding the half-stubbed candle his grandmother's personal maid would have used to guide her mistress up the stairs. He relit it with his own small tinder box and saw at once what had remained hidden in the dark. Several unexpected problems became suddenly obvious.

He asked, "Someone crashed through your window?"

"Isn't that what I said, boy? I was fast asleep and in she swung. I swore at her, but she didn't seem shocked."

Crossing the room to the mess of broken glass he had seen, Dominic stared down and sighed. This meant that the glass from the window in the room above was also broken. Not only was glass immensely expensive and usually involved considerable delay for repair, but the damned woman had almost frightened his grandmother to death. Marching back, he helped her under the sheet, and replaced the eiderdowns for warmth.

"What did the girl say?"

"Oh, she puffed on and on," spat the countess, her original fear having turned to fury, "silly nonsense about not knowing anyone was here, and pointless apologies."

"She didn't actually attack in any way?"

"Oh, for mercy's sake," the countess sat forwards. "Of course not. I'd have killed the wench. She just hopped around, bare footed you know, I hope she got glass in her toes. Then she opened my door and disappeared. It's all your fault, boy. You will never again house one of your strumpets in these rooms, do you hear me? I screeched my head off for you to come and arrest the brat and protect me. Well, you're here now but it's an hour too late. I could be dead of shock by now."

"My apologies," Dominic shook his head. "I was at Westminster Palace for the evening. Talking with the king."

It was the truth, although only half of it.

"Well, it's about time he got married again," stated the countess. "And next time you see him, you should tell him the city's getting thoroughly lawless again. Females jumping through windows, indeed."

The bedside chest held a small cup of wine beside the now flaring candle. Dominic held it up for her to drink. "Last of the night's sleeping potion."

Within moments the Countess of Desford, was gently snoring.

Dominic quickly tapped on the door to the adjacent room, and when there was no answer, he opened the door and called through. If his mother's personal maid had managed to sleep through her mistress screaming her head off, then a new maid would have to be employed. "Look after the countess," he called. "She's been frightened while you've slept like the dead."

With a deep sigh of frustrated irritation, Dominic then ran the stairs up to the room where he had held Jetta prisoner. The two wide sheets from the bed had been tied and twisted into a long rope and completely ruined along the way. Clearly once strong, it had been used to swing someone from the inside through the presumably already smashed window, and then on return, to break and enter the window on the level below.

An empty plate, and a cup beside it, lay on the bed. Small scraps of smashed glass lay beneath the window, but most would have been scattered outside, and difficult to find and clear within the shrubbery. Dominic's anger rose.

Having already unlocked the door from the outside, he now returned to the ground level and the front doorway, opened it and strode outside into the wind. Since he was still wearing the warmth of his coat and gloves, having discarded only his hat, he was sheltered enough although the sting of the wind whistled into his eyes. He headed towards the river.

There seemed no sign of the girl, nor of the wherry boat she'd rowed. Dominic searched the bank and peered down into the water. It held only the moon's tentative reflection, disturbed by the start of a windy drizzle.

He considered letting the entire matter float into tedious forgetfulness. But his thoughts were inconsistent, on the morrow, his farrier's funeral would take place. He would not be present for the church service, but he would feel obliged to be present at the beginning. And that, if nothing else, would ensure the memory of murder, Jetta, and the relentless trouble in his mind.

Returning towards the looming shadows of his ancestral home, he heard a faint snap from one of the sheds leading to the stable block. Something occurred to him. Immediately he kicked open the door.

From the darkness within, he could see the brilliance of two staring green eyes. Dominic smiled and leaned back against the door which he pushed shut behind him. "So here you are. Not satisfied with frightening my grandmother half to death, now you prefer to sleep with the cows."

"There aren't any cows in here," snuffled the small voice from the blackness. "And I'm sorry about your grandmother. I couldn't know she was in the room below, could I?"

"What you should have known," said his lordship, "was to behave with civilised obedience, stay where you were put, and not break a hundred sovereign's worth of glass. You should have simply slept the night in comfort, thankful at being well treated."

"Being a prisoner isn't being well treated," Jetta insisted.

"So, what the devil are you doing in here?" Dominic demanded.

"Trying to get my boat back."

"Ah." Dominic smiled to himself. "Not inclined to swim the Thames then?"

The wherry had been stacked there under his orders and the girl appeared to have had no success in rescuing it. "It's my boat."

"It isn't," Dominic pointed out. "You stole it from some pier within the city. That alone was enough to land you in Newgate. Instead, I gave you good food, safety and an extremely comfortable bed."

"But you locked me in. I want freedom. I need it. I've never been free in my life. Now it's all I dream of."

Dominic regarded her. Having accepted freedom as his inevitable right from birth, what it would feel like to be imprisoned had never occurred to him. "Then," he murmured, "do not steal. Do not kill. And do not damage other people's property."

"I didn't – kill," she mumbled after a short pause.

"That's what I intend to find out," Dominic said, losing patience. He took her arm, gripping with some force. "I have another bedchamber for you, less comfortable I'm afraid, but even you, I believe, will find escape somewhat difficult."

He hauled her back inside the house and up the stairs. But when they reached the third floor, he marched her along the winding corridor until they came to another set of stairs, narrow, steep and dark. Jetta was out of breath, but Dominic remained silent and continued to drag her. He was aware of the soft patter of her bare feet, he was aware of the warmth of her frightened breath, and he was aware of hurting her with his fingers digging into the soft skin of her upper arm. It did not, however, make him release his hold until they arrived at the top of the stone steps.

Dominic pushed open a small door, ducked his head, and tossed Jetta inside. Still in silence, he locked the door behind her. From outside, he called, "I shall order a breakfast brought to you in the morning, but it is unlikely to be early. I intend to sleep in. It has been a late and frustrating night and I've no intention of rolling from my bed for your convenience."

She heard his footsteps on the stairs and knew she must be locked into some sort of attic. Without light, she searched the walls for the window. Tracing her fingers up and then down and crosswise across every wall, she was soon aware that no window existed. It was an attic purely for storage – and for scullery maids suspected of murder, and so treated with a complete lack of consideration.

A pallet bed hugged the far wall. After the luxury of the previous two beds with their deep feather mattresses, their down-soft pillows, and their thick blankets and eiderdown topping, this lump of straw was suddenly as uncomfortable as the stone steps outside. There seemed to be nothing else except bags and boxes piled shut in the corner. Jetta tested the door. Locked of course. No window, no chimney, no knife and no possible means of escape.

Lying down without bothering to remove her tunic, Jetta snuggled beneath the two thin blankets, and slept sooner than she had expected. She was, considering the day's activities, utterly exhausted.

Without a window to tell its story, she had no idea of the time when she awoke, but she was quite positive that she had slept long and deep, and now felt strangely rested, strange since she had not expected either rest or contentment.

It was as she curled, creased but warm, that she wondered what was happening to her life. After almost twenty years of abuse and misery, she had scraped up every possible shred of courage still pattering at the back of her mind and had escaped from her torment. She had swept herself into a future of the unknown, but surely of better luck and less cruelty. Freedom was, after all, the ultimate goal, and she had grabbed it. Never suspecting the future could be worse than the past.

Until a man unknown, arrogant and unpleasant, had dragged her backwards. Captured, hauled from her glimpse of painless freedom, at first, she had been terrified. Terror and anger combined, and she nursed bruises and a sharp pain across her chest, probably a cracked rib. But she had not been whipped, nor given to the sheriff. And at least, for the first time in so many years, she was not hungry. Indeed, she knew she had been eating too much and it felt unnatural.

Jetta was startled at the light tapping on the door. "What?" she called, since opening the door was impossible.

A voice called softly. "Mistress, I done unlocked the door. There be a good breakfast awaiting you downstairs in the main hall. His lordship done invited you down."

Chapter Five

It had been the morning of the day before when Dominic had spoken to his household, though first to the sons of his farrier, murdered beneath the willow on the riverbank.

The private discussion, expression of sympathy and revelation of details had taken place only with Pip and Samuel Pike, sons of the farrier, and their mother Ilda who worked in the kitchens.

The news was no revelation since the gossip had been spread within moments of the body's discovery. But little time had passed. The dead man's family, however, had not seemed distraught.

"I have spoken to the priest," Dominic had told them. "The funeral will be held tomorrow. Each one of you is excused from work for the entire day. The rest of the household will be excused for the morning so they might attend the church service and burial." He had paused, looking at the three glum faces. "I have one person under suspicion, but personally I doubt she is the killer. If any of you have any information to offer on the subject, it will be most helpful if you tell me as soon as possible."

They had stared back without speaking. Finally, Pip, hanging his head, muttered, "Our dad weren't a nice fellow, my lord. But I ain't got no idea who could have done him in."

"A few times," whispered the dead man's wife, "I thought of pushing the fool in the ovens."

"Not what you'd call a happy family my lord," said Sam. "He beat us every day he could grab us. I'm mighty glad the fellow's gone. T'will be a relief at last."

"I'll kiss the hand of whoever done the deed sir," said Ilda, staring down at her wooden shod toes.

It had been an unexpected discussion, but afterwards the gathering of the entire household had been more energetic.

"Catch the swine and I'll hang him from the rafters," one said.

"You took a chit of a girl, I seen you my lord. If she done it, then I'll march the wicked lass all the way to Newgate."

"Perhaps she done us a favour."

"That man was hard working and honest. His killer must be punished."

"Yes indeed. Thrashed till he bleeds, and then hung at Tyburn."

Those who had known the farrier well, seemed less inclined to rant at the possible killer. But not one had a clue to offer, no one had seen or heard anything which might have brought the criminal to light.

The funeral was over when Jetta took a deep breath and hurried downstairs. The grounds were crowded as everyone returned from the church, with clearly no possibility of an easy escape. Instead, she followed orders, although this was exactly what she had hoped never to do again.

Entering the hall, she strode past the pages and those serving at the long table. Lord Stark, leaning back with only his cup in his hand, watched her. She sat opposite and sighed.

"I'm doing exactly as I was told. So, what are you going to do with me this time?"

"Feed you, although not personally," Dominic told her. And while you eat, you'll answer my questions accurately and honestly."

He watched her as she glared back. "Does the offer of food annoy you? Strange. Now, will you take ale or water?"

Ham, fried bacon, fried onions and sausages were piled on bread, and her plate was already overflowing.

"Water. Thank you," she mumbled.

Dominic raised a finger and summoned the waiting page. "Drinking water," he said, "for Mistress Jetta." He then turned back to her. "Eat. But also talk. I don't have that many questions, but what I ask, you must answer."

She had started to eat and was particularly enjoying the smoked bacon.

"You don't need to ask me questions, I'll tell you," she said, swallowing the mouthful. "I didn't have proper parents, when I was old enough, I went to work in a big house – in London. I kept getting punished. The master of the house was – abusive. His son was worse. I hated it there and I dreamt about how wonderful it would be if I was really free. Like you. So, I crept out when I had an opportunity. Yes, I stole a wherry. It was the smallest on the pier, and it wasn't chained. I didn't know how to row so I was horribly slow, but I kept going. I hid most days and travelled most nights. When you found me with the boat tied to the tree, I'd been asleep for hours. I hadn't seen your farrier. I didn't see him, and I heard nothing except the wind and the water. If I can have my boat back, I'll just travel on and I'll never bother you again." She took a breath, sipped her water and waited for his response.

"An interesting answer to not a single question," Dominic nodded, pushing his platter away. "Now let us try again. First, you give your name as Jetta Lawson. Where did this originate if you had no known parents?"

"I was given to a priest when I was a few weeks old. And the woman who left me at the church gave my name and then ran away. The priest told me later." Jetta swallowed quickly. She appeared to be enjoying her breakfast.

"The next question. How long did you stay with this priest? Or did you run? You certainly appear to have a habit of running."

Jetta gulped down the last of her water. "The priest gave me to the convent behind the church. I hated the nuns. They weren't kind, they weren't even nice to each other. I was about six when I ran away."

When Dominic stood, he was smiling. "An early desire for liberty, I see," said his lordship. "Most six-year-old children prefer security. Who did you run to?"

"To the fields up past St. John's Woods," Jetta said. These weren't memories she wanted to relive, but they weren't the parts of her life she would refuse to admit either.

Dominic regarded his reluctant guest. She was painfully thin and the cheeks on her face were sun burned in the manner most women would find appalling. The skin was pretty in fact, but sunken, pushing out the sharp edge of her bones. She did not look, to him, like a woman who had suffered from birth. He expected lies. But as yet, he saw no proof of it.

"You lived in a forest as a child? What in the devil's name did you eat?"

Jetta blushed. The first indication, Dominic wondered, of a lie. "I begged at back doors. I begged at kitchens, or I climbed in windows. I learned about mushrooms that grew under the trees. There were fruits and seeds and nuts. I never ate much but sometimes people were kind when I went to their doors."

"You spent years in this way?"

"I think so. I couldn't count them. They didn't roll evenly. Sometimes time was very, very slow. I knew when I was six. I didn't know any of my ages after that. I don't know how old I am now, but I can't be less than twenty."

"You were adopted?" Dominic had not intended these questions. He wanted to test her, to see how much she lied, and discover whether there was any possibility that she had killed his farrier. But now he asked everything for a very different reason. He simply wanted to know. The story interested him.

"In a way." She looked increasingly uncomfortable. "I went begging at the kitchen doors of a huge house in the city. The cook answered the door. He was nice and went to fetch me what had been left over after dinner. But then the steward came and pulled me in. He presented me to the man and his wife sitting there. He said I was a beggar and a thief. I hadn't stolen anything, but the house owner ordered me whipped. He said I could be a scullery maid in the kitchens as long as I did as I was told. So, I did as I was told. Well, some of it. I was told to do – the most horrible – things."

"And that's why you've run away this time?"

She nodded but avoided his dark eyes, looking into her lap. "Yes. And I've never killed anyone in my life. And if you let me go, I'd be so incredibly grateful. And if you don't want me to have the stolen boat back, it doesn't matter. I'll just walk and follow the riverbank. You'll never see me again."

For a moment, Dominic decided that would be a shame. He did not say it. Eventually, he spoke, "You may not have noticed, but there's not a visible scrap of you that appears even averagely clean. You also have what I might call an unusual – odour. Now, I wonder if you'd take a bath? I can order the tub set up in one of the bedchambers not covered in broken glass. A fire could be lit. Hot water, soap and towels would obviously be supplied, but you would then be left alone." He watched the distrust grow in her expression and smiled. "Personally, I have somewhere important to go and someone to see. I can consider your position while I'm away. But I'll be back this evening." He waited, then asked suddenly, "Do you read?"

"I don't see why you need to know," she frowned, "but yes, I do."

He lifted an eyebrow. "Unusual for a beggar girl."

"The nuns taught me." She waited for an explanation, then spoke into the lack of it. "But I would – very much – like a bath – as long as I can bathe myself."

"I'll arrange it." Dominic stood facing her. His face seemed placid. She was unaccustomed to his less ice-cold expression. "One of the maids will take you up to the right room while they fill the tub from buckets of water heated over the fire. And unless you have managed meantime to escape down the well, I shall see you at supper. And to fill the time between bath and supper, I'll arrange for a couple of printed books to be left in the room."

"To be left alone with a boiling hot bath," Jetta murmured. "It sounds so wonderful."

Dominic was smiling as he left.

―※◇※―

Once outside in the morning sunshine, he turned, speaking to the steward who had opened the front doors for him. "The stolen wherry," he said briefly. "Have it returned to one of the London piers. I don't care which one, I have no idea how you'll arrange it. Work it out yourself."

He then strode on through his own grounds and down to the river's edge. Half a mile perhaps, from the stable block through the heavily wooded pathway to the riverbank. Once again, he studied the old willow tree where his farrier had been found. It had seemed strange, for here it was partially hidden yet not entirely. Looking again, it seemed unlikely that the man had been killed in that place.

In the middle of the night, past midnight at the earliest, it seemed illogical and therefore unlikely that Fillip Pike would have been sitting in that precise spot. There seemed no obvious reason.

Yet if the farrier had been killed elsewhere, why then risk being seen while carrying a corpse to such a spot.

The man had been discovered in a dark and sticky puddle of blood. Not surprising, since his head was partially decapitated by knife or axe, and there was also a deep cut across the belly. The corpse remained fully clothed, but those clothes were also thick with drying blood, and one sleeve was ripped, leaving the arm, mottled and bloody, naked on the ground.

However, from the stomach wound, no blood had leaked to the grass beneath, and to Dominic, long aware of the devastating appearance of a battlefield once the carnage was finished, found this strange. Indeed, unlikely.

The method of killing also seemed excessive. He doubted whether a young woman could easily have found such strength, especially one as skinny as a knife herself. There was, however, no proof of anything and a hundred more questions floated around him like the dark smelling smoke from a chimney.

No rain had fallen but his people had thrown buckets of boiling water, and the blood was no longer lying in a great black puddle. It had spread diluted, though remained visible as a winding trace of unpleasant ribbon. Just a month previously, the entire area had been a slope of bluebells, silent in the breezes. But the mass of such beauty had faded as it did every year when spring approached summer. Dominic had walked the riverbank then, enjoying bird song, the spring colours, and the river's delight in catching the first rainbows.

It was no longer a place he might remember as a favourite to wander. But now Dominic explored every tree, every damp slope, and every shadowed spot beneath the drooping branches. He could find nothing which might add an explanation to his questions.

Once impatient with the useless wanderings, his lordship briskly turned and marched back to the stables. He ordered his usual mare saddled.

His huge gleaming destrier saw his master and kicked at the door, demanding attention. Dominic laughed. "Perhaps it's a warhorse I need today after all, Kram, my proud stallion. But no. I shall order an extra helping of turnips instead, and you can munch your boredom away."

The young groom Pip Pike brought the mare, fully saddled, and Dom mounted, heading towards the road that led back into the city. He rode slowly, enjoying the wind in his horse's mane as it twisted back against her neck. He stroked her, leaning forwards as he saw her ears twitch, waiting for his voice.

VESPERS

"My beautiful Felicia, how sweet if you learned to speak. You might have seen exactly what will now take me weeks to discover."

Ambling in the sunshine, seemingly without any particular desire to arrive, Dominic headed west. He took only two other riders with him, one being the head groom, and the other as a guard. Being attacked or needing protection did not occur to him.

Chapter Six

The hot water was as glorious as she had expected. Jetta lay back against the wooden lip of the large half barrel, unperturbed by the uncushioned ledge. No splinters attacked the vulnerability of her neck. She sat long in steam.

As a child at the convent, she had, under orders, bathed fully clothed. As a servant at the small Maddock Estate, she had bathed rarely and never alone.

Now the experience was one of joy. It was, perhaps, less joyful to watch the flakes of mud, dirt and grime which floated from her body and scummed the top of the water. She attempted to scoop this off with the cupped palm of her hand and dropped it onto the tunic she had previously been wearing. Now the threadbare shift lay flat and filthy on the rug beside the tub. Since it was already foul, more sludge would make little difference. But she didn't want second-hand grime on the thick rugged luxury of the floor, nor back on the emerging cleanliness of her body.

That vile man had blatantly informed her that she stank. She believed it but hadn't wanted to be told. Now at least she'd smell of soap. Not so bad.

More than anything she wanted to escape. Not to be remembered. And yet, absurdly, she hated the thought of being remembered as a slut who ruined what was beautiful by adding only what was ugly.

It had been sometime since she had seen herself naked, and certainly since she had stood both naked and alone. The heat of the water was deliciously soothing. Where she had been hurt, whipped, grazed and bruised, the pain eased into memory.

Soaking both physically and mentally seemed so relaxing, but the sweet peace turned gradually to determination. Jetta could see herself leaping into action. There could be little likelihood of her achieving anything amazing, but now she felt she could run, or even fly. Hot water and soap, she decided, were far more magical than she had expected.

There were problems of course. For clean sparkling skin to re-immerse itself in the filth of the only item of clothing she owned, seemed deeply disappointing.

Another problem quickly announced itself. She couldn't get out of the tub .

Her knees were scrunched to her chest, the tub was too restricting for her to stand and even if she miraculously managed such a feat, the only escape would be to tip the whole thing over, hot water and all.

In fact, the water was no longer hot. She had soaked for so long, the water was now clouded with soap and dirt in a tepid scum. Looking around, feeling trapped again, Jetta grabbed the sides of the tub with both hands and tried to rise. It wasn't working. All over again she felt foolish.

There was a careful tap on the door. Jetta stayed quiet and sat almost paralysed. Then the soft voice floated through the keyhole.

"Mistress, are you finished? I was ordered to bring you towels and new clothes once you were ready. May I help you dry yourself? And dress?"

It was the perfect offer at the perfect moment. Jetta called, "Oh do come in. Yes please."

Without any unlocking of doors, a small plump woman bustled in and deposited her armful of linen on the bed, then stretched out two buxom hands. "Looks hard to climb out, I understand, mistress. But just take my hands."

Not so hard. Once she was helped, it was just one leg out and then the other. Those same strong and sturdy fingers, disappearing beneath a wide white towel, began to dry her. Brisk, more scrubbing than soothing, Jetta barely had time to think. Something cool and white was draped over her head.

She squeaked, "But my hair's wet."

"We'll wrap it warm in a small towel until it dries," said the woman. "Then I shall help you comb it out. "

"You're - so kind."

"I'm just Mary, mistress, doing as I'm told."

A long lead backed mirror hung beside the door to the garderobe. Jetta stood there, amazed. The surface had been cloaked in steam from the bath, but now gradually it had cleared, and a young slim woman stood staring back at Jetta. She wore a soft gown in palest pink with red poppy embroidery around the neckline and at the end of the flared sleeves. It was tied tightly beneath her breasts with a wide silken band and below this the material swirled in impressive folds. The high band made her breasts look a little larger. Beneath she wore a white linen shift far nicer, she decided, than the tunic she'd worn as her only covering for several years.

A stranger stood looking back from the mirror.

Jetta couldn't move away, and then noticed that Mary was sniggering. "Like it, my lady? Good. Now let's untangle that lovely hair. Would you like me to shave off your eyebrows?"

"I'm not a lady," Jetta whispered back. "So, no. But I'd love all the knots to be cut from my hair."

"Combed, dear. Not cut." And Mary began to do as she said. Jetta sat meekly, her hands clasped in her lap. Even when the combing made her jerk with pain, she accepted the grooming and said nothing. When eventually Mary announced, "All done," Jetta scrambled up and once more hurried to the mirror.

Now the stranger who stared back, was a woman so amazingly sophisticated, Jetta felt suddenly shy of the person she had become. Her hair, now drying quickly in the fire warmed bedchamber, was a sleek cloak to her waist, thick, and dark brown, beginning to curl up just where it had dried.

"It isn't me," Jetta whispered.

Ignoring this remark, Mary began to tidy up, bundling the damp towels, comb and soap into her embrace. "Well, mistress, I hope you feel a little better. I'll get a couple of lads to clear the tub."

Jetta danced. Her skirts flowed out around her legs, and she felt the swirl of her hair around her face. She wore shoes now, the first in a long time, brown leather, flat soled, buckled and very comfortable. Beneath these were warm stockings, held just above the knee by black lace garters. She pulled a stool in front of the mirror and looked at herself for a long, long time.

There was one realisation accompanying this dramatic change, and Jetta realised it almost at once. The sense of captivity, the belief that she was incapable and born doomed, had been all her own self-pity. A wash followed by clean clothes had altered everything. She was the same person inside but felt entirely different.

Midday sunshine glistened on the pork chops she was served for dinner at the long table. No one else sat there, so she ate alone. Lord Stark, therefore, had spoken the truth when he had explained he'd be gone for most of the day. But she had not been taken to dine in the kitchens beside the servants, nor even in the annexe with the steward, the principal housekeeper and chief cook himself. Jetta sat alone at the great table just as if she was indeed the lady, she now thought she resembled.

With the large linen napkin over her shoulder, her hair tucked behind her ears, and her hands remembering the correct use of spoon and knife, Jetta ate everything she could and found it all delicious.

Sadly, perhaps, since it would be a long time before she might eat so well again.

But having been supplied with excellent clothes and even shoes, she knew she could leave the great house and begin to walk the long road to freedom. No boat unfortunately. But neither was there someone lurking to grab her as she made her escape. Indeed, it was likely that the great generosity of his lordship was a disguised hint for her to disappear and leave him without the trouble of keeping her and visiting the sheriff.

He had clearly disliked that sheriff. But she had the impression that he disliked her too. She had not, after all, been the ideal guest. This made his wish for her to leave more probable.

Leaving the dining table, Jetta approached the front door. No one made the slightest move to stop her. Indeed, no one guarded the front doorway at all, and the doors lay open to the sunshine. Jetta had no idea where her cloak might be. But the weather was fine, and she could now travel without shivering to death, even when sleeping under trees at night.

Hesitating at first, she walked from the great house towards the higher slopes she could see in the distance. Away from the stables, and away from the river. She felt the sunbeams on the back of her neck and adored the comfort of it all.

A cobbled pathway led from the house through a garden of hedges and golden flowers waving at her in the breeze. The hedges were grown in a vast pattern, which she avoided, and kept to the one path. Just for a moment, she was tempted by a wooden bench beneath a birch tree, and she sat, gazing up at the light through the leaves. The bird song was constant with the chaffing of the chaffinches, the twitter, the chirp, and the glorious liquid warble of blackbirds.

Leaving the bench, Jetta walked on and continued to listen to the bird song and the crunch of her feet on the path. No limping as pebbles cut into bare feet, but almost a skip of leather shoes to flat stones. She felt the swing of the expensive skirts at her ankles and wanted to sing with the birds.

It was a long way, she realised, from the house to the public road. His lordship's private land stretched endlessly, it also seemed endlessly beautiful. It was a walk she had enjoyed much more than her earlier escapes. But the public thoroughfare was less enjoyable. Although the road was well kept, being cut back at either side, little seemed attractive. The birds still sang, and a cuckoo called from the high branches. Beyond the roadside and a short cut hedge, she could see a farm stretching to the horizon, crops in neat rows, and beyond another neat hedge was a small group of sheep, two with lambs hiding motionless in the grass. Young ones hid from foxes, eagles and owls, and Jetta felt increasingly uncomfortable. Her own doubts grew, as if she should also hide in the grass from danger. The beauty of the vast grounds she had left, now seemed to remind her that her freedom could be at risk with every corner she turned, even as she passed each village she could not avoid. One of those villages, inevitably, would house the sheriff.

Abruptly the sky clouded, and the sunbeams shrank. It reminded Jetta of her guilt. To have taken the food, the expense of the bath and the care of the woman Mary, and especially, to have dressed in the clothes without thanks to the lord who had supplied them were by no means the actions of a polite, gracious or thankful female.

And clothes that had actually fitted. Even the shoes. Had the man correctly judged such matters without measurements taken? He had never even touched her.

Untrue, perhaps, since he had grabbed her and hurled her into the various rooms where he had locked her in. But there had been a reason and Jetta did not resent it. She had resented him though, there had been little to like. Yet he had sent away the sheriff. And he had supplied clothes, clothes of a lady. Simple but the prettiest Jetta had seen and far, far prettier than any she had ever worn.

She continued walking straight while her mind whirled in circles. At a point where the road forked, she stopped and read the signs.

They pointed to Chiswick back the way she had come. Further on two villages east and one north were listed. Then, another signpost announced Oxford further east. All appeared to be many miles ahead. Jetta sighed. She didn't need to make a specific choice since there was no specific direction she needed. Oxford, she decided, might be beautiful with a chance for her to find work in a brewery, a laundry, an inn or even a tavern, yet the arrow to Oxford appeared far too distant to consider. Had she still been wearing her tunic, she would have sat on the grass verge to consider her decision. But she was not going to spoil her beautiful new clothes. Instead, she hovered, bit her lip, and sighed again.

Then, without any thought, she simply walked straight on.

She had walked quite some distance, or at least it had seemed to be, when the thunderous noise floated from far behind her. Growing louder as it came closer, Jetta heard the shattering echoes of men shouting as they rode full speed.

Backing to the side of the road, Jetta pressed herself to the bushes, accepting bracken and blackberry thorns to her shoulders and neck. Sudden fear made her wonder if this was Lord Stark come to drag her back and punish her for yet another escape.

A party of men galloped past her, mid road, heading into the wind. But no one stopped. No one looked at her. Clearly it wasn't her they wanted, and Jetta exhaled deeply with relief.

They would, Jetta still smiled to herself, reach Oxford far sooner than she would. The horses were moving at full tilt, the men had heads down to their mounts' necks, clenched leather fingers grasped the reins, and the sound of the hooves on the cobbles was a hurricane of speed. Politics, lords or guards. Of no consequence to her. Although surely of importance to others. For this was a world she did not understand.

Standing very still until the dust settled and the sounds died away, Jetta shook her head, not at the riders but at herself.

Abruptly she turned and refusing to think in pointless circles any longer, she began to walk steadily back to the manor house, keeping now to the roadside where the cobbles faded into the weedy verge, and even enjoying the wind in her hair now blowing behind her, as if trying to quicken her journey.

    Hardly a breeze, but nor was it a gale. Not strong enough to tangle any of those beautiful silken curls that Mary had combed, it was simply a fresh wind, and Jetta was once again smiling when she eventually arrived back at the great open gates leading to the hedges and pathway of the Stark Manor and the imminent possibility of supper.

Chapter Seven

He spent several hours with Andrew, Lord Leays, his friend of some years.
"That wretch'll be back. I assume you know that?" Dominic said. "He's discovered a rising ambition after years of sitting as a sunken exile, I assume his mother is encouraging him."

"The Beaufort woman has been trying to get her son back for years," said Andrew Cobham. "But our dear King Edward refused every attempt. He disliked and distrusted the Tudors. Hardly surprising."

Dominic stretched out his legs, head back as he gazed up at the vaulted ceiling, its painted patterns and the great wooden ceiling beyond. Unlike most homes, however grand and including his own, no spiders spun their webs from beam to beam and no splatter of mouse droppings spoiled the colours. "You know the complicated story, I assume?" He grinned at Andrew.

"At the time I was living in a wreck of a house outside the Wall, with the destructive stench of the tanneries brought to me as a gift by the wind." Andrew was also grinning. "My friends were the riffraff I welcomed to live alongside and used as spies. I knew more gossip

VESPERS

than truth, though I heard some a little closer to the truth from His Majesty's court in past months."

"My family was never close to the mismatch of Margaret Beaufort's life," Dominic answered. "But she was one of the wealthiest heirs in the country. She deserved a better life."

"I saw her at Richard's coronation. We've never spoken."

Leaning back, Dominic sighed. "Permit me to bore you. Tudor, the first in the new line, was the illegitimate son of the wretched French queen left a widow by Henry V, poor soul. She had two bastard sons by her Welsh steward. Her royal son was Henry VI, the boy tried to be kind to his woebegone mother and declared these two bastard children legitimate. He even married one off to the wealthy child. Edmund Tudor, whom I never met, but sounds like a bastard in more ways than one since Margaret was only thirteen when he married her, and instead of waiting as is the civilised custom, he immediately got her with child. She was just fourteen when Henry was born, and nearly died."

Andrew shrugged. "A vile story from every angle. I imagine it's not what the poor woman wants widely known."

"But at least both survived. Then Edmund Tudor himself died of the plague. God given justice, I imagine."

"I met the aspiring Henry Tudor several times." Andrew sipped his wine. "He suffers from a complete lack of humour but fosters an ambitious aspiration to any position above his rights. Naturally he resents the treatment he's suffered from years of exile and the distrust of our gentle English folk. Of course, as we all know, he's attempted an invasion already."

Dominic drained his cup, and took the jug, replenishing both cups. He sighed. "And was turned back by storms, not by England's mighty forces."

"So yes, indeed. He will try again."

A rummage of disjointed thoughts delayed Dominic's answer. There had been battle after battle to remove the erratic Lancastrian king, the wretched Henry VI. A king of fading mentality, poor sick

Henry remained on the throne only through the determination of others. He was, finally, a pitiful creature who could not command a wherry across the Thames. He died by the new king Edward's orders.

The crown, after battles across the land and the deaths of more than had even been killed by the plague, they said, went back to the Yorkists. King Edward IV was long reigned despite many failures both mental and physical. And now his younger brother Richard, was gradually, after only two years, earning respect and popularity.

Lord Stark, supporting the Yorkists through the long tradition of his family, had little argument when faced with the possibility of a Tudor invasion. He was thinking aloud, as Andrew nodded. Dominic sighed, "Though I've always supported the Yorkists as my father did, I can understand why the Lancastrians battled for their own position. But this Tudor creature is a bastard of bastard stock and even in the Lancastrian line, stands many miles from any right to the throne."

Andrew lifted his cup in salute. "We all know this, my friend. I believe your mind wanders. You're thinking of something else entirely."

Dominic had been invited to discuss the threat of a Tudor invasion. But it was an entirely different invasion which dug into his thoughts. He nodded. "You know about the girl," he said. "My suspicions of her as a murderer have faded. I should set her free and think nothing more of her."

"But you do think of her, even while I speak regarding Henry Tudor and the French threat." Andrew chuckled. "You can't help yourself, my friend. Perhaps I should meet this strange servant girl. Or bring her to meet my Tyballis."

"Your wife is too generous and loves everybody."

"Even myself."

"So back to matters of state," Dominic dutifully leaned forwards again. "Apart from his mother, Tudor's backing was once very small. An attempt at friendship from the Breton duke towards his polite visitor brought some tentative backing. But now Tudor's been frightened off to France, he's in a far stronger position. Now the French king is backing him with a good strength of mercenaries, and he'll haul his criminal prisoners over to fight as well. Ludicrous."

"You know full well, the French have no interest in Tudor. Their interest is purely in finding any excuse to fight against England and wither our strength for when they next choose to cross the Narrow Sea."

Dominic lowered his voice as though the French might be listening. "They'll pay for Swiss mercenaries. And all England's staunch Lancastrians, even those who have long accepted the fall back to York, will now realise their chance. Old anger will resurface."

"It sounds to me," Andrew said, gazing at his friend, "that you suspect Tudor might win. But we have great military strength here too, my suspicious friend. And some great leaders, including our king; Richard's no sluggard in battle, whereas I doubt Tudor's ever lifted a sword in his life."

"But the English," Dom once again stared at the great beamed arches of the ceiling, "are bitterly tired of battle. Half our nobility will assume Richard can win easily enough without them. So many will cuddle down with a cup of wine and pretend they know nothing of any battle. Our dear king, much loved as he is becoming, will muster the entire country but may not bring them all.'

"What grand pessimism," Andrew said.

"I hope to be wrong. But with the French, mercenaries and prisoners fighting for their freedom, half of Wales and a few of the Scots, all the Woodvilles and the old Lancastrian supporters?"

Andrew frowned. "I supported Edward, but I'll support King Richard with twice the enthusiasm. I will continue to believe in our Lord's inevitable success."

"And there's Stanley," Dominic said, draining his refilled cup. "Will he back the son of his wife?"

Again, Andrew shook his head. "You worry like a child learning to ride his first pony when he can still hardly walk. Stanley has no love for Margaret, especially since he's never even bedded the woman. Tudor's mother lets nobody near her, whether married or not. She won't risk the agony and near death of bearing another child. Besides, Stanley only ever supports the side he is sure will win."

"Life," murmured Dominic, "is a jumble of luck rising to help us, then falling to destroy us. And whatever we do to deserve either the bad or the good, luck will make its own choices."

Andrew was shaking his head, not with disagreement but with the weight of his own experience. "Many men are drunk on passion and love to fight. The battlefield is a drug of delight. Some men will fight on without knowing what they fight for. I've known men who'll kill a friend once that energy blinds them. Others cringe. They'll slip away, or pretend they never heard the call."

"I hope I'm neither of those," Dominic murmured.

Now Andrew was grinning.

It was sometime later when he left his friend and dismissed his groom with a message for the countess to say he would be late returning for supper. Dominic passed the Palace of Westminster and took The Strand towards the River Fleet. Before the river's small bridge, however, he turned north and stopped at the old priory of St. John's.

The ancient stone building spread itself south of the farmlands and fields cultivated and hedged beneath the sunshine. But his lordship rode directly to the doorway of the priory itself, where he dismounted and threw his reins to the stable boy loitering there.

Look after her, Cooper. I won't be long."

The door was opened to him not by a monk but by a page.

"My lord?" Dominic's clothes made his station obvious.

"I wish to speak with your abbot," Dominic said. "I have no idea of his name, but I presume you do?"

The page seemed confused. "Abbot Frances leads us, my lord," he said. "But he rarely sees visitors outside church business."

"And how old is your unaccommodating abbot?" Dominic asked.

The page shook his small head, puzzled. "It's not common knowledge, my lord. But he is certainly an elderly man."

"Then take me to him," Dominic said, walking past the boy and into the long dark corridor. "Elderly means he has been here long enough to be the man I need. The business I have may not be vital to the church but it's vital to me, and that is sufficient. Take me directly."

Abbot Francis woke with a jolt and sat in a hurry, trying to straighten his habit. His anger faded as he saw the tall man leaning over him, unknown to him, but clearly a gentleman of importance.

"My apologies for the interruption, sir," Dominic said without any apologetic expression, "but I have some important questions. They do not regard your ministry, nor any recent situation within this monastery. However, I need your help and consider it urgent."

He sat opposite the aged abbot and began to explain. Rubbing the sleep from his eyes, the monk started to take an interest. "I remember her," he said, smiling faintly. "I'd barely seen a baby in my life before. Then this chubby little bundle was put into my arms. I was no abbot back then, just one of the monks, and when this tiny hand clasped my finger, I was delighted. I understood our Lord God's great design all over again."

"Yet it was the child's mother burdened you with this infant?" Dominic asked, "and told you her name, I believe, before she then disappeared?"

"Ah," sighed the abbot, sounding even older than he looked. "I cannot remember such details from so long ago. Years pass slowly, you know, in the Lord God's sublime service. I shall have to discover my old parchments. I must have it scribed somewhere. If you wish to wait my lord, I shall send one of the novices with the details once I discover them. But I cannot be sure to discover what you hope for, my lord."

Frowning, Dominic sighed. "Yet you remember the infant herself very clearly?"

"A great pleasure," smiled the abbot. "We remember our pleasure, do we not? But details and what was spoken, ah no, that's what fades into time."

The two men stared at each other. Dominic still frowned. The abbot still smiled. "I have been told some details," Dominic stated. "But I need both corroboration and facts that can then be proved."

"Proof?" sniggered the abbot. "That's a matter of Christian faith, my lord. Forget the need for proof and accept the trust we live in. Is there proof that the sun will ever shine again? Is there proof that one day we shall all die?"

"It depends," Dominic's frown deepened, "what you mean as proof. I have all the proof I need that children are born of mothers. I wish to know something of Jetta Lawson's mother when she brought her child here." His smile showed the wide gap where his front teeth had fallen away. The abbot snapped his mouth shut, and simply stared. "And I am not referring to a virgin birth," Dom added.

"I swore, on the Lord God's holy book, that I'd never repeat the words of that sweet woman," he murmured. Even as his voice dropped low, his accent remained strong, and to Dominic, it sounded distinctly Italian. The abbot continued. "And I will never break my oath." He stood slowly and pointed through the small window. "But there behind the priory is a convent, where the holy mothers of our same church, although with the name of their own saint, live in great sanctity. It was there that I took that little child all those years ago. As a man and a monk, I could not nurture and raise a female child on my own. Go there, my lord, and ask for the Abbess. But whether she also swore silence, I cannot say."

With his horse led by the reins, Dominic left the stretching green of the monastery grounds and took the short pathway to the larger stone building behind, crouching beneath its short tower, and the great brass bell which rang each hour. Its echo pounded through the trees but did not disturb the birds which appeared accustomed.

Three times the bell rang. There was, it seemed, time for everything and although the clouds swept in from down river, the sunshine continued to warm the day.

Dominic knocked loudly. Eventually after the third knock, a very young girl peeped through the small, barred flap opening high within the closed door.

VESPERS

"May I help, my lord?" the child asked in a whisper. Dom was sure she had to be standing tip toe.

He told her, "I trust so. I need to speak with your abbess."

The novice shook her head and stepped back. "Abbess Adelina refuses to see anyone without an appointment, my lord." She half closed the flap. "May I take a message. Or shall I make an appointment for – perhaps – the following week?"

"You may make an appointment for this moment, should you wish to," Dom told her. "But I have an urgent number of questions and intend seeing her without delay. Now open the door."

Somewhat surprised and intimidated by his tone, the child did as he demanded. She pointed down the corridor. "The second door on the right, my lord, just past the great hall."

Without waiting for her, Dominic followed the direction, and knocked once on the narrow door lying deep in shadow. No one opened the door, but as he knocked again, it opened itself. An elderly woman heavily covered in the thick grey flannel of her habit, looked up in surprise. She was sitting at a table, reading from a scroll, still half rolled. Her lips moved as she read. Then she turned in a hurry.

"My lord, what are you doing here?"

He bowed. "My Lady, I have questions which are of considerable importance both to me and to others. Some events occurred here some nineteen or twenty years ago? May I ask, were you already resident in this convent?"

"I was, although not as abbess," she said softly. "First, sir, give me your name. Then we can discuss your unexpected urgency."

She pointed to a small stool. Dominic sat, and he began to explain who he was and why he was there. He did not mention that Jetta had declared the convent cruel at that time, but he explained that she had run away when roughly six years of age and had not wished to become a noviciate.

The abbess smiled back with tolerant patience.

"Not everyone finds the discipline of servitude an easy following, while Latin and the constant reading in Latin of the Holy Book is not easy to a simple mind. I remember the girl you mean. We frequently have orphans delivered here, babies found on our doorstep, others handed in at the church. Sadly, not such a rare event. We bring these infants up in righteousness and encourage them to enter the sanctity of the church. The one you mention, if I am remembering the right child, was not either suitable or willing. She may have suffered from certain mental deficiencies, or even loose morals at birth."

"I cannot see," Dominic tented his hands, fingertips meeting below his jaw, as he regarded the woman, "that an infant has the remotest understanding of morality. However, that is not what I asked. I simply wished to know how she came into care here. Was it the abbess at that time who accepted her?"

"Indeed yes," the present abbess said, leaning across the table. "But that was not myself, and nor did the blessed lady speak to me of it. Abbess Randella was a kind and gracious lady, much admired and much followed. But she did not sink to gossip and would not have told others what was not their business. I therefore have no idea surrounding that girl's parents or her destination when she left of her own free will. You would do better to ask Abbot Frances at the priory."

"He sent me here," Dominic said.

"Then I cannot help you," the abbess answered. "Now I must ask you to leave as it is almost time for five o'clock prayers."

"Five of which clock, I wonder," Dominic smiled, "and does a child of just six years leave any place of her own free will. And without being followed to ensure safety?"

It was less than an hour since he had heard the convent bell ring only three times, yet Dom nodded, thanked her, and strode impatiently from the tiny study and back out into the corridor.

But as he left, a very small woman passed him, scurrying in the shadows. She seemed placid, but her face was deeply wrinkled. Dominic abruptly stood solid in her path and bowed. "My lady," he murmured, "Might I have a word with you? I am assuming that you were present here when the Lady Randella was abbess some years ago? Would you object to answering a few brief questions regarding what happened at that time?"

"My lord?"

"Or are you rushing off for the five o'clock prayers?" he smiled.

"My lord, it's only half of the hour past three of the clock," she said. "I'd be happy to help."

"In that case," Dominic smiled, "you are exactly the lady I'd hoped to meet. I am Dominic, Earl of Desford. I have questions, though nothing personal. Shall we sit in the great hall for a few minutes?"

"I've no objection to that, sir," the nun said, seemingly unhurried. "Come with me. The hall will be empty at this hour, and we can talk in privacy."

Chapter Eight

That night as the spring month of May trailed to its last hours, Jetta chose her own bed. There seemed no particular need to stumble back up the narrow steps and into the dismal cupboard they called the attic where she had passed the night before. The straw pallet had felt like returning to the years she had slept on the floor, the grass, the wooden planks of the wherry or the piled straw in the kitchen where she had worked.

Lord Stark was absent so neither he nor anyone else was determining her destination.

The first bedchamber allotted to her had been the one she loved, even though she had escaped it twice. Now she relished the warm comfort of the bed and was soon asleep.

She was aware, without particular concern, that Lord Stark had not returned home within her hearing. She had wanted to show herself, proving that on the one day when escaping would have been unrestrictedly easy, she had chosen to stay.

"His lordship," had said the steward, "has informed the household that he will be back for a late supper."

Jetta had not needed to wait for that. Now eating enough in one day to last her a week, she decided to wait and see his lordship on the following morning. There was no urgency, he probably wasn't interested any longer any way. And so, she slept.

Waking in the night while the rich darkness enveloped the bedchamber, she realised she had been dreaming of the man she disliked. She knew it for a dream and had no fears of strange visitations but seeing him in her sleep had seemed strange. He had come to her asking for something she couldn't understand. Now she remembered shouting, "I'll sleep where I want. Go away and leave me alone."

He had answered without words. "If I cannot find myself, how can anyone else find me?"

The next morning, absurdly, she traced back through the dream, and remembered how she had watched the man. There had been desperation in his silent words, yet only being a dream, she had been more interested in how he looked. Her dream-self had smiled at the muscled strength of his naked arms, and the long reaching fingers, flat knuckled and wildly flexible.

Certainly, she had never seen him like that when awake, and was quite sure that she never would. Half-naked, yet his thick hair pushed back from his face showing the bruises along his jaw, a deep graze across one high cheekbone, and a heavy swelling around one dark cold eye. There was blood on his neck which seemed to come from the back of his head. He had been attacked, although Jetta could not imagine why.

No velvet coat, no peplum from any doublet, Jetta had seen only a torn tunic top over bare arms, and the leg hugging hose, black silk and knitted, that followed those long thigh muscles and curved down the calves before then covering the feet. No shoes. The figure was slouched on a crude stone floor, slumped back against a stone wall.

Enough of dreams. It had been strange, indeed absurd. Now she wanted the reality.

Jetta jumped from the bed as the sunbeams slanted through the window and dressed herself in the one new set she had been given. Since it hooked up beneath her arm, not too tight since she was pathetically skinny, she was able to fasten this without help. Then she virtually danced down the stairs to the hall. Breakfast was indeed being served, and she sat where his lordship had sat her several times before.

But he, once again, was not present. Instead, a tall woman with a glacial expression glared at her from across the table. The food, as usual, was delicious. The atmosphere was not.

Yet since the dour and elderly woman ate in silence, Jetta raised her cup of breakfast ale, and spoke softly. "May I introduce myself, my lady? I'm Jetta Lawson and I believe you are – the Countess of – Stark? Or Desford? Should I perhaps apologise for appearing as a stranger at your dining table?"

The countess scowled back. "I am Lady Stark, Countess of Desford, ignorant child," she hissed through her remaining teeth. "And yes, I should certainly expect an apology from one of my grandson's whores who should never appear in my presence. But since my grandson is missing, I cannot speak with him concerning this, or anything else. I have no intention of speaking with you instead."

Jetta shrank, hurriedly placing her cup back on the table. "I'm, honestly not one – of them, my lady. I met your grandson – well, in odd circumstances. I'm sure he wouldn't even call me a friend."

"He'd not call you anything at the moment," the countess said still through pursed lips. "The wretched man has disappeared." She fluttered a bejewelled hand, and then grasped her cup and drained it with a gulp. "The horrid boy disappears often enough, but he always leaves some scrap of a message. Besides, the message that he *did* leave me, was quite inaccurate." She stood abruptly, hands flat on the table as she leaned over and stared down into Jetta's worried expression. "And *you*, miss, are the disgraceful harlot who smashed through my bedchamber window and attempted to attack me."

"Oh dear," Jetta sighed. "Yes, I am, my lady. But no, I'm not. I mean, I was trying to run away. I certainly never intended attacking you, nor anyone else." She inhaled and finished her ale. "And I'm no harlot."

"Then where's my grandson?" the lady demanded.

Her hair was grey beneath a small veil of netting which was pinned around her head, with one silvery curl escaping. She had shaved her eyebrows and hairline as was the custom but appeared to have done this herself without a mirror. She did not, Jetta decided, look remotely like her grandson.

"I have no idea where he is." Jetta now frowned. Lady Stark's glower was far too close. "I know he was expected back for a late supper, but I went to sleep before that." She did not mention his strange appearance in her dream.

Still standing, Lady Stark clapped her hands and roared for Benson. The steward entered immediately. "What exactly may I do for you, my lady?" He bowed. Clearly, she demanded more deference than did her grandson, although he was now the earl.

"Benson," she said, "his lordship has not returned. Where did he say he was going?"

Bowing again, Benson said, "My lady, my apologies but his lordship did not offer me his entire itinerary. First, I know, he intended visiting Lord Leays at his residence near Westminster. But beyond that, my lady, he told me nothing, simply to expect him for a late supper."

"Very well." The lady marched from the table with the same continuous glare. "I shall visit Lord Leays and demand to know when my grandson left there, and where he went. Benson, arrange a horse and litter."

"My lady, I shall do so immediately, and will arrange your retinue. Do you wish your private maid to accompany you in the litter?"

"Goodness no, she's a frightened little thing without a brain in her entire body. She can't even cut my hair properly." Lady Stark looked around. "You," she pointed at Jetta. "You'll come with me. You seem happy jumping through people's windows, so I assume you won't be frightened of me or anyone else. Get yourself a cloak and hurry up. I expect to meet up with you at the front door in less than half an hour."

Absolutely wordless, Jetta stared back. Finally, she managed the words. "But my lady, you've accused me of – all types of horrid things – and yet you want my company?"

"You'll do as I tell you without complaint and without bursting into tears as my maid would. And Dominic would never have invited his whore to breakfast, so I assume you are just some lost chit begging for food. Now, come along and get ready. Don't fiddle around, I'm in a hurry."

"Yes, my lady," Jetta almost stuttered, "but this isn't – and he hardly knows me – and I hardly know him -,"

"I don't accept excuses," said her ladyship. "Do as I tell you, and we won't have any quarrels."

"But – in a litter?"

"Oh, for goodness sake, child," the countess raised her voice, "there's too much danger without a litter. Horses bite, you know. Then there's all those huge ugly bears and lion creatures ready to jump from the bushes."

"My lady," it was pointless, but Jetta whispered, "I don't think any lions -,"

"I've seen those things outside the Tower, so don't you go arguing with me, brat. I am considerably older and have far more knowledge and experience. Now – hurry."

For a brief moment, Jetta sat still. She was having to do as she was told again, without the slightest hint of freedom. The situation, however, was more interesting than the usual scrubbing of steps, sweeping of floors, and washing dishes. The woman issuing the orders seemed highly unpleasant, but the orders themselves were not.

VESPERS

Sitting comfortably in a horse drawn litter was not something she had ever done before. And now, after the strange dream that still refused to leave her mind, the order itself of discovering not only the correct title Lord Stark, Earl of Desford, but the gentleman himself in company with his grandmother, seemed oddly attractive.

Lady Stark headed for the stairs. "Benson, two guards, and two grooms for the litter. I don't want any gold ribbon sort of nonsense. And hurry. There's no time to waste."

Looking rather blankly up at the steward as he began to march towards the door, Jetta said, "Mister Benson, do you have any idea where my cloak has gone?"

"I shall make sure it is in the litter madam," he said, and disappeared.

There was nothing else Jetta considered as any part of getting ready, so she wandered outside. Because still sunny and warm, she thought the day would be delightfully relaxing in a litter. Already she could hear Benson shouting out the message, the clank of something on large wooden wheels, and the neighing of a horse which didn't like orders any more than Jetta did herself.

Two horses, two drivers, a large, covered litter, and two riders close behind all thumped and rattled to the pathway directly outside the door. Benson stood waiting and opened the door of both house and litter for the countess when she bustled out. He set a large step enabling her to enter the litter more easily, and as she settled on the cushions inside, then he held the door, blank faced, for Jetta. As promised, she found her cloak folded inside waiting for her. She curled herself into it, but soon discovered that the welter of comfort which she had always assumed accompanied a litter, did not exist at all.

The countess, as might be expected, made no effort to leave space or cushions for her despised companion, but Jetta understood it would be a short journey and didn't complain. As the horses trotted forwards, the litter wheels began to bump and heave, and Jetta almost laughed. Walking would have been more sensible. Meanwhile the countess gritted her teeth and remained silent.

Lord Leays's manor was not at a great distance, although the horses had been kept at a strictly slow pace, ensuring somewhat less discomfort. Once they arrived, Jetta almost fell from the litter, gazing in wonder at the huge mansion in front of her. The Stark mansion was larger but older and darker, and the brighter brick of this more modern residence impressed Jetta considerably. The countess did not show the same reaction. She told her people to wait and thumped on the door. It was opened immediately, rather surprisingly, by Lady Leays herself.

"Goodness gracious, Tyballis,' said the countess. "What on earth are you doing acting as your own steward?"

Jetta stood back but saw the uniformed steward standing politely behind his mistress. "Well, I happened to be passing," the young woman said. "But I didn't expect you, my lady. Do come in. How are you? Is there a problem?"

So, Jetta followed the countess as if she was the maid, but never having been one, had little idea how to behave. She stood behind the countess's chair as she sat, carefully arranging her unaccustomed skirts, having already passed her cloak, and the countess's, to the steward.

"My dear girl," the countess was saying, "I have lost my idiot grandson. With all this scaremongering about invasions from France and the Breton duke running around in circles, I admit to being slightly worried. After all, as I'm sure you know, Dominic rushes in where any sensible man would stand back."

"He was here yesterday morning," Tyballis, Lady Leays said with a slight nod. "Let me call for wine. Will you stay for dinner? Andrew has gone to discuss matters with his highness, but he should be back by midday."

"Yes, I know the wretched boy was here, which is why I'm here," said the countess. "But it's information I came for, my dear. Not dinner. I simply hoped either you or Andrew would know where he went when he left you."

"Unfortunately, I've no idea," she said. "I do know that Dom came with a retinue of just two – groom and guard – and sent them home when he left, I think. I suppose he expected to be a very short time, and without difficulty. But I don't know where."

"Bother," spluttered the countess.

Wine was served, although not to Jetta, who was disappointed. Wine was completely new in her life, she'd not even been allowed a small sip before. But what she had been given over the last few days at the Desford Mansion had been delicious.

"Excuse me," she said into the pause, "but is it normal for anyone important to travel without a retinue?"

Tyballis looked up at her in considerable surprise. "I – well – no," she said. "But some do. Excuse me, but are you a friend of the countess? I'm sorry, I had no idea. I had assumed – but that is irrelevant. Would you like a cup of wine?"

"I'd love one," Jetta said in a hurry. "But no, we aren't really friends. Sort of -,"

"Acquaintances," interrupted the countess. "But she can have some wine if she wants it."

"In that case," Tyballis called for the page to pour it, "won't you take a seat? Some lords on an important mission, or leading an entire household south for summer, will have a retinue of fifty or more. A gentleman who is in a frightful hurry or doesn't want others to know where he's going, will take only his groom or perhaps no retinue at all."

"Thank you," said Jetta, wine cup in hand as she sat down. "His lordship didn't want anyone else to know where he was going then."

"No one would attend the palace, for instance, without a suitable retinue," Tyballis said, looking at the odd young woman with interest. "And where do you suppose his lordship would go, wishing to keep his destination secret?"

"Perhaps," Jetta kept her eyes riveted on her lap, "a monastery. Or a convent."

"Why, in the name of the Almighty," swore the countess, "would my boy go to such places? He's shockingly irreligious, not that I should be telling you this of course, but he has the morals of a stud horse. Oh, naturally he attends the local chapel on Sundays, but what would he even consider doing in a monastery?"

Embarrassed and now sure she was wrong in her guesses; Jetta shook her head. "I'm being silly," she said, blushing slightly. "I know nothing about it. No, he wouldn't ever do such a thing."

Aware now that she was being silently stared at by two women, Jetta returned her gaze to her lap, where her fingers were tightly clasped. She didn't even dare pick up her cup from the table, now sure she'd spill it.

"Fiddledy doo," said the countess with a hiccup. "Speak up, girl. What do you know that I don't? Is there a whore he likes living nearby?"

Jetta's blush increased. "No. Definitely no, at least not that I'd know about," she told her lap while squeezing her fingers into fists. "It's to do with my past. But I'm sure he wouldn't have been interested enough to go and check on my story. No – and even if he had gone to the convent or the monastery, why would he still be gone? He wouldn't be joining the order would he."

"Well – not the nuns," smiled Tyballis.

"You were a nun yourself at some time?" the countess demanded.

Jetta shook her head a little wildly. "I was supposed to be, but I ran away."

This did not clarify matters in the least.

The countess stood. "It seems highly unlikely to me," she said, "that Dominic would go anywhere near such places. Nor can I imagine you as a novice let alone a nun. I shall take the litter back home with the hope that my grandson has already returned." She turned to look at Tyballis who had also stood. "If Andrew does have some idea where my grandson went," she said in a softer voice, "would you kindly send me a message, my dear? It would be most helpful. In the meantime, I can only presume he's with his mistress, or he's ridden off on some absurd adventure."

Tyballis smiled and promised to help if she could. As they left, Jetta stopped briefly, saying, "I've had a slightly unusual past, once involving a convent. And his lordship wanted some of the details. It was the convent behind the priory in St. John's Wood, so very close, which made me think perhaps he went there, making use of everything being just down the road. But probably not. I have no idea of his mistresses. Does he have a lot of them?"

Now Tyballis was laughing as she answered. "I don't imagine so, but he's not going to discuss such matters with me. He's a good friend but not an immoral idiot. You go home and hopefully you'll find him there."

She watched them leave, wishing they had stayed to dinner after all. Considering Dominic as one of the most courageous men she knew apart from her husband, and both of them totally able to look after themselves, she had no worries for Dom. It was the girl who fascinated her. She would have liked to know a little more. If Andrew had any knowledge concerning Dom's disappearance, she thought she might take the message herself, starting a conversation regarding the odd activities at Desford House.

The short journey back home in the litter was as horrendous as the journey to Westminster, but Jetta now thought of little except Dominic. The large wooden wheels jerked and tumbled over the cobbled road, finally easing into the beaten earth, but adding the lurch of sudden holes and bumps.

Then, hurrying into the house as Benson opened the door, the countess demanded, "Well, Benson, is my boy back?"

"I'm afraid not my lady," said the steward. "But you have a somewhat unexpected visitor in the main hall. I attempted to eject her but have found it virtually impossible to make her leave. I do apologise."

Benson looked both apologetic and definitely ruffled. It seemed that the new visitor was not only unwanted, but had forced herself past him, and into the great hall.

The countess slowly removed her hat, gloves and cloak. "If it is someone who knows my grandson's whereabouts," she said hopefully, "I shall be quite content."

But as he took the countess's outside clothes, Benson was shaking his head as both women marched past him.

Chapter Nine

The small plump woman sat straight backed, her stool pulled away from the table, but she stood quickly as Jetta entered a little behind the countess. The countess, as usual, glared. Jetta had no idea who this was, but she was pale haired and blue eyed with lashes so long they seemed to graze her forehead. Indeed, the woman was exceedingly beautiful, but the countess was not impressed. "Now, who is this?" she snorted.

Although short and small waisted, the woman's breasts almost burst from her plunging neckline, the dress beautiful in white silk with lace and ribbons. Jetta, wiping away a pang of envy, promptly sat at the table. The woman looked her over with obvious contempt, then returned to the countess.

"My lady, I am a friend of his lordship, and only three days ago he swore he'd return to speak with me the following day. But he has not come. In the years I have known his lordship, I have always found – what can I say – that he keeps his word without fail. I have wondered if he might be ill. Even then I would expect him to send a message."

Lady Stark stared at the beautiful young woman with a blush of utter revulsion. Once again, she spoked through her teeth. "You will leave this house immediately and you will never return. My grandson's business is his own, but I will not entertain his sluts in my home."

Jetta, fascinated, smiled at the woman. Looking closer, she was not as young as she had first seemed, but she was certainly beautiful. Jetta said under her breath. "He's not here. Come, I'll see you out." The countess simply glared and said nothing else, so Jetta stood at the outer doorway and looked with considerable interest at the woman she guessed was Dominic's mistress.

The small stranger scowled, pouted, and followed Jetta to the front door. "His lordship's grandmother is a rude lady. I was simply worried. There's no excuse for throwing me out." She pulled her hat straight and the scowl remained.

"I'm Jetta. Do you love him?"

Abruptly the scowl faded but the woman seemed uncomfortable, even puzzled. "I don't speak of love, though I'm no harlot. My name is Teresa. You say Dom is simply your – friend? Are you the daughter of some lord, my lady?"

"Definitely not," Jetta grinned. "I presume your father isn't a duke either. I must say, it's rather brave of you to come ready to talk to Dominic's grandmother. She's much too pompous to speak with – well – most people."

"I presume you know who I am," Teresa said, puffin out her chest and gazing up at Jetta.

Nodding, Jetta said, "Well, I expect so."

The puff disappeared. "I never thought to see the countess. I thought I'd find Dom here. But," and she paused, sniffed, and said, "I'm respectable. I'm not a whore, but though she won't speak with me, it seems that horrid woman speaks with you."

"I'm not Dominic's mistress."

Teresa glared. "You say it to my face. And call me a whore."

"I didn't," Jetta pointed out. "I don't like the word. But you said you didn't like the word love."

"Oh of course," the other woman sniggered, now sounding angry. "It's make-believe. Naturally I tell him that I love and adore him all the time, but he knows it isn't true."

"Does he say it to you?"

"Not that I can remember. It's all a bit of a show, isn't it? A pretty game. But I can tell you this. I rely on him completely. He's my life. If he dies, I shall die too." Her hair was loose around her face in a cascade of blonde curls but held back from her forehead with pearl tipped pins through a small blue cup-fashioned hat. Indeed, she looked quite pearl-like herself, with a round face, round blue eyes, a little round pink mouth, a round tip to her short nose, and cheeks as round as pie crusts.

"You rely on him because," Jetta gulped, "why? Is it just the money?"

Teresa flopped back against the old stone wall just outside the main doorway. Her anger and her scowl all blew out. "I can't risk him taking back the house. He bought it for me, you know. But I'm not going to tell you my private business. I just want to know where he is."

"So do we." Jetta stiffened. "He's nearly a day late. Just disappeared, no sign, no message. I really have no involvement, but the countess is terribly worried."

"Only one day late?" Teresa tapped at her hair, re-setting the pins as she felt the wind through her curls. "Perhaps it's not such a worry. Perhaps – he might have forgotten he promised – but I do worry as well you see. Anyone in my position would understand. As I get a little older – well, men aren't always kind. They don't trust us, perhaps, but I certainly don't trust any of them."

The sky was clouding over, and the streaks of sunshine blinked out. Jetta no longer wore her cloak so shivered. "I'm not in your position," she said. "But I sympathise. I never had anyone to buy me a house, let alone anything else."

"He got as much out of the bargain," Teresa looked annoyed once more. "The nobility won't just stroll off to whores in brothels, or the sluts in the street. They think they're special, so they want someone special in their beds. But don't you go judging me."

"That rather spoils my sympathy."

"I don't want your pity, whoever you are."

"To be picked out by such a man certainly doesn't deserve pity." Jetta smiled rather coldly. "Though I suppose you have to be beautiful," she added, soft voiced.

"It's the Lord Almighty made me pretty," mumbled Teresa, "I was born rat-poor in a rat-infested hut in Hammersmith. It stank like a tannery instead of a place where a poor woman tried to look after four children. Then when I was about seventeen, I met Dom in the local tavern. I was working there, cleaning up. He talked to me."

Jetta was interested again. "How long ago was that?"

"A long time. Years. He was only fifteen, but he kept looking at me. He came back lots of times, then he came to my house and spoke to my mother. Gave her some money. And then – well, things sort of developed."

"I understand." She did. Dominic had actually bought the penniless slum girl he wanted as his mistress. "And you're both loyal to each other?"

"I won't answer that." Teresa turned away. "He isn't. Of course not. Though I never ask him."

Still shivering in the new chill, Jetta realised that this woman needed more money. Living rent free didn't pay for food or candles. So, when Dominic said he'd be coming the next day – and then didn't – for Teresa it could be a disaster. It wasn't a man she adored that she missed, it was the comfortable living he brought her. "I'm sorry," Jetta said. "I haven't any money at all. Not a single farthing to give you."

"I didn't ask," Teresa frowned, and the small snub nose wrinkled up as though some nearby smell disgusted her. "I don't want pity from you or him, and I never asked you for money. But I do need some money from somewhere."

Blushing, Jetta asked, "Aren't there – other men? Surely you could, being so beautiful. And never tell him."

"Just tell him I came and tell him I need him when you see him," Teresa said, and turned again, flouncing the circle of white silk that swirled around her small invisible legs.

Then from the silence behind her, a large flat hand clamped itself with considerable weight, to Jetta's shoulder. "You're going nowhere, miss. I've an idea I know who you are." He looked up at Jetta while holding her very firmly. "I've been investigating and I've an idea it was the three of you."

Jetta stared at the sheriff. "There are two of us."

"You two," snarled the short man, "and the poor fellow's wife. When some woman is done in, you can wager it was her husband. Always is. So, when some hard working fellow has his throat ripped open, it will be his wife and her friends."

Teresa was shivering and not from the wind, but Jetta no longer felt the ignorance and fear that had pounded in her head when first faced with arrest. Having been about to say goodbye and return to the hall, ready to settle for supper with the countess, this time it was Jetta who glared.

"That's ridiculous," she told the sheriff. "Just because something happens once or twice, it's not proof for every time. His lordship is not at home. Actually, I wondered if his lordship might be with you. Now, leave that woman alone and come back some other time."

"I'll do no such thing," the sheriff objected, unaccustomed to being spoken to in such a manner by a female nobody. And he eyed Teresa's deep neckline and the swelling flesh that protruded. "I've seen you before and know you for a harlot. You'll both come with me. Where's the poor farrier's wife?"

"I don't have the slightest idea," Jetta said, shrugging his hand from her shoulder. "And this woman is a friend of his lordship and has nothing whatsoever to do with any of this. Let her go."

The sheriff spluttered, released Teresa and quickly grabbed Jetta again, both his hands on her arms.

Feeling the strength of his fingers and the threat of his grasp, Jetta was not frightened. She was furious. Jetta pulled but could not break the hold. She kicked out, once to the sheriff's shins and then to his knee. With a howl of pain and shock, Sheriff John Kettering tumbled over and fell to the cobbles. But still caught in his grasp, Jetta fell too.

The sheriff had not released her as he collapsed, and both struggled. Jetta, skirts entangled, managed to kick him again and this time directly to the very large expanse of his stomach.

Teresa hurried forward, bent over and punched him in the nose. What he was yelling was hard to understand for his fury was now all jabber. Finally free from the sheriff's reaching hands, Jetta grabbed Teresa and pulled her inside the house, slamming the door shut behind her, and leaning back against it. The steward, having heard an echo of the commotion, was already approaching.

Jetta yelled, "Benson, don't let the sheriff in. Don't even open the door. Actually, you'll have to lock it."

"Madam," hesitated the steward, "without the orders from her ladyship -,"

But the countess now stood in the archway to the great hall and nodded. "Anyone attempting such unbidden violence on my property without the agreement of myself or my grandson will not be tolerated. Benson, send one of the kitchen lads down to the stables and order two of the guards up here and remove that man from my grounds."

"At once, my lady." Benson hurried to the back doors, while the pounding and cursing of the sheriff continued outside.

Both women stared. The countess called, "Jetta come with me. Leave that wretched harlot where she is. I'll see to her later."

Jetta whispered, "Sorry, I'll try to help," then followed the countess into the main hall.

Addressing Jetta, the countess sat stiffly, tapping her fingers impatiently on the arm of her chair. "I will not have whores and tramps in my home," she said loudly. "Once the sheriff has been removed from my premises, you will remove the harlot."

Jetta flopped down on the settle. "I imagine she'll be ready to leave, my lady," Jetta said, "I don't know her. But since she knows his lordship very well, I don't want to be rude. He might be – upset. Indeed, at least, perhaps we ought to take her with us. Perhaps she'll lead us to the more probable places."

The countess turned to Jetta with her usual glare, "What is all this about? Sheriff? Females of low-virtue and females without identity, and my son disappears. Explain yourself."

The shouting from the front doorstep had faded and it seemed even the knocking had stopped. Benson reappeared, looking a little flustered.

"My lady, Sheriff Kettering has been shown from the premises, but he insists that he will return, and has asked me to inform your ladyship that he is now convinced that he knows who the killers are and will take them into custody once his lordship returns."

"Pooh," said the countess, once again immersed in scowls. "Killers indeed. There are enough corpses on battlefields. He'll do as I tell him, and if someone has been killed with my grandson's permission, then it must have been the right thing to do."

Benson blinked in surprise, bowed and left the hall. Catching her breath and trying to ignore the two painful bruises the cobbles had left on her body when she fell, Jetta followed him, asking him to wait. The cracked rib had partially healed, and the cut on her head had finally closed. Jetta sighed, accepting that pain was obviously her fate. "Mr. Benson, there is a young lady waiting inside the front door. Is there any possibility of giving her a little money? I presume you know who she is?"

With a slight shiver of disapproval, Benson sniffed. "As you wish, madam. And how much should that be?"

Jetta had no idea. She'd never had any money herself and considered two pence a fortune "Umm," she tried to look apologetic. "How much would someone need for a week's food? Five shillings, perhaps? Can you take it from some sort of kitchen collection her ladyship keeps here?"

The contempt was a little more obvious than Jetta would have liked. "Madam, all matters of supply are bought with his lordship's permission, the venders do not require immediate reimbursement. However, some shillings are kept for business in the market. I shall endeavour to arrange matters with the young woman. And then do I ask her to leave?"

"I think that would be best."

The countess, still stiff backed, was not pleased at being kept waiting. Jetta decided she had probably annoyed everyone, Benson, the countess, certainly the sheriff, Dominic's mistress Teresa, and no doubt Dominic himself once he arrived home. This prospect, however, seemed momentarily irrelevant. She faced the countess. "My lady, my apologies. Now I'm at your service."

"About time," said the countess. "And only with relevance to my dear grandson's disappearance, tell me exactly who you are, why you are here, why my son has permitted your presence, and whether it was you who murdered whoever it was the sheriff was twittering about."

Jetta related very little of her story. It seemed of no consequence, and she wanted to maintain her privacy. She didn't trust the countess. "But I can see no reason for his lordship to have decided to investigate my story. It's far more likely he's been investigating the murder of his farrier. But apart from the sheriff and the farrier's family who live here, where would he go for that?"

Waving a delicate hand, dark spotted with age, the countess answered with an imperious lack of logic. "Hopefully he has understood part of the story that we do not yet understand. I shall wait another day before trying to follow this mystery. You, miss, will do nothing until I order it."

"The sheriff," sighed Jetta, "accuses me and is suspicious concerning the farrier's wife. But that's ridiculous. Perhaps his lordship has found a clue."

"Hopefully concerning that other immoral tramp of a female." The countess's voice was chewed grit. "Of all the wickedness for a wench like that to enter my home."

"Surely it's not so bad?" Jetta wondered if she was being a fool, but said it anyway, "the woman might not be someone you could approve of, my lady. But she's equally worried about his lordship. Doesn't that make her more likeable? Couldn't you approve just a little bit?"

The countess shrieked. "Rubbish. Disgusting harlot. It might also explain why my dear grandson has gone off without explanation."

"To escape his mistress?" Jetta hooted with laughter, tried to stop and couldn't. "But honestly, I'm sure that's not the explanation. He must surely be searching for an explanation concerning his farrier."

The sniff was as loud as the laughter. "It's a possibility," said the countess. "And the lad has only been gone for a little over one day and one night. But," and the sniff turned to snort, "if my boy doesn't return tomorrow, I shall have to do something. Hopefully Lady Leays will be here with an explanation, or better still Andrew with Dominic beside him. Otherwise, we shall have to be off on another search."

"I hope you find him easily," Jetta said, "I shall stay here and hope not to meet up with the sheriff again."

"You'll do no such thing," announced the countess crossly. "You will accompany me, and it's not open for argument, my girl. You spoke of a priory and a convent. I may consider those worth a visit if nothing else comes along. This is a serious matter, and you'll do as you are told."

Jetta spent the rest of the afternoon with her thoughts in a jumble. She had no conceivable notion where Dominic might be, felt no attraction for the countess, her snarls and demands, and was beginning to wish she had kept walking and had never decided to return to the house. Having done so purely to prove herself honest to Dominic, it now seemed utterly absurd.

The perfumes travelled from the kitchens through the narrow corridors to the great hall and the vast dining table. Supper was served.

"My grandson," insisted the countess with her mouth full of pork and rosemary, "is permanently strange but that's his problem, not mine. However, with the knowledge that I intend to drop dead at any moment without unnecessary warning, he always tells me when he intends returning to the house. Even on occasional nights away," here she glared at her platter, "he'll warn me beforehand, and then in he trots for breakfast. I assume that is when he visits his trollop. Besides, why has the death of that farrier become so important?"

"Are you accustomed to murder on the premises?" asked Jetta.

"Why not?" demanded the countess, cutting another piece of sausage, "but if you speak to me that way, young woman, it might become a good deal more common. At least try and squeeze in the occasional '*my ladies*'." She pushed half a sausage into her mouth and added onions. "Besides, we all die sooner or later. And the farrier is of no interest to me whatsoever. Does he have a wife?'

"Yes, my lady."

"Well, she can fuss about him," the countess decided. "But I shall not. And I'll tell Dominic when I see him, not to go calling sheriffs anymore. I dislike that man, shouting and raging on the doorstep."

Jetta stifled the laugh. "If you intend a quiet day here tomorrow, my lady, would you object if I leave? I have other things – other people – to see."

"Yes, I would object." The countess heaved herself forwards, clasping her cup of burgundy. "You'll stay here and look after me. Aren't you my personal maid, for pity's sake?"

Confusion squeezed out the humour. "Definitely not, my lady. I'm Jetta Lawson, who you've never met in your life before. I don't work for you, and I don't work for His Lordship either."

"In that case, you'd better start," growled the countess. "I'll not employ some ragged young girl who comes flying into my bedchamber without asking first, and then gets employed here for nothing other than breaking glass."

"Umm," said Jetta, working this out.

"You shall come with me," the countess announced, "unless Dominic has arrived back home in the meantime. Tomorrow I rest. I'm past the age of climbing mountains every day. But only for one

VESPERS

day. I'm certainly not going to sit silently at home just waiting like a cup of wine for someone to come along and drink me."

Jetta's second, 'Umm' sounded much the same. She said quietly, "Umm, my lady, would it be possible, for me to retire to bed this evening? I am – quite exhausted."

The countess frowned, then yawned. "Very well," she said. "As long as you don't tell anyone who you are or what you are. And if you see that cheeky little harlot again, tell her to stuff some respectable linen down the front of that gown. I refuse to permit my son to mix with half naked females."

The thunder came in the night and rattled the little leaden window frames. Wind and rain dribbled down every chimney and tipped over the dried flowers sitting in jugs on every hearth. Jetta woke to the noise, sitting up with a hope that it was Dominic slamming the front doors behind him. But as the rain torrented against the glass, she realised what it was, pulled the eiderdown over her head, and snuggled further beneath the blankets.

Unfortunately, now thoroughly awake, she found herself thinking once again of Dominic. She laughed at first, imagining him as another thunderstorm. But her thoughts drifted, and she was abruptly seeing him in the river, calling, helpless, and drowning. Jetta could see herself rushing to help, pulling out the wherry boat she'd rowed upstream, pushing it back into the water, almost crying as she leaned over to catch the drowning man beneath his arms and haul him to safety.

But he did not seem a man so weak to slip down the wet embankment, nor to be arrested, improperly captured, killed in a brawl, or lost in the countryside. Dominic was strong and knowledgeable, arrogant and determined. He was a friend of the king. He was an earl. How could such a man be in trouble? Jetta sighed and eventually once more fell asleep.

The following morning, she woke to a grey sky and the threat of more rain. At the dining table where the breakfast was already being served, Jetta quickly wished her hostess good morning, and sat, drawn by the now familiar perfumes of good food. Eating considerably more than previously in her life, the allure of food had captured her. It was, however, clear that his lordship had still not returned.

"Well, girl," said the sticky eyed countess, "see for yourself. My grandson hasn't appeared. I was out of bed far earlier than I approve, hoping to find him back home. But he did not even send a note."

"But my lady," said Jetta, "it's only a day and a half. If he rode north to Yorkshire perhaps, it would take a lot longer -,"

"And just why would an intelligent man ride to Yorkshire?" complained the countess. "Do you think him Luna-crazed? No. Something very unpleasant has happened to my grandson, and we shall set off early tomorrow, and find him. I shall order the litter brought around for nine of the clock. The weather today isn't ideal for rutted roads, but at least we'll be under cover. Besides, I shall pray for sunshine tomorrow. It's bound to be a nice day."

"Glorious," murmured Jetta. She would have sooner ridden a horse beneath the tempest than climb back into the endless jolt of that litter but kept it to herself.

It appeared that the holy deity had not been listening to the countess, for on the following day they woke to a darker grey sky, black clouds and more rain. Her cloak wrapped tightly around her, Jetta climbed into the litter and at once, dutifully obedient, she spoke through the small hole between herself and the riders, telling them that her ladyship was ready to leave. The litter wobbled, the large wooden wheels began to roll, and the soaked horses grumbled and neighed. The countess complained at every jolt, of which there were hundreds, but the pounding of the rain drowned out the constant rattle.

It was unexpected when the rain stopped. The horses shook their manes and picked up pace, while both drivers flicked their whips in the air, steadied their hats, and sat back cheerfully.

A few small rays of sunshine glistened with reflection and suddenly the world was as pretty as a newly painted picture. The wood pigeons were cooing and a host of fledgelings were squeaking from their branches until a buzzard flew over.

Though, when the litter stopped, it jerked its occupants into each other's arms. Jetta felt her heartbeat double, as loudly as the pounding rain. She knew they were back in the heart of London, and this was the very last place she wished to be.

It was the countess, as the steps were set for her and the door opened, who snapped, "What is it, silly girl? You look as scared as a chaffinch escaping an owl."

"I have – bad experiences of the city," Jetta whispered.

"We're only visiting the sheriff," the countess said. "Not that horrid little fool in Chiswick, this one is a sensible man who knows his business."

Chapter Ten

T he night's pelting rain seemed to have seeped from stone to stone and now the blackness within was damp with a stench of stale decay and the underground growth of things unseen.

Waking into what seemed blacker than any dream, Dominic stared around, tried to stand, and for a moment could not discover his feet.

With both hands to his head, he tried to remember what the hell had happened, where he was and why? It bothered him like knives stabbing into his head while his head pounded and his eyes blurred, his memory slept even though he knew himself awake. For a moment he could remember only his name.

Finally, as his situation clarified, Dominic realised that he had been somehow imprisoned. Yet he still did not know how. Nor could he remember any circumstances immediately before the unconsciousness had overtaken him. Slumped against the black stone wall, he allowed time to pass while summoning both memory and logic.

The chill was significant, and the cold dampness seemed to leak into his body. He was naked to the waist, wearing only his hose.

They, at least, were tight knitted in black silk and kept a snug fit from toes to codpiece. The waist band was wrapped tight, but above that he was bare, his flesh marked with cuts, bruises and deep scratches. It felt as though he had been whipped although such an attack was nowhere in his memory.

After some moments of considerable effort, he managed to stand and began, very slowly, to examine the room he was in. He could find patches of the stone where seepage of something smelled foul. Beneath his feet were pavings, uneven and cracked. Pulling up one broken corner, he discovered only muddy earth. Wherever he walked, the smell was lesser or greater, but always there. The darkness was continuous, no window existed, and even more strangely, Dominic could find no door.

If there was no door, then he had entered this dismal cell from below or from above. Or a door existed but was so well camouflaged that in the pitch black, he had yet been unable to find it.

Nor was there any sound. The silence was haunting and only the soft scuffle of his own feet interrupted it. He could see no ceiling, and whatever was there, was higher than his arms could reach. The pain continued. Dominic knew he must have been severely knocked out with some heavy object from behind. Gently smoothing over his head, he felt the swelling where the pain concentrated, and the sticky patch where blood lay thick. He had suffered other attacks over the long and invariably uncomfortable years of his life, but never one so confusing, and the motive for undressing him was still obscure. Every part of him ached or wrenched within him. He had been dragged, beaten, perhaps kicked, but all while unconscious and unable to defend himself.

His last memory was the sweet, crinkled smile of a small nun beneath her small, starched coif and wimple.

"This way, my lord and I'll tell you everything I remember."

Those words still lingered in Dominic's mind, but he could not imagine that he had been struck over the skull and imprisoned by an elderly and helpful nun.

The necessary memories did not return. Some glimpse of the convent doorway, and raising his hand in goodbye. Yet these thoughts were obscure and Dominic wondered whether this was simply his imagination. He must surely have left that place in order to enter this one, but his eyes summoned no further reminders.

Where he was, Dominic decided, was no room at all. Perhaps a cave, but which surely had no place in a convent or priory, nor would such inhabitants have any motive he could think of to imprison him. Slumping back down, Dominic again leaned against the wall, head back and eyes closed. Very gently, as his mind drifted, he directed himself backwards over past hours, even past days. But nothing except his own imagination interrupted the black nothingness.

He could for some moments, remember the girl Jetta appearing before him. She spoke, but her words did not impinge. He had asked for help, and she had nodded. But although the picture remained at the back of his mind, he knew this was a fantasy. There was no possibility of such a girl suddenly entering his prison. And there was no conceivable recollection of how she could have entered – or left.

Sleeping was his only escape. Unaccustomed to damp stone as his only bed, he slept poorly, and his headache did not ebb. He woke many hours later to the sound of footsteps over his head and sat up abruptly. No light permitted further understanding yet Dominic was sure that someone strode across a floor which sat over his ceiling. This left him wondering whether the cave simply lay below some other building, or if a cell had been built underground, especially since he had found only earth and mud beneath one broken paving. If true, this, would certainly make it more difficult to escape.

Escaping, however, was now his only determination. He had never surrendered in his life and the thought of doing so now did not even occur to him. But the other thing which did not occurred to him, was how he could do it. Without a door, and locked below ground, left him little option.

Not knowing whether food would be brought to him, and if so, how – he decided that in some manner and for some reason, he would be expected to live. Otherwise, why had someone not killed him immediately? He had been badly injured and imprisoned. To do this without killing him was illogical unless someone wished to keep him alive. Living meant eating. And drinking. Which meant a door – or at the least a tunnel from below or a funnel from above.

The other possibility was that someone had no intention whatsoever of bringing him either food or drink and hoped he would die of starvation very slowly and in the greatest pain. This was not, he knew, Newgate or any other gaol, for that would include inevitable differences.

But there was a door. Dominic discovered this not long before it opened to him. More slowly this time, he had pressed his palms to the walls, and had felt the place where a flat impression indicated a possible doorway. An absurdly and remarkably narrow one.

Less than an hour later, a deep grinding sound interrupted his thoughts and a slit of blazing light practically blinded him. The cell was small and only two steps took him to the light, but it had already gone. At its base lay a small platter and a dented cup. The cup held water and the platter held a chunk of smoked bacon heavy with fat, and a roll of rye bread, seemingly stale.

Dominic ate. He could not see what he ate, but judged it from its taste. This was not the type of food he was accustomed to eating, but that was of no consequence. But proof now, he was unlikely to starve to death, and therefore his gaolers did not want him dead. At least, not yet.

The many hours that then passed drifted into sleep or self-hypnosis while Dom considered what he might achieve, sliding from possibilities into absurdities. He also discovered, surprisingly, that he thought of Jetta.

After his business with Andrew, he had visited the priory where the girl had claimed to have started her life, and where the abbot had met her mother and known her name.

This desire to know more of the girl had been a nagging insistence, although at first a relatively small one. The possible, indeed probable, invasion of Henry Tudor and the French was of far greater importance, but it was not yet on the horizon. The girl Jetta, however, was already in his house. So was the possibly connected business of his farrier's murder. An investigation into such a strange pair of events had seemed an interesting alternative to his normally mundane daily pursuits, usually ridiculous conversations with his mother, dinners with half drunken friends, and nights with his increasingly less appealing mistress.

That such a step led by curiosity had turned into the worst moment of his life so far, should be, beyond doubt virtually impossible.

The insistent reappearance of Jetta into his dreams, his thoughts and his memory began to annoy him.

One dream took Dom to the river with the sunshine blistering above, and the water below as silently hot as a jug over the fire. He and Jetta stood together on the bank, and he told her that he intended swimming to the opposite side. He asked the woman if she could swim. She had shaken her head.

Dominic had promised, if she agreed to undress, that he would teach her to swim. For a woman who wished to travel the river upstream, this might save her life. She was hardly an experienced boat-woman.

When she agreed to undressing, it was Dom in his dream who undressed her. He tied back the long silken veil of her brown satin hair, and felt the soft sheen of her forehead, cheeks and mouth under his fingertips. He wanted to kiss her mouth, but did not. Instead, he unclipped the fastening of her gown beneath her arm and it fell open. Her skirts were still held in place by the wide silk sash, heavily pleated, but this he also unclipped, and the gown fell from Jetta's shoulders. His dream self gazed at the woman. She was still wearing her shift, but he delighted in watching the wonder of her outline, the curves and shadow through the linen, seeing her so desperately thin and yet so beautiful.

VESPERS

Sinking deeper into sleep, he lost the dream, and remembered it only vaguely when he awoke.

Now sometimes, trapped in total inactivity, Dominic was only vaguely aware of whether he was asleep or awake. Both soon felt the same. But he lay, or sat, tight to the wall where the doorway offered no draft. Yet this way he knew that if it opened again, he could and would grasp the leg of whoever opened it.

There was no way he could count hours, nor even days. He was convinced that more than one day had passed since the last and only meal. Yet he could not be sure of that, nor sure of anything else. Desperate to be active, he kicked or punched the walls, but this was wasteful pain, bruising feet and hands. Indeed, the walls were rough stone, some parts even jagged, and the damp chill emanated from them. He marched the parameters of the cell, but two strides in one direction and four in the other, allowed no more than irritated absurdity.

Life slowed. An hour became a day. A day shrugged itself into weeks. Utter inactivity had never before dulled him. The boredom of little or nothing to do at home had seemed to him as inactivity. He dreamed of returning to what would now seem bliss. He could wander the grounds. There were books, both monk-quilled and those now printed in the fresh manner. He could ride out, visit friends and relax with good wine.

The only possibility now was the raging fury and confusion of his mind.

He was able, when tired, to lie back and think of the past, imagine the future, renew memories and explore the puzzles of history, of friends, of religion and of unknown science. Yet without company, his thoughts eventually, inevitably, leaned towards the pointless wandering of question without answer.

Once accustomed eventually to the great darkness, Dominic saw only the rigidity of rock. Yet within that rock was the narrow streak of a doorway without sign of lock nor handle. Clearly it could be opened only from the outside. An outside as yet forbidden.

Yet another fruitless avenue for a wretchedly frustrated mind. To leave this hole and discover a river raging through a city, surpassing mountains, or leading underground to palaces as yet unseen. Although Dominic knew when his thoughts waded into nonsense, he permitted the discovery of gold pits, of unicorns galloping the forests, and of mermaids washed up on the beach.

So the days passed. His anger grew, then abated, then grew once more. Sleeping more, walking less, thinking in circles and knowing nothing, gradually Dominic discovered himself without brain, without understanding and without hope.

Yet it was never apathy which dissolved him. He was swollen with the urge to escape and discover, and was itching, fingers ready, to grab any and every opportunity of whatever source or style.

He was sleeping again the next time the door was pulled ajar.

Light blazed into his sleep. His eyes snapped open and as he had planned, immediately his hand reached through the narrow slit in the stone. He grabbed what was there, and hauled it into the cell. His arms, although now naked and half-frozen, were strong muscled. His grasp was unbreakable. The door-slit remained open. The cup of ale and a lump of bread scattered beside him, and in the ooze of light, Dominic realised he held the bony ankle of a small man.

Blocking the doorway, Dominic threw the man onto his back, one leg in the air as he kept hold of the ankle, forcing it upwards.

"Who are you?"

The man struggling on his back yelped. "I'm Peter. You'll not hurt me. I ain't done you no harm."

"Except keeping me prisoner. Now explain at once. Who ordered my capture, and why?"

"I ain't got no notion," squeaked the man. "I doesn't see nobody special, mister, hardly nobody at all. Tis hard getting down here, but I brings yer grub and you ortta be thankful."

Dominic threw down the man's leg, but placed his own foot hard on the small plump belly. "Who do you work for?"

"I ain't telling. I got orders not to tell you nothing."

VESPERS

"You tell me the name. Immediately. Or you'll die as quickly."

"You reckon to kill me?" the man whimpered. "But if I tells you his name, then tis him what'll kill me as quick."

Dominic glared. "He! So neither nun nor other female from the convent. So, the name." Yet the small gaoler had rolled over on the ground, bleating and blubbering against the stone floor. Escape was the more important. Ignoring the man still on the ground, he saw only a pointless risk in staying, so Dominic strode across the wriggling body, snatched up the fallen bread, squeezed through the barely existing doorway, and then stopped abruptly, standing a moment, amazed.

He had expected to be attacked by other guards beyond the doorway, or at least to be surrounded by gaolers. Instead, all he felt was the ice cold on his nakedness.

Rubbing his eyes not only to reduce the blindness brought by the light, but Dominic also found difficulty in believing what he saw. He stood in no tunnel, nor cellar. Outside his prison there was neither house, nor shed, nor priory.

The wind was in his hair and slashed against his skin. Yet as he moved, he did not shiver. The air was suddenly warmer than it had been in his cell, and out in the open air a mild warmth felt more like a caress. Yet after so long in utter blackness, his eyes stung in the insistent light. Midday perhaps, and the sun pushed through the dancing clouds.

All he saw now was a vast expanse of rock and rubble beneath a vast grey clouded sky. All he heard was the small man's wails behind him.

Dominic stood on chalk, looking out over the abandoned and vast chalk pit. In the distance he could see a high slope of green leading to a ledge, a hillside which blocked any sight of the land further south. Further north he thought he could see marshland, suggested by faint streaks of reflection on water and bog. No human nor any building was visible. Only the wilderness of white chalk cliffs and the occasional darkness of holes and caves.

With one step back, he shouted to the man still inside the cell. "Get out here and explain. Otherwise, I shall enjoy strangling you."

The man whimpered, then called. "Tis the old chalk mine. No folks does much mining anymore. The marshlands is leaking in."

"Who do you work for?" Dominic demanded again.

"I told you, I ain't saying, or I's dead. You wants to do me in and they wants to do me in too. It ain't proper fair."

"I can discover your master for myself," Dominic said. "Simply tell me the direction of the city. London – Westminster – wherever I should go to find those less frightened to speak."

The small man pointed to the upwards sloping ledge. "You climbs that, reckon you'll see where to go."

Now ignoring all other difficulties, Dominic began striding towards the southern hillside. The black silk hose covering his feet now turned chalk white in the flying dust, and he ate the piece of bread as he walked. There was chalk up his nose, and in his mouth, but the sour smell came from the marshlands.

A chalk mine. He knew nothing of it. Instead, what he knew and now could not dismiss, was the pounding pain in the back of his head, the sharp stab of the smaller wounds on his upper body, and the cramp in his legs.

He discovered, which did not surprise him, that his legs were weaker than before his capture, his muscles ached, and the impatience of his stride did not make him quicker. Once having finally climbed the hilly slope, however, Dominic could stand and catch his breath, exulting in his freedom. The knowledge of it blew in the wind and he felt almost as though he could stretch out his arms and tell that wind to carry him onwards.

The sky had been huge, such a vast expanse of cloud bringing no colour to the nothingness below. But immediately arriving at the sloping peak, the new horizon was rich green with the flurry of a small forest.

At once Dominic smiled. The relief was like a sudden warm breeze. Now he knew exactly where he was.

Chapter Eleven

The day after the inconclusive visit to the sheriff of the west wall, the countess threw her wine cup at the window, her platter of kidney and ale pie at the page who had served it, and an empty jug at Jetta.

Jetta both confused and surprised, was simply glad that the countess had an extremely bad aim. Tempted to chuck the jug back, she restrained herself and took another spoonful of her own pie. The countess was now her hostess, even though it certainly hadn't originally been that way. Besides, an elderly woman who forgot everything within minutes and constantly contradicted herself, did not deserve anger.

"How long is it now, girl?" The countess's glower was virtually permanent.

"Three and a half days, my lady, and four nights." "It is becoming quite urgent, I agree. Even a little bit – frightening."

"I am never frightened," said the countess. "That's only for simpletons. But I am certainly worried. The sheriff yesterday sounded distinctly unhelpful and had no ideas at all. He even suggested," she looked ready to faint, "that perhaps my grandson had sailed off to France to join the Tudor traitors."

"There is another possibility, my lady, however unlikely," Jetta said, "that we have discussed before, but with slightly different goals. The priory and the convent at St. John's. They aren't connected. The priory of St. John's was originally dedicated to the Knights of Jerusalem, but the convent isn't. They are the sisters of St. Alkeld, I was there when I was very young. I loved the priory and the abbot, but I could hardly become a monk, so I was sent to the convent. And I hated it. I really don't want to go back there, but maybe Dominic went. He talked about it with me once and he wanted to know more."

The countess looked down her long thin nose. "You actually think my grandson went all that way just to find out about you?"

"Probably not. But possibly yes." She was blushing and shook her head. "I expect it's not right and I don't want to go anywhere near the place. I just thought I should mention it. Otherwise, we've run out of ideas."

"Call Benson," the countess stood, "and tell him to get the litter ready. We are going to church."

The weather was bright, and a vague warmth was blown in a pleasant puff of wind. The litter, however, discovered the parts of the road where puddles remained and where grass had slipped into mud. Several excessively uncomfortable hours dragged, the countess dozed and Jetta, although hating the ride, became gradually more excited.

The priory stood proud in age, and as the litter finally jerked to a stop by the open doors, Jetta jumped out. The abbot had heard the horses and came slowly to the doorway. He had aged considerably but he was the man Jetta remembered with such affection.

Neither short nor tall but now somewhat bent, the abbot walked forwards with a smile of recognition. "Do you really remember who I am," Jetta grinned. "After all this time?"

"I remember you very well," he said, leaning on his walking stick as he approached his visitors. "I didn't see you only as an infant, my child. Hopefully you'll remember that I spoke with you many times over the years. And it is a real joy to see you again, my dear. Especially since you look well provided for, and comfortable in your new service."

She didn't bother to tell him that she was in no service at all, and had escaped from what she had considered a nightmare. "I'm searching for the Earl of Desford. This is the countess, his grandmother, and we are both worried at his disappearance."

The old man frowned. "I believe I met the nobleman you speak of, my dear. He came to ask about you and we talked for some time. He is an impressive and intelligent gentleman, and he wished for further information regarding yourself." He turned at once to the countess and bowed. "My lady, is it possible that the earl has now travelled north? After we had spoken at such length, I advised him to visit the convent, where I had sent Miss Lawson after she came here as an infant. But I did warn his lordship that the convent has changed somewhat since I first came here. Those ladies now deal with matters which are, let us say, beyond my interest. Which is why my own monastery takes no new noviciates. I spend many of my days in solitude."

Both the countess and Jetta stared at him. "That," sniffed the countess, "sounds quite troubling, sir."

He nodded, almost bowing his head. "It is something I have found troubling for some time now and have prayed that my Lord God saves us from whatever may be happening. As for the connection up north, I know little about – but there is a larger convent where the previous Abbess travelled often. I should perhaps inform you, that the Lady Margaret Beaufort has become affiliated with the convent. She has not taken the veil, but she comes here often. We all remember her son's attempt to invade, but we must also remember that she is a great lady and devoted to the sacred teaching."

"I wonder if Dominic met her." Jetta swore under her breath and turned to the countess. "We have to go to the convent here. It's within walking distance. There's certainly no need to travel north until we understand more."

"I share no acquaintanceship with the Lady Beaufort," he smiled. "However, I have been uncomfortably aware for some time, of the traffic and communication between the convent and those exiles now in France. Letters from Henry Tudor once arrived here, clearly by mistake. I did not open them."

"I shall not be travelling north into those heathen jungles," the countess said crossly. "And I shall not be walking anywhere either, silly miss. We have a litter and that's where I shall be."

Jetta turned back to the abbot. "I'm sorry, you sound so unhappy. I was hoping you'd tell me more about who I am and what my real mother was like. It's been like a dark cloud hanging over me for most of my life."

"Change that to a rainbow, dear child." The abbot smiled. "But I swore silence on the Holy Book and cannot break that oath. I hope to see you perhaps later."

With a warm clasp to Abbot Francis' hand, Jetta followed the countess back to the litter. Having always suspected that the abbot was beginning to retire into his own little hermitage within the church at the entrance to his monastery, she wished him great joy and thanked him again for his help. But she had never before heard him speak of the convent as if it was dangerous. Jetta immediately expected that many living there, whether or not in secret, were helping with the future invasion in some manner.

Jetta heard the prior call, "Keep safe, child," and waved back.

The day had brightened and the ride to the convent gates took only moments up the old beaten pathway to the great iron gates. They hung open and beyond them was the stretch of grass, and rows of herbs, fruit vines, the twists of berries and vegetables growing neatly. Two donkeys grazed in a small field, and seeing visitors, they hurried to the fence, curious and hoping for food. Geese pattered behind another fence, flapping feet and wings, also curious about the new arrivals.

Rattling and bumping, the litter arrived at the huge wooden doors although they were closed. High in one was the little iron railed opening where visitors would be questioned by one of the novices. But Jetta neither bothered waiting nor knocking. She simply pushed open one of the doors and walked in.

Jetta knew every part of the convent, the short straight corridors leading to the chapel, the many nuns' dormitories, the single room which always housed the abbess, the privies, the hall for dining and discussing problems and doorways to the small sanctuaries and alters, and then out to the grounds. She expected no change. A convent, and the attitude of those running it, rarely changed, so she walked directly to the small room where she knew she would find the abbess. Asking to meet her was unlikely to produce a welcome response.

The countess, having discussed this with Jetta already, went directly to the dining room. It was midmorning, and both too late for breakfast and too early for dinner. And was therefore probable to meet the younger nuns and novices cleaning, sweeping, scrubbing, or on their knees in front of the small corner alter, praying to the tiny plaster image of the Virgin Mary, and the great bejewelled cross behind her. Yet many of the elder women would be speaking quietly to each other around the dining table or reading in solitary reflection.

"My child," the countess told Jetta, "speak to whoever might know about his lordship. The wretched boy can't still be here after all this time, and after all, he can't join a convent or become a nun. But now we know he came here, so I shall question every girl I see."

"And if you hear anything of invasion -,"

"Pigs tails, girl," the countess scowled, "as if anyone takes the slightest interest in that dreary Tudor fellow. Now, I presume this place is genuine, and not a brothel in disguise?"

Jetta sighed as she walked on, avoiding the need to reply.

Several women looked up in considerable surprise as the countess entered the huge hall, dressed in considerable finery.

"I am the Countess of Desford," she said, standing to face the elderly woman who looked up from the table. "I have questions, questions of upmost importance."

Straitening her wimple with a twitch of one plump finger, the elderly nun smiled and welcomed the countess to sit with her. "My lady, what a delight," she said. "I am Sister Deira, one of the eldest here. You ask me whatever you like, my lady and I shall be delighted to answer whatever I can."

It seemed like a good beginning.

Jetta opened the door to the private room of the Abbess, without announcing her arrival, and stood at the small scrivener facing the tall woman sitting and writing on the parchment spread there.

"Sister Adelina?" Jetta frowned. "You're abbess now? What happened to Abbess Randella?"

The abbess also frowned as she stood. "You have neither been invited nor welcomed, Jetta. What are you doing here after all this time?"

Jetta's small smile was both haughty, which was intentional, and sarcastic, which was entirely unintentional. "I'm here because I want to know what's been happening," She placed both palms on the scrivener and stared down at the abbess. "I see you've managed to rise in power since I was last here. Did Abbess Randella die?"

"She became seriously ill." The abbess spoke softly. "Very sad. But she still lives and receives great care within our northern sisterhood."

"Sent north?"

"She lives in our holy sanctuary near York," the abbess replied, carefully keeping her voice sweet, soft and gentle. "But you were never her friend, Jetta. I cannot see why you ask after her."

"I was never your friend either."

"Perhaps," the abbess continued, "you were too young, and our rules were rather too strict for you. "I sympathise, Jetta my dear. Abbess Randella was older, and believed in some of the teachings now considered just a little out of date."

"I'm not your dear and never will be," Jetta said, leaning closer, her green eyes cold. "I was tormented here for years, by Randella, by Deira, and by you. We worshiped the God of love, yet you only taught hatred."

"That's your childish memory," the abbess said, her smile also turning to ice. "Remember you were only a little six-year-old when you ran away."

"So where," Jetta demanded, "is the man who came here several days past to ask after me?"

"Good gracious," the abbess said in a hurry. "What an absurd idea. No gentleman came here."

"Then how do you know it was a gentleman? It could have been – a farrier."

"You simply wish to cause trouble, Jetta, and I certainly won't surrender to your games. Why bother coming here after so many years?"

"Because," Jetta raised her voice, "I am accompanied by the Countess of Desford, who is the grandmother of the young man who came here three days and four nights ago. Abbot Francis at the monastery clearly told us that he sent the earl up here to speak with you. So forget the denials. I know full well that you saw him, and so does his grandmother. These are the nobility and friends of the king."

"Very well then." The abbess scowled and looked back down at her parchment, ink tub and quill. "He came here, but he asked me not to let anyone know if they came asking about him. Now I expect he's ridden north."

"Why?"

"To speak to dear Randella, of course. Now stop being so bad tempered, just as you used to be as a child. You obviously haven't learned manners after all. I'll explain the way north if you'd like, although I really cannot be sure where he went. Going north was discussed. It's perhaps more sensible to just go home and wait for his return."

Jetta stared, bit her lip and sighed. "Something's not right. He wouldn't have gone all that way – for nothing important. Nor for something quite pointless, that would take so long. And if he had intended – well, he'd have contacted his grandmother. Even Teresa."

"Who," she demanded, "Is Teresa?"

"None of your business." Jetta turned quickly, and abruptly asked the one question she knew was mostly certainly not *her* business. "Knowing Abbess Randella, she'd have hung on until her dying breath. So when you started dealing with the Lady Beaufort and Randella objected, did you simply decide to get rid of her? Plonked her over the head, perhaps, and sent her out of the way. Instead now are you secretly helping the Tudor usurper? Is that right?"

The abbess stood immediately, her chair fell back, and she pointed fiercely at the door. "Treasonous brat. Out, or I shall have you thrown to the donkeys."

Now Jetta turned once more and marched out towards the principal dining hall without another word.

The countess was sitting comfortably speaking with the small plump nun that Jetta recognised immediately.

"Ah, there you are, my dear," said the countess. "Come and sit here and join the discussion. It's most interesting. And a great relief, since finally I've discovered where my wretched grandson has gone. Sister Deira has been a great help. Such a kind nun indeed. Your idea to come here was very wise after all."

"Then what," Jetta demanded, "happened to Dominic according to Deira?"

The countess stared at Jetta, frowned, and waggled one finger. "Now, now, my girl. You can be very abrupt, and it is particularly rude when others are being so especially helpful. The sister has been explaining and I am extremely grateful."

"Did she tell you how some novices were locked up and starved for days if they fell asleep during prayers? A delightful practise indeed. And did she explain that others were whipped when they didn't even know what they'd done wrong? And was she delighted to describe how some of us were made to sleep outside with the geese when we misquoted the bible? I became very fond of the geese. They got to know me rather well. And, by any God given miracle has she told you how the previous abbess, who was vile anyway, was forced to resign and travel up north so this convent could collaborate with the Tudor son of the Beaufort woman?" Jetta huffed.

For a moment the countess sat with her mouth open, but then closed it with a snap. "I cannot believe you, Jetta. That is a ludicrous story."

Sister Deira scowled. "You exaggerate, girl. Yes, you were punished. Your Latin was particularly poor, and I don't believe you even attempted to improve. Your behaviour as a child was shocking. And seemingly it still is. As if holy women would become involved in politics, especially that sort of thing."

"So what happened to the earl when he came here?"

"There are two possibilities," growled Deira. "The most likely is that his lordship travelled north to York, for the abbess gave clear directions. But the second possibility is that we suggested he visit Lord Brian Maddock. Our other convent and the great sanctuary lies in the Yorkshire Dales, and Abbess Randella, who was the abbess here when Jetta lived with us, is there. She has problems with her memory, but we feel she may remember what happened to Jetta after she left us. Alternatively, Lord Maddock is where Jetta finally ended up in service, since Abbot Francis of the Knights of Jerusalem did actually worry over the child, discovering where she finally ended up. He told us several years past." She paused, with a somewhat smug smile. "You see, we actually troubled ourselves regarding your future, in spite of your lack of religious understanding and rebellious behaviour."

Jetta was staring down at the table. Rings still marked the wood with its own fleeting memory of cups for wine, ale and goat milk. Eventually she muttered, "I wasn't helped. It was years of one punishment after another, and Abbess Randella liked to think she was doing the Lord's work. But really, she just liked to watch me cry. And you liked making me lie on this table while you whipped me. When I ran away, I never wanted to see a nun ever again."

The small nun stood, straightening her wimple which seemed permanently askew. "Then I have no further interest in directing you," she said through a tiny, pursed mouth. "A nasty child you were, and a nasty child you are still. Leave and do whatever wickedness you want, no doubt you'll end in Newgate."

Looking down at the countess, Jetta nodded. "You see how sweet these women are! This place is alive with the cruellest memories. It makes me feel sick. Abbot Francis doesn't realise what this place is like, and I hope he never finds out. Whether you come with me or not, my lady, I'm leaving. I know where to go."

With puzzled discomfort, the countess also stood. She gazed helplessly at Sister Deira. "Sister, I apologise deeply for this girl's behaviour. I am simply searching for my grandson. So we shall be leaving, and I thank you sincerely for your help."

"May the Lord bless you," mumbled the sister, trotting off with a sullen scowl.

Almost running, Jetta left the convent and once out on the soft grass, she exhaled as though she had not breathed fresh air for months.

Then, quite suddenly she grinned at the countess. "I expect you think I'm crazy. Perhaps I am. But I told you I'd run away from here when I was just six years old, now you know the reason for it."

The rueful smile did not amuse the countess. "Convents are places of love and virtue. You must have been a most troublesome child."

"Perhaps I was, though I only remember the punishments. But that convent was never a place of love. A few other novices were treated just as badly. The abbess believed in discipline. She was wicked. And I wager she deserved all the horrid things they did to her and deal with Margaret Beaufort and Henry Tudor instead."

"Enough." The countess marched to the litter. The two riders leapt to attention, set down the step and held open the door. "Are you coming, girl? Or have you taken offence with me too?"

Jetta had hesitated. "I'm sorry, my lady. But there's something I need to see again, though it means walking in the forest. Just – well – to remember what I did when I was six. Would you mind waiting at the church? Or go back home, if you'd prefer."

"I shall certainly not be walking in any forest," the countess sniffed. "Indeed, I shall visit St. Paul's just inside the city wall. It is some years since I attended there, and once you've finished talking to the rabbits and foxes, that's where you'll find me. And if you find that wretched boy of mine, tell him where to come."

"It's quite a distance from here, my lady."

"I'm not a fool, girl," spat the countess. "I shall be sitting comfortably in my litter. You, on the other hand, will probably find yourself in a thunderstorm, not to mention attacked by wild pigs and lions." She settled herself in the litter and ordered her riders to drive on. The two guards mounted and yelled at the horses to stop chewing the vegetation growing at their feet.

"I don't know how long I'll be," Jetta called, but with the neigh of the horses and the calls of the men, no one heard her.

The silence soothed her, and she started walking towards the shadows of the small forest to her east. The smell of the undergrowth and the burrows delighted her. Once under the trees she stood a while, watching the sun steal through the leaves like a candle flame in a breeze. It was only after two joyful moments there that she knew exactly where she was. It had been perhaps ten years, but the perfumes surrounding her, the scrubbing beneath and the bird song above, reminded her of her happiest memories.

She walked through the shadows of the trees, delighting in her feet scrunching in the old leaves, and the sunshine on the back of her neck. She had to admit that this was not good for her beautiful new skirts, but she did not stop walking until she came to the tiny clearing she had been looking for.

The hut cuddled within those shadows was considerably smaller than Jetta remembered. Having lived there for some years when very tiny herself, this had seemed like a mansion. She was frightened only of finding the owner gone or replaced by someone else.

Jetta called, "Ned," and her voice shook.

But he didn't come from the hut. He came from behind her, startling her even more.

"I know who you are," the voice said, and the huge hand patted her shoulder, almost knocking her over. "You, little one, my best and only friend. Little Jetta, my precious, show me how you've grown up."

She turned at once, with a smile so wide it lit her dimples and her eyes seemed to reflect the sun beams.

Chapter Twelve

Standing at the top of the slope, Dominic breathed in the first dregs of cleaner air, and pivoted, assuring his direction. Behind him stretched the Chalk pits in a vast open stretch of dirty white crags and splits. To his right the moors stretched even further. Tiny twists of dirty smoke rose from the endless ugliness, yet he also saw the high steps of the hunting herons, the fervent buzz of flies, wasps and mosquitoes. Birds flew above, calling in strange distant echoes.

But ahead of Dominic the mounds were sprawling beneath thick grass and the birds and insects hunting there were almost hidden. A sweet warm breeze flitted over the green of grass and clover, the tiny white flitter of daisies and the glint of dandelions.

Further towards the horizon the haze of the clouds dipped below an outline of buildings and the soaring shape of the new Moorgate. But he turned from that, although every familiar speck breathed of escape and freedom.

Closer, however, edging out from the slope and the grass, was the start of a small forest, its leaves busy in the breeze. Immediately the trees grew closer and the small animal tracks through vegetation and undergrowth were the delights Dominic recognised and knew that it was through the woods that he would find the way back to Chiswick and the glory of his home. It called.

Dominic wrapped his arms around his nakedness, ignored the wet holes in his hose and the bleeding toes pushing through, and began to march in the direction of his comfort and sweet protection.

She rushed into the elderly man's embrace.

"I suppose I shouldn't," Jetta muttered. "But I can't help it. It's wonderful to see you again Ned"

Ned's laugh was a guttural chuckle that sounded a little like the crows watching from above. "Well now, my poppet. You was nine or even ten years I reckon, when you left."

"I don't know," she said. "I don't even know how old I am now. Perhaps twenty."

"No knowing and no matter. What matters," he grasped her hand, which then disappeared into his massive palm, "is you coming back here, little one, for a cup of good ale, and maybe a good chat if you've time."

"Oh, I've time to talk," she assured him. "For hours, except I'd keep you from your work."

"My work doesn't matter none," he brought her into the hut, opened the shutters, and let the light stream in through the windows. Without glass, parchment, bone or covering of any kind once the wooden shutters were taken down, the warmth cradled those inside. Ned sat Jetta on one of the stools and filled a mug with ale from the tap on the side of the barrel. "Now then, my little one," Ned smiled, sitting opposite her and grasping his own well filled cup, "tell me of your life since you left me. Looks like you've done well, lass."

He had pointed to her clothes, and the expensive embroidery. But Jetta shook her head. "An odd story, I'm afraid," she said. "Like most of my life. A mother I know nothing about, passed to Abbot

VESPERS

Francis, and then to that terrifying convent. It was those years with you, Ned, that were my happiest."

"So, tell me you wedded a duke, my dear, after leaving me all alone."

She laughed. "Not quite. I went begging for a year or possibly more, and I usually slept on doorsteps. It was winter and snowing when I went to the back door of a big house in Cripplegate. The steward pulled me in. I was never sure if he meant to be kind or cruel. But anyway, they gave me a job. That was alright. Hard work wasn't a problem and proper food and clothes instead of rags was a blessing. There were even a couple of women who tried to help me. But the owner of the house was a pig, and his son was – well – perhaps it sounds silly, so I won't bother describing him. But I was there for years and slept under the kitchen table. Not so good but not so bad at first until the son grew up. Then it was dreadful, I eventually managed to run away again. I found a wherry on the Thames embankment and rowed upstream."

"What a clever girl," Ned crowed. "I always knew it. Always said it. Now me – I love the trees but there ain't much brain in this little head of mine."

"It's rather a large head, you know," said Jetta, regarding the high brow beneath a flock of nearly silver hair. "And a very nice one too."

"Now, now, my sweet one," Ned insisted. "No need to try making me better than what I know I am. I'd never leave here, I love my work more than myself. I kiss the trees, and they kiss me back. I'll chop them, but they forgive me for that. I'll plant, prune and stack. I leaves some uncut, I even worked the charcoal for a year and more, remember?"

She smiled at the memory. "And you loved all the birds and the animals and even the insects."

"That 'ain't no less important, my beauty. Them bees, they make it all grow anew. And the red squirrels, well, they don't like the bees but I do."

Jetta floated back, disappearing into memories. "I loved the beavers and the hedgehogs best," she sighed, "and all the birds, every single one of them, the ravens used to come to my hand." The sigh turned to smile as she drained her cup. "But it was you, Ned, who made it all so happy."

"Me, a big brute of a fellow with this tiny little might of a child to look after? It was my best time too. I remember making a ball from some old bladder left by scavengers, and we played for hours till you were far better than me. Catch a feather, you could, or a pin in the dark. I reckon you were the best thing I ever had in my life."

"You should have come with me when I left."

But he shook his head and the wild silver tendrils spun across his nose. "I love it here too much, you always knew that. Looking after every tree and every bird. Helped feed all those little wanderers in the winter when food was scarce. And I wouldn't let poachers come into my wood for trapping them rabbits for their fur, nor them sweet deer for their meat. This was the king's land, loaned to the Knights o' St. John of Jerusalem and there ain't no one else can live here, my little one, 'cept me – and you. And his royal highness our blessed King Richard who pays me, and I won't ever do him wrong."

He paused and Jetta reached out, taking his hand. She squeezed it, enjoying the rough toil of the skin, the ridges made by years of work with axe and knife, and the warmth of its affection. "Somewhere there's another man, a young one with dark hair, nearly as tall as you but never so muscled. Have you seen anybody like that? He might have come here looking for answers. I know him but he wasn't looking for me, just wanted to know a few things. About me, I mean. But his grandmother's worried because this man never came home."

"I'll go looking, lass, if you want me to," Ned said, leaning closer across the tiny table. "Are you worried too? Or is it something' else, like you want him gone? Just you let me know. I'll have him up a tree or under the ground in a day. Just you tell me."

"No, no," Jetta clutched Ned's hand even harder. "No. He's nice. Actually, I'm not so sure about that. He probably isn't very nice, but he doesn't want to kill me or anything, and I certainly don't want to kill him. I just want to know where he is. He went to the convent and that's all we know."

"Those females would eat any man alive, I reckon." Ned finished his ale and offered a refill to Jetta. She said yes at once, needing anything that might help her relax. Seeing this man again was wonderful but she knew it meant more sadness when she had to leave. And it seemed he knew nothing of Dominic.

"So you've had no visitors?"

Big grins again. "There was a robin in the trees as I made my soup nigh on three days back. But my best visitors, apart from you of course my special one, were a whole family of foxes. Mum, she had three babies and I gave her the two dead birds that had fallen from their nests, poor little scraps I tried to save, but died anyway. Some call wild foxes' vermin, but they've the hearts of puppies and I ain't never hurt one. Nor never will."

With another tight embrace, Jetta smiled at Ned. "I loved the foxes to. But I meant a tall man with black hair."

Ned shrugged his shoulder, "how about you and me, being well-nigh dinner time, we have some duck eggs, and some of the herbs I steal from the priory garden?"

"I'd love to." She had forgotten about being hungry, but it had been quite some time since she'd eaten.

Ned cooked in the large iron pot on a trivet over the little fire. The smell of the fresh herbs brought a perfume of sheer heaven and when he added just a tiny spoonful of dark wine, Jetta remembered how much she had always loved his cooking.

She had spent five Christmases with Ned, but she had been a child. Living with him now would be impossible. Yet the memories were sweet enough for dreams. "Ned, this is wonderful. What a clever cook you are."

He chuckled again. "Reckon I'd be chucked from every kitchen in the land, if I'd the courage to cook for other folk. No, I ain't no good, but I know what I like. And if you like it too, then I reckon I'm happy."

"I remember our Christmases," she told him. "Venison that made my mouth water, and the only time you'd ever let us eat meat. And after dinner, we'd sit and sing together."

"It was the old king," Ned nodded, wiping his bread over the platter to scrape up the last smears. "He came bows and arrows at the ready every winter, and he shot the deer I loved. *They have to be culled,*' he always said to me. And every year he left one of those sad corpses for me. You need to hang venison for a good time before eating, and that would be enough for well-nigh a month."

Jetta finished her own platter, and copied Ned, wiping the surface with the bread. "Doesn't this new king come hunting?"

"I reckon he does in some places," Ned nodded, "I was told he goes hunting when tis a sad time, like when his little lad died, and then the wife. A terrible sadness and folk saw him cry like a man in pain. But he doesn't come here much. I met him once when he was still a duke, and was mighty proud to kneel to him, I was. But ever since the coronation, when I stood outside the Abbey to cheer and fling my hat in the air, the poor fellow, he's bin so busy. What with rebellion, then his little boy, and then the Lady Anne. So he's been grieving and once I saw him with tears all over his face, shining like a rainbow. He came here then, but not hunting with a bow. He held a beautiful great peregrine, and wandered alone with her, hunting in solitude. And yet being king, well, he's still working day and night."

"With the threat of Henry Tudor and the French."

"I'll fight, I will, if ever that bastard pretender ever dares come for our true king. But, well little cherub, I confess, living here alone I don't get news, nor even gossip."

Jetta was nodding, but her thoughts were far off. She knew this was a rare pleasure, and she had to leave soon and walk down to the Fleet, the London Wall, and through to St. Paul's. Already she had taken far longer than she should, entertaining herself while no doubt the countess was counting the minutes, hoping that Jetta had found the earl.

And of course, she had not.

"I should leave," she sighed, although not standing nor making any move to leave the table. "The young man's grandmother is waiting for me, and I've been ages. When I manage to settle somewhere, can I come again?"

"You can come, as often as you want my dear," Ned poured more ale, bending over the dusty barrel and wiping the little steel tap. "You come and live, if you want, and old Ned will take hisself to sleep under a tree. Nor you won't cook, little one, nor you won't chop no wood nor scrub no floors. You'll be my little princess."

She genuinely wished that she would and could. "I'm afraid not, Ned dear," she continued. "At the moment this is pure indulgence, and such a pleasure. But I'm needed elsewhere unfortunately. And I still have to clear my name from a horrible crime." She shivered but did not mention her growing interest in the man who had now disappeared.

Presenting her with another cup of ale, Ned once again sat opposite her at the small table, balancing his huge frame on the wooden stool. "Drink up, my little princess," Ned told her, leaning forwards again and taking her hand. "Now you tell Uncle Ned what's been happening to you. For you ain't capable of no crime, and that's the truth."

"Oh dear." She groaned, she wished she hadn't mentioned it. Not only was the situation absurd, and Ned could hardly help with it, but she seemed to spend half her life these days in recounting her past. So she gulped more ale and started the story.

Horrified, and equally indignant, Ned roared, "And they accuse my little lass of such a wicked thing? Well, that's as bad as bastard Henry Tudor wanting the throne when he's no crumb o' rights to it."

"Don't worry, Ned." She tried to laugh. "Of course I didn't do it and of course they must realise that. Except for the half-witted sheriff. The earl knows. Otherwise, he wouldn't have me sleeping under his roof in one of his best guest bedchambers. And now he's disappeared himself." A sudden thought crossed her mine. "And in case anyone thinks it – no – I haven't killed him either."

Ned's chuckle turned to cackle. "The mighty monster of the forest."

"I wish you were. You'd be awfully useful."

Now both laughing, they drained their cups, and as Jetta stood, ready to leave, she squeezed Ned's hand once again.

"I shall try to be useful, my little apple blossom," and Ned refused to release her hand.

"I'll be back sometime soon, honestly I will. But in the meantime, there's nothing you can do. None of us have the slightest idea where he is, or why, or doing what. He might even have been killed, but I don't think so. Can't think so. That would be awful."

"No point thinking of such things," Ned told her softly. "You ain't had an easy life. We both know your life till now has been mighty hard and cruel. The Lord God, He doesn't bring the rough stuff all the time. Tis bound to be happier times on its way."

The draught was sudden, like a slap of cold wind abruptly gusting into the room. And the deep voice said, "An unexpected blessing. I seem to have come to the right place after all."

Chapter Thirteen

Those heavy brows lifted, and the cold eyes had turned warm. The faint smile curved Dominic's mouth at either corner, but the enormous tiredness was what spoke the loudest.

Jetta leapt up, staring, and Ned stared, stunned.

Since Dominic was naked to the waist and wore only the snug black hose, the lack of shoes while striding across the difficult miles of varied terrain meant the hose had ripped. He had crossed over rock, chalk, and tree roots. But it wasn't the ladders in his hosiery that Jetta was staring at.

She wanted to run into his arms but didn't dare. Yet, while silently telling herself that she couldn't possibly do such a thing, she did it anyway. She felt the heat of his body against hers, the hard pressure of his nipples, the slide of his skin over the pronounced muscles, the tickle of the hair across his chest, but more delicious was his far thicker hair, tousled and windswept, across his brow.

Dominic's chin was bristled, not having shaved for some days. The half nakedness, much as she loved it, was surely not by his own choice, and although the day was just slightly warm with little sunshine, his lordship was gleaming with sweat.

As she flung her arms around him, his automatic response was the same. He embraced her as though she had saved his life.

Then he looked at Ned. "I should introduce myself and apologise for such an abrupt entrance. And I can assure you I rarely walk half naked through the forest. It seems you already know Jetta, but you and I have never met before. I believe you must be the official Guardian of these woods."

Ned, who was dressed in a huge brown tunic, belted low at the waist, brown hose beneath and boots like boats, now grabbed the new arrival's outstretched hand. "I know who you are, my friend. If you don't mind me saying, friend, that is. Anyhow, you're the grand earl by the name o' Dominic, gone missing for days and left my little princess worried sick. Now your gran's waiting, reckon she's praying for her lad's safe return."

Dominic's smile spread across his face. "Dom," he murmured, "although at the moment you could call me Tudor and I'd barely complain. A comparatively easy release after some very dark days of imprisonment, brings a sensation of freedom I doubt I've ever felt before."

"Well, you be mighty welcome here, my lord." Ned sat Dominic on his own stool, and promptly poured another cup of ale. Dom sat, drank the entire cup without pause, wiped his mouth and looked grinning at Jetta, then Ned, and reached to refill his cup.

"You must be the local woodcutter," Dominic smiled, thanking him for the wine. "I admit to being rather thirsty, and extremely weary. I am not at my best, but your kind welcome has helped." He looked across at Jetta. "Is this – a family member, perhaps?"

She had moved back into the shadows. "No," she was mumbling and rather flushed. "Just a – friend." The following silence felt embarrassing, and with a hiccup, she realised that once again she had to relate more tales from her past. She now retold the years of strange adventure as a child.

VESPERS

"Running from the covenant, I spent a few nights getting lost and almost climbed into birds' nests. But Ned found me and took me home."

Although it was Dominic she spoke with and it was Dominic she watched, she realised that Ned was listening avidly. "It ain't no lies, yer lordship," he interrupted near the end. "And this poor little princess o' mine, after being my little sister, she reached the vast age of twelve or so, thought she'd grown too much for living with an old gent like me. She went off for work and ended up with the worst lord you can think of."

"I'm not sure," Jetta whispered, "but I think I was about thirteen."

"I have heard that part of the saga," Dominic said. "Except I did not know the man's name. But you, my friend, were not explained. Perhaps," and he laughed softly at Jetta, "she wished to keep you secret. I understand the desire to keep the best parts to yourself."

"Like Teresa," whispered Jetta without thinking.

Dominic stared back. "Teresa?" His laughter died, and his eyes were ice once again. The sudden stab into his private life after days of incarcerated misery and the exhaustion of his escape, slammed against him, as unwelcome as his own pains.

Jetta immediately looked down. "Yes. I suppose I shouldn't have mentioned it. But she came to your home, you see. I met her and she told me who she was and how she missed you. Your grandmother wasn't very pleased."

"How interesting." Abruptly, Dominic's voice fell quite flat. No flicker of interest was discernible in either his voice or his expression. The tone was pure angry sarcasm.

"No good blaming me, it wasn't my fault," Jetta grumbled, then, with a panic-stricken rush to change the subject, she said, "And your grandmother. We've been talking for some days, and trying so hard to find you. She has been terribly worried. This morning we went to the convent, and they said you'd been there. Now your mother's waiting at St. Paul's Cathedral – praying – I mean – waiting for me in the hope I'll have found you."

Again, Ned interrupted. "Might I ask, being mighty important, I reckon, where your lordship's been?"

Once again Dom leaned forwards, his naked elbows to the little table. Now the warmth once again lit his eyes and etched his smile. "I must thank you for your concern and apologise for my distinct lack of clothing. But sadly, I also have a distinct lack of memory." He nodded to Ned and smiled to Jetta. "I had a meeting with Lord Leays in the morning. A close friend. Then, since it was not far off, I rode on to your priory and they in turn suggested the convent. I do remember some of what was discussed there. My mind then blurs into darkness, but I regained consciousness in what seemed like a cell. I was trapped there for some days, but had no method of counting the time passed." He raised an eyebrow to Jetta. "How long was I gone?"

"If you count that same day – and this one – it's five days and four nights."

"Shit," Dominic said under his breath. "To be held imprisoned for that long is a damned humiliation. At least I eventually kicked my way out. But I have no idea who put me there." He paused, then added, "Or why."

Jetta stood. "It must be my fault, surely. It was either the abbess, whose quite wicked. Or, perhaps more likely, the man I used to work for. Did the abbess tell you his name and how to find him?"

"I have no idea." Dominic leaned his head on the backs of his hands where they were clasped on the table. "The unconscious hours, or however long it was, have entirely disappeared. That's left me with no notion of the two answers most important to me. Indeed, all that remains in my bedazzled brain, are the interminable hours spent in a dark and empty cave, and my joy at breaking out. The miles I've walked since have been long and nothing pleasant until walking into this forest. Why half my clothes disappeared, I can only guess they became blood stained and so were taken to disguise some of what presumably happened."

Jetta watched, the outline of his backbone clearly visible, the tied belt of his hose slipping down over the gentle rise of his buttocks. She took a breath before speaking. "So you've walked miles. You must be exhausted. I'll leave you with Ned while I go and collect your grandmother. I have to put her mind at rest."

"A great kindness," Dominic breathed without lifting his head. "I thank you."

Pausing, Jetta looked down, then across to Ned. Her whisper was even softer as she slipped through the half open door. "Is it alright to leave him here? Please don't wake him. I'll try and be quick, but I'll be some time walking all that way."

Ned followed her. "I wish I could do it for you, little cherry blossom," he sighed. "But not knowing her ladyship nor her knowing me, would be mighty hard."

Jetta nodded in agreement, smiled at a sleeping Dominic and left quietly.

He watched her slip into the shadows between the trees then Ned returned to the table and the slumbering stranger. Not exactly how he had planned to spend the day, but it had brought an interesting break in his usual routine. "I might be a tree-feller and gamekeeper," he muttered to himself as he took the second stool over to the window. "But maybe I can be a clever fellow after all, and maybe help them folk more powerful."

It was sometime before Dominic awoke. The sunshine had been warm on his naked back, bringing sleep to seal out the exhaustion. He woke, only vaguely aware of where he was.

"Where's Jetta?" He leaned back, pushing himself upright from the table and looking around.

Ned grinned. "Just me here. A proper disappointment I reckon, but naught I can do about it. Our little friend Jetta has gone to London to find your gran."

Dominic blinked, still fuzzy from sleep. "Ned. I sit in your home, thankful for your generosity." He stretched his legs beneath the table, and Ned saw the drips of blood falling across his floor.

"No generosity of mine," Ned said, leaning back against the

window as Dominic leaned back against the wooden planked wall. "I only gave you a mug of local wine. You want another?"

"With the greatest pleasure, yes indeed." Dominic was breathing in the fresh blast of freedom, but also the smell of trees and gentle sun on the bracken, the bright music of bird song and the perfume of dinner from the pile of platters still holding the smears of egg and herbs. "But if I have interrupted yourself and Jetta -?"

Shaking his silver tousles a little wildly, Ned said in a hurry, "There ain't no stuff between us, other than friendship. Don't you go thinking Jetta and me is a couple, nor ever was. Me? I'm old enough to be her grandpapa, I knew her first as a tiny scrap of a child, beaten ragged and as miserable as a rabbit in a trap. I looked after her, poor little thing, she was. Besides," he grunted, "I ain't never been into that stuff."

Dominic regarded his new and unlikely companion. "You are telling me, I gather," he grinned, "that you take no interest in women? Or have I confused your meaning?"

"I was born in Newgate," Ned chuckled without shame. "My ma was pressed within the month, and I was given to an aunt. I made me own way in life and didn't have money nor bloody sense neither. I found this job, and I love it. Most of the time I see no one. I see the foxes and the wild cats, deer and hares, voles and badgers, and enough birds to make you want to sing along. I don't need women."

"The wonder of nature." Dom was also laughing softly. "Though I doubt if I could live long without a woman in my arms."

"I gathered that," Ned grinned.

Dominic delighted in uncontrolled laughter. Laughing now seemed alluring. "After misery," he told Ned, "laughing is obligatory."

He stood, stretching, felt the strength return to his legs, and walked to the window. A wood pigeon bobbed and cooed from a tree branch. A tiny leaf swathed hedgehog was scuffling at the half open doorway. Ned reached over, hauled it up onto his lap, and began to pick the old leaves off the spines.

VESPERS

"You appear to be more of a father than a game-keeper," Dominic said, watching, still amused.

"They all need a little loving care," Ned explained, laying a platter of river water on the ground, then the animal beside it. It drank, snuffled into the platter, then turned and waddled off.

Dominic nodded, smiling as it disappeared under the trees outside. "I assume you don't hunt. Do you capture the fledgling falcons?"

"I do, but I don't like it over much," Ned answered, "but I know how King Richard is mighty kind to his birds. Not so keen on bows and arrows, he isn't. But loves his falcons. I got three just fledged for him after his queen died. He wasn't a happy man. But he rubbed his fingers in them falcon feathers and his face in the downy growth, and I saw him kiss the beaks. But don't you go telling anybody I told you that."

Two more mugs of ale, talk of politics, of the threat of invaders, while trying to remember the twenty or so other names of those who could claim the throne of the Lancastrians before Henry Tudor, the making of leather, the weather, which was not at its best for June, but nor at its worst, the expense of the new paper from Italy replacing parchment, the new fashion of codpieces becoming more prominent, and the new printed copies of the Bible appearing in the English language.

"They reckon it's wicked."

"The king approves."

"Wouldn't make any difference to me," Ned sighed. "I can't read Latin, I can't even read English. Nor Greek neither. But why must that beautiful book be in Latin?"

"I gather Jetta can read." Dominic responded. "She would have been taught in the convent no doubt. I'm surprised she didn't teach you."

"Wot for?" Ned demanded. "Wouldn't be any use to me. But I taught her hunting with falcons, though don't you go telling anybody since it ain't proper for a little lass. She might have got a merlin, I reckon, but I gave her the peregrines I trained, and she learned it and all. Swimming, climbing trees, cooking, and all sorts."

Clasping his hands behind his head, Dominic sat, smile now permanent, and compared his own past to Jetta's. A different life beyond comparison. "And yet she's walking all the way to St. Paul's. It's a long walk. And the gates will lock soon."

"Told me they have a litter with two horses. So coming back won't be so bad, as long as the wheels can get through the trees. I told her, sure to be better to leave the litter at the Fleet and just walk through."

"I doubt my grandmother would agree. She tends to believe that walking is an immoral sin."

"Could ride one o' them horses?"

"For my grandmother, that would be almost as bad as walking," Dominic laughed. "She's no longer young, though she won't admit it."

Ned shrugged. "Reckon we all do as we want if we can."

"Which is why imprisonment is a frustrating thing to experience," Dominic said softly. "In that black cell, I discovered fear. Perhaps there had been moments of fear as a child though I remember none. In the cell, it felt completely new to me. Fear pumps the heart and head at a speed I would never have expected."

"You ain't never been affrighted before, my lord?" Ned was impressed. "I wager you live in one of those palaces, places big as a litter just for a privy. Must be mighty nice."

"I have never considered an alternative," Dominic said without pride. "But nor have I ever been kind enough to walk from here to St. Paul's simply to help two other people, one of whom, at least, has not offered her the kindness she deserves."

"You've not been kind to my little Jetta?" Ned asked in surprise. "But we talked plenty before you turned up, my lord. And she said plenty about you, she did. Didn't say naught bad. Spoke well of you, and said how she wanted you rescued quick."

Lifting an eyebrow in immediate surprise, Dominic began to answer but was interrupted. The tramp and whiplash of the litter could be heard like a storm, and the countess's voice in high pitched complaint.

Dominic strode outside. The litter stopped with a scrunch of undergrowth, the driver opened the door and the countess virtually capsized from within. The horses bent their heads to the interesting growth under their feet and fell contentedly silent.

"It's true," the countess squeaked. "My darling boy, it's really you." She hugged him with eager hands, then frowned. "Was it really that hot? It's not – well, what I'd expect."

"I did not strip purposefully," Dominic laughed. "I can explain later, dear." Though it was actually Jetta he was looking at over his grandmother's shoulder. He turned to Ned. "I thank you again, and greatly appreciate your kindness," he told Ned. "I will visit again, if you can put up with an errant visitor at times. Next time, I promise to dress a little more appropriately."

"Dominic, who is this fellow?" demanded the countess.

"A friend," Dom said softly, disentangling himself from his grandmother.

Jetta, having scrambled from the litter which now stood lopsided as the horses grazed, was short of breath. She said in a rush, "I expect you want to go home now."

"I expect I do," Dominic smiled, "but not in a litter. I'd rather not submit myself to more torture yet. If the litter can trundle with one horse, then I shall claim the other and ride home."

"My lord," said one of the drivers, "poor old Spot ain't got no riding saddle. She's only bin pulling the litter."

"I can ride her bareback," Dominic smiled. "Though if I may borrow your coat, I will perhaps cause less scandal than riding the highway naked." And he turned again to Jetta. "Well, my saviour. Which do you prefer, litter or horseback?"

"Horse back," said Jetta at once. "But we only have the two horses, my lord."

"Then you shall sit in front of me. I'll keep you safe while we ride somewhat ahead of the litter and cause a scandal of a different sort."

Dominic grinned as he struggled into a coat that stretched too tightly across his broad shoulders.

The countess was obviously put out at the idea of losing her companion, so huffed at the pair of them, though neither pouted nor scowled. Finding her grandson was sufficient pleasure after all. She managed a small smile as she was helped into the litter.

Jetta turned back to Dominic warily and realised that her own smile was echoed in his. Hers became the wider as he then lifted her on to the mare's back. "Arms to her neck, my dear," he said, and mounted behind her, reaching around to take the reins. She was pressed back to his chest though she tried to sit straight. Yet as his arms pulled even tighter around her, and with the strength of his thighs against her legs, Jetta could hardly breathe. It wasn't the pressure on her lungs that troubled her. It was the excitement of his body holding so close, his own breathing thumping against her back, and his steady heartbeat which she could hear against her spine.

He asked, "Comfortable?"

She could only nod in reply.

Chapter Fourteen

The countess, litter-weary, had since fallen asleep three times, once at the table, once in her cushioned chair, and once in the privy. She had therefore been escorted to bed by two pages and her maid.

Dominic's story had already been told, but it was once alone with Jetta that he told the tale again with more detail. He was wearing a long black bed-robe over his shirt and had stretched himself across the well cushioned settle.

"Do you think it could have been anyone in the convent?" Jetta asked softly, rubbing her finger around the top of the pewter cup she held. "I hated so many of those nuns. But it makes no sense, why would they hate you? I'm sure it must have been someone else." She sat on the high-backed chair facing him, though his piercing gaze caused her cheeks to redden and her hands to fidget.

"I've told you all I remember," Dominic said, his voice equally soft. It was not a story for the servants, or even his grandmother. "I have now washed, dressed, and eaten. Such banal and common practices, but the liberty to behave as I wished and enjoy the comfort of my own home seems literally heaven. I now understand your need for freedom. Yet I was only a few days in that hole. You were imprisoned for years."

"But I had light and I wasn't alone."

"Your fear. I admit to never having understood such a sensation before. Life was often sad, although more often dreary and unchallenging. Yet I'd not experienced fear since my childhood."

"And so," Jetta murmured, "you are now desperate to know how and who it was?"

Dominic nodded, though his frown remained. "It's the 'who' more than anything. Not knowing means the possible risk of it being attempted again – maybe even to you, if the convent is truly involved. So, tell me your thoughts. And then perhaps, we can piece it together. Why was it done, by who, and how do we prove it?"

Jetta tried to make sense of it before speaking, but under Dominic's heavy stare she had no choice. "Alright, But it's still only a guess. While I was there, the sisters mentioned that they knew where I had been employed before, the place I was running away from when you found me on the river. Well, I think one of the sisters must have gone to him, to ask him to meet with you to answer your questions about me. I think perhaps they meant well. But that man, I doubt he ever meant well in his life."

Jetta was feeling flustered as Dominic's stare turned into a smile. She reached to put her cup down but changed her mind and grabbed it back, only just avoiding spilling it over her skirts. Keeping her hands busy seemed to help calm her bewildered thoughts. "I believe that it was him who attacked you. No matter how much I hated the nuns, I can't believe they would have almost killed you and kept you prisoner." She took a breath, relieved that he was taking her seriously. Not many in her life ever had.

"Yet you believe a minor lord of the city could have wished me dead, never having met me before?" Dominic sat now with his elbows to his knees and drained his third cup of Burgundy. "What's this man's name?"

Jetta had still barely drunk her wine, wanting to keep a clear head. "Lord Brian Maddock. His wife is Lady Mary. His son is Percival, who is vile, much worse than his father. They live in Cripplegate. He's the third grandson of the late Baron Stanley. I think it must've been him that imprisoned you."

Dominic took another long gulp of wine and raised his head with a bemused stare. "By all that's holy, why?"

"Because he's a pig and his wife's a sow and his son's a devil. Because you asked after me, someone he hated. Or perhaps he said something to someone and realised you could have overheard. Maybe he supports Tudor."

"What difference would that make? I'm a friend of Richards, but it's not generally known." Interested, Dominic sat forwards.

Jetta frowned over her own muddled memories. "I'm not sure about any of it, just trying to bring the threads together to see what we find. You say Abbot Francis seemed to hint about Margaret Beaufort. That's Tudor, isn't it?"

"It remains nonsensical. Had I not been the one taken, I doubt I'd have believed it." Dominic dragged his fingers over his face in frustration. He was unaccustomed to chaos, and both liked and expected control. This had never been questioned before.

Sensing his mood, Jetta continued. "I confess I didn't care much about politics back then. I was only interested in trying to survive. But you'd be amazed at the amount of gossip that goes on downstairs in the kitchens and laundries. Servants live on gossip. It's the only diversion. And apparently, Lady Mary spoke often of visits to Margaret Beaufort. When I heard about that, I was surprised. The Maddocks aren't important enough to have such close relationships. And I can remember the family stopping talking quite suddenly when any of the staff walked in. Lots of different reasons of course."

Dominic didn't answer for some time. Then he leaned over, grabbed the jug of wine and refilled his cup. He offered it to Jetta, but she shook her head.

"Drugged, poisoned or knocked unconscious. There's no other possibility." He drank deeply, setting his cup back beside the jug.

"And not, you believe, by your party of delightful nuns? What about the abbot you liked so much?"

"Oh, I don't think so. But how could I know for sure?" She now slumped in her chair realising that she was of little help after all.

Dominic stood and walked to the large fireplace before turning back to her. "Then you'll accompany me to the Cripplegate house of the gentle Maddocks."

Jetta stood up quickly in surprise. "Oh no, please, not there. They'll drag me back. They'll whip me for running away."

He laughed as Jetta spoke, which made her glare back at him. "I've shocked you?" Dominic was still laughing. "Can you really imagine that these people would take my companion and chuck her back into the kitchen? You, my dear, will come with me as a friend. A close friend, let us say. No, you'll be perfectly safe with me."

His words calmed her somewhat, though her fear would not disappear so easily. He had called her '*my dear*' and that had been surprisingly pleasant. "I suppose they wouldn't dare, but what if it *was* them that attacked you? Surely it would be asking for trouble?" She responded, staring back at him, hopeful rather than simply disobedient.

Dominic lapsed into silence, but a small, strange smile curled the corners of his mouth, turning his eyes unusually warm. Then he laughed, saying, "Well, I'm sure we can deal with whatever happens. But tomorrow we shall visit this devilish Lord Maddox, his reaction will be extremely interesting. We shall, of course, take a larger than usual retinue."

⁂

Jetta, sitting late that evening by the window of her bedchamber, watched as Dominic left the house and marched to the stables, calling for the mare to be saddled. She knew exactly where he was heading and didn't mind in the least. She smiled as she climbed into bed and pulled the eiderdown over her head.

VESPERS

At his invitation, she had ridden home from Ned's cottage with Dom's arms tight around her and his naked chest against her. He had called her '*my dear*', and now he wanted her company travelling to London. She expected no protestations of affection, but she believed herself accepted.

The next morning, dutifully dressed as the sun inched up from the black horizon to a faint peach glimmer, Jetta prepared, both mentally and physically for a day of challenge and quite possibly danger.

Her riding gloves, she decided, were stout enough to enable her to punch, and perhaps even strangle. Though her fingers were not suitably strong for most of these tasks. She could only hope there wouldn't be the need.

She was not so pleased with the rest of her clothes. Unfortunately, they were not sufficiently grand enough to convince anyone that she was the Earl of Desford's friend. But there was nothing she could do about that unless she borrowed from someone else. She wondered whether Teresa might lend her something prettier, but knew that even if she did, they wouldn't fit her purpose. Teresa was both shorter and plumper. As for borrowing from the countess, forget it. Nothing would fit, and certainly nothing would be offered. At least she wasn't dressed in the clothes she'd arrived in just a few short weeks ago.

Hurrying downstairs to the main hall and the dining table, she discovered Dominic already there, but no sign of the countess. At least it meant that he had not stayed the night with his mistress, and Jetta silently told herself off for being so childishly pleased.

Dominic looked up. "Ah, your clothes," he said, more to himself than to her. "I shall have to think of something."

"Yesterday you were barely clothed at all," sniffed Jetta, "and I didn't complain."

"Not clothed at all?" He grinned. "I was, I believe, wearing hose. Otherwise, I would have probably been obliged to jump in the Fleet."

Jetta quite suddenly felt the need to study her fidgeting fingers to hide her blushes.

"My lord," Benson bowed.

"Yes, I require a lady's cloak," Dom said, returning to his cup. "As grand as you can find. Steal one of my grandmother's if you have to. Fur lined and large enough to wrap around." He then turned back to Jetta, now sitting opposite across the white linen tablecloth. "Our plans are changed," he told her. "His highness the king has been exceedingly busy and needs to discuss some urgent issues. I'm called to attend Westminster Palace this morning. Naturally you won't be needed in audience, so you may have to wait a wretchedly long time in the annex. They'll bring you wine, and I doubt I'll be gone for the entire morning. Then we ride to visit your friendly demons."

"Gracious, could I not wait outside for both?" Jetta stared and nearly choked on her cheese and breakfast ale. Going to the palace, even though she would not see the king, was a nerve-wracking thought.

Benson entered at that moment to deliver the cloak as ordered, and Jetta prepared, now wearing a cape of superb quality, dark red velvet and lined in thick black fur. Ned would not have approved, but it was the most beautiful thing she had ever touched.

"You look the part now, and no one will think to question you my dear. The annex will be fine." Dominic reached for her hand. "Now we leave, I cannot keep His highness waiting."

Westminster Palace breathed back at her, the glory of it leaving her breathless. She had seen it before from outside but had never entered. Sitting quietly in the annex with the black fur wrapped tightly down to her ankles, was an experience she would long remember, and the thought of it helped her sit patiently quiet for a little over an hour.

VESPERS

King Richard, still involved with the rituals of burial, looked tired and strained.

"Anne rests in Westminster Abbey," he said softly. "But the head piece is not yet complete. And there are other duties, less urgent, but must still be attended with some speed. And always, at the back of my mind, is the threat from France. This is a bad year for expecting an invasion."

"Is any year better or worse for invasion?"

Richard smiled. "You do me good, Dom. You're the tonic that the medick cannot supply. But yes, I've twice dealt with unexpected treason, and for me – from the least likely – Hastings, then Buckingham. Hastings was intelligent and should have known better in spite of his greed. Buckingham was a simpleton, but even he should have known that he stood to gain more with me than against me."

"Morton let him imagine he'd soon become king."

"Wretched fool. But I accept my own fault in the final affray. I should never have put Buckingham forwards as Morton's gaoler. But no matter now. I think mainly of Anne. I miss her, and I cry for the loss. She was a friend when I was little more than a child. Then through many years living so close brought feelings I'd never known before."

"It'll be a busy year." He was well aware that the king would not want sympathy.

"And highly important, distractions are good for a man who might be tempted to disappear into sorrow. I turn the misery of loss into the fury of betrayal."

"We all loathe Henry Tudor," Dominic answered, nose back in the silver cup as he drank the wine. "I've never met the man, but I can loathe him for his treasonous ambitions. Supporting the Lancastrian cause still gives him no rights for he's neither next in line, nor a trained candidate. He knows it himself and will use the French for support. If he really believes himself the true king of this land, how can he bring over our erstwhile enemies to slaughter his own people?"

"If all those who desire to be king knew the life of disappointments that kingship requires, they might change their goals."

"I hear that Andrew has gone back to spy out the situation. Not Brittany this time, but France."

Richard nodded. "Yes. Andrew left yesterday." Looking up, he gazed directly at Dominic. "My friend, I've a job for you too. I know the most obvious traitors of this sweet country. I expect the remaining Woodvilles to turn against me, and I've brought Baron Stanley into line, concerning his own dilemma. His son has joined my private entourage, and Stanley would risk losing him if he turned traitor for his unpleasant wife."

"Stanley may be married to Margaret Beaufort," said Dominic, "but they rarely see each other. I've no notion if they share loyalty, but they are unlikely to share a bed."

Richard nodded. "I understand the situation with Stanley, and I understand his difficulties, since his wife is Tudor's mother but it's other potential traitors I want unearthed. Find out whatever you can. Who will answer when I call the muster, and who will turn traitor? I have others with their fingers in the treason pie, but you are a good deal more than simply trustworthy. You are an eccentric individual. You like to search the burrows and cross both over and under life's bridges."

"It's an apt request, sire." Dominic sat forward. "There's a lord of low standing, Brian Maddock, to the best of my memory I've never met the man nor any of his family. He lives in Cripplegate with a wife and son."

"I know of him," Richard said, "but do not know him. He sits on no councils nor advisory meetings and has no position. What of him?"

"I believe he'll fight on Tudor's side," Dominic said, "Just one fool with no following. I need to know more. And within the next month I promise I'll scour the whole damned land. Messages will have to be sent in code to wherever you are."

"My duties take me both north and south," Richard said.

VESPERS

"I won't follow you, sire," Dominic answered, "but I'll also target north and south, and hope not to miss either the obvious or the subtle."

The king stood, taking his friend's arm. "There is another man, of somewhat higher standing, related, I believe to your Brian Maddock. I know him slightly, but I dislike him. He's probably another Tudor supporter, once close to the Woodvilles, and perhaps still is. He avoids me. I find that both convenient and suspicious. Howard Tambar, 1st Earl of Plymouth, a distant relation of Stanley, and also of the Maddock family. I believe he could muster a reasonable following."

Nodding, Dominic paused, remembering, then said, "Yes, I've heard of the man, and met him many years gone. I understand he never comes to court. I know little of him, nor wish to. Yet now, perhaps, he becomes more interesting."

This time the horses were ready saddled with the palace guards outside, hands ready to help. Those personally claiming audience with the king himself would be treated with special courtesy. Dominic lifted one hand to Jetta's elbow. She did not ask anything of what his highness had said, stifling her curiosity. She smiled gracefully and didn't speak.

Together they rode slowly, following the curves of the Thames where the road was wide, and the smell of the water was not quite so bad as the smells of the city's cesspits overflowing and uncovered.

Jetta sat straight, her small feet pressed into much larger stirrups as she tried to overcome the escalating swamp of fear in her stomach. It was therefore some time before she noticed how closely Dominic was riding, and how often he glanced sideways, checking on both her riding skills and her confidence. This brought with it a feeling of relief and safety, thankful that he was by her side. Her fears started to melt.

Entering London through the Newgate, the stench in their faces, they turned north and headed towards Muggle Lane and the large brick building which now stood, newly built, on the corner. A little south of Cripplegate, this was a useful position pointing towards the two gates out of the city, both north and west. The house itself, without grounds or private stables, was restricted.

"This is the one," she whispered as her heart hammered beneath her ribs.

"With the stink of the wall and the piled rubbish in the ditch outside?" Dominic's expression did not hide his disgust.

"No matter," Jetta mumbled. "The stink inside is almost as bad."

Dominic's two principal guards marched forward, crossed pikes knocking against the door. It was immediately opened by the steward who was clearly startled.

"Lord Stark, Earl of Desford, wishes to speak with Lord Maddock. Inform him that the earl is waiting."

"At once, sir, at once," the agitated steward responded, and looked up at Jetta with recognition. Although she sat high, elegant on horseback and glorious in a cloak of velvet and fur, the steward obviously recognised her and stared in even greater astonishment. Stepping back, he pulled open the hinged entrance, blinking, embarrassed, at the metal squeal. "Please enter, your lordship, while I make your arrival known to Lord Maddock. I shall have wine brought immediately."

He watched with fascination as Jetta followed Dominic through the doorway and into the dark corridor. From there the steward showed them into the entrance chamber and Jetta, who already knew the house in detail, kept quietly to the rear. The steward bustled off and a page appeared with wine and three cups, pouring a cup for both Jetta and Dominic.

"Not the best." Dominic sipped at the pallid red water.

Jetta raised her cup. "It's the first time I've ever had wine in this house, I can hardly believe it."

"Also the last, I imagine," Dominic smiled. He was leaning

VESPERS

against the doorway, arms crossed. Jetta sat on a chair beside him. "Don't speak too much," he looked down at her. "I don't know yet if the problem will exacerbate or be easily solved."

Within the dull entrance chamber, the plastered walls were bare, the floorboards unpolished, and only the rise of the stairs and the two wooden chairs where Jetta sat, broke the emptiness. This was not a household of great wealth or importance.

"I'd rather not speak to anyone in this house," Jetta sniffed between gulps of wine. "Joseph, the steward's not so bad. Everyone else is horrible."

Dominic's intended reply was interrupted. A wide-shouldered man marched from the main hall, neither old enough for the lord, nor quiet enough for a man of sense.

"Visitors, eh, uninvited ones at that." he announced, licking his lips as though contemplating a meal already laid out for a cannibal. "And one I certainly recognise. Found a grand friend, have you, cleaning girl?" His sneer changed as his lip upturned to a smirk.

Jetta's glare was as black as her cloak, but before she could say a word, Dominic spoke, his words soft and his sneer threatening, brows lowered. "How interesting," he said. "A young man who has never learned manners nor understands the use of tact." He now stood tall, the menace came from more than his expression.

The young man stepped forwards and raised his fists. "I don't know you and don't want to. But the whore at your side, she belongs here and damned well deserves a whipping for running away."

"Indeed, your charming greeting gives me the pleasure of answering in the same manner." The smile faded and Dominic's eyes were now hooded. Since you are clearly Percival Maddock, a creature without title or brain, you will not speak to my friend ever again in any manner or I shall call for your immediate removal. Now, back to the point. This young woman was in your father's employment, she was so badly treated that she left, as any person no matter their station, is entitled to do. I therefore insist on hearing no more on the subject." His smile grew once more, as Percival Maddock stared in shocked fury. "Now, there is another situation I wish to discuss with your father. He is, I assume, hiding somewhere in the house."

Percival choked slightly. "My father is out," he said with the defiant pout of a small boy. "And so is my mother."

"Outside in the street," Dom said, "are eight of my personal staff, four of them armed. Unless you call for your father to appear immediately, my men will enter and search your house."

"You have no right –,"

"True." Dom nodded genially. "No rights at all. It will not stop me however, I shall act precisely as I wish. Now call your father."

From the small step inside the doorway where Percival had been standing, unable to resist the temptation, he strode up to Dominic, both hands still fisted. "This is my home and for all your fancy names, you have no right to make demands in my father's house sir."

Before Dominic had a chance to respond, Percival had swung his right fist, fast and accurate, towards his visitor's face. Yet it was Percival who now lay on the ground, flat on his back, while Dominic remained standing exactly as he had been, and with the same smile.

"You need to practise a little more," Dominic told the young man beneath him. Slowly he nudged Percival in the side with his foot. "Get up," Dominic said, "and find your father."

Humiliated, furious, but trying to hide both anger and pain, Percival stumbled up and scurried from the hall.

"I enjoyed that," Jetta told Dominic softly. "Could you do it again?" He smiled, shaking his head in amusement.

It was some moments later when Brian Maddock marched into the room and stood close to where both Jetta and Dominic now sat, not as tall as his son, but equally outraged.

"Whoever you are, sir, I must ask you to leave. You have befriended an erstwhile scullery maid Surprised as I am, I've no desire to take her back into my employ. You may both now leave my property at once."

"A few questions first," Dominic said without moving. "You say you don't know me. Is that true?"

VESPERS

Maddock was flustered. "My son and my steward gave me your name, sir, and so I know who you are. But I've never seen your face even at a distance, and never wish to again. You've attacked my son with no explanation, and bring this strumpet with you. Why are you here?"

Dominic ignored the belligerence in the man's eyes. "You will not refer to Miss Lawson in those terms again, sir, or you will regret it. So far, I have no reason to doubt what you say. And you have never met me before, which was my first question. I have more. Are you acquainted with Howard, Earl of Plymouth? What is your relationship with the Lady Margaret Beaufort? And when do you expect the fleet to arrive from France, will Tudor aim to land on the English or Welsh coast?"

Flustered, then angry, it was obvious that Brian Maddock had no idea how to answer, and managed only, "How could I possibly know such a thing?"

Dominic's smile reappeared. "You have answered my first and fourth questions very clearly, sir, and I now know full well that you side with the Tudor faction and consider yourself a Lancastrian. But I'll offer a small piece of advice before I leave. Once the invasion occurs, as it will no doubt, sometime this year, you should stay home and lock your doors. Since I now know you as a traitor, once the fighting is over, you might very well find yourself on the gallows." He frowned again. "Now I shall repeat my second question. How often do you meet with the Earl of Plymouth and when did you see him last?"

Lord Maddock's anger seemed to fade, and confusion took its place. "Howard? Yes, I knew him, but he never comes here. I've not seen him for years."

Percival did not reappear, and his father stood and simply gaped as Dominic and Jetta left. It was the steward who opened the doors, bowed, and wished his lordship a good day.

Dominic smiled as his groom brought over the two horses. Mounting, he turned to Jetta. "Neither as useless nor as useful as I had suspected," he told her as they headed towards the bank of the river. "However, my questions were clearly answered. It was not the father who attacked me. Perhaps the son, though I doubt it. Maybe your sweet nuns, although any reason remains obscure. This family supports Tudor but is of too little consequence to matter."

Jetta shook her head. "Perhaps the nuns then. They could be supporting Tudor too I suppose."

"Though such support would be of minor interest on its own," he murmured. "Someone more important behind them possibly. But a parcel of women, most elderly and some little more than ten years, would neither help Tudor, nor explain why I should be locked in a hellhole for discovering the facts. No, I'm no closer to understanding the situation."

"Well," Jetta grinned, "thank you for hitting that pig-face Percy. He was the one who kept trying to – though he didn't manage it. But he had me whipped over and over and over. Stripped and lashed. And he stood and watched."

Dominic looked over at her and the smile had left his eyes. "I should have hit him harder."

"I hope there isn't a next time. But do you want to go back and talk to the nuns?"

"There is something strange about that convent," Dominic sighed. "But for the moment, I intend taking you home, and then preparing for my own travels."

Jetta looked aghast. "You're going away?"

"On his highness's business, yes," Dominic smiled. "But I'm not throwing you from the premises. I now call you friend. After walking from John O' Groats to Land's End on my behalf –,"

She giggled, "Not quite that far."

"I invite you to live peacefully in my home," he answered her, "try and ignore my grandmother, keep the bedchamber you already occupy, don't die of boredom, and I shall return in a few weeks." He studied her disappointment. "Visit Lady Tyballis," he suggested. "You have a few things in common, and there's not a soul left in the country who dislikes her. Besides, Andrew is also out on the king's business and she's alone. I leave tomorrow, but I'll be back within the month."

"I won't run away anymore. I can promise that."

"And your wherry boat, which was never yours, has been returned to the London pier. So, you don't have the means either." He was laughing at her, but she decided she didn't mind at all.

"Thank you," she mumbled, very small voiced.

Chapter Fifteen

"I haven't the faintest idea why you think such silly things," said the countess over the breakfast table. She gulped her ale and pulled a face. "And why do they bring me this when they know I only like hot milk in the morning?"

Jetta answered neither objection. She planned on several visits to Tyballis over the next few weeks, walks down by the river, sitting in the sunshine on golden days, and afternoons spent dreaming of what she might one day do with her life. Not used to a life of leisure, or in fact even a minute, she had no trouble at all thinking of things to occupy her time.

The amazing, almost explosive change in her life had neither been planned or expected. She had done little to create it. The change had floated from a dark summer evening with its last glimmer of sun which had indeed seemed like a disaster. Then – the sun had risen. And now it seemed that the shadows had turned to rainbows.

Yet despite all the glorious improvements, Jetta was not fool enough to expect miracles. Staying here forever, perhaps even one day acting as nurse for Dom's children, seemed the most she could possibly hope for. Unlikely, but there was nothing wrong with hope.

VESPERS

She would do all she could to prove herself useful. He had called her friend, but she was not entirely sure what that could mean.

He wouldn't whip her perhaps. And he wouldn't bed her. You don't bed friends. He surely now believed she had not murdered his farrier, nor anyone else. But a friend cannot live on charity forever.

The old house was magnificent and that alone gave her enormous pleasure, but she could not imagine staying forever in a bedchamber designed for far more important guests. But as yet, she'd been made no offers that even smelled of servitude.

The countess changed her attitude on an hourly basis. She asked Jetta to fetch her scarf and order the litter. But at other times she curled in cosy conversation and cheerfully discussed her only grandson's childbirth, (*'I was there. The wretched boy took hours and hours to come and then popped out yelling his head off. But he's always been a difficult boy, then as now, my poor daughter-in-law. She was very ill for some days, and then died.'*) his upbringing, (*'Not that I arranged much of that but my son told me he was doing well and three years ahead of his age group'*), and his many varied faults, (*'My dear girl, it would take me all day to list them but drinking too much wine probably heads the list. And he's arrogant, oh dear me yes. Extremely arrogant.'*) And I daresay he snores. What do you think?"

"I'm sorry my lady, how would I know?"

"You don't sleep in his chamber then?"

Jetta coughed and swallowed. "Never, my lady. Of course not." Her cheeks now glowed quite pink.

The countess waved off Jetta's response as if it had no bearing on her thoughts. "Where's he gone, anyway? The wretched boy's never here when I want him. I need him here. The Scottish army could arrive any day at our stables."

Jetta was accustomed to the countess frequently living more in the past than the present. "I'm sure it won't be the Scots, my lady. The king has made a Peace Pact with them. I heard this some time ago. It's more likely to be the French. But not quite on this doorstep, I hope. As for where Dominic has gone, I don't know. He's working for the king I believe."

"Well, I'm going to bed, dear. It's getting late. Look at that miserable sky. When Dominic comes back, tell him not to wake me."

Jetta, also quite accustomed to this type of remark, nodded politely. "I shall certainly tell him if I see him, my lady. Though I don't expect him back for many days yet. Perhaps a month or more from what I was led to believe." She took a sip of her own ale, and wiped a drip from her chin, and smiled, "I do hope you sleep well, ma'am, but we've only just started breakfast, though the morning is hidden behind the storm."

The thunder swam with the glinting threads of lightening and the rain abruptly split open the clouds.

"Time to get up then?"

"As you wish, madam."

"As it happens, I don't wish," the countess frowned." I had a most interesting dream last night, and we need to follow it up. We should go to the stables."

"You dreamed of horses?"

The stables were at no great distance from the main house, but the rain was increasingly heavy, pounding now against the windows. The clouds were dense. "Surely you don't want to ride in such weather?"

"You're such a silly little girl," the countess sighed, leaning back in her chair. "No, not at all, I never ride. Horses clomp and thump and make horrid noises. I dreamt of that dead man, whoever he was. He did things with horses, didn't he? Don't you want to find out who killed him. I need something to keep my mind from the invading Scotsmen, so that's what we shall do."

"My lady, I promise the Scots will not come here. Not today or ever."

"I suppose they don't like the rain either," the countess nodded with a faint smile. "And I've heard they ride on elephants. I never met an elephant, but I believe they are large and fat, so they wouldn't like the rain either."

The murder had almost been forgotten even by Dominic, Jetta sighed, she would rather forget it had happened at all.

"I'm sure Benson will gladly accompany you, my lady."

The countess scowled. "You think I want Benson fussing about and getting in my way?'

"You actually want me with you?" Jetta stared in both disbelief and disappointment.

"Well, child, why not? You need to make yourself useful."

Jetta stared at the table. "I'm never useful," she objected. "I know nothing about dead farriers. Other than the look of his dead body, and I really wish I didn't know that."

"Good," said the countess. "I knew you'd be just the companion I need. And if you're good and do as your told, you can borrow my cloak again."

So, she borrowed the black velvet cloak later that day, once the storm had died down, although it seemed rather an extravagant manner in which to visit the stables.

The double-sided stable block was busy. Although the grooms started work just after dawn, the large number of horses meant long hours. With or without a farrier, this was a job, feeding, and exercising, grooming and attending to the great stacks of equipment, which rarely paused. The heaving rain, however, had made exercising a very short and miserable affair, the grooms were more soaked than the horses, who now stood within their stables munching happily on the hay and the unusual treat of turnips.

"My lady," the head groom looked surprised and dropped his bundle of saddle in need of cleaning. "Can I help?"

"I want to see the one who died," said the countess, pulling back her hood.

All the staff were accustomed to the countess's odd behaviour. "My lady, the unfortunate man – well, he's buried in the churchyard. But I can send his sons to talk with you."

"And his wife too," the countess nodded.

Jetta stood back, stroking the grey mare she had ridden, fingers into the soft white mane, and almost nose to nose. The horse whuffled and Jetta jumped back laughing. "Beautiful Felicia," whispered Jetta. "Maybe I'll run away with you one day?"

She was interrupted. "Come here, Jetta. This is Pip and this one's name is Sammy. Is that what you said, boy? Good." The countess carried on without waiting for the answer. "Pip and Sammy have lost their Papa, and *We* shall do something to help discover the culprit. Their Mama is on her way."

"She helps in the kitchen, lady," said Sam, before wiping his nose on his cuff and sniffing.

The younger grooms slept on straw on a ledge built high over the stables which formed part of its roof. The farrier's tiny house, now housing only Ilda, the widow, was not far on the left. The head groom had a hut on the other side. Jetta decided this was considerably better than the accommodation she'd ever been given before coming here – and being treated as a princess.

She was thinking of that and smiling as she walked over to the countess. But Pip and Sammy knew exactly who she was, remembering her arrival, and didn't smile in return. The younger boy scowled. But then their mother hurried over, wiping her hands on her apron, and quickly the boys wiped the sneers from their faces.

"My lady?"

"Shall we sit somewhere, Ilda?" said the countess, looking around for some suitable bench.

"There's a wooden one just around the corner there," Ilda pointed and led the way.

The bench would possibly seat four, but it was obvious the countess had no notion of sharing it. First Pip spread one of the horses' blankets over it, though it wasn't much cleaner than the bench. Although the rain had stopped, drips slipped occasionally from the gaps in the stable roof. The mare Felicia was kicking her stable door and Pip promptly disappeared.

"Questions first," decided the countess, turning to the widow. She did not look like a woman in mourning. "Who do you think murdered your husband?"

"I don't know, my lady." Her breath smelled of the morning ale.

"No ideas at all?"

Ilda shook her neat head with its neat white cap. "Ma'am, he was a good farrier but not such a good husband. He wasn't a religious man, and he didn't believe in the church. He was never faithful, nor truthful, nor bothered to leave the tavern at a decent hour. I didn't talk to him often, but he often beat me. And, my lady, I have to confess, I'd long stopped loving him. Perhaps I never did."

"I'm not sure what love has to do with marriage my dear," sniffed her ladyship. "Now, what about you boys?"

Pip had returned, and he and Sammy stared at each other. "Dunno, my lady."

They stood under the drips which escaped the roof above, not daring to step away as they looked down at the woman on the bench. Sam said nervously, "I can tell one thing, ma'am. Being late, we'd gone to bed. We bed early cos we rises early. I was downstairs sleeping on the pallet. Pip were above the stalls wiv all the other lads in the stable. We never heard no one nor no folk busting in. Mum were fast asleep upstairs in the bed. We didn't know nothing till the morning when Rustin found our pa dead."

Ilda glared at her son. "Mind your language. This is the countess you're speaking to."

The boy mumbled an apology.

"You don't seem to be in tears about it, young man."

"Didn't have none, ma'am. My pa was a nasty bugger. Got pissed most nights and whacked us bloody when we was younger. Not so much when we got big enough to hit back."

"Mm," murmured the countess. "Well, spare the rod and ruin the child they say. So, you've just carried on working as before?"

"No reason why not, my lady," mumbled Pip.

"Wasn't it rather a messy sort of thing, his death?" she asked. "I remember my grandson telling me he must have been killed elsewhere and then carried to the riverbank."

Both boys muttered beneath their breath and stared at the toes of their boots. Jetta looked quite green.

The countess frowned. "We'll never get to the bottom of it if we don't look at the facts."

Thunder bellowed out again over the horizon. The storm was returning. The sudden wind slanted the rain at the stables and Jetta shivered. Black clouds disguised the sky and as the wind gusted sharper so the rain turned black and slammed down in torrents.

The angry voice came abruptly and most unexpectedly from behind them.

"Ah, that's right handy that is." The voice was low and gritty, and everyone turned. "All you guilty buggers sitting together, just as I wants you."

Sheriff Kettering was an unusually short and stocky man, but he was well muscled. He now carried metal wrist clamps and a bundle of rope, and swung them with a large grin on his face. "Now then, I thank you all for that. I know a son would never kill his own father, so it's these females I wants."

"What?" screeched the countess.

"Not you of course, my lady," said the sheriff, briefly embarrassed. "But it's always the wicked wife, and that wench that was found right next to the crime. I arrest you both in the name of his majesty, so now put your arms out. I'm not risking you wenches running off. You'll come with me."

Ilda stared. Jetta shook her head in astonishment. "You're mad."

Both Pip and Sammy jumped in front of them. "You'll not touch my ma," Pip shouted. "She just lost her husband and you're stupid enough to think she done it?"

Sammy raised both fists. "You ain't taking my ma. Nor this other lass neither. A good woman, she is. And there ain't none of us done nuffing. What you reckon we's doing sitting here quiet wiv the countess? We bin trying to think who done it."

VESPERS

"I know exactly who did it," insisted the sheriff. He grabbed Jetta's wrists and clamped them into the padlocked irons. "First you, Jetta Lawson, arrested for murder. And now you –,"

The boys stepped towards the sheriff, growling like hounds, almost knocking him over. Stumbling into where the tackle was stored, the sheriff shouted out into the rain, the thunder echoed him. At once four of the sheriff's large assistants appeared from the stable shadows, leapt on Pip and Sammy, hauled them away and literally threw them into the rain. The courtyard cobbles were turning muddy, and the puddles splashed in every face.

Now the widow did what she had not done on the death of her husband, and burst into tears. In spite of the rain, it was not difficult to tell as the farrier's wife howled louder than the wind.

The sheriff stood, shaking rain from his hair. "Jetta Lawson and Mistress Ilda Pike, I'm arresting you both for wanton murder."

"What on earth," demanded the countess, attempting to wipe the drips of water from her own face, "do you all think you're doing? You have no authority here. Get off and get out before I have you in the stocks."

But now Ilda felt her arms twisted behind her, and like Jetta, felt the metal rings clamped around her wrists. Both were quickly led out, and hoisted past the stable courtyards, avoiding the house, and on to the main entrance. Pip and Sam pelted through the rain but were already too far behind.

The countess was still yelling while wondering whether this was all her fault. But unfortunately, with all the fuss and bother going on, no one took any notice. "Perhaps I should have brought Benson after all," she sighed.

⁕◆⁕

The lightning struck closer, sizzling white flames over the open cart that waited in the street, pulled by one very drenched ox, and driven by a man with his hat over his eyes. Ilda and Jetta were pushed in.

The rope now connecting them was tightly doubled, and climbing into the cart made both of them trip, both falling into the straw above the wheels. The cart began to trundle. It jolted and swayed, far worse, Jetta knew, than the litter had been. The sheriff mounted his horse which had been tethered to the railings at the gate. So did two of his assistants, one leading and one following. The other men walked, heads down.

Jetta glared over at the sheriff. "You'll be sorry – this is ridiculous and probably against some law or other." She turned back to Ilda. "Don't be frightened. Don't worry. I'll get us out of this."

Ilda whispered, "I pray so."

"I'll prove we are both innocent," Jetta said. She was almost shouting. "This sheriff is a corrupt idiot. And if he wants paying to set us free, then it's too bad as I haven't got a ha'penny and he wouldn't deserve it anyway."

"And unfortunately," Ilda hiccupped in misery, "his lordship is away, or I believe he would have the wretched man arrested himself."

"Hopefully," Jetta said, softer voiced, "he'd punch the sheriff and kick him into the puddles."

Chapter Sixteen

They were taken to a cell not too far away, and Jetta thanked the silent lords of luck, that this was not at Newgate at least. It was one room, stone and windowless, beneath the ground of a building where the sheriff and his assistants appeared to spend most days, no doubt punishing more innocents and feeling good about themselves.

Still tied together, Jetta and Ilda stared around them, their eyes not yet accustomed to the darkness after the murky London daylight. Jetta's and then Ilda's hands were unlocked, and their rope bindings were untied before they were pushed into the black nothing, and heard the metal door clan shut behind them, followed by the sound of the key turning.

They smelled sweat and urine, and tried to see what they could already feel. The press of unknown bodies was unpleasant.

"Who's you?" someone asked.

No separate cells for men and women then. "I'm Jetta. Do we get fed in here?"

"Sort of," said the same voice. "Dark cheat bread. If you're lucky enough to grab it afore someone else does. And water. Ale and cheese if you pays well-nigh double for it."

"I was working when I was grabbed," Ilda mumbled. "I don't carry my purse while I'm cooking." She wiped her eyes. "If my sons can visit me, they'll bring money."

Jetta wondered whether the countess would even think of visiting her. She doubted it. The grandmother of an earl, beautifully dressed in satin and velvet, a mansion full of comforts, would surely not consider coming to a prison like this, especially to visit a nobody.

"Wot did you do, lass?" someone else asked.

"Nothing," replied Jetta at once. "Is it all men here? How many are we?" She only received grumbles in response. "I can swear on the bible and the crown, I'm innocent. That stupid sheriff just decided my guilt. There's not one crumb of proof."

"There ain't no sheriffs need proper proof. Otherwise all them cells would be proper empty."

"Even Newgate."

"Watch yourselves. Guilty or innocent, there's some gents in here would like to know you better, though not sure they'd be considered gents by most."

Ilda began to cry all over again, sinking down to the stone where she stood. Now Jetta was trembling too.

"Anyone touches me, I'll report him to the sheriff. Aren't there any other women in here?"

Silence followed. Then a rough voice said, "You sits next to me, little lass. I can protect you. Get you the bread and water afore tis all grabbed by others an'all."

"I'm sorry," Jetta whispered. "But how do I know I can trust you? You might be – just one of them."

"True," the man said. "But I ain't got no prick so I can't hurt you in that way, lass. I doesn't tell this to folks much, but I were castrated in Newgate a couple of years back, bloody it were too. They said I were a bad man. I don't reckon I was."

Jetta wasn't going to ask for proof. "I appreciate your – offer."

"Yer welcome, lass. I likes you. But no matter. I can protect you both, what is it – Jetta and wot?"

"Ilda." She said softly.

"Good names. I's Gimlett. Come sit here wiv me."

The crowded cell was too squashed to be cold, but the stone floor was damp. Soaked themselves and dripping rainwater, Jetta and Ilda sat beside Gimlett on that same damp stone. Jetta was grateful for his large warmth, although he stank of unwashed flesh and sweat. Yet he brought heat as well as protection.

"Thank you so much, we're both innocent you see and really don't belong here."

"Reckon that ain't summit I can helps wiv," Gimlett said. "I bin castrated when I done hardly nuffin. But I done plenty wot no one knowed about, and never got hung yet, so's I can't complain. But reckon you can shout yer head off every day saying how you's innocent and it won't make one fart o' difference."

Nodding, Jetta believed him. She wanted Ned. Better still Dominic, but she had no idea where he was. He said he was working for the king, so much more important than a murderous brat caught for crimes she didn't commit, and he would never be interested in her rescue anyway.

It was also likely, and horribly sad, that Dominic would now believe the sheriff. He had thought her guilty before. Now perhaps he would have no doubts.

She mumbled to Gimlett, "I'm very good at picking locks. But I'd need a knife point or something like it."

"Wouldn't do you no good, lass," he told her. "These locks is them big padlocks on the outside. You can't even see the buggers, let alone pick at 'em. "Sides, outside is steps and then a room all full o' sheriffs and chunky big louts ready to chuck you back in again."

The fear she had denied began to slip into her mind and was difficult to force out. But at least Gimlett had made a good bed. Having no idea of what hour it might be, she curled to sleep against Ilda. Gimlett's huge frame, double folded around the middle, made her think of Ned. But Ned was lean and bore no fat, only muscle.

She thought it might be dinner time but without appetite, the vision of food seemed as nauseating as eating slime or weeds and she was pleased when Gimlett put his arm over them both, and listened as he fell asleep and began to snore, his throat and nose blocked with sweat and sludge.

Ilda whimpered and sniffed. Fear stopping her from sleeping. She whispered to Jetta, "You know what the king did?"

"What on earth has the king to do with this?" Jetta sat up with a start waking Gimlett in the process.

"It's a new law. He's made things better, I heard. But I don't know if it's reached here."

"He's brought new laws to stop corruption in the law courts. I doubt these horrible sheriffs bother about that?"

"I suppose not."

"You two young ladies gotta stop worriting about stuff you can't do nuffin about," Gimlett snorted. "More you's awake, the more I gotta be awake, and that be a waste o' time." He grunted again and turned over.

"How can you sleep?" Ilda whispered. "Will they hang us? Will they whip us?"

Jetta felt sick with nerves as once again Gimlett began to snore.

"I wish I could sleep," Jetta whispered back. "It would be an escape. I don't want to see, and I don't want to think."

Eventually she managed to doze a little, but Ilda hadn't closed her eyes at all.

Three of the bulky assistants brought food at supper time and kicked the door open, chucking stale rye bread into the room, then passed earthenware mugs of unclean water. Gimlett reached up, glared at any other prisoner who pushed past him, and took the free bread and the mugs.

"The water ain't good," he said under his breath. "Folks gets gaol fever. But we gotta drink. No drinking, no living."

Jetta drank little, and with difficulty. The taste was foul, the smell almost as bad. The ground beneath them was slippery and chill, but the cell was squashed with shifting bodies. With no fresh air to breathe, now Jetta sweated too. Eventually they all slept, fitfully and uncomfortably.

The next day, breakfast was stale rye bread once again, and more stale water. Jetta looked up at the small man who carried the bread. Her eyes had adapted now. She saw him and she saw his sneer.

"How long do we wait for the trials?"

"It comes when it comes," he growled and slammed the door behind him.

With better sight, there was more to see. Yet what could be seen was of no interest and perhaps better not seen at all. Ilda was crying softly, her head buried on Gimlett's blanket. The cell was low ceilinged, and stone walled without space to hold the twelve men it held – and now two women as well. The corner where a hole in the stone counted as the latrine was avoided by everyone until they needed it, but some were forced to sleep close.

One skinny man called over. "Two proper dressed ladies, we got now. You two is pinch purses I reckon."

"No," Ilda called back. "I have never done that and never will."

"It ain't no shame," the man said. "We all gotta live somehow."

"I'm a respectable cook in a great house," Ilda said with a sniff.

Jetta looked up. "I'm sure this sheriff is corrupt. He's arrested us with a story he's invented himself. Do we get the chance to buy ourselves out?"

"Dunno," the same man muttered. "I ain't got the pennies to try."

Gimlett interrupted. "Reckon he'd be affrighted to do that, mistress. Could get hanged hisself."

"He deserves it," Ilda said. She lay back down. There was nothing else to do. There wasn't even the space to move without stepping on someone else.

There was the usual stench and the shuffle of the discomfort, the heavy snoring and the words cried out from sleep, when the door opened once more. The sheriff himself poked his little bearded face around it, and for a moment fresh air seeped inward.

"Who is it knows a smart fellow called Benson?" Jetta stood so quickly she stumbled backwards into Gimlett's lap. He chuckled and gently pushed her upwards. Jetta waved both arms to help her balance. "Come here then, girl," the sheriff called, so Jetta squeezed through legs and bodies and followed to the steps outside.

The air was no fresher and stank of damp and an overflowing cess pit, but no bodies pushed against her, and the arid breath of other men didn't sting her eyes. Then, arriving at the top of the steps, she saw Benson. She wanted to throw her arms around him.

"Miss Lawson," Benson smiled but looked more as though he desperately wanted to hold his nose, "her ladyship has sent a purse to cover for you and Mistress Pike, for food and hopefully some comfort. And she wishes to inform you that she has begun to work on having you both released as soon as possible."

Jetta had hoped for it, and yet had never been sure. Now Jetta almost collapsed. "Thank her a thousand times for me. I know the earl can't be traced at present, but if she can make a protest – anything possible." The danger, which still existed, was that the countess would forget, or even consider her guilty of the crime. "Please Benson, I beg you, if her ladyship forgets about us in here, would you please remind her."

He bowed, trying to hold his breath. "I shall do my best, miss." He handed over the heavy purse and hurried from the office to the cleaner air outside.

During Benson's visit and the passing of a purse, the sheriff had remained polite. Now he reverted to being a bully. Jetta was pushed downstairs, tripped and almost tumbled, feeling as though she had twisted her ankle. It screamed in pain, and she almost screamed back. Once thrown back into the cell, Gimlett shielded her.

"No need fer pushing and shoving," he glared at Kettering. "We ain't trying to escape. Not yet anyways."

"Give me the money," the sheriff ordered Jetta. "I'll see you get better meals. Maybe a blanket."

"It's stuffy in here so I don't need a blanket," Jetta glared. "But I'll pay for the meals when you bring something decent. And decent ale, no more filthy water. For all three of us."

"That stuck up fellow said nothing about Gimlett here," the sheriff objected.

"I'll pay for who I want," Jetta objected in return.

The day drifted. They slept. Everyone slept. One of the men was dragged off for his trial, and then another. Although Jetta felt great sympathy for the punishment they were likely to receive, it improved the squash down to a slightly more open space, and she could almost breathe.

For dinner, she, Ilda and Gimlett were brought hot lamb pies, and mugs of ale. The difference was amazing, and Jetta's appetite returned with a flitter of recognition. The ale instead of the water was an even greater improvement. Two of the men watched with obvious envy, and one crawled to Ilda's side,

"Give us a bite, lass. Just one little bite and one little sip."

"I would," Ilda sniffed, "but I know you'd snatch the lot."

"I never would. You got Gimmy beside you. Eat wot you wants, then leave me a sip."

With a nod, Ilda did as asked. She remembered her own boy's half starving when her husband had spent all his wages at the tavern. She ate, knowing each eye followed her every move from platter to fingers to mouth. She left a fair dribble in her cup, and a good-sized bite of pie. Handing both to the man who had begged her, she watched him stuff the small slice into his mouth, drinking the entire slurp, and barely having time to enjoy either.

He burped and grinned. "Thanks, lady. That were kind. And most welcome."

"You ate too quick," Jetta shook her head.

But the man shook his back. "Some other bugger would've gobbled it off me if I'd bin slow."

Another man directly behind, had indeed been reaching out ravenous hands. Jetta said, "I'll do the same for you when we get supper."

She did as promised, and when the elderly man was taken off for trial the next morning, she felt that whatever happened next, release or the gibbet, at least he'd enjoyed a few scraps of his possible last meal.

As usual there was nothing to do but sleep. Gimlett snored into her ear, and she wondered if it was the fear or boredom which she dreaded the most.

As the days passed with an incomprehensible lack of change, Jetta thought increasingly of Dominic. She wished it was him she could sleep against, and then thought of his own recent imprisonment, a cave, he'd called it, and no option to buy himself proper meals. In fact, he'd said that most days had passed without food of any kind. No light. No company. And no possibility of discovering where he was or who had put him there.

At least she ate every day, she had company, she knew where she was and why, and she had the warmth and protection she needed. Who had put her there was definitely no secret.

Time, however, held no relevance. Breakfast meant morning. Dinner – the day was half over. Supper – then it was time for bed. Few bothered to count. Supper might be bedtime from the day before – or for the day after.

Jetta had finished breakfast, knowing the time of day only by which meal arrived, when a greater commotion echoed down from the office above and the altercation was loud enough to make the downstairs ceiling vibrate. Gimlett, however, slept through it. This sort of racket was evidently normal life to him.

At first, trying to take no notice, but when she saw Ilda sit alert and suddenly jump up, Jetta sat up too. They were both alerted by the voices, although entirely different ones, from upstairs.

"Oh, thank St Joseph, my lovely boy," Ilda squeaked. "Tis Pip come to help us."

"And Tyballis. That's amazing," squealed Jetta, wishing she was tall enough to bang on the ceiling.

Their reaction woke Gimlett, who sat up and roared.

"Please thump on the ceiling if you can, Gimlett, we can't reach and we need to get their attention," begged Jetta.

He was tall enough to make it easy, and as he reached up both arms, he beat what seemed like a pattern of drums, and shouted at the same time. It was only moments later when an assistant came pounding down the stairs and flung open their door. For less than a blink, everyone was silent.

The assistant demanded, "Wot's all that bloody noise?"

"Those visitors upstairs are here to see us," Jetta yelled above the clamour. "One is the son of my friend here, and the other is the extremely important Countess of Leays, wife to one of his majesty's closest allies. If you don't let us meet with our visitors, they will certainly let the king know."

The assistant yawned and seemed not in the slightest interested. He did, however, open the door, letting them out. "Oh well, best come up then. But just you two females. Naught else. The rest of you shut your noise."

No one was shutting up, Gimlett in particular, who roared about the lack of justice and lingering corruption. "You's all thieving bastards," he yelled. You'd better not have killed off me friend Arlon yesterday? Did he get a fair trial?"

"He got let off. Now shut the shit up, and let these two females come up fer their visitors."

Jetta and Ilda were already halfway up the stairs.

Chapter Seventeen

Tyballis hugged her close and Jetta burst into tears, leaving a tiny puddle on the velvet shoulder.

Jetta then pulled back. Cringing at her clothes, a gown that had once been pretty, embroidered sleeves, and soft shoes, were now torn, her skirts badly stained, and her shoes were thick with mud. Her hair was dirty and tangled, and her face streaked with tears that she could not wipe off. She felt more self-conscious now than when she had first met Dominic. Ilda who had been very plainly clothed in plain linen shift beneath an apron, although now definitely stained, managed to look almost normal, and curtsied low to the woman dressed as a princess. Yet Tyballis didn't smile. She was frowning with concern.

"Neither of you should be in here. This is disgraceful. I know well that Jetta is not only innocent but has nothing whatsoever to do with this crime. And you, Mistress Pike, you are surely innocent, for how could any woman murder her husband in that way?"

Tyballis did not mention that a long time ago before meeting Andrew, she would have been delighted to murder her own husband.

Both blushing and nodding, "I didn't your grace." Ilda turned quickly and embraced her son. "Pip, how on earth did you get here?"

"Benson come to tell me and Sam. And said her ladyship might help, so I rode to the Leays mansion and Lady Leays was as proper kind as Benson said." Ilda seemed afraid to let Pip go and tightened her arms around him.

"I never imagined," she said, muffled, "that a real lady would help me."

"My husband is on the road," Tyballis said, "working for the king. So is your own master, so I've no way of contacting either of them, but I shall send word and hope it reaches one or the other. If your trials are set before I discover them, then I shall ask for an appointment with the king himself. But I'll not do that until I need to. His highness is facing many other problems at present, and is still recovering from the death of his wife and son."

Jetta sniffed, "Thank you so, so much. I can't believe that the sheriff will ignore the king, even though he obviously ignores all his laws."

Tyballis smiled. "I've warned the sheriff my dear, but he's not a man to be frightened of women, and he still refuses to release you. The town beadles and even the mayor's aldermen have been congratulating him on his fast and efficient arrest of the two shocking killers. He's not going to give that up so easily."

She had a large basket of food and blankets which she handed directly to Jetta.

The sheriff barged through. "Time's up, my lady. All very well for a countess having criminal associates, but I'm not having no female, whatever she may be, tell me my business. I'm a freeman and duly elected."

Tyballis glared at him, "And can just as easily be unelected sir. Be careful who you choose as an enemy."

As Ilda and Jetta were thrust back down the dark steps into the cell, they heard Pip calling, "That bloody sheriff is breaking them new laws. Don't you worry, not neither of you."

The door clanked once they were pushed into the cell. Ilda slipped, but Gimlett caught her. The three sat together peering down into the basket. Jetta smelled a kidney pie, no longer hot, but as tempting as anything straight from the oven. Ilda held up a shawl, thick knitted in deep green. She wrapped it around herself in delight.

Jetta grinned. "How can you? It's sweltering in here."

"Not at night," Ilda said. "That dampness pushes in. There's a blanket too. You should have that."

There was more bread, and Jetta gave a large chunk to each man in the cell, and a bowl of steamed cabbage with sultanas and slices of bacon, which they also shared. The pies, Jetta, Ilda and Gimlett kept for themselves, but the apples were enough for everyone.

At the bottom was another purse. Jetta tied it to her belt and looked around. "I'll share some of this too when we get to leave, as long as no one tries to steal it."

She faced the man who trotted down with the suppers, chucking stale bread and handing out mugs of water as murky as the rivers themselves. The two meals for herself and Ilda were brought immediately afterwards, mugs of ale and wedges of cheese and smoked bacon.

"You two wenches does mighty well," the sheriff's assistant said, holding out his hand for payment.

Jetta handed over six pennies, three for each of them, and one extra for the service. But she said, "How much would it be for a good meal for all of us for tomorrow's dinner. A *really* good meal, with ale?"

Staring in shock, unsympathetic, the man spat. "Forget that, wench. We ain't got the facilities fer so many."

"Then let some of them go."

Sniggering, the man counted the fingers of both hands. Nine fellows and two wenches. Now that would cost a fine purse. Maybe a sovereign."

"Rubbish," Jetta glared back. "We've been charged three pence

VESPERS

each plus one. For eleven of us, that's thirty-three plus one. That's – well – about three shillings."

"You ain't got that much. I doesn't believe ya. Nobody's got that much."

"I have, and more. Don't spill anything, and I'll give you another penny."

Every man was now her friend, and they slept with a peaceful and more trusting atmosphere. The possibility of theft was as strong as ever, but Jetta kept her purse safe and paid for one meal a day brought to each man.

Days following reduced their numbers. One man, dragged off, waved to Jetta. "Well, little lady, you done given me a bit of comfort afore I face the swing."

But when they tried to take Gimlett, both Jetta and Ilda cried.

"No. You can't. Leave him here until there's an official charter."

Standing, stretching, and shaking the dust and dirt from his hair, Gimlett faced his new female friends. "Don't you worry now, my girls," he said. "There ain't no man dares to touch you now, and you's as safe as when I bin here. And I ain't scared o' no noose. Tis wot I always knowed would happen. Wot I never knowed, was a nice full stomach. That makes a difference.

Ilda grabbed his hand. Gimlett squeezed her fingers and raised them, kissing the back of her knuckles. He turned to leave, but Jetta stopped him. "I don't care what you've done. You're a good man and you don't deserve this."

"Fer the past, little lady, yes, I does. Fer wot they says I done now, no – fer I never done it. Not sure if that makes me a rotten fellow, but I sure ain't no saint. Anyways, now I gotta go. If I be late fer me trial, they'll have me guilty fer stuff wot ain't even happened yet."

Jetta reached up to kiss his cheek, but could only reach his chin. So he bent over her, and kissed her forehead.

"Get a bloody move on," shouted the sheriff's assistant from the stairs.

Gimlett turned to face the silence in the cell. "Now you lot, you look after these two lasses, or I shall prove me innocence and be back to smash ya stoopid heads together."

They heard the door lock behind him and settled back down in the darkness. No one spoke. Finally, one man muttered, "Costs you less for food now, lass."

Someone else added, "The jury ain't all buggers what's bin bribed. Maybe Gimlet's gonna be freed yet."

"Don't be a fool," someone said, and another snorted.

"No chance. Gimlett was an old gang leader in Southwark, and when he found something wicked to do, he did it."

"But that was years back and not in Chiswick."

"And this sheriff is a corrupt bastard."

Jetta settled back into a miserable pile in one stone corner. The chill leaked in. Including herself and Ilda, only eight bodies now filled the cell, which left space to breathe, but also the misery for those who had gone.

She used the blanket folded double on the ground beneath her, and had nothing to wrap over. Ilda used the knitted shawl as a blanket. Both were cold. But Gimlett did not return that night and Jetta cried silently for some hours. Gimlett had been safety. Now she felt alone and scared. She breathed in the clammy echo of the unknown and the constant reminder that guilt or innocence held no promise of freedom.

Unable to eat the supper brought to her the next day, she gave it to Ilda. "Eat what you want. Give the rest to anyone you like." The nausea crept like an ice-cold finger up her spine.

There was no change to the darkness, but once supper was well gone and the last slurps were finished, the men stretched or curled, and they could imagine the stars outside. As expected, Gimlett had not returned. Jetta imagined him swinging, the noose around his broad neck. She imagined those long legs kicking. She imagined the man cursing. Could you sleep while hanging on the gibbet? No, of course not, how stupid. She thought herself a fool, wondering if it would happen to her in the same way. Shivering, half sobbing, Jetta finally fell asleep.

And then she dreamed of everything she feared.

Waking, whether late or early, Jetta pushed away the shadows of nightmare in her head. *"Come to the call of the death knell, murderer. The rope awaits you."*

"You think it makes any difference whether you are guilty or not? A quiet woman dies in agony in a house fore when her trivet falls, the fire rages. What was she guilty of? The Lord God takes us when he wants us."

Jetta shook her head, rubbing her eyes and thumping both feet on the ground. Ilda looked up. "What's the matter, dearest? You slept badly?"

Jetta shivered and sat beside her. "Yes, I did. Now I'm awake and it's just as bad. We've lost Gimlett."

"We don't know that. Maybe he's been found as innocent, and he's marched off home with a smile big as the sky."

"No. If he'd been released, I'm sure he would have come back to tell us. I know he would. I'm sure of it. And now I can't get the idea of him hanging out of my head."

Ilda patted her shivering shoulder. "Never think the worst, my dear. Tis wrong half times, and even when you get it right, you never saw it and you can't be sure." Managing a smile, Jetta once again lay back down, curling again as Ilda wiped the hair back from her eyes. "Must be time for breakfast. And you didn't eat much supper. You must have food now dear." Ilda paused, then settled. "Listen, when we first got here it was you who cheered me and told me good sense. When I moaned you were all positive and stopped me thinking the worst. But now we've changed places, and it's my turn to help you through."

"Thank you. Maybe the Lady Tyballis will bring good news. How long have we been here now?"

"Not the faintest idea," said Ilda, leaning back and closing her eyes. "It feels like months."

"Two weeks? More?"

"More I think."

As usual, they heard voices from upstairs. The sheriff was talking politely to someone, but no words floated clearly, and only the tone was obvious. More time passed, the discussion upstairs ended, and the sheriff seemed to have drifted, or dozed as they did downstairs.

But then the door crashed, and the sudden boom of a deep voice brought her back vividly alive, the words vibrated. "She surely ain't, but reckon I does," bellowed the voice into her ear. "Wot you wants, my sweet little lass?"

Sitting up with a jerk that banged her head into the new arrival's chin, Jetta stared. "You're back!"

"I ain't no ghost neither. "Gimlett laughed and produced a large scarlet linen cloak where the dye had run at the hem, but its sheepskin lining was a thick warmth that seemed to cuddle her almost as well as Gimlett had done.

But now he pulled her into his arms, lifted her high and her feet left the ground as he swung her and swirled her around him, grinning and laughing as he lifted her in circles.

"You'll make me dizzy," she yelled, more laughter than words.

He slowed, then stopped, but didn't release her. "Let off, I was," he was practically singing. "Found not guilty alright, like the innocent little lad that I is. But I had to go and sign stuff, so spent last night at the mayor's bloody big mansion on the river. Lectures and a bed in the stables. But now I's back, and I can tell you this, my little sweetness. I'll be off to find that fellow you told me, the one what chats wiv our king. Then there's the high and mighty lady what came here, and then the fellow you says almost lives in them trees by St. John's. And I's gonna make bloody sure they all find you and Ilda as innocent as babes, that I am."

Chapter Eighteen

Time passed in clouds before he left, and the sheriff marched downstairs to shout at him.

"Only because the mayor had a few words to say to me, I've been more than generous, now you're going. Out, and quick about it."

Gimlett hugged Jetta, then Ilda, and then Jetta again, whispering, "I got a good thing going, I have. Just wait a bit, and I shall make bloody sure you're free."

They hugged him back, but Ilda cried when he left. The chilly nothingness returned like the plunge of a sword.

Two more of the dismal crowd were hauled out for trial, and one new man, shackled and furious, changed the quiet hopelessness of the underground cell. With her money almost gone and no magical appearance of more, Jetta now paid the price of ale and better food only for herself and Ilda.

Gimlett had returned so she knew him free, she was so relieved. He'd confessed before regarding his guilt of other things, but Jetta had lost her sense of justice. There seemed little difference between right and wrong. You could be innocent and hung, even dismembered. You could be guilty, pay up, and go free. He had explained nothing in detail, but it seemed Gimlett had done some sort of a deal with the mayor.

Tyballis had certainly bribed no one but had perhaps threatened. A cleaner method without doubt but however it had been done, there was a delay put on the expected trial. As yet, nothing more. The sheriff was as proud as a man in full armour as he received the compliments of those thinking he had somehow solved such a difficult crime in such a few weeks.

The trial, of course, had not been cancelled, only delayed. The sheriff smiled. He expected no problems. Although the two countesses needed a careful eye, they were only female as were the captives. The Countess of Desford and the Countess of Leays were ladies of power, one married to an important man, the other a grandmother of an earl possibly more important still. But neither man had turned up. Either they held their families in contempt, or they were too busy elsewhere.

Half dozing, half remembering, Jetta was counting. "I feel we've been here a year. Every separate day takes a month to finish. Every hour is so slow. Is it only three weeks?"

Someone called from across the room. "It ain't that long lass. I were here when you first come tripping in that door, and I were mighty grateful when I got the good food you paid for. And then in marches Gimlett, free as a bloody magpie. Tis eighteen days today, mistress, and that be two weeks and four days. I bin here longer."

"Me too," yelled a deeper voice. "I ain't complaining. Whilst I's here, I's alive."

Jetta did not feel alive. She felt only the inactivity and meaningless sleep of death.

A third man mumbled, "there's folks can be in prison fer a year or more. In fer debt, in fer sommit what the sheriff's well night forgotten. Not me. I bin four weeks though and that's bin bloody hard."

"Can we have lawyers or barristers at the trial?"

"If you can find one and afford to pay him you can."

Now Jetta wished she had saved her money for a lawyer instead of eating it away. "How much do lawyers' cost?"

"Dunno. Never met one."

The night passed like a stagnant stream of mud. She dreamed of slow trotting pigs falling into the dark water to sink. Watching, crying for the loss of life, she sat on the muddy bank. Then she realised she was slipping and already her feet were in the stream. She was sucked down. One of the pigs called, but she couldn't answer. The mud filled her mouth and she choked.

A hand rested gently on the side of her cheek. She twisted, trembling and crying. Then two strong hands lifted her.

Despite the dimness in the cell, Jetta recognised the voice immediately, it was loud, imperious, and angry. "You, Kettering, have not heard the last of this. These women are innocent of the crime you accuse. You've not the slightest proof against them, not even a thread of probability."

Standing behind Lord Stark, Earl of Desford, Sheriff Kettering stuttered, seemingly choking as he tried to respond.

"My lord, it was not idle supposition, I swear it. I was given good information from another young female."

"What foolish nonsense." Dominic glared down at the sheriff. He supported Jetta with one arm, while Ilda, tottering a little, stood beside him with a glowing smile of pride and relief.

The sheriff, confused and more miserable than angry, cringed back. "She came right to my office. A proper pretty young female saying she's a good friend of yours, sir, and knows the dead farrier and these two women. Claimed she knew exactly what happened. Described it. Said she saw it. Knowed all the names and promised as how you didn't want them released."

Eyes narrowed beneath lowered brows, Dominic spoke with the

shadowed threat that Jetta recognised so well. "Her name? And did you verify that name?"

"Well, not exactly my lord. It was a very pretty miss called Isabella Brigg, sir."

"And you made no effort to prove her story, nor her name?"

"Not seeming necessary, my lord –,"

"The necessity is indeed now sunk beyond trace, since I say they are innocent which is more than sufficient. They leave here now with me." Dominic now openly glared. "I know no person of that name, and she therefore cannot know me. I am also fully aware that these women are entirely innocent. The cruel and illegal absurdity of this situation will be judged in the future. You've not heard the last of this, Kettering."

The small belligerent sheriff was now wringing his hands. Behind him several men were grinning. One cleared his throat. "That lass you got there, sir, she got money off some posh lady. That lady says about not being guilty, but there weren't no proof o' that neither."

Dominic's eyes had turned to an ice even colder than usual. Then he turned away. He neither answered the man nor spoke, but placed one arm around Jetta's waist, while also guiding Ilda. The cell door was open, and Dominic marched to the steps, then slowly up them, keeping both women close.

Warm security and the tempting sensation of affection made Jetta feel half drunk. She leaned against the guiding strength.

The sheriff and his men ran upwards, looking back as they insisted on how careful they had been, and that the authority was theirs, which they had used only within their rights.

Indeed, carefully and slowly behind Dominic, two other men, keeping to the side shadows, were now escaping. But the sheriff saw nothing except his own possible incarceration looming closer.

Outside Pip and Sam waited for their mother. Excited in their saddles, they held the reins of another horse, and helped Ilda to mount.

Dominic nodded. "Go on ahead and settle your mother at home.

VESPERS

She'll need food, a comfortable bed, and a peaceful rest. In the meantime, I shall look after Mistress Jetta and then move onto other problems. Report to me tomorrow." He then assisted Jetta to mount his own horse.

Jetta sat and leaned back against him, and in spite of the previous endless sleep, her eyes struggled to stay open. His embrace, arms around her as he held the reins, soothed her into the sweetest dreams. She could feel his breath on her neck.

"Well, my little one," he whispered. "We are not too far from home." He had flung his cape around her shoulders, and she relished the dark blue velvet. The cape was thinly lined in another layer of velvet, the same colour and richly embroidered in scarlet and cream. She thought it amazingly beautiful but loved it more for another reason. It brought her more than warmth for it somehow smelled of him while it also disguised the stained and torn rags she wore beneath.

"Are you hungry?" he asked as the horses moved into the trot.

Jetta tried to shake her head, but it hurt. "No. I had enough food. The Lady Tyballis brought money and I paid for our meals. A few months ago, I was used to hunger. Now, my lord, thanks to you, I'm accustomed to so much wonderful food. Ale and wine as well."

He laughed softly. "Perhaps Gimlett needs your thanks too?"

She was astonished. "You know him? You know he was there?"

"It was your friendly giant who found me," Dominic said, his smile fixed. "He explained what had happened. He had some knowledge of where I might be since, surprisingly and certainly secretly, he is also a spy for the king. He's no lifelong friend but while working for Richard, I've met Gimlett a hundred times, and I understand him."

Jetta's mouth popped open. It was not what she would ever have guessed, but it made sense. "Will you see him again soon?"

"It's probable." Dominic nodded. The ice in his eyes was melting. Jetta could not see his eyes, but she felt the widening breath of his smile. "I liked him. It was not part of his work to befriend you and help towards your release, but he did so anyway, and with considerable success. That's a character I value."

"And you came. That's so kind as well, really amazing and the last thing I expected. Coming to get me like this – it's kindness beyond kindness. And have I interrupted important work?"

"Not yet," Dominic said, "over the next two days', I intend to instruct you and then you will start working with me."

"As a – spy?" Her astonishment grew.

"Does the idea seem unattractive?"

"Oh, absolutely no. It's exciting. I have no idea how you do anything like that, but I'll try very hard, and I'd love to feel really – useful."

In fact, Jetta felt bilious. She was engulfed by a combination of huge relief, the overwhelming wish to feel Dominic's warmth against her for the rest of her life, her exhaustion despite having slept for weeks, every part of her body ached, and she still trembled from shock. But the best tonic she could have, she was sure of it, would be excitement and something to give her direction.

"It's easy enough, once you know what to look for" he told her as they came within site of the mansion. "I shall naturally explain exactly what you'll be looking for, and I'll not give complicated explanations. You simply need some portion of courage, which I know you have. After your many escapes and stealing a boat and rowing it into an upstream current, I am quite certain that courage is something you don't lack, my dear."

She loved the '*my dear*' and thought she could now count them. "I'm not even sure what courage feels like. What you do in desperation isn't really courage, is it. But I'm not often scared witless, though these past weeks have certainly tested that." Jetta knew the memory of it would haunt her longer than the nearly three weeks she had spent there.

"Come inside." Dominic dismounted and threw the reins to the groom whilst Pip and Sam could already be seen closer to the stables, where they were helping their mother dismount. Dominic lifted one hand. "Take my hand and slide down," he instructed Jetta. "Now – follow me." As he strode to the main hall, he nodded to Benson. "A light dinner for both of us, plenty of wine, and tell my mother we can't be disturbed. If I'm needed, knock on the door."

Jetta blinked. She hadn't expected him at all, and still his behaviour confused her. She was also sorry to lose the cape, taken by Benson. Dominic pointed to the stool opposite the place he sat himself.

"You're going to teach me now?"

"Not today. Tomorrow. It won't take long."

Jetta could smell her own filth. Her clothes carried the stench of over two weeks of built-up grime. She could smell her own body, the accumulated sweat and the unwashed knots in her hair.

"May I take a bath first?"

"Later." He didn't bother to smile. "For the moment, I can put up with you."

Jetta blushed. She sat back from the table, but she still disgusted herself and his words hadn't helped. "I've still got my old shift so I could at least change into that."

"That wouldn't help over much," he said. She immediately felt considerably worse.

Jetta stared down at her lap beneath the table. "Sorry."

"You should not apologise, neither to myself nor to anyone else." She blushed again. His gaze became more insistent. "Now listen," he ordered. "This is more important and you're wasting time."

Dinner arrived. Two large jugs of wine accompanied the platters, and so did the countess. Her complaints were shrill outside the door.

It was Benson's voice which answered her. "My lady, my instruction is that his lordship should not be disturbed. Both his lordship and Mistress Jetta are inside, I apologise, my lady, but I must obey his lordship."

"You can tell him, when you see him," the countess announced very loudly knowing that it would be heard, "that I shall smash my own dinner over his head the next time I see him."

"Very good, madam." Jetta could imagine Benson hiding his smile.

But Dominic was talking again, ignoring his plate and his grandmother but cheerfully sipping from his cup. "The idea came from Andrew. Indeed, Tyballis helped him in the past before their child was born. He spent some time abroad with Henry Tudor and brought a good deal of information back to the king here."

Jetta leaned forwards, excitement bringing her increasingly awake. "We're going to France?"

"Not at all." Dominic shook his head. "Neither of us leave this country but there are two of our more powerful traitors living here, and what they intend is of considerable importance. His highness believes that getting either of them to give the smallest clue of what they intend, although unlikely, could become invaluable. I intend to try, and I intend to engage your help."

"I can guess who you mean."

"Good." He drained his cup and reached for the jug. Lady Margaret Beaufort is a woman of haughty dignity and determined privacy. Yet, as you well know, she constantly works against the Yorkist cause. How much do you know of her?"

Surprised, Jetta said, "The Tudor mother. That's all."

Dominic nodded. "Very well. I have met her many times but do not claim to know her personally. However, I'm well aware that her life has been both interesting and unpleasant. Born as an heiress of magnificent fortune, she also had a rigid guardian, and a good deal of illegitimacy in her ancestors. Her marriage to the Tudor son, also descended from the illegitimate line was no insult, since he was declared as King Henry VI's half-brother, Edmund. She gave birth to Henry when she was still extremely young. A frail little child as far as I've heard, she damn well could have died in childbirth, and her baby with her. The son dying might have proved a blessing but both survived."

"So this interesting lady is working to get her son on the throne?"

"Not at first. She was far too young. I doubt it occurred to her."

Jetta felt the strange pang of sympathy for the woman who was surely both lonely and missing her son. Jetta had been lonely for half her life.

"Poor girl. Only a child herself? Her husband should have been beheaded."

"What a sweet natured child you are, little one. Indeed, the wretched husband died of the plague soon after. God's gift of justice perhaps. But the child-widow he left behind remembers him with respect, and almost idealises him as the father of her son."

"Well, she's mad."

"I tend to agree. Edmund Tudor had her into his bed when she was only twelve. Consummation ensured that he'd inherit her wealth if she died before him. Luckily, he died first. The plague is no quick death. But after a life of mistreatment, the child had a baby to cuddle and so blessed the husband who provided it. And," Dominic continued, "while still young, the son was taken from her and then sent into exile in Brittany. She asked the late king to give him leave to return, but this was denied."

"Has she asked the new king?"

"She has a far more ambitious idea now. Are you aware that she backed the Buckingham revolt? Once her treason was proved, Richard confiscated her fortune, and gave it instead into Stanley's safe keeping. Naturally as her present husband, he allowed her access. But since Tudor's right to the throne is virtually non-existent, if he wants it, it will have to be claimed by conquest."

"He tried that before, didn't he? And it didn't work." Jetta was now drinking. Having crunched a few nuts and eaten some sort of bread, she wasn't enthusiastic for the food. She was for the wine. The thought of a little girl being taken by a man so old, had made her feel nauseas. The wine was a good medicine.

"Yes, he attempted an invasion. But the weather stopped him more than we did," Dominic said.

"So he's coming again?" Jetta was enjoying the conversation. With neither interruption nor the long silences she usually accepted from him, he was now her teacher. He wanted her. Perhaps he even needed her.

"Yes, without doubt," Dominic said. "And it will be this year. That was the news my friend Andrew brought the king, but there's no knowledge of the month. Therefore you, my dear, will infiltrate that house, discover what has been arranged, and whether the lady's present husband will back her. If Stanley fights for Tudor, then the numbers will change and King Richard would have little chance of success."

For some moments Jetta sat aghast, neither looking at Dominic nor at her plate. Then she slowly lifted her cup, and drank it dry, finally pushing it to Dominic for refilling. She knew of Lady Margaret Beaufort yet had certainly never seen the lady. However, the city gossip liked to spread its stories, true or otherwise. Jetta also knew more since the Maddocks spoke of this and had been overheard many times

"Is the new husband a better man than the one before?"

"I've lost track of her husbands," Dominic told Jetta. "She was married at one year old, and again at twelve. Another husband died, and now she has Thomas Stanley. A highly intelligent man who changes his ambitions every few weeks. Treason this week – loyalty the next. But it's a marriage of wealth and convenience. No co-habitation, being of no importance except to the church which might call it invalid." Jetta was leaning forward, Dominic was leaning back. "The lady's very small and very thin but as intelligent as Stanley. She'll know more of Henry Tudor's plans than he knows himself."

"And I heard them say she's a nun."

"No." Dominic refilled her cup and passed it back. "She dresses like one and refuses to be touched. But it's more pretence than truth, and aids her privacy. She's taken no holy oaths."

"I don't like nuns," Jetta muttered.

"That's not of the least consequence however." Dominic smiled. "Stanley does not live at the same property, but he keeps in touch and in such circumstances, what you would attempt to overhear could be invaluable. Now getting you in, and having you work closely, that's my objective."

"And that's spying?"

"Indeed it is." Dominic smiled, eyes half closed and unblinking, cup still in hand. "Discovering whether Lady Margaret backs her son and supports his claim is of no importance, since the entire country knows well that she does. What is important, is whether she has talked her husband into supporting Tudor. You cannot possibly work for him. Stanley is neither a fool nor looking for a young woman to wash his damned feet. But if you're clever, you can find the answer from Margaret."

Now Jetta was drinking as much as Dominic, but she was still longing for a bath and the comfortable bed she remembered. "I think I can pretend, but I've never done anything like that before."

"I'll teach you. I believe you're quite as intelligent as required."

Jetta sniffed and refused to blush. "You only say that because you're teaching me how to work. I'll do it of course. I want to. What about this husband?"

"Stanley's an important man and has enough men on his properties to call and win this battle all on his own. But his son from an earlier marriage is being kept at the royal court by Richard. Virtually a hostage."

"Kept against his will?"

"The court is a place of utter luxury, and all expenses are paid by the crown. Not such a hardship."

"I know people like this King. Well, I suppose some don't, but he's made some very good new laws. I keep hearing about them. Kings like money but he's reduced a lot of taxes. So why would anyone fight against him?"

Jetta watched Dominic's face change. A little warmth lit his eyes and the tuck at the corners of his mouth raised slightly. "I expect the details of a king's reign don't reach the kitchens, but Richard has achieved a great deal more than that. He's an excellent king, he's also a friend of mine. But after just two years, the people can't be sure.

And what the lords want from a king is personal gain, power and recognition. They really don't care whether he's a great king, unless there's something in it for them."

Jetta risked smiling just a little. "I understand. And I'll do whatever you tell me. I'm only here, I mean only alive, because of your help. I could be hung on the gibbet if it wasn't for you. But even apart from that, I want to do it. It'll wake me up and stop me feeling like a squashed parsnip and no use to anyone. Though," she smiled again, "I honestly don't see how you're going to get me in there."

"You don't object to working as a servant after your last brutal experience?"

"I'm sure this would be very different."

"Indeed, it would." Dominic's eyes remained warm. "Finish your wine and then go up to your bedchamber. I'll have a bath brought in and a fire lit. I'll also arrange for new clothes. Those should be burned. I'll see that you get some more."

"And after the bath?" she asked, a little hesitant.

"Then you go to bed and rest. I shall be busy but will send up the clothes when I can."

Draining her cup, she sighed with disguised relief. She had wondered, couldn't help wondering, whether Dominic would want her to pay her dues. That might mean his bed, not her own. The thought had made her almost dizzy. She had tried to find Dominic when he had been imprisoned himself. And he had been grateful and told her so. Yet he had already rescued himself. This had been a much bigger and more successful rescue, and her own gratitude was immense.

With the Margaret Beaufort plan, she wasn't sure whether she should be horrified or excited, yet the excitement burst larger. She was being treated with a dignity she was sure she didn't deserve. Now on the way up the stairs to her bedchamber, she also wondered what the alternative call to bed would have been like and whether, one day, she might discover the fantasy.

Chapter Nineteen

Sitting in the wooden tub of steaming water, Jetta watched the dirt from her body dissolve, and giggled to herself. The most beautiful feeling accompanied the washing of her hair. The heat and the liquid soap soaked through to her scalp, and she massaged every trail and curl over and over again.

It left the water less than clean, so she sat in her own dirt, but once she stood, although with considerable difficulty, she climbed out of the tub. She had now almost conquered the knack. With even more difficulty and a considerable number of splashes, clambered in front of the small dancing fire and dried herself. She felt clean at last. Sitting on the bed, she managed to dry her feet and toes. She felt almost perfect.

Climbing into the soft luxury of her feather bed with its embroidered eiderdown covering, Jetta settled in utter peace. She was clean. She smelled clean. Then with the excitement of the mysteries to come, and even while attempting to remember how many times Dominic had called her 'my dear', she fell asleep.

It was dusk when she woke, and the first pale silver of a rising moon showed beyond the trees outside her window. It overlooked the front of the house and down the narrow cobbles to the stables, but it was the sky she watched. For some time, she stood there waiting for the stars to multiply and the moon to stretch its aura and smile back at her.

The window remained unshuttered, her nakedness, however clean and beautiful, was not how she should be seen so she kept carefully to the side, just a tiny black shiver to anyone below.

And what she saw spoiled her peace, for down at the main entrance she saw a horse being led from the stables, and then saw Dominic mounting and grasping the reins, and without the accompaniment of a single guard, he was riding off into the distant shadows. It being that time of the night, Jetta knew exactly where he must be going.

Watching him ride to visit his mistress had not bothered her previously. Such a wealthy and powerful lord would not be a gentleman of chaste habits. But somehow now it felt different. She knew she had no right to cry, but she sniffed softly to herself, held back her tears and climbed slowly back into the bed.

The tub of soapy water had been removed, the fire had been allowed to burn out, but the warmth remained in the room, and the ashes were still hot. Over the back of the one cushioned bedchamber chair, a pile of clothes were folded. Their colours were hidden by the darkness, and only the flicker of red from the hearth brought the hint of a scarlet cape. But Jetta didn't want supper and didn't want to face the countess alone, so she stayed where she was and did not explore the clothes.

"I am," she told herself very softly but aloud, "a complete idiot. I am falling in love with someone I really don't like. What on earth am I doing?" But she looked forward to the following day when she might start training for the most amazing job of her life.

VESPERS

Dominic rode the riverbank, watching the reflections of the moon and stars shimmer across the darkening blue. His pace was easy but not slow. He had every intention of being back home by midnight. The scurry of small animals retiring to their burrows was a friendly reminder, a final whisper announcing the end of the gloaming, and the arrival of the night itself.

Then, as he turned the street corner towards Hammersmith Square, he permitted his destrier to amble, and stop outside the cottage he had bought for his mistress. He tethered the horse, dismounted, and opened the cottage door.

In effect, the house was his and he owned the key for it, but the door was not locked and as he entered, he laid the key on the first step of the stairs aiming up to the bedchamber.

Teresa, even more beautiful in the shifting shadows, was curled on the cushioned settle, attempting the paper stitching she had been learning now for some time. She leapt from her cushions and ran to Dominic, but he held her off. He simply gazed down at her, eyes cold.

"My dear Teresa," he said softly, "what a shame you have spoiled it all. There was a small vague chance, you know, for a greater and prolonged success."

She stepped back and frowned. "Dominic, my darling, you sound very cross. What have I done now? I've been waiting and waiting for weeks for you to turn up. I can't remember the last time you were away this long."

"We are not shackled together, Teresa. I go where I wish."

"Well, never mind, dearest. You are my beloved hero, and I've never denied it. But sit, be comfortable, and I'll fetch the wine. It's a little late for supper, but if you're hungry?"

"Neither hungry nor thirsty, Teresa. I have come only for a brief discussion of my intentions."

She gulped. "My lord." skipping around to his back, she flung both arms around his waist, resting her face against his surcoat, "You know I love you. But are you angry with me? What have I done?"

Taking both her hands in his, he unclasped her fingers and

unwound her arms, pulling her to face him once more. "You don't love me, Teresa, and you know it. Nor do I love you. But we've both enjoyed some intimate friendship. You're beautiful. And you're experienced. You'll soon find someone else."

With a squeal of disbelief, she began to pummel his chest, and when he removed her hands again, and sighed, she flopped back into a chair.

"You frighten me. You can't mean it. Are you teasing me, naughty boy? You know very well that I adore you." He stood, looking down at her without smiling. "Now you're cold, you have such cold eyes. I promise, I've done nothing, absolutely nothing to make you cross."

"I am not cross, Teresa," he told her calmly. "I am furious. And therefore, our friendship is finished. You may keep the cottage and its furnishings. You may keep whatever money still rests under your mattress. But you will not see me here again."

Dominic turned, as if to leave. Teresa rushed to stand between him and the doorway. "I don't understand. What's wrong? You've found another mistress? It's that -,"

"I assume that's why you did it, thinking I'd taken another woman to my bed in your place. But, my dear, you misjudged. I have not."

Teresa was shaking her head wildly, the pristine curls in her eyes. "I didn't mean – so I didn't know, that is, I don't understand you, my darling."

"You have, to my knowledge, entertained numerous men over the years while I've paid for your so-called exclusive attention. I have never minded. And I'm quite sure you know that I've never been faithful to you. Without any love between us, neither of us have been obliged to keep exclusive friendships. Yet on this occasion, you have imagined absurdities. More importantly, you have reacted with appalling spite and stupidity."

"I love you, Dom." She was crying and the tears were genuine. Her voice was muffled, and she was terrified. "Without you – I can't go on."

"Simply frightened you'll not afford it? But with the house and furniture, expensive clothes and whatever you've stashed away which I'm sure must be substantial by now, you'll manage very well, Teresa. And you are, as I'm sure you know well, still beautiful. You'll capture some other man fast enough."

Teresa attempted a sideways giggle, fluttering her eyelashes in all their thick curling darkness. "It's only you I want, my dearest. I'll die without you. Are you trying to shock me into some new adventures? Whatever you want from me, I promise to do it. With you, I'd never say no."

"You're making this considerably longer than need be," Dominic sighed. "It's me who says no, Teresa. I am finishing our relationship and you are well aware of my reasons."

"I never said no. I did everything I could to please you. You know I did. Don't tell me I didn't do enough? You always fell asleep exhausted and smiling."

"Since explicit details appear essential," Dominic said, "even though you already understand very well, I will tell you that earlier today I rescued both my cook and a friend from the local sheriff's hole. Did you imagine that I would not have the authority to do that? And while informing the sheriff that he lacked even a spittle of truth, he related the story of Isabella Brigg, and a detailed description of how my farrier was murdered. Not only do I know that story to be nonsense, but I also know who swore to it as truth."

"And you think that was me?"

"Naturally. Not simply thinking, Teresa, I know without doubt. And I will not continue a relationship that includes lies and cruelty."

"You know you can trust me," Teresa mumbled. "Of course, that wasn't me."

"I've always known I couldn't trust you," he said, "since you've always denied the many affairs I know you've had. But it didn't matter to me. This does. It is an intentional attempt to cause pain and great harm, possibly death. But your arguments are a waste of my time. I'm leaving now, and I'll not return."

She grasped the door frame, leaning hard against it. "So it wasn't that silly Ilda you wanted to save. It was the bitch Jetta, because you want her in your bed. You complain that I was lying, but now you're lying to me. Of course you want her. You've given her a luxury bed in your own home. You let her speak to your grandmother. They share a table for breakfast, for goodness sake. You've never allowed me such privileges. I'll wager you've already been up her skirts."

His cold eyes narrowed and turned to ice. Dominic pulled her from the doorway and flung her across the little room to the settle. He then strode outside into the night, mounted his waiting horse, and rode back to the river and took the direction for Chiswick, returning home to a solitary and irritable night.

Having slept over too many hours, although disturbed by nightmares and self-recrimination, Jetta was up and dressed early the following morning. The clothes she found waiting for her were even more wondrous than she had expected. The gown was low-necked, but a tuck of embroidered damask was fitted for modesty beneath the deep V of the dark green satin. She thought she might need help with the clasps beneath her arm, but found she could cover them with the green velvet planchette. There were still knots in her hair, but she managed to comb out some now that her curls hung clean. When she found she was pulling out more hair than knots, she stopped, pulled on the pretty flowered garters, and trotted downstairs.

No one sat at the dining table and so she wandered outside, relishing the fresh air and the early warmth. After the cell, fresh air seemed more luxurious than anything else.

Having noticed the peep of one nipple, she was fiddling to straighten the tuck of embroidery that would hide her breasts, when she looked up. Dominic was watching her with a smile considerably warmer than usual.

"You shouldn't be watching," she said. "But the clothes are

wonderful, so thank you. The clothes were meant for me, weren't they?"

"Most certainly." He neglected to tell her they would never fit anyone else since they had been made for her.

"They're glorious. Incredible. Thank you. It's awfully kind."

She didn't ask what she was expected to do in return.

"But it will be a long day," Dominic told her. "There's a great deal to tell you and a lot to learn. For instance, in spite of the details I told you yesterday, the story of Lady Margaret Beaufort, Duchess of Richmond, has a great deal more history. With the war between two ancient families both claiming a superior rite to the throne, underground hatreds and suspicions rule. That can cause more misery than a battle. A good deal of this is quite irrelevant. A lot more is imperative."

"I know some of that," Jetta said, sitting at the long dining table, already crisp in the white starched tablecloth, awaiting breakfast. "But since I'm neither Yorkist and not a Lancastrian, I never know the ups and downs. I mean, I know some of the ones who are, and who isn't as well."

Dominic laughed. "Who am I then?"

"By birth, I haven't the faintest idea. But you're friends with the king so you're a Yorkist."

"Very true," he told her. "Which means you need to be a loyal Yorkist as well."

Jetta laughed with him. "Now I know."

"There is, however, a great deal you don't know," he said, sitting opposite her across the table as he had before. "But I'll teach you what I can today."

"I know how to scrub floors."

Dominic was still laughing. "That's not what I intended teaching you. Nor is it one of my own talents. No doubt you could teach me. But enough of floors. It's the Countess of Richmond we will concentrate on for today. And you need to remember everything I tell you. For instance, her father killed himself while she was still a child. That is probably not so important to remember, but the more you know, the better you'll understand her."

"I'll try and remember everything."

"You'll need to. You also have to remember the salient facts concerning the Stanleys. They've been powerful for generations, but their history matters very little. They are amongst the richest men in England. There are two brothers, equally powerful, who invariably enjoy creating some conspiracy or other which guarantees the family safety in times of war, whatever side they follow. Splitting their loyalties has been the favourite game for many years. I expect the same this time. Or will they combine to back the Tudor side because of Lady Margaret of Richmond?"

"And that's what I'm supposed to find out? Oh dear, I mean I'm awfully sorry, my lord, but a countess isn't going to tell that sort of thing to her scullery maid."

The door had slammed open. "What exactly won't anyone tell me?" the countess demanded, trotting into the hall.

Dominic was laughing again. Jetta suddenly thought him two different men. One stood straight backed, almost stiff, with half closed eyes of ice and an expressionless voice. But the new man was utterly warm. She smiled at him. "You seem unusually cheerful this morning, my lord."

"Do I? Perhaps I am."

Dominic drank his breakfast ale, regarded his grandmother without explanations, deciding she wouldn't understand anyway. But he stood, took her arm and led her to the waiting table, then leaned back against the wall. This had been painted with a mural, covering the entire space up to the vaulted ceiling above. Birds of many kinds including a flock of herons flew across the dawning sunshine, the sun itself rising from behind the mountains. Below was a lake, and here three geese were fishing, heads below the water. It was a peaceful scene of considerable beauty.

Jetta gazed at it, wondering if it had been painted from real life. But the peaceful beauty reminded her of the stagnant danger of past days. Now she began to wonder if working for the Lady Margaret Beaufort might be far more dangerous. If she caused even the slightest suspicion, being entirely unpractised in such work, she might be killed after all. Doubts followed delight. Then delight followed the doubts. Dominic's smile called back the instant delight.

Chapter Twenty

From the sweet July weeks to those of the month's end, the weather burst from warm to hot and the new personal maid in the Lady Margaret Beaufort, Countess of Richmond's private home was accepted as efficient, quiet, and respectful. Within the hierarchy of servants, Jetta's position was medium to low, but she still worked tirelessly in the great bedchamber, changing the bed, overseeing the personal laundry and checking that the garderobe had been cleaned.

Cleaning was once again a tiresome and exhausting job which she had accepted for many years, but this was nothing in comparison to the demands of the Maddocks family, now involving only the proper tasks without the extra orders and the endless punishments.

Jetta frequently saw her mistress, curtsied and kept her silence. Her opinion of the Countess of Richmond gradually became both defined and detailed, but she did not speak much with the other servants. She saw little of them except at mealtimes, and that suited her. Known for her strict and silent respect, some of the staff grew accustomed to speaking in front of Jetta, not caring if she heard or not. They felt secure, for after all, she was not the type of woman ever to repeat their secrets. Many of the staff thought Jetta remarkably stupid, even deaf, and they insulted her within her hearing. They gossiped endlessly and this included those matters Jetta wished to know more about, and so remembered. She reminded herself, however, that gossip rarely included more than a grain of truth.

This was not a habit copied by the Lady Margaret.

Jetta was privately half dead of boredom after she had pottered within the lady's bedchamber for three weeks. July was approaching August.

Sitting idle on the window seat one afternoon, finally Jetta heard something she thought interesting. Lady Margaret was in the grounds below that open window and was passing a tight-fisted hand to a young man on horseback. It was impossible to see what she had given him, yet could not have been more than a scrap of paper. And then she heard the lady whisper, "Early in August, depending on tides. Landing as arranged, Milford Haven."

The man answered her, and immediately Jetta recognised that voice. For some moments she could not remember where she had heard it before, but then, realised. Sitting almost aghast, mouth open, Jetta finally had something useful. As the messenger rode from the small, cobbled square, Jetta also saw that his surcoat was embroidered with the Stanley coat of arms, but ahead of him rode the gentleman whose voice she knew, and he was dressed grandly, and in no livery at all.

She wanted to jump up and down. Instead, she managed to grab her own messenger, a young Yorkist groom from the stables, to pass on that same information, knowing it would go directly to Dominic.

Another day passed without any noticeable activity. Jetta had no doubts that her new mistress would be working harder than anyone, but was far too practised to permit anyone in her home to hear what she was busy arranging.

She wore the clothes of a nun, and within the house she had her own chapel which she attended at some length every morning. Her staff, however, were not invited. They were simply ordered to keep her home in the strict cleanliness of a convent, without either decoration or indulgence.

But then something else happened. Lady Margaret, since the Buckingham revolt, had been ordered to stay within her property. Only Buckingham himself had been executed, whilst Morton had escaped. Known to have helped in the conspiracy, Lady Margaret was not now permitted as a royal visitor. As king, Richard had been easy-going with punishments, and the lady had been forced only to give her property into her husband's safe keeping and stay within her own walls. But those interested in the lady's conspiracies, came to her. Principally Elizabeth Woodville, as much a meddler as the lady herself.

Jetta saw many visitors, invariably without knowing who they were, and without hearing what was said in private. Quite unaccustomed to listening at key holes, this was something she did not dare risk.

Then quite unexpectedly one morning, another visitor arrived, carried by litter, and difficult to identify at first. The small woman wore a veiled turban, and plain dark clothes. But as Jetta recognised her, she ran immediately into the shadows. In the woman's company, alongside the litter, a man rode. He neither spoke to the woman, nor looked at her as she climbed from the litter, but rode ahead of the large retinue, dressed like a king, Jetta now recognised him almost as clearly as she recognised Mary Maddock.

Lady Mary Maddock picked up the hems of her skirts and trotted up the steps, smiling as the door opened for her. She entered the property, and very quietly gave her name and title to the steward. She then followed him into the bright annexe where several windows, large enough to light the room in sunbeams, were carefully shuttered against such unwanted trespass. The man strode in behind.

Jetta still did not know his name, but certainly knew he was the same lord who had once visited Sheriff Kettering, and had many times come to the Maddock house while she worked there. He had seemed less of a friend and more of a master, but the relationship had never interested her. She had disliked him, his attitude and his almost permanent expression of malice. Yet she knew little of him, not even his name or title, nor had ever wished to do so.

She promptly walked along the outside brick, and muffled by ivy, discovered the room where she hoped something of interest might be overheard. Half covered by ivy, she huddled back and listened. Yet the windows were fully shuttered, and more than an occasional word was impossible to understand.

The voice was focused though silky, but as she concentrated on listening, a hand gripped her wrist painfully, Jetta immediately recognised her attacker. "Stupid bitch. What are you doing here?"

She stood in both fear and fury facing Percival Maddock. "I work here, I work for her ladyship. Let me go, you've no right to touch me. Take your hands off me or I'll complain to the countess."

He pulled back, partially releasing her, but suddenly stepped forwards again. "You think she'll believe you over me? I'll tell her I caught you stealing. But for now, I'll get you down amongst the bushes." His smile was certainly sinister enough.

"You didn't manage it before, despite how many times you've tried. But that was your house, and this isn't."

Percival Maddock swung Jetta back against the wall and her head smashed against ivy protected brick, yet she felt both the blood and the pain. "Don't forget I've seen you stripped down for a whipping many, many times, and I always watched though there's nothing attractive about you. But I'll have my revenge for all the times you've bitten and kicked. This time I'll get you. You're nothing but an ugly brat but I'll have you, not in my bed but on my floor, and then I'll squash you like the nothing you are."

His contorted face, with cursing and spit, came too close. Jetta bit as hard as she could, teeth to his chubby chin, she ground harder until she felt his blood on her tongue. He howled, pulling against her with his fists to her stomach, but she kicked and scratched as she bit.

His cries of 'bloody whore,' 'doxy' and 'ugly trollop,' were easy to ignore.

But it was his voice, that attracted considerable attention. In his own home, it would have been ignored. Lady Margaret was not the sort of woman to ignore anything of that nature.

Jetta heard her, and quickly stepped back. The front of her gown beneath the apron was torn. Without a moment's delay, Jetta quickly dropped to her knees and began to cry.

The countess stared. "What is the meaning of this?"

It was Mary Maddock who realised and spoke quickly, "this girl, my lady, does she work here? I know her, she used to work for me. A treacherous harlot, my lady – a trollop of the worst kind."

Margaret pointed. "Then who ripped her uniform? Are you trying to tell me she did this herself?"

"No. Well yes, obviously to make my boy look bad," Percival's mother glared. "And who made his face bleed? He could hardly have done that himself."

"Unless he walked into a wall. I presume he's capable of that?"

"No, my lady, he's not blind." She flopped back against the wall herself, and the ivy broke its leaf and twig in her hair. "This little thief stole from me several times. I therefore dismissed her."

"You told me before," said Lady Margaret looking down the considerable length of her nose, "that the girl had run away."

"She did. When I sacked the trollop."

The countess raised an eyebrow. "I trusted you, madam. I had supposed we might trust each other. I find this behaviour quite upsetting, and especially that of your son. If you try to protect him, that I can understand. But he was attempting rape. Admit it."

Mistress Maddock hung her head. "He wouldn't dream of it. He's not like that, my lady."

Lady Margaret turned her attention to Jetta. "Although we've never shared conversation," she said, "I know you've been working for me for some weeks now. You work well, you're quiet and well behaved, but I know little of you. Tell me what you know of the Maddock family."

VESPERS

"You ask that whore about my family?" Mary demanded. "You've known me for some time too, my lady."

Ignoring this, Margaret gazed at Jetta. For a moment Jetta was disturbed, for the eyes staring at her were as cold as Dominic's so often were. She tried not to shiver. "My lady." She did not look away. "I was taken to work for this family for some years, and was never permitted my freedom. I worked hard, as any servant should, but I was frightened of them. I did nothing wrong, I would have been too scared my lady. But Percival Maddock often attempted to abuse me, and when I tried to protect myself, he ran to his father. Then I was stripped to the waist and lashed until my back bled. So I found an opportunity to escape."

The countess nodded. "Please return to your work. I shall speak with you afterwards." When she began to talk with Mistress Maddock, Jetta hid just inside the corridor, trying to overhear. "I am deeply disappointed," the countess was saying. "I had thought you would make a welcome ally. You travelled with my trusted friend, the Earl of Plymouth, which seemed to be proof of your intelligence. Naturally, I shall not mark you as a traitor to our cause, but I must carefully consider the consequences, abuse of any woman is abhorrent to me. Thank you for coming, but I need time and will contact you when ready."

Only moments afterwards, The Countess marched into her own bedchamber, and surveyed Jetta. "You bit his face?"

Jetta nodded. "I did, my lady. He attacked me and I didn't have time to think, I just did whatever I could. It's not all that long since I escaped that house. I wasn't going to let them drag me back."

"I have no objections to a woman protecting herself." The lady sat neatly on a small wooden chair beside her bed, her hands clasped in her lap. Her face was narrow, and her expression seemed to carry permanent disdain.

Having disliked the woman for some time, Jetta now discovered herself grateful. "Thank you, my lady, that's most understanding." She waited. What she wanted to know was impossible to ask.

Lady Margaret remained straight backed, stern and cold eyed, yet her words, although with a sniff of discomfort, were kind. "This is no easy time for a woman, and I approve of the determination some display in order to survive. As a young child, I had no choice. I was told of my fortune, my title, my importance. And yet my fortune was never mine to spend, my title seemed a weight around my neck rather than a boon. And I was treated as little more than a servant without a brain. Now I exert whatever power I can claim. I am entitled to title, and my entitlement is a constant comfort." Jetta stood, hands behind her back. "I am not used to speaking of such matters," the countess said. "Nor shall I do so again. But I will not permit that man onto my premises in the future, and I can promise you greater protection. I have an idea that you are more intelligent than you seem, so I believe I owed you the explanation."

"I thank you and with deepest respect, my lady." Jetta stifled the questions she would have loved to ask. "But I wasn't born with title, inheritance nor even the possibility for learning clever skills. So, I'm somewhat stuck with this life."

"Marriage? Children?" The eyes were small chinks of ice.

"No, my lady." She was careful to look down at her own feet. "There is no likelihood of that as yet, and I don't seek such a life."

"I'll not discuss this matter again," the Lady Margaret said. "I have explained my opinion and that's enough. You will now return and continue with your work."

And Jetta did, curtsied again, and left the room. She hurried to the laundry which was about as far as her allotted work could take her. She did not see the man who had accompanied the Maddock family, but she did remember his name.

Four days later, when Jetta found herself virtually drowning in her own tears of frustrated boredom, she asked the steward if she might give in her notice. "I would," she said with a deep breath, "prefer to look for more interesting work."

"Here?" inquired the steward.

That was the last thing she wanted but could hardly admit it. "I doubt there would be a place for me, sir. I wish to be – something more."

The steward laughed. "As if anyone would take a chamber maid's wishes into account," he said with contempt.

"Forgive me for arguing sir," and she tried to smile, "but I can read and write well, and might find more intelligent work."

Jetta knew she would miss the house itself. It was spacious and wonderfully clean, always scrupulously tidy while bathed in quiet serenity. Yet it lacked decoration and remained devoid of personality. Every room was kept dark and little light was permitted to enter except in the kitchens where it was necessary for the staff to see exactly what they were doing. In the laundries the mangle squeezed riblets of water from the constant arrival of identical clothes, first the nun's habit duplicated over and over. The only activity which ever took place was the endless cleaning, and keeping distant from the private conversations between the lady of the house and her secret visitors. Better, perhaps, than a place of fights and constant noise, which she had worked in previously.

What was secretly required of her was quite different and she had succeeded in that, although hardly to any great extent. Her random thoughts were interrupted by none other than the countess herself.

"Miss Lawson, you wish to leave my employ?"

"I have loved working for your ladyship," said Jetta in a hurry. "But the work itself is – I'm sorry to say it – is repetitious and –. I apologise, but I'm hoping to find something more challenging."

"You will soon discover," said her ladyship loftily, "that quiet work permits your thoughts to gather and flourish. Noise and chaos are the worst thing for an active mind and serve only the simple minded. You will no doubt discover your mistake. Your remarks are frankly idiotic, girl. But I wish you a prosperous future. You may soon discover that there are great changes to come in this country which will affect all our lives, so stay determined and do not be afraid. In spite of what you say, I assume it was the attack from the

Maddock boy that has frightened you away. With that I can sympathise."

With relief, Jetta marched to the stables, reclaimed her own mare, and called the young groom who had accompanied her. Within half an hour of saddling and preparing the horses, they both rode from the premises.

It was as they left the main gates out into the wide road beyond, when they were passed by two splendidly and colourfully dressed riders leading a procession of guards, guides, grooms and a retinue of liveried staff.

Jetta and her companions were pushed aside, their horses slipping amongst the blackberry bushes of thorn and bud.

Muttering to herself under her breath, she bit her tongue, waiting impatiently. She now knew one of the men, and the other seemed even more richly arrogant. Jetta wondered if this was the lady's husband Stanley, though she recognised the livery, but could not be sure.

"Two damned wretched little moments after I leave," she mumbled, "along come the most important people for me to follow and overhear." At the same time, she held a certain respect for the woman who had suffered so much without surrender in any shape, yet no respect for a woman who had continued unfailingly to try and alter the country's peaceful existence for the sake of her son.

She was only angry with herself, knowing she hadn't found the information that Dominic had asked for, and now perhaps it had arrived when she was helpless. Useless.

Edging her horse from the thorns, she stopped again.

It was then that the larger of the leaders called to his companion. "But remember, Howard, I'm making no commitment. Everything depends on the day, and I'll not risk the obvious. My brother will be the closest, as I've told her. He'll make his final choice on the field."

As they slowed, approaching the mansion's open grounds, the other man answered. "She'll understand, and she knows I'm backing Tudor."

VESPERS

Jetta heard every word, grinned, delighted, but decided that as a spy, she had proved herself utterly unworthy.

Back on the open countryside, Jetta knew her riding skills were improving. She wished she had other skills to polish. Cleaning a commode wasn't something she ever wanted to do again, but she had a nasty feeling that this might have not been the last time she'd be told to do it.

There was no point in stopping for refreshment but her back ached from the hours riding so she dismounted and wandered the riverbanks, enjoying the sunshine on her neck, the reflections of it on the water, and the sudden leaping of the small fish with the tiny ripples they left behind. But she repeated to herself the name of the man she had recognised, the Earl of Plymouth, and wondered what connection he had to the sheriff she despised.

If the Beaufort Countess and her constant conspiracies and treasons brought about an invasion by her wretched son, there would be a battle. Jetta could not imagine Tudor winning, but any battle would cause tragedy. The death of friends and the heartbreak across the country. Many would die. Yet they had the courage to face such slaughter. A thousand men and more would follow their leaders, some holding little more than a fork for shifting hay, or a knife once used for sheering sheep. What any battlefield would actually be like, sound like and smell like, she could not imagine and hoped it was something she'd never experience.

Yet ambition, whatever pain it might bring to others, was always the motive. The ambition to rule, to claim the ultimate position whether entitled or otherwise, was sweeping in like a gale. To invade a country inevitably meant slaughtering those you wanted as your own people.

"I'll never meet any king face to face," she told her mare, stroking the horse's soft white face. "I like the sound of King Richard. He's changed laws from being greedy and corrupt, into being just and helpful. We can save our own money and not lose half of it in taxes or corruption. He knows how guilty and treacherous Lady Margaret is, but he nods and puts her into the care of her husband. As if that's going to keep her quiet. If ever, the Lord God forbid, Henry Tudor comes over here again to steal the throne, then it's his mother's fault. And Richard might wish he'd executed her after all."

Wondering whether she would ever be able to stand and watch a woman swing from the traitor's noose, Jetta closed her eyes. No, obviously not. Some executions were publicly watched, even cheered. Jetta thought she'd be sick. She didn't like Lady Margaret, but never to the extent of seeing her executed. Not on the gallows of course, but decapitated. She was imagining the blood and the head bouncing on straw and was glad when the groom woke her from the dream.

"Mistress, it's getting late. We've still got a long road ahead."

So, Jetta rode on into the twilight and finally arrived at what she now called home by midnight. Her groom, riding constantly a little behind, dismounted and helped Jetta to do the same, then took her reins and led the horses away.

Jetta gazed up at the house. A candle was still burning.

Chapter Twenty One

With the warmth of familiarity and the escape from the saddle, this truly felt like home. The trees she recognised. The front squares of low hedge, neat and formal, led to the informality of scrub and thorn in the distance. Daisies and clover could be seen in the glimmers of the moon as they sprang through the grass and the gaps between cobbles and pavings.

Jetta could hear an owl very softly calling, but there was utter silence as it flew over her head.

A candle flame flickered in one of the great wide windows of the hall. Jetta wasn't sure whether she should see who it was or sneak straight to bed. But a lit candle at this time of night wasn't going to be the countess and surely not any of the staff.

As quietly as she could manage, she held her breath, pushed open the front door delighted it wasn't locked, and wished she had the courage to peep inside the door of the hall. Closed, but surely not locked. It never was.

Anyone up at this time of night could only be Dominic, with a large pewter cup of wine in hand. There was, as usual, a choice. Do what she wanted and creep in to see him. Or behave like a dutiful servant and go immediately upstairs to bed.

As was becoming a habit, something completely different immediately occurred. A deep man's voice from behind the closed doors roared out, "Sounds like you've got a visitor, I reckon. Now at this time o' night I wonders who it could be. No way it ain't Lord Dom creeping bloody quiet in his own home. You come in here, little cherub, and say good evenin' to yer friend."

There was no mistaking Gimlett's voice, so Jetta, delighted, ran into the hall at once, coming to a halt quite suddenly.

The vast room seemed to be full of her friends, and the only one missing was Dominic himself. Tyballis sat comfortably beside Andrew on the settle. On a chair back in a corner of shadows was Ned her oldest friend from the forest, and Gimlett sat on a large chair with his feet up on a stool.

Clapping her hands together in astonished delight, Jetta grinned and sat herself with a flop on one of the cushioned chairs. Tyballis had hopped up at once and embraced her.

"Dearest Jetta, none of us expected you tonight. We're all dutifully waiting for Dom."

"He's expected?"

"Within an hour or so," Andrew said, his eyes like stars glinting through the darkness. He leaned over and lit another candle stub.

"Humph," Ned was keeping his opinions to himself, but didn't seem happy in such expensive company.

There were stories to tell, and Jetta told her own.

"You all know where I was and what I was trying to do. But I'm not a practised spy, not like all of you. There's not much to tell, just a lot of housework for only a few insights. I disliked Lady Margaret, though sympathise with what she's been through. Does anyone here know her?"

"I've met her a few times. But that is not the same as knowing her." Andrew shook his head, still smiling. "Does anyone really know her? I doubt it. Not even her latest husband Stanley."

"She's quite unlikeable, so lacking in warmth and so austere. But there was one day when she spoke to me. I was attacked by a visitor of hers, someone I know. A – vile boy. Lady Margaret heard me scream and came down and dismissed both the boy and his mother from the premises. Afterwards she talked to me – a little as if she actually understood my predicament. Then she spoke a little about her own miserable childhood and explained how small and insignificant she'd always felt. So that presumably explains why she's so cold. It's as if she's the Virgin Mary and every soul around her must obey."

Tyballis smiled. "Well, she wears the clothes to fit. I suppose she feels as if it's a suit of armour she can hide behind."

"We all needs to hide sometimes," grinned Gimlett, "though not her, with all that coin and title."

"I've met Tudor too," Andrew leaned back on the settle. "Now him, I dislike intensely. He lacks humour and he lacks warmth. He's also a sanctimonious prick." Both Gimlett and Jetta giggled as Andrew continued, "And without either training or even the slightest experience, I doubt he'd be a king to welcome."

Tyballis nodded. "Surely he won't ever be king," she argued. "How could he win an invasion – without a single thing in his favour – or even much in the way of supporters."

"He has a few, and possibly more that we know nothing of as yet. Not that many love him. Very few have met him." Andrew picked up his cup of wine from the table and stared into it. "Nor do people hate our King Richard. If anyone knows him, they respect him. He's very much admired. But it's too early for the public to hail him as a hero yet. People usually want whoever they think will make them better off."

"But Tudor just can't win. It wouldn't make any sense." Jetta now felt she knew a good deal more than previously.

"Sense," said Ned suddenly from the shadows, "doesn't play fair. "You of all folks, little almond blossom, know that only too well."

Becoming an almond blossom seemed suddenly most attractive. Jetta smiled but turned to Andrew and carefully related the little she had overheard during her work at Lady Margaret's home. "But," she stared down at her lap, "it's all known anyway, isn't it?"

"Nothing is ever all-known, my dear. It seems you've brought back some highly useful information yourself," Andrew said to Jetta, "which I'll carry to the king in the morning. Tudor's invasion will come at us within the month. And depending on the weather, will land at Milford Haven. It seems the Lord Stanley won't back the invasion as Richard holds his son at court. A hostage is always helpful."

"And what about the other Stanley?"

"What you overheard may be useful. So far," Andrew added softly, "none of us know. According to past habit, Stanley's brother will join the winning side at the last minute."

"Which won't be the French." Ned nodded. "The steward's in bed, so I'll fetch another jug of wine." He stood, smiling down at Jetta. "How strange it is," he said, "I still remember you as my little girl, not much more than a babe, and even though I helped when I could, you ran to the mansions, begging at the kitchen doors. Now look at us. You live behind the mansion's doors yourself. What could be more different?"

"Funnily enough," Jetta mumbled, "I don't feel different at all. I'm still just trying to run away from life."

"It's hard to escape the past," Andrew murmured. "We live in the present. Why do we hang onto the past? Yet I do it myself."

"Because the present's too fleeting," smile Tyballis. "One blink – and it's gone. It's the past too."

"Wine helps, fair enough." Ned left the hall and Tyballis turned to Jetta.

"Speaking of the past, did you ever find out who you are? Who took you to the abbot?" Tyballis asked her.

"No. But it happens all the time, doesn't it? Illegitimate babies abandoned, mothers desperate to keep their mistakes secret. There must be hundreds every year. The nuns told me that over and over, whenever I wanted to know about myself. So I gave up and I don't care anymore. I feel so sorry for the mothers, and mine too, whoever she was, poor soul. The bastard children, like me, well most don't care I expect. Abbot Francis knows but he's promised never to tell."

"Don't you never be ashamed of it, my little blossom," Gimlett sat forward. "There's this daft Lady Beaufort herself, what's of a bastard line, and were told years back she can't never be royal, nor whatever brats she has. And she takes no notice o' that at all, and nor do her rotten son."

"Good for her, in one way," Tyballis smiled again. "That's a woman who lives in the future instead of the past."

"Destiny." Jetta shook her head.

"Is it always? Living in the future is a sure way of being disappointed," Andrew sighed. "Or perhaps that woman is simply ashamed of her past. People have often thought I should be ashamed, but why? I am what life shaped me. And that's destiny."

"I'm not ashamed," Jetta said. "I just wish I had a childhood worth remembering, with a mother to hold. And perhaps sisters or brothers."

"Nasty buggers they is, all of 'em," interrupted Gimlett. "You ain't missed nothing, lass."

Ned returned with another cup and two jugs of wine which he cheerfully set on the table. "Now then," he said. "I'll pour, who wants what?"

Nobody refused, instead finding some relaxation in their cups, the exhaustion bringing blurred thoughts of sleep.

The outside door slammed, footsteps were loud, the hall's double doors opened up and a deep voice called, "There's no time to sleep but plenty for drinking. It's nearing dawn and we all have a great deal to do."

"Jetta's back," Gimlett called, "and we got some news an'all."

Striding across to Jetta, Dominic placed a welcoming hand on her shoulder as he grabbed a cup of wine of his own, smiled and drank. The tingle of exhilaration woke her from exhaustion. She almost wanted to dance. Each of his fingers felt like a separate delight.

"Yes, a little bit of news but nothing much. I'm sure you probably know it already." She wished quite desperately that she had some startling secret to tell him.

'It's all been cancelled. No one's coming. Henry Tudor dropped dead this morning. Lady Margaret and her husband are just going to stay in bed forever.' But sadly, nothing like that.

"The invasion? yes. When and where?" Dominic did not see her blush. It was far too dark in the room.

"They say he's coming this month if he can. And it'll be Milford Haven unless there's a storm when he's already on his way. But he's leaving as soon as possible."

"Excellent," Dom smiled, "And that's as detailed as we can expect. Many things make a difference. The French generals, and whoever else they intend sending. It won't be Tudor in charge. He's never fought anything in his life. The French will lead and do all the planning. And some of them can be damned impressive. That's what I've been looking into myself. They're paying Swiss troops and offering a pardon to any French prisoner who agrees to fight for them. I doubt the Woodvilles will impress us over much, but one or two can fight like dogs. We outnumber them so far, but we can't be totally sure." He turned back to gaze down at Jetta. "Do you have any clues as to the Stanleys?"

"A bit, but they don't seem certain themselves. I don't think Lady Margaret's husband will fight. But everyone says his brother will come in at the last minute on whichever side he thinks is winning. And it's that Plymouth earl you mentioned too. He's a definite Lancastrian. I saw him twice."

Dominic's hand remained firm on Jetta's shoulder. She could hear her own heartbeat racing, and hoped that he could not. "Yes, that's the general opinion. It's a Stanley habit." His eyes had warmed from their usual ice.

Andrew looked up from where he sat. "And what's the Desford habit, my friend?"

Jetta heard Dominic's voice directly in her ear. The warmth of his breath cocooned the top of her head. She could hear his smile. "Loyalty, my friend, loyalty. Enthusiasm, genius and loyalty." And, with that same heated loyalty, he stayed where he was. "I've had a few moments with the king. He expects news of the landing any day now. He'll be riding north himself."

"And we'll be following." Andrew spoke softly for a moment, looking only at his wife. "His highness will be calling on everyone to follow, of course most will. We should outnumber the French two to one."

"Except possibly for the Stanleys."

Gimlett grinned, "I'm on me way day after tomorra. I reckon on getting there first and doing some reckoning around. The king knows. I already told him. He laughed. Got a good chuckle, he has."

Ned was frowning. "There's no one will miss me, except for a few trees and perhaps a badger or two. I'll be off with Gimlett in the morning after tomorrow, soon as the sun's up. So no bed tomorrow night. It'll be a long march. But as for tomorrow itself, I know the plan, my lord."

"There's no long march necessary. You know I've told you both to take my horses. The head groom knows exactly what to bring you at dawn after tomorrow. The king rides to Nottingham. Keep the horses there and use them in battle according to orders. You already have the weapons I supplied."

"We do, and damn good 'uns they is," Gimlett replied.

As Dominic turned, moving away from her, Jetta whispered, "That other man you mentioned once, he seems to be friends with the Maddock family and Margaret Beaufort too. Hugh somebody, Earl of Plymouth. He was riding with the Stanley husband. Thomas, isn't it. They were definitely friendly."

Turning back to her, his hand moved across her neck, his fingers caressed her chin without conscious intention. "Plymouth. Yes indeed. I've heard his name several times of late. Perhaps I should search for this illusive creature. He knew my parents, but not as a friend. I've not met him since."

Andrew stood with Tyballis tight beside him.

"I'm leaving in two days, as well awaiting the king's word. A little private time alone with my wife first is all I need. Dom, send word as soon as you need me, or when we have word that they've landed. And if this Plymouth earl looms anywhere close, I'll let you know."

By this time, they were now standing at the open doorway. Jetta smiled at Ned. "I'll miss you. I've only just found you, Ned. Now I'm losing you all over again."

"I've been loyal to this king since before his coronation," Ned smiled back at Jetta. "I'm prepared to fight for my country, whether I'm needed, or not."

Dominic followed them out onto the dark steps, speaking softly to each man as they left. Even to Tyballis he murmured, "Swear to stay safe, you and the child, and help Jetta too if you're able."

The moon had risen over the willow trees, their falling branches whispering in the night's breezes. As each of his visitors disappeared into those rustling shadows, Dominic quietly locked the door behind him and returned to the hall where Jetta remained sitting.

Not knowing what would be considered proper, Jetta had been unsure whether to slip up to her own bedchamber, or to wait for Dominic to wish her goodnight and to give instructions for the following days. So, wanting to see him for perhaps the last time, she waited.

One of the candles blew out as the door swung closed. Just a stub remained, its tiny flicker across the table.

Sitting very still on a chair beside the empty hearth, Jetta watched as Dominic wandered over to one of the great windows, and stood there, staring out.

His voice was so soft, she could barely hear him, and he did not turn to face her. A muffled sound of hooves as the last of the horses left the grounds had disappeared when Dominic finally spoke.

He remained with his back to her. "This is a vulgar question, and one you do not need to answer if you don't want to." He paused. Jetta could hear his slow inhalation before he spoke, and then his words startled her as he said, "But has any man ever taken you to his bed?"

Jetta was stunned. She felt a rise of panic and gulped. She whispered her response, "No. Never. Not ever."

She said nothing else. It was almost a nausea that rose into her throat. That was the last question she might ever have expected and now her thoughts flew in dark circles. Did the man only bed experienced women? Would he hold virgins in contempt? Surely his Teresa had been a virgin at some point. Perhaps that had been before he met her.

Dominic came back to her, standing behind her chair as he had before, though this time both his hands gripped her shoulders. He bent his head, speaking quietly into her ear, warm breath as delicious as an embrace.

Yet no embrace came. Instead, he murmured, "I will wish you goodnight, my little one, and hope that your dreams bring you the kiss I wish I could give you myself."

He left her, sitting there all alone, and she stared into the darkness, wanting to cry. For a moment, she didn't understand what had happened, nor why. Then the obvious filtered through, and she knew she'd cry once she curled into the lonely embrace of her bed.

His touch had delighted her, his words had chilled her, and now, floating in ridiculous visions, she dreamt of him rushing towards her, partially naked, limited only as her own imagination could supply.

Jetta stood, and trudged slowly up the stairs. The last candle stub blew out.

Chapter Twenty Two

While Jetta lay awake but still in bed the following morning, Dominic rode briskly northeast and headed for St. John's woods and the great stone convent and its grounds. Three guards, his chief groom and his principal secretary rode behind, bright in green and gold livery.

"Tis almost as if you're off to battle already," Ned said, as they arrived at his home with a snort from the tired horses.

Dom dismounted, drinking the ale Ned brought out to him. "Are you coming. I've no objection if you've changed your mind."

"Just like my trees, I never bend backwards," Ned grinned. "I'm ready and I'm coming."

The small party then rode west, riding more slowly towards the Covent. The fields of neat growth lay under the late July sunshine, cabbage, parsnip, carrots and onions, a long strip growing garlic, and hemp grew massed across the rise, used for most of the sisters' clothes and their bedding. Fruit trees grew off into the sun blaze, and beyond that as the slope slipped into the gentle valley were the rows of vines and wheat.

Several of the nuns, bent to the knees, were working amongst the stretches of such enthusiastic growth, sweating in the avid heat beneath the thick habits of their holy orders. The day was too hot for such clothes.

But it was beyond the perfumes of fruit and growth that Dominic led his men and dismounted at the convent doors. As usual they were closed and only the tiny, barred window within one door was opened as Dominic knocked.

"You may remember me," he said at once, "I've an important matter to discuss with your abbess. My guards will remain outside, I promise, only one man will accompany me."

Almost immediately another sister unlocked the door, Dominic marched in with Ned beside him.

Abbess Adelina sat calmly behind her small table, hands neatly clasped in her lap with the great carved wooden cross covering the wall behind her. A small window welcomed the sunshine. "Please sit," she told them both. "You, my lord, found conversation difficult the last time you were here. It would appear that your religious faith does not always coincide with the deep and true faith that we preach here. But if you have some of your ungodly actions or opinions to confess, I am willing to hear your confession."

"Not at all what I had in mind, I assure you," Dominic grinned. I'm here to ask a question which I consider of utmost importance – not to you but to me and to another person most intimately involved. I can see no reason for you to deny the knowledge, since the answer should bring you neither trouble nor benefit."

The abbess sighed. "You ask again about the girl Jetta, so many years ago. Yes, I knew her, but not well. I was a senior and took the daily service at Prime while she was an adopted child known for her bad behaviour, training to join the convent but with very little chance of success."

"I am interested only in her identity," Dominic said. "I wish to know the details of her arrival here, of her mother and what that woman said."

"Abbess Randella," Abbess Adelina replied, "as I am sure I have told you already, sir –,"

Dominic interrupted. "Indeed yes, Sister, that is precisely as you told me before. But since my previous visit, I've become acquainted with the gentleman now sitting here beside me. He works in the woods, and has, in the past, been acquainted with your previous abbess, and also with Abbot Francis at the monastery. I imagine you remember meeting with him, Edward Campion, usually known as Ned, as at the time you were working with the crops and needed instruction."

"As I have informed you, I took the Prime service each morning."

"And then spent the day pruning and caring for the trees on your grounds," Ned said. "I know you well enough, sister, and you know me well. Indeed, first time I came it was proper inspired by the sweet lass I knew as Jetta. She told me how cruel you all were, what with beatings and locked up all day with no food. Two were worst, she told me. That was Adelina and Dierna, both hated her. But when I came here to find out if this is a convent or some place of beatings, I ended friendly with Dierna. And she told me loud and clear how you knew exactly who Jetta was. It was the abbot told her, being worried about what the lady mother had told him. But he'd sworn on the Bible never to tell, and being an abbot would never break such an oath."

"I'm sure you've spoken with him," the abbess said without expression. "And I'm equally sure that he refused to tell you what he knew."

"Of course." Dominic leaned over the table. "I have also spoken to him on the subject. But an abbot will not break an oath he considers unbreakable. However, since he considered the information difficult to keep private, evidently, he came here and divulged the details to you, Sister. He felt that divulging what he knew to a nun on her way to becoming abbess was not a breaking of the oath. It was sharing the information with the daughter of another holy order, and therefore did not break the secrecy he had promised."

"Sister Dierna told you this?"

VESPERS

"And trusting any abbess of holy orders," Dominic continued, "the abbot would not have insisted you swear to the same secrecy." He stared, then sank back to sit opposite. "We are expecting a great upheaval and bloodshed over the next month. I believe you already know, and indeed support, this expected upheaval. This is treasonous, yet not heresy and I cannot judge you for what you support. Not that fighting will take place on consecrated grounds. But what I am told about the young woman I now consider a close friend, is of considerable importance both to her and to myself."

Lowering her eyes to the papers on the little table, she nodded. "I have sworn no oath. I simply took the abbot's confession, and of course, no confession can ever be divulged. Especially to someone not within the holy orders. Yes, I do know the details that you ask. I can, I believe, inform you that the child who left here had an interesting and unexpected background, which the woman who brought her here explained in some detail. But everything else was part of the confession and therefore cannot be repeated, it being a deadly sin to divulge any man's confession to the Lord."

Ned, impatient, thumped the table. "And why can't the sweet girl know her own identity? For now, she thinks she was another bastard child dumped on the church steps by some pitiful ashamed mother, unable to look after the baby herself. And I know that ain't true or there'd not be all this daft secrecy, would there! But I know naught else."

"Nor will you, sir," the abbess said, "since I have no intention of breaking the privacy of the confession."

Dominic stood. "I am extremely disappointed," he said, nodding. "But I understand, and I accept your decision as regards the confession. Yet you inferred that what you know is not entirely from the confessional. Do you refuse to let the girl know anything of herself?"

She avoided the heavy brows and cold eyes. "What I know, I must keep to myself, sir. The girl will not suffer from ignorance. She is neither princess nor slave brat."

Then Dominic turned abruptly, adding one last question. "And while I'm here, sister, do you personally know the Earl of Plymouth, one Howard Tamper?"

"Gracious no." The abbess showed her irritation. "I am a holy nun and through my faith and love, I have risen to the state of abbess. I know none of such men, titled or otherwise."

"He has been seen close to here."

"Hardly my concern, my lord."

It was as they left the convent, talking softly to each other, that another sister walked over, opening the front door to them. As they left, she followed, standing quietly on the doorstep.

"I am Sister Josephine," she said softly, "and I wonder if I may have a word. I may be able to help you. I also know another newly arrived young novice, sir, and she knows something of this from quite another source."

"Please tell me what you can, sister." Dominic took the reins of his horse from his groom and walked slowly beside the elderly nun.

"I am breaking no oaths, though neither should I relate anything said to another under oath," she said. "But I cannot help but believe that the girl should know something of who she is and where she came from. So I shall tell you what I overheard the abbot tell Sister Adelina. I heard every word. I was praying in the chapel, and the abbot's confession was made in the confessional directly behind me. I've never told this to anyone else and never will. The confession was never made to me, and I feel no special guilt in telling of it to you."

Dominic, leading his horse across the sun beams on the grass, and nodding to Ned to stay where he was, answered her. "I can swear to you, sister, on any book you wish to produce, that I will divulge this information to no one other than her."

"Then let's walk through these budding vines," the sister said. "It is private there, and only Jesus Christ and yourself shall hear me."

The perfumes of damp grass and budding growth floated on the small morning wind, and the young sister spoke softly as they walked. Dominic listened carefully and without interruption until his unexpected companion paused. "Not the usual story," she smiled.

He frowned in reply. It was not disbelief, but he had been exceedingly surprised. "Since I know her well," he said, "and better almost every day, I had not thought her some backstreet woman's child, nor the daughter of a scullery maid. But what you've told me is remarkable and nothing I could have imagined."

"Which is why she should know," said the nun.

When standing beside Ned once more, Dominic thanked her, then thanked her again as they left. "You have," he said, "amazed me. Yet I half expected to be surprised, so perhaps it's no surprise after all. You have my thanks and the assurance that I'll tell this to no one except Jetta herself"

Ned had waited with the guards. "That took longer than I'd expected. You believed her?" Ned asked.

"I did. There was no conceivable reason not to," Dominic said,

"And you'll tell her now?"

Dominic frowned again. "I must, and have every intention of doing so. That's the only reason I had to ask. Though it's not an easy decision when we're about to ride away into the unknown future."

He and Ned spoke little on the way back to the forest, and Dominic did not dismount when they arrived at Ned's door. Ned lifted his hand, but then turned. "I could die, my lord. And – well, so could you, sir. Should she know before you leave?"

"It might seem more nightmare than blessing." Dominic took Ned's raised hand. "But enough of that now. I'll be seeing you again soon," he said. "Although not in such pleasant circumstances. Now, get yourself to the smith. You need the armour I've ordered for you. Gimlett should be there already. It needs adjustment to your height – and width."

Jetta did not see Dominic for the next two days and spent much of her time sitting with the countess in the hall where the sun streaked in the wide windows. But the countess occasionally forgot who she was, and either told her to be careful bringing in the soup, and not to forget the salt, or told her to take a message to the queen.

"Sadly, my lady, there is no queen at present. And even if there was, I'd be in no position to see her."

"Then tell the cook I want kidneys in burgundy for breakfast tomorrow," and this was a message that Jetta could carry cheerfully, knowing she'd also enjoy her breakfast the next day.

But the following morning when the kidneys were served, the countess would only stare at her platter, and object to having such rich food so early in the morning. Not that it was ever that early, for the countess was not an early riser, but if Jetta was present, she was perfectly happy to swap her bread and cheese for both servings of the kidneys, and ate them with considerable pleasure.

The countess had other problems. She saw small children running down the stairs, and sometimes they fell. She heard packs of stray dogs rushing through the gardens, destroying the hedges, and often in the evenings she heard the singing of the angels. "Most sing very well," she told Jetta. "A few are not so good. There's one, red hair, quite startling. But she's elderly, poor dear, even older than I am. She can't keep those pretty musical notes going without stopping for breath."

"Do angels breathe?"

"Don't be absurd, dear. Of course they do otherwise they'd flop down dead. And it must need a lot of breath to keep those heavy wings flapping."

"I've never thought of wings being heavy."

"Well, of course they are," the countess scowled. "All those feathers. You're such a silly girl. They call to me sometimes, but I've told them I'm not ready yet. They'll have to wait."

Often Jetta sat beneath the willow trees and listened to the sweet drift of the river behind the long loose branches, remembering how she had arrived here months ago, dirty, exhausted and frightened. But now her life had changed in so many ways. Most changes were remarkable and glorious. Not all.

Sitting in that cold and terrifying cell, trapped by the sheriff she hated, Jetta had believed she might be hung. Then there had been the blissful rescue again by Dominic.

But it was Dominic himself that filled her mind, whether in her own bed, sitting by the river, at breakfast, dinner and supper, and even when talking to others. Smiling at herself when she remembered disliking him, at least she understood the reasons. He was arrogant. But perhaps all earls had the same fault, except for Andrew, Lord Leays. And Dominic's eyes under those heavy lids could turn so cold they had seemed like a stab of steel, and capable of killing. He had accused her and believed in the possibility of her guilt.

'What? Innocent me?'

From a man like that, she had expected whippings and rape. So her own trust in him had been as weak as his trust in her.

Then everything had changed, and she wasn't even sure why. The man she disliked had somehow turned into the man she loved.

And all because of the farrier's murder. Though now she knew exactly who had killed him, and why. It was something she had no intention of telling anyone. Not even Dominic.

Chapter Twenty Three

It had come. The time had arrived. Now the word was out the shrill warning of the bugles announced the call. The mayor of each township rode every street, holding high the great flag of the country. Every evening the Watch marched through the City of London, held their flaming torches high, and shouted the news.

For the muster had begun and England was called to prepare for war. Landing on the Welsh coast, the invasion had started.

The rush, the shouting and the bustle sprang along every street, horses returning to their stables for reharnessing, examined carefully by the local farrier, then galloping out to the fields to upgrade their training. Every destrier flexed his muscles, and a dozen other stallions raced the hills, charging the sudden signals that other horses would avoid. Along the riverbanks the lords trained their mounts to ignore the flash of a sword or the challenge of a sudden trumpet, the call of a bugle and the screaming of men. Every war horse rode only to his master's commands and gloried in his own armour and the colours that he wore. The harness, bells and reins of every battle horse were polished and updated.

It had been many years since England rode to battle. The new

VESPERS

king's rule was marred by a small Lancastrian rebellion which had twice threatened the peace, and once a new threat had sailed from across the seas, yet never landed. But now the country's new prosperity, the success of trade and the improvement of the laws bringing great hope for a better life, were cut short by a nationwide call to arms.

There was excitement as the forges blew great gusts of smoke, the smiths smashed their hammers on steel, the thrust of metal into sword and arrow, and the embroidery of banners and flags.

Although the muster was unknown as yet to younger men, their fathers instructed them and excitement blared, more common than fear. The bugles of heralds called from the guild halls, every armourer and every smith working into the night, and chain coats were fashioned on every forge as the flames rose and the billows blew them higher.

Most lords already owned armour, and had fought in years past, but some steel boundaries needed loosening as his lordship had been feasting well and exercising little. Recently knighted, some younger men as yet owned little to proclaim their worth. Horses also needed armour, but this could be adapted, so no destrier would gallop into battle unprotected.

Sir Dominic, Earl of Desford, checked the buckled lining, then passed his armour to his blacksmith for immediate repair. It had once been his fathers, but had been much adapted since then, and flashed from upper arm brace down to gauntlets, from thigh cuisses to the protection of the knees with poleyns, down to the greaves and sabatons. Dominic regarded his helmet, then tossed it over to the settle. Battle now seemed inevitable. What he had planned, as always, had been smashed by the ever-spinning wheel of misfortune.

As the excitement rolled through the streets, so others sat in their shadows, praying for their lives, their husbands' lives, and the safety of their children. Many would follow their lords without armour or longbow, without chainmail or sword. They would leave their wives to sob for them, and perhaps to starve without the payment of their protector.

Small farms might no longer prosper, sheep and cattle would wander searching desperately for food, a thousand successful businesses would cease to exist, and new-born children would never know their fathers.

Their king would win, he *had* to win, but inevitably so many of those who fought for him would still lie dead beneath mounds of others dying.

French soldiers would march into villages, rape the women and steal their food. They said many of the French were criminals released from their prisons in exchange for risking their lives. Winning or losing, such men would practise their hatreds on the wives and daughters of their enemies.

Between the fear, excitement, the panic and the desperation, there was also great confusion. Gossip travelled fast, but changed its story six times along the way. News was not always true and had more chance of accuracy if written. Some only believed what they wished. Another pointless invasion from a foreign stranger was neither welcomed nor accepted.

'Like last time, the fool will drown before landing.'

'This Tudor bastard is clever with his lies. But not so clever with his right to the throne.'

'The bastard of a bastard. An exile and a fool who knows nothing of us, that won't know if York is south of London, or Warwick is north of York. And he marches with the French. They hate us and we hate them.'

'What rightful king invades hand in hand with England's enemy of centuries?"

'So the ambition of one solitary man will bring the destruction and death of thousands.'

The bright hope of August smiled across the countryside, and as yet there was no news of the French landing. Yet the warning had come, for the enemy was already at sea and was threatened by neither storm nor rough waters.

Luis of France was the spider who wove webs and hated the

English. For more than a hundred years they had spat contempt at each other and fought to prove their own superiority. Yet for some time it was the French who had laid down their arms and run. But the spider did not forget his grievances, and although Luis and his daughter knew little of Henry Tudor and cared nothing for him, they knew a great deal regarding England and would grasp any opportunity to challenge and to overcome.

The Countess of Desford saw little of her grandson. He avoided her and the strange questions he was sure she might ask. He discussed strategies with Andrew, Lord Leays, with Sir Francis Lovell, with the Duke of Norfolk, with Gimlett who sat like a lord in his company, and with Ned who was received with respect by the others. Dom also spent time with his Highness, King Richard, for all his mighty battle experience of the past, was deeply interested in the ideas and knowledge of his lords and his friends.

Dominic was avoiding not only his grandmother but also the girl now part of his life, Jetta, who had first appeared in the oddest way. He no longer believed her capable of murdering his farrier, although he was still not sure who had. But he was in danger of losing something even more valuable and wouldn't risk it at such a time. The entire country was about to fall into bloody drama, and he would fight it, not add to it.

English power was much loved by some, and bitterly hated by others. And even within the country, envy and long-standing resentments continued. The Woodvilles had always backed the Lancastrian side until their friendship was bought in marriage by Edward IV. But the children of that marriage had been proved illegitimate and the Woodvilles could never forgive Richard for accepting his right to the throne in their place.

The hatred of the Stanley brothers was always a threat. Their long-standing feud with Richard was unlikely to make them close allies. Margaret Beaufort would slaughter bishops for her son, and even though his own son was held as a cautious hostage by the king, her Stanley husband was still capable of conspiring with his wife and brother.

"Do you have faith in the outcome?" Dominic asked his king.

"I never expected to be king," Richard sighed and leaned back, his eyes almost closed. "Does a fourth son ever expect to inherit a crown? I'll take what comes to me, Dom, but I have faith in my right to success."

It was Ned who said, "My liege, I believe in the treachery of William I, a conqueror of greed and lies. But he won, he succeeded, and he flourished even without justice. Our Holy Lord has His own plans and tells us nothing of them. It's not always good men who wear the crown."

Richard smiled. "Do any of us truly deserve the honour of such a holy title? Only Henry VI believed himself chosen by God. And, sadly, he was quite mad."

"Sire," Andrew interrupted, "since you are neither coward nor madman, we can trust in the right of the man born to be king."

Richard raised his cup. "Sweet words, my friend, thank you."

Dominic had also raised his cup and now drank. "But as my spy told me, sire, Lady Beaufort's husband will not risk his son's life, and won't fight against you if Tudor dares to march. But I'd not trust Sir William with a toothpick. He's had a long-standing feud and he's a man who never forgets."

"And that's something I won't forget," Richard smiled again. Nor do I forget the fame of the French general they say will lead alongside Oxford. De Chandée is known as a fervent and remarkable warrior."

"And Oxford also carries a dangerous reputation."

Beneath the blazing August sun, the packed ships had crossed the tranquil waters of the Narrow Sea, and swept up to the Welsh beaches, dropping their anchors in the shallow surf. The French troops led by Philibert de Chandée, the Earl of Oxford and Henry Tudor landed at Milford Haven on the Welsh coast on the seventh day of August. On hearing the news, every lord and the troops owing him allegiance, prepared to march.

VESPERS

The enemy had arrived. There were varied reports on the size of the army they led, but it seemed that the French forces numbered about two thousand, the Swiss mercenaries were small in number but huge in skill, and those following Oxford and Tudor added almost another two thousand. Cutting through Wales, they were able to recruit more, although fewer than they had expected. However, Tudor, they claimed, was the descendant of Welsh nobility, and some believed it. Those, nursing Lancastrian sympathies also joined as well as those with grievances against King Richard. Those rushed to Tudor's side, gathering the men of their families and scuttling to join the march.

They cut across Wales, and although no town or village blocked them since a population of a few hundred would not fight against a marching troop of five thousand, some, for their own reasons, ran to join.

With the warning of more than a hundred ships at sea, King Richard had called his troops to muster and rally. Most were well prepared but where news took longer to arrive, some were tardy, late, or delayed. His staunch followers in Yorkshire were amongst them.

Immediately on hearing the news of the landing and so knowing the invasion was in progress, Richard rode north to Nottingham Castle, a place of comfort, light and allies where he had often taken up residence before when planning and organising whatever was to come. Expecting Tudor to aim for London, Richard was wary. However, because of the route taken to muster his army, he decided to cut off any advance by taking his own men north, and so called his followers to join him outside Nottingham.

All across the land, the lords loyal to their king and country, roared out their own muster. Every man of age sixteen until sixty gathered their arms to follow their lord. Troops marched every road, dragging carts of armoury and rode destriers or younger horses now trained for battle.

Villages along the route closed doors and hit their cattle, pigs, goats and poultry, but stood beside every lane to cheer the heroes of their country, out to shout victory against their enemies.

Long days dragged in sweating and weary miles, from the south to the north, and from the north down to the south.

So, the troops stopped, bivouacked, and prepared for battle. The heaps of guns, ammunition and thousands of arrows began their journey. Ten cannon with cannon balls were already housed in Warwick Castle, and these were trundled out and onto the old Roman road of Fen Lane.

By the twelfth day of August, Richard was waiting in Nottingham. When the news reached him that Tudor's invasion was again moving, he rode through the Midlands, the massed armies of England behind him. He stayed overnight at the monasteries and priories, his lords sometimes with him or at the local inns and taverns.

The weather welcomed them, high summer, and cloudless skies. Men fighting for their lives in full armour would find the heat uncomfortable, but when fighting for life, comfort could never be expected.

Both Dominic and Andrew led their own men, no great armies of a thousand warriors, but some hundreds of those eager to follow their lords. Ned followed Andrew. Gimlett followed Dominic.

Those wives who followed the armies themselves were eager to set up tents, prepare food, and comfort their husbands. Other women had only themselves to offer. Boys too young to fight but eager to learn and watch, rode the carts of weaponry, packed the arrows into their quivers, and the quivers to their straps.

Some men would sleep in the open, surrounding a small cooking fire. There were tents, large, small, oiled or not. The skies smiled, promising no rain. At night the flame's dancing sparks spat high to join the thousands of stars blinking in the moonlit shadows.

Dominic had his own tent, Gimlett on a pallet at his side. They spoke quietly together as night closed in, discussing what was ahead of them.

"I ain't scared o' dying," Gimlett said. "I done plenty I shouldn't. I followed the late king, and done what he asked, was more spying than fighting. And I liked this new king plenty too, so I done offered meself once more, and he laughed, and done took me."

Dominic tried to be interested. He had concentrated on every aspect of the battle to come, yet it was Jetta who pushed aside the raised swords and the flash of the arrows in his head, and crept persistently into his thoughts. She had taken up residence at the back of his mind and sat there, docile yet confident, smiling – and waiting. He wondered, too often, if she ever thought of him just as he thought of her.

A hundred times he imagined her in his bed, visualising what he had never seen. Tiny, delicate, with huge green eyes and the figure of an imp. He wanted her slim body within his embrace and longed to kiss her. But now knowing Jetta was a virgin, he brushed away temptations. She'd surely never wish to be his mistress.

With soft apologies he turned his back on her. it was the upcoming battle that roared, imminent and cruel. Yet Jetta remained. Only death could now bring distraction.

"Has anyone reported our numbers yet? Them other bastard lot?" Gimlet asked.

Dominic sighed, closing his eyes. "The present count is around five thousand. It should stay that way unless the Stanleys swoop."

"And our little chicken coop?"

"We outnumber them with roughly eight thousand. But William Stanley stands a mile off, six thousand men behind him." Dominic lay back, half imagining the possibility of Stanley's treachery and what that would create. "But is it treachery if a lord fights for his brother's step-son?"

"Damn well is," Gimlet said, gravel voiced. "Tudor ain't Stanley's son, they even never met, and he must fight for his king and country, or be bloody executed for treason."

At times of war, with the battle almost at each man's feet, many drowned themselves in ale, jugs of wine for the lords, prayers and the writing of final testaments stuffed behind belts. But whatever other reaction battered each man, terror or courage, the marching and the work at the start and end of each day was exhausting and they slept already bathed in sweat.

They woke at dawn the next day. It was the twentieth day of August. Richard, rising as early as his men, addressed them as the sun turned from grey to peach, peach to scarlet and scarlet to gold.

"The enemy is very close. By tomorrow we'll be camping in sight of one to the other. I will seek the high ground and oversee. Your lords will call the orders as always, you will cut off the enemy at the right of the marshes, and the archers will be led to the hedgerows for their initiation of the battle. We have a thousand long bows and two hundred arrows for each. Once all longbow ammunition is used, the archers with crossbows take up the three back wedges, adjusting their targets. Every troop will face the enemy in lines four deep and as closely as is possible. The enemy must see no space between or beyond the onslaught They face. Meanwhile the cannon will move, circling to the enemy's rear, and our artillery will dismount and take both right and left positions, avoiding the marsh. I tell you this so that when your lords speak the same words, you will follow without difficulty and if one word disappears behind cannon fire, you will still know it. You will also know that I watch, and love your courage with all my heart. When the moment comes, I take my men and charge. I shall be proud to fight at your side."

The men cheered him. The women sitting astride the wagons and carts at the back of the camps clapped and hooted, having little fear of anything except rape, which few feared anyway.

Remaining mounted, the king stroked his destrier's mane. He rode a grey stallion, a warrior as much as its master.

Both the Duke of Norfolk and the Duke of Northumberland flanked their King, and declared themselves leader of the right hand advance, and the overseer of the rear, while Andrew Cobham, Lord Leays and the Earl of Desford sat their stallions close behind their monarch, and eighty other great leaders and warriors of the infantry with them.

Andrew smiled across his horse's great mane, decorated with a scarlet flash of ribbons. "For me, the first military charge I've ever ridden. "

"Galloping a battle ground behind your king must be the greatest challenge and the greatest inspiration of any man's life." Smiling back, Dominic slumped a little, relaxing in the saddle. "First I shall dream of it. But the dream is never as powerful as the act."

Richard once more faced his men, standing high in his stirrups, both arms in the air. He wore the crown of England which flashed, catching the brilliance of the sun.

"I am your king," Richard now announced. "I love every man amongst you and will protect you with my life. They say that an army fights for their king. But let me swear to you that this king fights for his army and the precious love he feels for his country."

"This Tudor usurper," called Norfolk, his voice like thunder, "will be killed or sent back to his exile. Or remain for the rest of his life in the Tower. He has no more right to the throne than a fox which comes snooping at the chicken coop."

"We will fight for you. And you will fight with us," Northumberland shouted.

"And I herewith promise you my life," the king called. "I accepted the crown for the good of this country, and for the good of this country I will now fight off the invader who wants only glory and power for himself, and the death of those who own this land."

Chapter Twenty Four

"Jetta, come here girl. Are you there?" Well, you shouldn't be, you should be here."

"How about a clue?" Jetta called back. "If I know where you are, I can maybe find you quicker."

"Silly girl."

"And no, I've heard nothing of the king's forces or where Dominic might be. I doubt the fighting's started yet, or the news would be on fire all over the city. So I'm going outside for some fresh air unless you want something important."

"Of course it's important. But you've been such a fiddle-dandler, I've forgotten what it was."

"Wine? Ale? A shawl, though it's far too warm for that. Slippers? Or just a chat? My lady, if you can't remember, then I'll find you later. I need fresh air."

"A ridiculous idea, it's no good for you," the countess screeched. "And don't go jumping in the river."

Promising not to jump anywhere, Jetta hurried outside and breathed deeply, gulping the sweetness. It was warm, perhaps hotter than warm, and the sky was softly cloudless, a drifting sweet azure. Jetta knew that both the young Pike grooms had ridden north with their lord. But Ilda would still be sweating in the kitchen, baking bread and tending the ovens. She'd not trouble every cook in the mansion, Jetta hoped only to attract Ilda's attention.

A blast of heat knocked Jetta backwards as she opened the outside doors, and smoke like a billowing attack swooped out, rising to replace the lack of cloud above them.

"I won't come in. I don't want to get in the way. But is it possible to have a word with Ilda?"

It took quite some time before Ilda was able to come to her, so she leaned back on the wall and let her mind wander. She jumped when Ilda finally came out.

"You want me, Jetta?"

Taking Ilda's arm in hers they walked the cobbles from house to river, and past the stables. "Have you heard from your boys? Any news from anyone?"

Ilda dipped her sticky hands in the river and wiped them on her apron, then lifted it and wiped the sweat from her forehead. "Not what you'd call new, miss. The troops are gathered, and they've camped in Nottinghamshire. It's all farms, you know, and the farmers will watch their land trampled, but can't do nothing about it. The invaders are on the western side, they say. But news from there takes days to get here, even if the horse gallops till it collapses. Anything might have happened by now."

"Lord Stark?"

"I pray every night, mistress. What more can I do? But I reckon I'd know if my boys were injured. And I don't feel it. What's the day? Do you know?"

"Two days off St. Bartholomew's."

"Late August then?"

"I believe it's the twenty first," Jetta said. "But that doesn't help. We have no idea what might occur on any day."

"The victory of our king, miss. It has to be."

"It has to be that, but even I'm not stupid enough to celebrate our victory before the battle's even taken place."

The birds were singing, the chiff-chaff of a chaffinch from the bushes, the beauty of the new black bird family, the soft crooning of two wood pigeons, and the harsh call of a raven. It all seemed beautiful, safe and so placid. And yet both women breathed tears, swallowing back bile and the panic they would not admit.

As Ilda slipped back into the kitchens, it was the elderly chef who poked out his nose, waved a wooden spoon, and called to Jetta. "They got men all along the way, you know. We'll get the news by the evening as each one rides just an hour to the next on the route. I recon we'll be hearing mighty soon. That bastard Tutor won't be sitting on a tussock waiting for curds and whey, waiting for King Richard to send the spider."

Jetta laughed but it was fake. Nothing felt safe enough to smile about until they heard some news.

She wandered again down to the river and sat beneath the willows. Here even the tiniest breeze, ruffling the leaves, cooled her forehead. This far upstream the river was less polluted, and Jetta watched the fish jump, the shine of their scales catching the sun.

With the sharp girlish voice behind her, she was unable to see who spoke, yet knew exactly who it was.

"You told him, didn't you?" Teresa demanded, her words clipped in fury. "You wanted me in trouble. You wanted to get rid of me."

Jetta had no idea what Teresa meant, and said so. "I haven't seen him for days. A week and more. He's ridden north for the battle. And how could I tell him anything about you? I don't know you nor anything about you. Not much more than your name."

"Lying fool," Teresa spat. "You know damn well I was his mistress. You certainly wanted rid of me. You want Dominic for yourself."

They were staring at each other, almost as though they spoke different languages. Then Jetta whispered into the sunshine. "I like Dominic. I think we're friends. But I'm nobody's mistress and never will be. I wouldn't be – comfortable. And I promise you, I haven't told him a thing about you – not good – not bad. Isn't life horrible enough at the moment without you getting so angry over nothing?" She remained sitting on the sloping warm grass, but had turned, looking vaguely into the sun.

Peering down at Jetta, Teresa sneered and raised her voice. "I spoke against you. I admit it. I told the sheriff you were guilty. I said you'd killed the farrier. Perhaps you did for all I know. But I never said a word to Dominic. It was you who bitched about me."

"You got me arrested?" The sun made her squint, but Jetta glared.

"Of course. But only to get you out of the way."

"As if that makes it right." Jetta clambered upright and fisted both hands. "You actually told that vile sheriff that I killed the farrier? In case Dominic dropped you and took me for his mistress instead? And then you have the spite to blame me for telling about your disgusting lies. But I had no idea it was you and never told Dominic what I didn't even know myself."

The sun still burned into her scowl, but she blinked it back, now furious. Too angry to argue, Jetta swung one hand, her knuckles to Teresa's jaw. Jetta had not planned it, not even thought of hitting back, but although now her hand stung, she was pleased. It felt somehow comforting.

Teresa, more startled than hurt, toppled back, skirts up to her knees and head in the grass. She sprang up again like a button in the wind, and rushed towards Jetta. Each had expected the other woman to be incapable of fighting, yet each did what they could.

Now out of breath and fiercely infuriated, Teresa's voice was a screech. "Dom came to me, and he was horrid and said he knows so you must have told him."

They were on the ground, Jetta with both arms fully around Teresa's neck, when the sheriff and his assistant arrived striding into the chaos, grabbing both women, the sheriff hauling Jetta to her feet.

"Little whore," he shrieked, grabbing both her hands behind her and kicking out at her legs.

The assistant was far kinder with Teresa and Jetta watched as he made no effort to hurt or insult her. "Unjust," she now glared at Kettering. "So you think she's your spy now, and you believe the nonsense she told you. Just believing her that easily? You really are a stupid useless sheriff." She scowled. "What are you going to do now? You know dragging me off to some prison will get you into more trouble than me. I've committed no crime. And now you have."

"How dare you," the sheriff spluttered.

"Corruption – and it was proven."

"Well, there won't be nothing following on from that now, will there!" the sheriff grinned. "Don't matter who wins, there won't be no time for that suff. Accusing a legal sheriff? Disgraceful. Now you come with me." The menacing and self-satisfied grin faded again into scowl. "Tis the earl will back me, he said it before, and did it when he could."

Spluttering, "The earl backs you?"

"Not *your* earl," Kettering spat. "One more powerful and mighty strong too. Off north for the battle, he is, but he'll be back, and he'll have you carted off, like he did before."

Now on her feet and as happy as she could be, Teresa danced along. Small and pretty, her hair had fallen loose in the squabble and now seemed more beautiful in the sun. Her short plump legs and large breasts bounced as her skirts swept from her tiny waist to her wide hips.

Ignoring the woman, Jetta yelled at both men, "You should be up north fighting for your country as well. And when *my* earl returns victorious, he'll know where you've put me, and he'll come after you."

"*Your earl,* trollop? He's a weakling. It was my friend the Earl of Plymouth had your feeble Desford locked up for well-nigh a week in the quarry, and he still don't know who dun it or why. But you'll not be telling him, for he'll be dead, and you'll be well guarded. And you never know, after a good thrashing, you might be dead too."

Jetta caught her breath, almost choking. "Plymouth. The Earl of Desford never even met him."

"Maybe and maybe, you're talking the rubbish I expect from an uneducated trollop. But you'll not be back in the same gaol as before, harridan. Now you get into that cart," and he pushed her in as though she was a sack of turnips for sale at the market. One hand tied to the cart's side and the other hand to the opposite edge, Jetta could not move of her own accord but was bumped and bruised by the rattle on the cobbles as the mule dragged the cart, heading east.

They were heading away from the dark cell at the sheriff's office, and passed neither the house, the kitchens nor the stables to ensure that no one would know where she had gone or who had taken her.

"And shall I tell him about you when *my* lord comes back? No, I bloody won't," Teresa sang to herself. She rode beside the cart, astride a donkey that looked underfed. "I'll tell him that his whore is dead. And as I climb back into his bed, I'll tell him how you spied for the usurper's side. Then he'll have nothing to do with you."

It was where they were going that troubled Jetta. At least this was a distraction from the agony of waiting –of wondering whether Dominic was alive – of which army had won the battle – of what would happen next and of just sitting around with nothing to do except cradle a sore head. Now the sore head had started to pound.

As the mule cart swung a little north and followed the line of the ditch beside the old Roman wall, for a dizzy minute Jetta worried she was being taken to the great goal at Newgate, the largest and most fearsome in the country.

They rode beneath the portcullis as she stared up at the filth of the rising brick and stone, both too black with soot and smoke to see the difference. The stench was hideous, and Jetta was thrown back with the strength of it. Then they were through Newgate and had left the stench behind. She could still hear the calling and the screaming, but they continued to drive east, and then north.

Immediately Jetta knew where they were going and pounded on the floor of the cart. "Not the Maddock house," Jetta yelled. "You can't. You don't know them. They'll surely have ridden north. You may be too damned short and stupid to fight for your king, but Lord Maddock isn't. You've no right to take me there."

"Lady Maddock is looking forward to seeing you," called back the sheriff's assistant. So, she was expected, which was terrifying.

Percival Maddock met them at the door, chortling like a magpie behind his steward. "Back home, eh, ugly bitch?" he called, as the steward opened the door. Jetta was untied, dragged down and thrust into the arms of Percival. Meanwhile the steward gave a small but heavy purse to the sheriff. Jetta was hauled backwards but she saw the purse exchange hands. She had been bought, she realised. She tried desperately to dig her heels in the ground, but she didn't have the strength to stop him. Hauling her upstairs, his hands clasped firmly around her arm, Percival threw her into his bedchamber. She missed the bed and tumbled to the rug.

Jetta was sure she knew what would happen next. The wretched boy was some years younger than herself but clearly, he had grown in strength and her arms felt deeply bruised. Now her new gaoler locked the door behind him and shuffled back downstairs to his mother. At first Jetta heard mumblings of what was said, but then the other doors were closed, and she heard no more.

Standing, brushing herself down and shaking her hair from her eyes, Jetta strode to the window, desperate to find a way out. It was not large and would be hard to climb through, but they were only on the first floor, and she always had the knife.

Indeed, she had two. The larger was tucked inside her belt, completely concealed, while the other was tiny, and clipped into place within its leather covering inside one of her stocking garters. Battle meant not only the slaughter of those on the field and the roads and villages close by, but it could also mean the slaughter and rape of anyone in the path of the excited victors as they marched home, or by the fleeing survivors, furious at their defeat.

At times of battle and war, self-protection was important not only for those on the battlefield. For days she had been free to wander the Desford manor and had armed herself in preparation.

Without any interest in the bedchamber of the man she despised perhaps more than any other, she examined the windows fastening. A tight clasp held it in position, but there was no lock. She sighed with relief. Three twists, just one minute, and the window was open. She pushed it wide.

Now she could hear the conversation floating from below,

"Can I do anything with the whore? You know exactly what I mean."

"Yes of course, Percy, but be careful my boy. After you've finished, bring her down for a good thrashing. But when your father rides home, he may not be so pleased. The whore lives with a powerful man now. Until your Papa comes home, we don't know if he's a hero or a villain and that may make a difference."

"What difference will that make?"

"Percy darling, use your sense. If Papa is a hero, you're free to lock your door and tear that little bitch to pieces. But if the king wins, and we are amongst those waiting for punishment – than you grab that girl if you must – and then we quickly escape south."

"I have plans. We'll win. I know it. And I know just what I'm going to do to that slattern." He smirked, leaning back against the table.

His mother growled. "So you will go quickly and order the steward to silence, while that silly little bitch screams her head off."

Percy sniggered. "Sounds like you want to watch, Mama."

But his mother scowled. "Definitely not, I'd be sick," she told him. "But the slut deserves whatever she gets, and I'll certainly not complain."

"Oh, she's going to get what she deserves and more."

Lady Maddock sighed and pointed to the door. "Off you go and have your fun. But don't forget she has to be passed on to Howard Tamper afterwards. The Earl of Plymouth wants fun of his own. We've promised to keep her alive."

"I know it, I'm not a fool. But he doesn't even know the bitch."

"But he hates the brat's master. I'm not interested in why, but he hates Desford and will attack the girl to hurt him. Of course, he'll hurt her as well. Plymouth's past doesn't interest me in the slightest and he's welcome to keep his secrets to himself. I daresay he'll eventually kill the whore with a beating. But that's something you certainly won't be watching, my dear."

"Fuck and cut? That's what I want to do – and more."

"You can watch her whipping as you always did, my dear. But now we have to be careful of who wins the throne."

Chapter Twenty Five

No birds sang. The dawn climbed in silence, just a pale light peeping over the horizon. At first the land had seemed empty, yet now the pastel rising sun changed emptiness into the rush of movement, and the silence swept into the urgency of immediate preparation. An eagle sat patiently on the chimney of the old farmhouse by Fen Lane, her great golden eyes fixed on the gathering below.

The two huge camps, some miles apart, had slept nervously, expectant for the morning. Some snored, some dreamed, but no one knew what could happen on the following day.

Marching boots had already settled, camping close to the marshes but well beyond the aim of any longbow, of the crossbow, of the infantry and of the cannon, spread in two rows on each side of the battle lines.

Richard was ready. He had slept deeply, one of his household pages, well-armed, lying across the entrance to the tent itself, and his armourer on the floor pallet beside him. No leader of such importance would sleep alone at such a time.

His dreams had been sweet, but the night was hot, and the

sweating had awoken him early. He had taken a breakfast of wine and wheat biscuits while standing, and while his armourer buckled on each piece of his padded inner jerkin, strapped on his mail, and finally buckled the armour itself from helmet to sabatons with every finger protected by the gleam of steel within his gauntlets.

Striding from his tent, the King of England and Wales was met by those he would lead in person, by his standard bearer and others, waiting their sovereign's word.

None of the night's cooking fires had been left burning, no smoke drifted from the camp, and little noise murmured in the stillness as the tent flaps were flung open and tied back.

So the hush of a hot black night hurriedly metamorphasied into the rush of nearly ten thousand men, their determination and elation, yet also the hidden terror that elation would turn to annihilation.

The Dukes of Norfolk, leader of the infantry and Northumberland who would guard the rear, strode forwards to speak with their men. The archers ran to their flanks, right and left. The cannons were already in place.

Across the divides of marsh, hill and field, the tents of the enemy were less numerous, but those who strode out to the rising sunlight were as tall, as strong, and as determined. Henry had not yet appeared but already his standard bearer, holding up the vast banner of the dragon and the arms of the Welsh, paraded and then stood waiting. Henry had hoped to muster more of the Welsh to his army, and some had indeed rushed to his flag. Many had not. Nor had the Scots come racing to the Tudor call. They had originally fought the Plantagenets and Edward IV, but King Richard had made peace with them, and most saw no motive for fighting either with the Welsh or with the English. This was not a Scottish battle, and they'd gain no more than their own deaths.

And so, both sides were camped almost within sight of the other, while the troops of Lord William Stanley, the younger brother, stood in great numbers behind the battlefield, under the orders of their lord

VESPERS

to keep aside, back behind the other lines, and not engage unless ordered.

The eagle fluttered its wings, ready for the battle's end and the inevitable blood-soaked bodies lying spread at its feet, open for the scavenge.

Two thousand of Henry's men were experienced French soldiers, under the command of Philibert de Chandée, a leader of some fame both in his own country and abroad. The Earl of Oxford led every other of Tudor's troops except for the Swiss mercenaries who had their own leader. Jasper Tudor kept close to his nephew and the small troop behind him. French, Swiss, Welsh and English Lancastrians, the Tudor forced numbered almost five thousand. After the battle for those not killed, the Swiss would be well paid, and the five hundred or so French criminals would be free of their imprisonment. But it was the Lancastrians who fought for passion.

Richard watched their preparations, and those of his own men. His numbers were greater but not so vast to easily outnumber the others. Some of the smaller lords had received their muster too late, and were only now struggling to leave their homes and march to battle. Richard's force numbered eight thousand, perhaps. It would be enough.

Amidst the flurry, both men and leaders murmured their last prayers, clutched the cross most wore beneath their clothes, marched to the huge carts and took their weapons, filled their quivers, and stomped out to join their lines, pressing and tightening each man to the next, ready for the first run.

Briefly alone with his priest, Richard took Mass, bowed, and prayed not simply for success against the enemy, but for the safety of his friends and lords, his men and his country.

At a mile distant, Henry Tudor took Mass beside his uncle, both praying for victory, but also for a painless death if that was the Lord's decision.

All in place beneath the summer sky, the march began, keeping the lines close and the thumping rhythmic beat of the boots on dry ground. Then the other side, first Oxford's men, the French keeping entirely separate.

As they started to move, each line so close, first slow and then faster, running to their own positions, reorganised, the archers on the rise, noise reached its own crescendo. Then Richard stood tall in his stirrups and raised one arm. A mighty cheer from his men, echoed and rebounded out across the fields, and the cannon fired. Henry's men scrambled away, and the cannon fired again. All along the lines the smoke rose, the stink of sulphur and the screams began.

The third explosion blasted into fire and the smoke was dark. There was blood in the air.

The eagle, startled, flew off but remained within sight of her eventual and extravagant meal not yet spread below. But she could smell blood and knew her feast was close.

Then the archers stepped forwards beyond the cannon and were immediately in position to loose on target, and at once nearly a thousand arrows cut the clouds, cutting even the breeze, high like silver spears attacking from above.

"Loose," cried their leaders, and the men fired, arrows zooming in both directions, some even able to pierce armour.

Beyond range of the enemy cannon, Philibert ordered his men to circle behind both the enemy's front lines and load their crossbows ready.

The English longbow men fired directly into Oxford's army and the small group of Yorkist artillery shot at the French as they circled the field. The flight of the arrows, deadly on both sides, pierced and killed. Then the archer's flanks retired as they grabbed what other weapons they could see either from the carts, from the dead or from the boggy grass. Now even where the marshlands paled, the grasslands turned to mud beneath the tramp and skirmish of boots, and many of the cartwheels were stuck.

Pierced by the great force of the arrows, men tumbled, clutched at their wounds, cried out and fell, their battle ending unmercifully soon.

Then the French troops crashed down on the marching lines of the English, fighting hand to hand. Each faction fought as they could, sword to pike, knife to axe, eyes of hatred or fear staring through each visor. A dying man watched as his own throat was ripped open, the heat of his blood weeping from neck to shoulders. As he died, next to him was the struggle to spin a knife into one man's jowls while locking his own sword with battle-axe and armoured knuckles.

Falling on his killer, a man with chest sliced to his ribs, could knock over and trap the one who had killed him. The crying eyes of a young man in pain would lock with the tears of another, and the son of a Lancastrian would recognise the son of his Yorkist neighbour, once a friend.

The stink of cannon fire and the stink of the smoke merged with the stink of sweat, the blood still wet and the blood sticky and then solid beneath the sun. There was vomit from men and from horses, and the shit of those dying in their own muck. Then, as the heat blazed down, what should never have been there began to cook, and smelled even more foul.

A line of men armed with guns, gazed down waiting for their signal to shoot. But a gun could backfire, and the man who fired it, however courageous, might lose his fingers, his hand, or his life. Yet when that gun opened fire and the sulphur blazed like an oven bursting alive, so someone would die, beneath the filth of the smoke.

Now noise was also an attack as men died shouting, the screams of those suffering would stop abruptly as death conquered everything, or another would lie weeping, his death as slow as the memory of the wife he'd never see again. As a horse screamed, the man squashed below would try to rise but find both legs broken and his horse now dead, its blood pouring into its owner's mouth, drowning the man as the horse died with him.

Death stank. Pain stank. No battle ran to order. Men cheered, praised themselves as they saw the point of their own sword sink into the eye of the man trying to kill first. Then into the grass below were the dead man's brains, a glutinous mess of bloody grey slime, and the last twitch of the feet.

Overall slammed the pounding thunder of men killing and being killed, no longer marching but rushing forwards or skirting back, the order which had kept them as one solid mass, too formidable to separate. Ten pikemen, solitary five for each side, rode the outskirts to force deserters back into the skirmish, but few were running. The weight of the battle held them as they thrust two handed with sword, Halberd, even a hay rake.

Less than two hours perhaps, and no clear sign of advantage. But then a howl rose, sank, and rose again. Two heralds rushed to tell the English king. His great and trusted leader, the mighty Duke of Norfolk, leading the vanguard and fighting like a wild boar himself, had died at Oxford's hands and now lay at the duke's feet, his skull and helmet crushed in a bloody trail.

It was bitter news. "Take this information to the Duke of Northumberland," Richard ordered the heralds. There existed no moment to mourn. That would come later. "He must be ready to close ranks and attack from the rear."

The heralds turned their mounts and rode into the smoke.

Without their leader, many of Norfolk's men now paused, shrank back, unbelieving or unwilling. Yet others raced towards the enemy, furious at the death of their lord. A man would stare into the unknown face of a frightened opponent, and slam his sword into those fluttering eyes. Another, pissing as he ran, would slam a hammer onto a stranger's head, then fall in pain as the next in line speared him, the point to his heart.

The king sat astride his courser, his battle-axe across his knees. Beside him, all mounted, sat his greatest warriors. Lord Leays sat silent, his visor closed, his black stallion snorting and kicking at the turf as his master held the reins tight to the side, his other hand with his sword already raised. So Andrew waited only for one word, and that was to charge.

The Earls of Lincoln and Surrey sat to the other side, each with

VESPERS

their visors closed, concentrated only on their king. Sir Richard Tempest sat his own charger directly behind, and although younger and less experienced, the Earl of Desford aside his stamping destrier, sat to Tempest's right.

The standard bearer, holding high the banner of the King of England, with the white boar and the arms of Gloucestershire bright shining against the cross of St. George, also waited beside his monarch for the order to charge.

The battle already lay scorched with bodies strewn beneath the August sun. Death was a heaving nightmare. Where cannon fire had found its mark, bodies lay in heaps, dead upon dead, others blown apart.

The Tudor invader was using the French, England's most common enemy, to kill the people he called his own. Yet now Henry Tudor, once Earl of Richmond before his exile and the attainder of his title, sat mounted within a large group of his bodyguards. He could see little beyond the heads of those around him, yet well protected, he stayed safely where he was.

There was no indication of success or failure, only of the battlefield splitting across the countryside, pockets of men fighting beneath the bushes, wading the streams and the marsh where blood coloured everything black except for the corpses which lay thick with mud, already half buried.

Dominic, standing in his stirrups and bending forwards, murmured to his king. "The Tudor bastard sits aside and doesn't expect to be attacked. He can't fight. He can't use sword or axe and is too cunning to leave himself exposed. He cowers there. I see only the top of his head."

The king's eyes narrowed. He wore the simple gilded substitute battle crown that sat neatly on his helmet, as he made no attempt to hide his title, nor the obvious target he made of himself. Henry Tudor was no shining target, instead closed and almost unseen between the shoulders of those taller.

"I see him," Richard said, his voice grating from within the helmet. "He hides as a coward does."

Dominic spoke again, voice as soft as could be heard over the tumult. "My king, I believe we are ready."

"We need only your word, sire." The Earl of Surrey sat close. His stallion, decorated and armoured, was snorting and impatient.

Andrew, tall in the saddle, stared ahead, waiting.

Richard spoke loudly, turning to those behind him. "The dead are too many. I see William Stanley's men close but standing back. His usual trick,. If we show him success, he'll join us. And while Tudor lives, too many others die."

"Northumberland guards the rear, but sire, you've called on him to advance. Yet I see no movement. Does he threaten treason, or has he lost sight of his duty?"

"A young duke and perhaps with less experience than he claimed."

"Now. Forwards, as arranged," Richard told his closest companions. Immediately he stood up from his stirrups, addressing those around and behind him. Calling, "Now we charge to protect our people and our land." His voice rang out in the breeze, "We fight here, not for our lives, but for the lives of thousands. For the lives of our people, of those we love, and for those who will die on these fields unless we kill the enemy first. You are England's proudest. We ride to save lives. " His voice caught the wind and shuddered like rolling thunder across the hillside.

He paused just one moment, pulling on his coat of arms over the silver sun beams of his armour. This silent declaration was understood by every man across the fields, and by the bodyguard protecting Tudor. It was a battle cry beyond all others. No retreat. This would be a fight to the death.

The reins of his stallion in one steel closed hand, his battle axe raised in the other, Richard began to ride. Golden sunlight sprang across the ring of his battle crown, and picking up speed, he stretched out his axe from the sloping grassy peak of the small hill as the movement began. Each horse stepped forwards. Each rider raised his sword, pointing his steel, the flash of reflected sunshine blinding those below.

The first steps, spurs pressing, the great destriers began the charge. One step. Two, the horses walked. The walk immediately turned to trot. The steam swirled out from nostrils, throats wide, and then, gathering rage, further forward and greater speed.

Eighty stallions now galloping, their speed whistled with the wind, hooves raced, thunder swelled, down the grassy hillside towards the small throng protecting the invader, which had kept so carefully distant from those screaming and dying.

Tudor, watching through the closed visor, jumped from his horse to make a smaller target. Before him massed the thunder of hooves, great lines of dust clouds rising over the vibration of the charge. The destriers' plaited, tussled manes blew out in streams behind them as they cut the wind. The charge, every second closer, every second louder, was a hurricane of fury.

Into the blaze of the sun rode the king's standard bearer, the great banner held high and flung back in the wind. So close behind they rose almost together, King Richard mirrored the banner as the sun caught the rich colours of the embroidery and the shimmer of the small golden crown above the flashing silver of armour. Every other man charged behind, screaming out their battle cries, flags and banners dancing high, horses snorted and roared, their riders roared as loudly, it seemed the sky opened, and the breezes were overtaken by the storm of the great attack.

Seen and heard as the coming of death, now inches from the bodyguards, Richard raced into the squash, shouting for Tudor to find his courage and draw his sword, so to face the attack and the challenge of England's king. At sight of the great sweeping danger heading towards them, De Chandee sent his best pikemen to surround Tudor and those ordered to protect him, a hundred men Swiss trained, with pikes as long as trees. They closed ranks in a three pointed palisade, too tight to break through and too late for any to swerve. The troop of pikers, one knee bent to the mud, remained still and silent, the great steel points outstretched.

Half the charging horses were speared in minutes, steel right through their bodies and out the other side, fountains of blood and the screams of dying horses and their riders. Ahead the king astride White Surrey had charged through before the pikes were raised within one mighty circle, and drove through the swirl of bodyguards, one aim now directly before him. His battle axe outstretched, Richard of England charged the ring protecting Henry Tudor, his visor down, his knees clamped to the destrier's sides, riding ever faster. His standard bearer beside him, he forced his own path towards Henry Tudor beside his own standard bearer.

Richard spurred his horse, killing the Tudor standard bearer who crashed to the grass beneath the flying banner, and then directly charged the first bodyguard, a giant of a man who died immediately beneath Richard's axe, beheaded like a traitor.

Yet for many of those in that battle charge who had not been able to avoid the Swiss pikes, it was their own speed, galloping forward, that killed themselves. Pike speared into bodies, faces and the horses themselves who lay thrashing, hooves now kicking out to enemy and friend alike. Both men and horses screamed. One horse ran free, its rider dead, leaving the manic cries of power and pain, racing across the fields towards freedom.

Other pikes were hurled aside, and Richard pounded onwards, his axe blade dark with dancing blood as he killed the next two men guarding their cringing leader. Already charging against him was the third protector, heaving over the dragon banner which lay thick with mud and blood. But the king thrust past, and his axe was one bloody point from Henry Tudor's life.

Bodies tumbled, blood spurted. Dominic veered his destrier, avoiding the pikes and encircling the groups around Tudor. He killed one, sword to neck as his helmet toppled and the sun sparkled red on the neck and down the shining breastplate. Dominic saw Andrew across the circle and raised his sword to him. Andrew nodded and headed directly towards the centre. The noise was too great for speech, the chaos too great for signals. Only Richard could be seen as the amazing pinnacle of that swirling crush of action.

Then once again everything changed. Reaching across the neck of his stallion, Richard had killed those three standing directly between himself and his enemy. Henry Tudor stumbled back as Richard's axe was inches from its aim. Then as the king rose, standing again in his stirrups to reach out and over, the attack against him came from behind. The clash of metal against metal was against the king, and the crashing weight, also against Richard, was an onslaught of inescapable violence. Concentrated only against him, the new hoard, a mass of hurtling bodies all against just one, ran, shouting, seemingly invincible.

Hauled from the saddle, thrust downwards into the mud, ten men pressing with massive weight onto his back, no longer a battle but instead a bestial bombardment, Richard breathed out and abruptly knew his own death.

Only moments before he had known his own victory. Now he breathed silently into the small cup of his helmet before that was wrenched from his head. Those enemies now lost in the determination of brutality, thrust their swords into the back of his skull, one very deep, one hard and just above the neck.

The attack continued, but Richard was already dead.

Those remaining from the great charge, stood staring in horror. Dominic from one side, followed by six of the Yorkist lords, and Andrew with five lords from the northern edge, first paralysed with disbelieving shock, all then headed further into the scrum, horses kicking, a hundred men screaming, others running either forwards or back. And so just for those few moments, the fighting continued.

Then it slowed, shrugging into disbelief yet recognising the pointlessness of further action. Their king had gone. Nothing now remained worthy of battle. There was nothing to fight for.

Dominic and Andrew, together now, came to Richard's side but were forced back. They realised instantly who they faced. These were not the Welsh, singing of their success, nor the Swiss pikers now retiring, moving backwards into their own formations, this was the jubilant army of William Stanley, who had stood far back, watching the battle until he knew who was winning, and whether he could utterly ensure his own success.

Six thousand of Stanley's men had been mustered. Six thousand now hollered and laughed. They finally felt the thrill of a victory previously denied them. They had no specific hatred of their king, but after standing at a considerable distance for two hours in the blistering heat, ordered to keep utter silence and rigid order, the invitation to prove their strength was irresistible.

Very slowly the vicious noise, the bombardment, the rush of fury and the slash of hatred slowed. Men stood close or at a distance as word of failure, and of success, was murmured across the fields.

The Earl of Oxford marched forwards, taking Henry Tudor's shoulder. Together they talked of the future, but Henry Tudor had seen his own death galloping towards him, and now prayed, thanking God and all the saints while King Richard lay in the marsh at his feet.

It had never been truly expected and now the excitement swirled into unbelievable elation. Tudor breathed hard and fast, ordered the dead king's armour removed, and pulling forwards the great destrier, the king's war horse, from the mire stuck around its hooves, it was ordered that Richard's dead body be slung across the horse's back as they rode to announce their victory at Leicester.

Astonishment and bitter disappointment spread amongst those thousands loyal to their king, and those not wounded now inhaled deeply, stood for long moments half unbelieving, many crying both for their king and for themselves. The horrified hush spread liked dark clouds, then split as the roar of success rose in cheers.

Those slumped in devastated and exhausted sorrow then began, heads down, to leave the battlefield, wiping their eyes on the backs of their hands, cursed under their breath and cleaned their weapons on the grass or across the backs of those wretched hundreds stretched dead in marsh and field, slope, valley and bush.

VESPERS

King Richard now lay naked across the back of his own horse, led by the reins as Stanley's men marched east. White Surrey, confused, carried his beloved master but obeyed the rigid orders of strangers.

From beside the stagnant reek of the battleground, many men stood in sad disgust as the whole world passed into miserable confusion before them. Richard's body lay pale, face down, as it was taken away into the bright sunlight and shadows. The body was well muscled, strong and impressive, but the spine was mis formed at one side, causing one shoulder higher than the other. Some pointed. Those who would miss him so dreadfully remained still as the destrier passed, crossed themselves, and prayed that their king would find happiness with his wife and son in the life beyond death.

Andrew moved closer to Dominic. He removed his helmet and stood very still as the sun sprinkled his tears with its own reflections.

Dominic had also removed his helmet, and was tear streaked. He waited, head down, as his slaughtered king passed. He watched the rise and fall of the naked body, blood streaked and humiliated. Yet more than eight thousand of the king's men knew their sovereign as a hero of justice, and had loved him, knowing they could never love the usurper, now unsure of the Lord God's motive.

The Holy God had first claimed the young prince, then the sweet wife, and now the monarch himself. It would, they knew, be a sweet family gathering on the other side of purgatory. Men removed their helmets and bowed as the king passed. But the victors snorted, and trudged behind their new leader, many still nursing their own wounds.

As the king's bleeding remains were led slowly away, more of his men rushed forwards, then stood in disbelief, horrified not only for the loss of their monarch but with fear for the future. More and more came to the roadside, standing in silent misery and disbelief. Andrew murmured, "We have not only lost our king, but we have also lost our own futures. With this fool in charge, what happens to our country? Are we attained, executed, or exiled?"

"The absolute brutality of Stanley's last moment treason leaves me dumb," Dominic said. "Yes, he's had arguments with Richard before, some huge, and never loved him. But he's fought beside the Yorkists often enough and this time swore to do so. Yet this Tudor creature is his brother's stepson. That inevitably guarantees him great rewards."

"I imagine it does. Although probably not beyond the next argument. With both Stanleys, some future clash is inevitable."

Dominic sighed with bitter loss. "And not of any consequence to us." His tears caught the sun.

"I'll not risk my men rounded up for gaol or for hanging by these wretched victors," Andrew said. "I'll lead them home, then I'll weep in bed beside my wife."

Dominic nodded. "I've no wife so will weep alone," he said softly.

Without speaking, both men watched the disappearance of their king, crossing themselves.

They then, heads low, blood still smearing their armour, rallied their men and trod the range of the strewn battlefield, a mile west where the dead bodies stretched across rise and fall, ditch, stream and marsh, and as the battlefield cleared, they took the road south towards London.

All across Leicestershire and into Warwickshire troops plodded, across the ruined fields of the local farms, slaughtered sheep and cattle left to rot, ready for the hungry victors and the scavengers waiting above.

Abruptly Dominic stopped and dropped to one knee, pushing back a great thorn bush, breaking the twigs and thrusting his hands beneath the pointed leaves. The thorns did not cut him as he thrust and pushed, pulling on what he had seen. Still within their armour, his hands grasped whatever lay beyond.

Gimlett lay twisted to one side, his body racked and thick with baked blood. One arm had been hacked from its great shoulder, the huge muscles chopped apart. The arm was raised with the hand still gripping the sword. But as the one-armed body was twisted beneath the thorn bush, the head had been wrenched the other way, the throat cut so deep both windpipe and larynx were spurting out like animals escaping from their cage. Yet the face was strangely peaceful, eyes open, watching the dance of the leaves in the breeze and the rich colour of the sun-stroked sky gazing down where it could. They smiled at each other, Gimlett and the sky.

His mouth was a little open, blood soaked and sweat soaked, a better meal, perhaps, than so often.

Dominic sank further to the ground and once more wept quietly. He stayed while Andrew waited, but then, with the tears still wet on his face, he whispered goodbye and remounted, again joining Andrew as they rode south. Their horses, exhausted as they were themselves, plodded along the London road.

The eagle flew down, silent, to find the dead meat spread before it. Other predators began to sweep in beneath the sun's glitter, eagles, falcons and buzzards, each careful of another more powerful, ravaging and ripping at bodies and faces. Cautious at first, the foxes slipped from the trees and their shadows.

Tudor's men, those unhurt, stomped the ground, searching beneath the bushes and kicking at the banks of swamp and stream as they searched for the enemy still gasping for those last moments of life. They killed the men already a breath from death, and those lying so close to dead, groaning and begging for help, yet unable to stand. Saving those on the point of death, friend and foe both, would help few since the medicine that would await, would never conquer the wounds now seen.

Then amidst the howls and final sobs, they hurriedly examined what was carried, reaching inside armour and jerkins, chain mail and boots, finding precious stones on rings and crosses, bundles of money, and silver handled daggers. They stole whatever they could, then moved on to the next. Some discovered King Richard's tent, and pushed inside, grabbing whatever they found.

The bodies were then dragged to their graves, those of their enemies dug into one great hole where the battle had ended, the dead of the winning side carted to the nearest church for burial in consecrated ground.

Surrounded by his guards, Henry Tudor felt the sense of glory so strong, his heartbeat pounded like a galloping courser. William Stanley rode behind, knowing that success was his and his alone.

Dominic, Andrew and their men along with many others, were already marching home, their heads dizzy with the terrible loss which had change their lives.

Chapter Twenty Six

That night both Dominic and Andrew stayed at an inn along the way, a scramble of staff summoning food and drinks, not having expected such arrivals, and more frightened of brutal retaliation and drunken fury from all those leaving the field.

The Leays and Desford men made camp outside, resting on the warm ground. Utterly exhausted, most slept like the dead, but others rocked themselves, unable to forget their friends who lay dead on the field. Bitter for the loss, they silently tried to sleep away their shame and misery.

Their lords took a room within the inn and ordered food, ale for their men and wine for themselves. They sat alone at the small wooden table, and spoke, soft voiced, of the pity they felt, and the dismal probability of a wretched future.

Two men had entered, they heard the footsteps behind them, looked over their shoulders, then returned to their cups. But one of the men spoke loudly, coming to the table, his voice loud and forceful.

"You are the Earl of Desford, my lord?"

Dominic looked up. "I am, sir. But I doubt I know you." He had no wish to make acquaintance with anyone now, nor from either side.

The smell of the battlefield hung. Drifting over those who had fought. Worse was the bilious memory and the stagnant exhaustion. The pain of wounds remained like a heavy black cloak on every man's shoulders.

The man stood tall. His armour was blood stained but it did not appear to be his own. He held his helmet, his sword thrust, also blood stained, through his baldric. He was pale haired, his face seemed twisted, and a long cut scarred his jaw. Seemingly elderly, his pale eyebrows closed in scrubby wedges across his nose, and his eyes were pale blue frost. He spoke loudly.

Beside him the other man wore no battle clothes, and stood shorter, half smiling. Andrew recognised him immediately. "Bishop Morton? Back in this country so soon after you're escape?"

Bishop Morton sneered, one booted foot pushing up onto the bench. "You think I had nothing to do with our victory? I have worked for Henry Tudor since King Edward's death, and will see Tudor crowned as our new monarch."

"A bishop who cheers invasion, backs blood and forgets the love of God he should be preaching." Dominic glared without standing.

"And from now on you'll be mighty careful if you want to live," the bishop spoke through gritted teeth. "It'll be me, you fool, who will help run this country. I shall be our new sovereign's right hand man."

"Then I hope Tudor is left-handed," Andrew said, scowling.

But it was the other man who spoke, pushing forwards. "And I am the Earl of Plymouth, sir, and although you may not know me, I know you well."

Dominic stood. His own armour had been partially removed, his sword left in the room above, and only a narrow cut against the back of his neck still showed smears of blood.

He said, "Never having met you before as far as I remember, my lord, I cannot interpret your fury. And no doubt you know me as little as I know you."

"You know nothing about it then," said the man. He was as tall as

Dominic, but his hair, free of the helmet's restrictions, now sat tousled in its pale matt curls, and threads had been glued by blood to the wound at his neck and chin. "You insulted and thwarted my cousin, and it's been sometime since I decided to ensure your punishment."

"I know your name but not you're nature, my lord." Dominic stared. "Several have recently warned me of you. I have no interest in petty revenge, but do I thank you for imprisoning me in that stone cave, half starved? What cowardly retaliation. And who, sir, is your cousin?"

Now the other man was laughing, not with humour but with fury. "My second cousin on my mother's side is the Sheriff Kettering, my lord is the new King Henry the seventh, and my intention is to throw you in the Tower until you promise loyalty and ask pardon for your arrogance."

Bishop Morton's hard jawed face was immediately creased in delight. "You sob for your failure? Then know this, you'll bend your knees to our new monarch, the Lancastrian. Victory is ours, and every man in England will know it and cheer for King Henry."

But Dominic sighed, sitting back at the table. His platter was empty, but he lifted his cup of wine and drank, his back to Plymouth and the bishop. It was Andrew who then answered.

"I presume you're aware that your cousin is a mangey rat full of corruption? We may now have a king who will forgive corruption, but there are still many who will not. Fate does not always side with the wicked."

Plymouth slapped both hands, palms down, onto the table between Andrew and Dominic. "You'll get no proof and in future no doubt I'll deny it," he hissed directly into Dominic's ear, "but for now, you log headed clout, know this. Yes, Lord Maddock and I arranged your imprisonment. Not to die, but to suffer what you deserve in that quarry pit." He spat on the table, then stood back with a grin of success.

First pausing, then Dominic spoke very softly, his voice as icy as his gaze. "You, sir have been a traitor for most of your miserable life. Now I know you are a foul criminal. Yet while I understand Maddock's childish and disgusting motives, I know you only as a traitor and a fool. I'll not speak with you again."

Andrew and Dominic remained sitting and turned away, speaking to each other while noticeably ignoring interruptions. Almost immediately the Earl of Plymouth and Bishop Morton left, but Plymouth shouted back, "We'll meet again, Desford. Prepare yourself. I am not one who forgets. You'll be in the Tower within the week."

They had gone when Andrew sighed. "You know nothing of this creature?"

"I still know nothing." Dominic paused, thinking, and added, "I know him to be a traitor, a fool, and a bastard. Had I known sooner of his guilt concerning that damned gravel pit, he'd have been beheaded on the block by now. Yet I still know nothing of his motives and cannot ever remember meeting him in the past."

"We saw little or nothing of him before, I presume, since he removed himself to Brittany, and backed Tudor. I only wish I'd met him on the battlefield. He would assuredly be dead now, even if I'd had no knowledge of whom I'd killed." Andrew ordered more wine, and raised his glass to his friend. "Beware any excuse this bastard dreams up to have you thrown in the Tower. Whether Tudor would make such an order without reason, we cannot know."

"I know as little of Tudor as I know of Plymouth," Dominic said quietly. "But I know what I suffered in that damned incarceration Plymouth ordered. I've wondered who could have arranged that, and why, ever since. Now I'd gladly kill the wretch myself."

It was on the morning of Tuesday, the twenty third of August that London heard the news of their loss and the king's death. They stood in amazement at the doors of their houses, or rushed inside to barricade their safety.

Victorious foreign troops on the march would rape and kill, destroy cottages and steal possessions. But already there were deaths from other causes, and they said more were now dying from a new disease. Some called it the Sweating Sickness. Some called it The Tudor Death.

Jetta had climbed from the first-floor window without trouble, inserting and twisting the point of her smaller knife to click the opening catch. There had been no padlock nor proper lock, but a small window unopened for years acts as its own fortification. Jetta, however, was experienced in such matters. This had opened for her without too much trouble.

"You see," she told it very softly as she climbed through, "nothing can stop a determined mind."

The only thing that slowed her down had been the size of the glass square, welcoming head and shoulders, but leaving little space for pelvis and legs. She wriggled forwards. The risk of falling became a genuine danger. Even Jetta realised the threat. She held to the top edge of the open window and continued to ease herself out. Stretching out one arm, she had grasped a tree branch. The whole thing felt absurdly perilous but with a snatch of bravado, she stretched out her other hand – and grabbed. Pulling, knees over a branch and holding tightly, her head swung out, and with a gasp of gratitude for success, Jetta sat in the sycamore tree and smiled.

Nobody had seen her, or she'd have been in the arms of some lout. With nothing except her stockings beneath those flowing skirts, she had revealed what no woman wants to reveal. She was laughing anyway as she ran quickly to the other side of the house and out onto the road.

She had then crept the cobbles from the Maddock house and through Cripplegate, intending to head north towards the old Marsh. It was at the great gate where she heard the news.

"They say that Welsh bastard has killed the king."

The crowds gathered, whispering, shouting, one woman screaming. "Will we all be raped in our beds?"

"We'll all be sent to Newgate?"

"What of the king?"

"They say he's dead, killed by the Stanleys."

"It was treason then. Stanley turned."

Jetta leaned against the old wall, looking around in disbelief. It would be pointless to ask about the other knights. Surely no one yet could give a list of the dead. Head down, she ran through the Cripplegate with tears streaking her cheeks.

Dominic and Andrew would both be known as faithful Yorkists, even Gimlett and Ned. She continued to cry, and as she ran the tears and sniffs stifled her and she stopped, gasping for breath.

With almost nobody about, she sat on the wide ledge that banked the road, dropped her face in her hands, and wept for the king. But now she was going nowhere, had no reason to run north or east. And so, she turned, heading back to Chiswick, praying that the information given her was mistaken.

Jetta did not understand how a small Welsh nobody from bastard stock could claim a throne, and grasp victory against some of the strongest knights in the land.

Yet she believed in the great wheel of fortune knowing that although the mighty Lord God punished the wicked and praised the pure, He never explained His plans.

It was supper time when she arrived again at Dominic's home, ambling slow, listening to the gossip along the way, but hurrying past Westminster Palace in case something had already changed.

And then, once home, and as she slid to the settle and laid her head on the cushion, closing her eyes, she heard Benson's voice and sat up with a sigh.

"It's true, isn't it, Benson?"

"Madam, it is, both parts of the devastating news are true, and I cannot even convey my sorrow at what has happened."

Now Jetta sat up straight, gazed up at the steward, and whispered, "Oh, Benson, he's not – killed – is he?"

Benson gazed back. "Our great lord king – yes. But our own lord Desford – no. At least that one devastation has not occurred, miss. It would be the end of the world indeed. But the Tudor invader has won the battle with his French army, and now marches south to claim London."

"And the other terrible news?"

"Miss Jetta, I cannot guess the right thing to do. It is our lady, the countess, who lies mortally sick. I have called the medic, but he is not one of fame, for those all travelled with the army and our king. But Doctor Frayman believes the lady will die any moment."

"I don't understand, what happened?" Jetta asked. She stood in a hurry, almost tripping, and ran towards the stairs. "She's in her bedchamber?"

"Indeed, yes," Benson said, "but miss, you can't risk going there. They say the sickness leaps one to another. No doctor fully understands, for it appeared in just days and we've never known it before. It was brought by the French, they say, carried in parcels, opened and blown out when they arrived on English soil."

"I have to talk with the doctor at least."

Brushing past him, she marched the stairs, her brain in a swirl. Stopping at the countess's door, she knocked. At first there was no answer, so she called. "Is Doctor Frayman there? I need to speak to him. Urgently." With no idea how she stood on the ladder of authority, she knew only that she was no servant.

A muffled voice answered. "My lady, are you the lady's daughter? Please come in, but as we've no idea how this sickness spreads, you had better stand by the door and don't enter too far." Jetta entered and stood obediently just one step inside the door. The room was stifling, everything closed, including the bed curtains on the far side. No candle was lit, and only dark shadows remained unmoving. The doctor continued, "It's the sweating sickness, my lady, and we know almost nothing about it. We believe it was brought by the foreign army."

The smell coiled up from the bed like smoke from an oven and made Jetta nauseas. "I'm not a lady, sir. But the countess is my friend and protector. How can I help?"

"There's nothing to do, mistress," the doctor muttered into his collar. "I'll speak with you downstairs. Staying here is dangerous."

Splutters drifted from the bed where the woman was muffled, naked arms waving from the eiderdown. "I'm so hot, Dominic. Get me free of this ghastly fire."

"Her ladyship is suffering from a violent fever," the doctor explained, following Jetta to the door.

Again, the countess called. "I'm in a lake where the water boils. It's cruel. Michael, help me. Bring me cold water."

"Sir Michael was her husband, the first Earl," Jetta whispered. "The countess is always a little vague with her memory."

"Rightly so, miss," the doctor told her. "The poor lady's not likely to recover." He hurried to the main doors, eager to leave. Turning briefly, he added, "Folk burn and then the freeze. Swathes of sweat turn to ice. Folks start the sickness in the morning and by the evening, they're dead."

Turning away, Jetta thanked him but felt no gratitude. This was a doctor who had no idea how to help. If he was right, there was no one able to help at all. Shivering, not with the cold but with nervous fury, she stood a moment, wondering what more might become a disaster.

The battle was lost. The countess was suffering, and the poor woman might die. Jetta would be alone.

But not alone for long. She had escaped the Maddocks and soon Dominic would be home. There were blessings beside the tragedies.

Back in the main hall, Jetta wiped her eyes and sat again on the settle. When Benson came to her call, she ordered wine, and when he returned she asked him to wait. "Please tell me everything," Jetta said. Her fingers gripped at her skirts, the tears already in her eyes.

"How long has her ladyship been ill? And what do you know of this sickness?"

"You're right Miss. It's the sweating sickness. I heard of a house nearby where three died within a few short hours. It was the shivering first, a cold like ice. The poor girl cried and said as how her little neck screamed at her, she was in agony and her head was running in circles. The same doctor that came here, miss, told me he gave her a mixture of willow bark and poppy seed, thinking perhaps she simply had a cold. Her mother helped and wrapped her in three blankets from her own bed. But the girl tossed and turned and cried out and then began to sweat. The sweating was so feverish, the secretions ran down her face and neck and she screamed that she was burning. Within moments she could hardly speak and was gasping for air. After another hour, the child was dead, and the mother was experiencing the same symptoms. Telling me all this, the doctor said as how he was terrified of catching the awful sickness himself."

"And she died too?" Jetta winced.

"She did indeed, and her second daughter after her. When his lordship comes home from the battle, he'll find a worse misery than he faced up there."

"Yet you have not caught it." Jetta squeezed her hands together. "And the countess?"

"It's the dreadful end, miss. As for me, maybe the Lord God has other plans. You go in there to look after her, you'll no doubt die beside her, so I suggest, if I may, you stay out. If her ladyship is still blessedly alive tomorrow, maybe she'll survive. Some do. Most don't."

Jetta finished her wine and noticed that her fingers were shaking. Quickly she placed the cup back on the table. Benson had always been efficient and loved his lord, but had been aloof as though he considered her unworthy, and an interloper. Now he spoke as though, quite suddenly, he was her friend. Disaster had obviously changed his attitude.

He asked her, "More wine, mistress?"

"Yes please, Benson," Jetta held out her empty cup. It seemed the only way to pull her thoughts from the inevitable.

Finally, having drunk herself tipsy and avoiding the countess's bedchamber and her own arguments and desperate guilt, she scrambled into her own room and fell onto the bed, not bothering to crawl under the covers. The day was warm. It would have been exceedingly pleasant, she decided, if only it had not been so monstrously unpleasant. Unpleasant? No, far, far worse than that.

She curled as though hiding from the cruelty of the world, not caring about her clothes since they were already torn, creased and basically ruined by the beast of a sheriff and Percival Maddock, and the ridiculous business of climbing out of small windows.

Now she was wondering if any of the servants had caught this wretched sickness and could pass it to everyone else, but then, her thoughts in chaos, she eventually fell into a deep sleep.

It was when she woke some hours later that Jetta found Benson and asked him if anyone else had been ill. "Has the doctor returned?"

The twilight was creeping between the trees outside, turning sunshine to shadow, and shadows to night. A slight chill ran up the stairs, but near the kitchen fires it was warm and bright. Benson seemed shrunk in misery. "Yes, mistress. The first who caught it three days past was a cleaner, and she tumbled down the stairs, poor lass. Then a young kitchen boy. Afterwards that boy's brother, who was a groom. All dead, miss, and in their caskets in the church. But now our lady, which is so much worse."

Jetta was whispering again, as if she didn't dare ask aloud. "And have you looked in on the countess since? Or called the doctor back?"

"I've not, Madam. But I will if you tell me."

"Thank you, but-," Jetta sighed. "I'll do it myself."

This time, instead of rushing, Jetta tiptoed slowly up the stairs and stopped outside the countess's door. For some moments she stood very still, listening. There was no sound of any kind. And so, with great care, Jetta opened the bedchamber door and peeped inside.

The darkness of before was hanging in huge swathes around bed and walls, windows and doors. The door to the garderobe stood ajar, but there was the same utter darkness. The bed covers did not move and no sound, even of breathing, broke the feeling of threat. One careful step at a time, Jetta crossed towards the bed. Twice she whispered to the countess, and then risked speaking loudly. There was no answer of any kind.

Unwillingly, not wanting to face the possibility, though needing to know, Jetta continued and took two deep breaths as she crossed to the bed.

Lying on her back, the countess stared upwards, eyes glazed and unseeing. Both withered hands were relaxed over her chest, yet she seemed so peaceful. She was certainly quite dead. Her mouth lay a little open, the dribble like cracked glass over her lower lip. The sweat remained on her face like a glittering sheen.

The little chair in the bedchamber was not comfortable but Jetta sat and watched the strange emptiness of the face above the eiderdown, its passive rest on the pillow below.

The countess had been a remarkably vocal woman, and although she did not always speak with the best intentions, she had always seemed remarkably alive.

They had never been close friends, but Jetta whispered, "Sleep well, my lady. I wish you beautiful dreams."

It was the amusement of their acquaintance which whispered in her head, the countess's voice as strong as though she was still alive and speaking. *'Where are you girl? You like my warm cloak? Keep it then, and when I die, perhaps ten years hence, I shall leave it with you'*

'Idiot child. Go wash dishes and scrape that smile from your face.'

But then, *'I need you in the litter, child. You should be my granddaughter. Your company keeps away my headaches.'*

She backed away. Then at the doorway, she turned. "Your grandson will be disturbed, I think, at your death. I'm sure he will miss you very much."

If he's alive himself, she thought as she whispered goodbye, and abruptly tiptoed back to the bed, holding her breath, and bent down, lightly kissing the dead woman's wrinkled forehead.

She knew it was a risk, but she also knew that more than half the men of the country had risked their lives days past, and many would never return, leaving wives and mothers sobbing and desperate. Quickly she turned and hurried downstairs to a household both in mourning, and wrapped in fear.

Chapter Twenty Seven

The victorious French and Swiss troops camped near Nottingham, arranged their departure, and sailed back to their homes. Henry Tudor's troops marched to the outskirts of Westminster and northern London, camping there until they knew where their new leader would be.

In Leicester, the church of the Greyfriars opened their doors to their king, and the body of King Richard III was brought in to lie in state beneath the pulpit and the cross of Jesus Christ. The wounds were terrible, but the friars washed the body, and permitted those who had loved him and fought for him, and survived themselves, to walk slowly past, cross themselves, and wish their lost monarch a happier life beyond death than he had known before it.

For some days the body lay, then it was quickly covered in a roll of soft material and was buried within the church.

Henry Tudor had problems. He had lived long in exile, spoke poor English and knew nothing of the English countryside. Nor did he know of normal practise for royalty, for acceptable procedures. Henry Tudor executed those he could and announced his right to the throne from the day before the battle when Richard III was still living. This would give him the improper authority to claim that every single man having fought honestly for his king and country could suddenly be counted a traitor.

Shortly after, he was dissuaded from this, and accepted that he might only claim the throne by right of conquest, and not by inheritance or by blood.

"He might have been a loose tongued idiot by name of Master Henry Smith," Dominic muttered as he and Andrew approached the long roads banking the Thames, and so approaching their own homes.

"I shall miss Richard," Andrew said, "desperately, both as a private friend and as the best monarch this country has enjoyed for many, many years. The anger and the disappointment will breed its own dismal doubts. But I have a wife I adore and a son I long to see again, so I'll soon be in the arms of those I love, and will have soft shoulders to lament on. You have no such help. But come to me, of course."

Dominic smiled. "My grandmother sometimes remembers who I am. And there's – someone else. Not that I've the faintest idea – she has probably left the house. It was a strange time, preparing for battle and possibly death. Then blocking that trickle of fire that wouldn't leave, yet still wanting me, perhaps, to genuinely accept the possibility of such an unlikely state."

"The girl? Jetta? She inspires this confusion? Perhaps she returns your feelings in kind?"

"I doubt it." Dominic remembered. "I must have been a combination of the road to gaol, and the road to freedom."

Remembering gave no ease to either man, just the clang of metal on metal, and the sweet call of the blackbird at dawn. Memories flooded over the wretched present, memories of meeting with their monarch as a friend, discussing matters of state, raising wine cups and laughing over other memories with the man who would always now be just a memory himself.

Neither man had followed the sad destrier, puzzled as it was led

VESPERS

over the battlefield, aware only of the fading presence of the master, and the loss of that deep understanding they had shared. Yet as the stallion plodded where led, it was also aware of the sadness and the disappearance of the master's caress. While Surrey kept his head low, distrustful of the noise and violence of strangers. He was covered in muck from the marsh, and with blood from his master's naked body. Indeed, many thought the king's stallion must have died in the battle, unable to recognise the forlorn and discoloured body as the bright beauty of the royal destrier.

Many had followed and walked into the church where the king's body was brought to lie as though sleeping.

Yet Dominic and Andrew did not attend as their friend lay in state, instead keeping Richard alive in their minds as they rode south, leading their men home.

When Andrew left, riding on towards his home near Westminster, Dominic turned to the open gate of his, wondering almost fearfully what he would find. He had been gone only ten days, but in that time the world had changed entirely. He hoped, with vivid colour, that Jetta would still be living in his home, but felt no sense of optimism and rode slowly on to the stables.

The two grooms and others of his household had followed and fought with him, so now he dismounted, wished them a welcome home, threw them the reins, and marched back to the front doors, lying open, with little more than shadows inside.

Benson, one of the shadows, bowed low, came to hold the door open, and greeted his master. "My lord, I know the news and we have heard both rumour and gossip. But I thank the Lord God for your safe return, sir, and although there is more sad news to relate, the greatest pleasure is to see you here again."

Staring back, Dominic stopped on the doorstep, passed cloak and hat to his steward, and lowered his voice. Only one thought lingered. "So, tell me the sad news, Benson, before I fall over it. I have become accustomed to dread and disappointment."

Somewhat uncomfortable, Benson also lowered his voice, and

bowed once more. "My lord, across the lower half of our land, a new sickness has taken strength. They call it the Sweats, or the Tudor Poison. It crept into this house just a few days ago and attacked three of our staff. To our horror and misery, this sickness also attacked your grandmother, the countess. We called immediately for medical attention, but with terrible sadness, my lord, I must inform you that your grandmother passed away yesterday."

Simply staring, Dominic remained standing in the entrance hall just inside the doorway, finding neither words nor any manner of comfort. He had been ready, on the verge of expectation, to hear that Jetta had died. Now a surge of guilt pushed out the relief.

Striding into the house, one step to the stairs, he looked down at Benson. "She remains in her bedchamber? Or has been removed to St. Nicholas?"

But the voice he heard from the top of the stairs was neither Benson nor any other man, but a voice he immediately recognised.

"She's here, Dominic. I've been keeping her company. But I'll go. This is all so sad, but we're all so terribly relieved that you're – that you've come back."

Dominic did not answer Jetta. His own relief blocked words and needed thought. When he entered his grandmother's bedchamber, only the faintly unpleasant smell hung like another curtain around the bed. He walked over and sat on the side of the mattress, taking the old woman's hand. It was soft and not rigid. Rigor Mortis had already passed. Dominic sat there, staring at the calm face of a woman he'd loved as a mother once, when both his parents had died.

From outside, Jetta heard his first few words. "Well, my dear, now you have the luck I missed, escaping the usurper and new king –,"

Returning to her own bedroom, Jetta lay down and tried not to think of death and devastation. The swirl of sudden relief knowing that Dominic lived and had returned, was not diminished by the knowledge of the enemy's victory. She knew nothing of royal business and trembled only for Dominic's safety. Yet, especially without the watchful company of his grandmother, she had no reason to remain, and she was perfectly sure that on the following day, perhaps after the funeral, he would throw her out.

At his suggestion, she had spied for the king. But her small discoveries had served no one. Before and briefly after, Jetta had dared call Dominic friend, but the battle could have, perhaps would have, changed everything.

Neither sat at the table for supper that evening, and the household remained in mourning. Window shutters were closed. Bright livery was removed, and mahogany replaced it. A white tablecloth also disappeared, and black linen was spread there. Jetta wished she could steal the tablecloth. She owned no dark clothes, so hurried that evening to ask Ilda Pike.

"Oh miss, tis good to see you again, and so good to know the master is alive, and home here. I can lend you a black gown, but it will be far too big for you."

"I'll try and tie it up," Jetta said. "I can't wear red or green."

Trussed with belts and ribbons around a long black gown, its dye fading at the hems, Jetta fiddled the next morning. The clothes and colours of mourning would be to honour the countess, yet there was also his highness, King Richard, whom they would continue to honour. All those who had fought for him would dress in the dark shadows they felt. Most of the country was in silent mourning.

There had been no further word from Dominic, and Jetta had one small, determined plan. She would attend the funeral, almost out of sight as most women did, curtsey to Dominic and thank him for giving her a place of safety to stay, would then pack her bag of possessions, and leave. She would head away from London, and sleep wherever something offered shelter.

The countess's casket was simple due to the number of funerals lately held in churches across the country, but across it was laid a tapestry of flowers and birds, presumably Dominic's choice, though Jetta thought it a great waste to leave such a glorious object in the dark behind stone. She watched it leave the premises, and then hurried back to her own chamber to change and prepare. The actual funeral would take place in three hours, when the abbot would speak at some length. It would be another day before being laid beneath the church tiles, but by then, Jetta thought, she would have left the sweet beauty of the house she had even called home, even for such a short time, the very first, and had enjoyed.

Wearing only a pleated white shift, Jetta had one leg bent up on the little clothes chest, trying to adjust the first garter to hold up her short black stockings, when the door flew open with a crash of thunder that almost made her fall. It felt as though the countess, had come back to life.

"Why the devil," Dominic demanded, eyes cold, "have you not come to see me yet?"

Jetta stared back at him, mouth a little open and eyes wide. "Pardon?"

Now Dominic's brows lowered, his eyes almost closed. He stood at her door, glaring. "You've not even bothered to discover if I'm still alive."

She gulped, almost choking, and stared back. "Not true. I spoke to you from your grandmother's bedchamber when you first arrived home. And you may not have noticed," coldly, "but I'm not dressed."

"Of course I've noticed," Dominic said through gritted teeth. "Do you seriously imagine I don't observe things? I've imagined you undressed a hundred times over the past weeks. I now see that my imagination was not accurate. But not once have you bothered to come and find me."

Although not naked, her arms were entirely bare – an unforgivable sin. Even worse, one leg was uncovered to the knee. Jetta quickly put both legs to the ground, pulled down the hem of her shift, and moved back into the shadows. His words were not helping.

"Go away," she shouted at him. "I've been alone all this time worrying about you and saying my prayers which isn't what I want to do all night and looking after your grandmother, though not very well as you can see, and got dragged off by that disgusting sheriff again, and waited and waited but then I thought I should leave you in peace because you'd seen horrible things and now there's your poor grandmother and the funeral, and you won't want me because you never said you did. You just think I'm a servant who scrubs floors and killed your farrier."

Both stared at each other, more anger than anything, both their voices raised, almost shouting.

Dominic said, "You make no sense."

She said, "How can I when you march in like that after days and days, left here crying."

His voice sank. "You've cried? So have I."

And abruptly, two quick steps, he walked over to where she stood, both his hands to her uncovered shoulders, pushed her backwards onto the bed, leaned heavily across her, and looked down at her, his eyes only an eyelash from hers.

His eyes remained heavily hooded, gazing so closely, intruding, forcing their path inwards, fire and smoke.

Staring back, Jetta did not close her eyes but absorbed his gaze, wanting to swallow every flicker. She had never thought this would happen and she still struggled to believe it.

Her head, back against the eiderdown, Dominic breathed deeply, and then kissed her.

It continued, Jetta thinking she might faint, Dominic drinking it in, drinking her breath and the taste of her tongue, drinking her willingness and the pressure of his body against her breasts.

And then, as abruptly as he had kissed her, he stood back and strode from the room. The door swung shut.

Entirely out of breath, Jetta sat up and stared. She wanted to march out and find him and slap his dammed handsome face and shout at him never to come near her again. To tell him she was leaving, and that he'd never find her. The trouble was that not one word would be true. She wanted to stay, and she wanted him to explain, to kiss her again, and even – perhaps – depending on Teresa – take her as his mistress. What did mistresses do anyway? She could hardly ask Teresa to explain. Teresa hated her now and probably always had.

And how could you ask someone about becoming his mistress in the middle of his grandmother's funeral?

Tasting his mouth still on her lips, Jetta scampered into all her clothes, had no mirror for seeing what sort of mess she looked, and tried to gather a semblance of elegance down the stairs. Benson stood at the bottom, directing each member of the household attending the funeral. Dominic had already gone on ahead. Jetta waited for a quiet moment, reached up and whispered in Benson's ear, "Do I look alright, Benson? These clothes aren't mine and don't fit well."

Pretending suitable civility, he whispered back, "Very acceptable, miss. The hat and gloves will help."

And Jetta hurried to enclose herself within the rest of the crowd until finally Benson locked up and headed towards the local church. It was a small church, not far along the country road and its banks of bush and daisy, its dull old stone awaited the parade. The priest stood at his doorway as the bell tolled. The crowd could be seen from some distance, led by Benson, trotting like a bunch of sheep led out to graze, keeping close and gossiping to each other as they came closer.

Washed, her hair covered by feathers over a black gauze, the countess had been swathed in a white shroud. The countess had, the doctor assured her grandson, received the last rights and the final mass before death. As she lay in a casket of polished wood and on a mattress of flock and down, her body now shrouded, the rest of the household took standing space behind. Dominic sat alone gazing at the casket, and it was behind him that every other person stood in their livery, the bright collars removed, now in the black drapes of their mourning clothes.

The priest said mass and proceeded to speak for some time concerning the immense religious purity of the dead woman, her beauty both physical and parental, and her determination to help all those she knew. Some of this was probably true, but exaggerations were expected. Jetta kept to the back behind most of the staff. She had no place to claim, being neither relative, neighbour, member of staff or household, and actually all she could claim was being a suspected murderer.

Nor was she thinking of the countess. Nor, in fact, of herself. Dominic had kissed her. He had not asked first and nor had he spoken since. After the bitterness of his experiences on battlefield and his dead grandmother's bedside, with his friend the king now dead in the north, Jetta thought perhaps Dominic had turned into a creature of determination while lacking kindness or consideration.

That meant she didn't want him.

Although, as she reminded herself, she did. Yet would be a fool to promise herself to a man who would not give her love, only demands. And might even beat her. And amongst other thoughts was the clarity of one thing more important than all the others, being that he had not actually asked for her. A kiss was a kiss. But there had been no sweet declaration of more.

Back in her own bedchamber she changed once more into her own clothes, sat on her bed, and cried all over again.

Chapter Twenty Eight

Henry Tudor announced himself as King Henry, the seventh of that name, and settled into a mountain of organisation.

Knowing himself a usurper and disliked by the country he had conquered, the new king surrounded himself with a large bodyguard. Whenever he appeared, so did the Yeomen of the Guard, the loyal protectors of a king who feared he might be assassinated at any moment by the people he claimed to rule. Where he walked, the guard walked, and surrounded him as a flowing scarlet wall.

The foreign troops had left, returning to their own countries, and now the Welsh and English Lancastrians slowly salved their wounds, regained their energy, had celebrated their victory by beating those villagers living close, raped their wives, drank as much as they could afford or steal, and began their wander home.

William Catesby, King Richard's loyal Chancellor, was the first to be executed. But after he was advised by his new council, the new king was persuaded out of his somewhat illegal and unjust ruling that his monarchy started the day before it actually did, and instead announced October 30th as the day of his coronation. The advice also included a warning. If too many old enemies were executed, as king he would be loathed and distrusted for life. Henry therefore announced that the lords who promptly gave him their promise of loyalty would not be executed or attainted and could retain most, perhaps all, of their lands.

He had previously pledged his intention to marry Elizabeth, the eldest daughter of King Edward IV, and parliament's official ruling that Edwards marriage had been bigamous and therefore his children illegitimate, was now quickly denied by Henry, wanting Elizabeth as his wife, thus doubling his right as monarch. But his own coronation took place some considerable time before the marriage. He would not risk his own claim being overshadowed by hers.

Henry liked detail but the sort of detail he loved tended to be bland and without flavour or colour. His confidence was born from control, and absolute control now centred in completing detail. He was competent within his limits yet knew nothing of kingship, but he had the tutorship of his mother, Margaret Beaufort. What he didn't know, she did. Settling in with his quill, ink pot and piles of paper and parchment, Henry Tudor knew one thing. He had the power to learn at his own pace, and change the country's habits of a lifetime if he wished.

London and the surrounding villages were nervous and kept to themselves, indoors if they could, not daring to speak against the new king in case they were overheard by spies, captured and tortured. Recriminations had begun, but not as many as expected. Under cautious advice, Henry Tudor began with private lists.

First on the list of those to arrest over the next month, was the name of Dominic, Lord Stark, second Earl of Desford. He had been amongst the closest of those who joined King Richard in the massive charge which had killed him and so many others. But the charge had comprised eighty men streaking down the slope like monsters in some myth, banners flying. Many had somehow survived. There were others he knew to have been particularly loyal to Richard III, but it was in fact Francis Lovell who set off the first rebellion.

Both the Lords of Desford and of Leays, along with many others, waited for their own reckoning.

Chapter Twenty Nine

Standing at his bedchamber window, Dominic looked out on the darkening sky and its first pale silhouette of moon, a scratch of pearl. A blackbird was warbling its last precious claim of territory and the wood pigeons were cooing from the trees. Just a few goodnight calls before the final silence.

But Dominic was murmuring very softly to himself. The rise of an entirely new dynasty seemed haphazard, and yet God had allowed it. And if allowed, then it was surely intended. Which might mean the fall of England, poverty, and misery. Or resilience might conquer the man who had conquered.

Dominic's bedchamber was unlit and only the moonlight slipped uninvited through the window. He leaned there, not entirely steady, nor entirely sober. He had sat in church for longer than he had intended, and on returning home, had called for as much to drink as he thought he might swallow before choking. Dry biscuits and a large jug of wine replenished once empty of all but its crimson smear of dregs.

Now the window, unshuttered, gazed out on darkness and it seemed Dominic could see more than was there. A scuffle of something equally dark ran from under a bush. A young badger, hungry. Above the long-eared owl peeped out from its nest in the barn roof, watching the run of the young badger. It spread its wings in utter silence. Dominic immediately turned away. He did not wish to see any creature die. Death had soaked his dreams for days.

Undressing without the call for his page or valet, he threw his clothes across the room, climbed into bed, and tried to sleep. When finally he dreamed, it was of Jetta, tiny and so thin, escaping the claws of the owl.

He woke to a sound which had also become familiar, that of shouting downstairs and the clank of metal on metal. Dominic took little notice. He yawned, wished he had slept longer, and without any sense of urgency, he pulled on hose and his heavy bed-robe over, tied tight. He then shuffled downstairs towards the probability of breakfast and discovered Benson, extremely agitated, at the open doorway.

Outside, attempting to push past Benson, was a young man in highly decorated clothes, brandishing a sword.

"My lord," Benson turned, "this is an outrageous situation. I will not permit this gentleman admission."

"Not if he wants to jump around with that thing," Dominic said, pausing at the doorway and seeming far more interested in food than the murderous visitor. "Who is he anyway? When is breakfast served?"

"Yes, my lord," Benson answered. "Breakfast awaits you, sir, in the hall as usual. This creature has given his name as Percival Maddock. Shall I fetch your sword, sir?"

"No, I'm hungry," Dominic yawned. "Shut the door on him."

Percival waved the sword again, and Benson stepped back only just in time to save the destruction of his nose.

Dominic turned. "You," he said, ice cold, "should sheath that thing quickly, or you'll find yourself in considerable trouble. What the hell do you want anyway? I have some vague memory of having met you once, but I don't believe I know you and I certainly do not want to. Leave immediately."

With a wide swipe of the sword against the large metal padlock, Percival managed to block Benson, shoved his foot inside, and forced his way in. Dominic and Percival stared at each other, both furious. The fury was ice cold in Dominic's eyes. Percival hopped from one foot to the other, red faced.

Between them, Benson tried to appear civilised. "My lord," he said, voice muffled, "I shall fetch your sword."

Continuing to regard the other man with iced disgust, Dominic blocked the way to any further entrance. "You are uninvited and unwanted here. Yet you seem to have come alone, which is most unwise. Damned tired of fighting and hatreds, I am not alone and if you do not leave, I shall be forced to make you."

"You don't understand," Percival shrieked. "I have the power here, since I supported Henry Tudor. But I'm here for more than that. You've got that little bitch Jetta hiding here. She belongs to me. I bought her years back, and then I paid for her again a week ago. But she damn well ran away again. Now I want back what belongs to me."

"Outright slavery doesn't exist in this country," Dominic replied, voice still quiet. "No human male or female can belong to you, even when married. It brings certain rights, but I cannot believe you married the girl?"

"Of course not," Percival spat. "She's a slum brat without parents."

"Then she belongs only to herself. I have noticed her skills, especially that of escaping. I'm pleased to hear she succeeded once again." Benson, marching up behind his master, held up the hilt of a long sword, which Dominic took into his own clasp, but did not raise it. He held it down, close to his leg. "You leave now," he told Percival. "My breakfast is waiting for me. If you refuse to leave, I shall enforce your departure."

"You haven't heard the last of this," Percival said. He sheathed his sword, attempted to kick the front doors open, found them locked, and marched out, blushing slightly, when Benson opened them for him.

"How unpleasant," Dominic remarked to himself, and walked off to the dining table. "Is the whole world dedicated to pain, I wonder."

It was some time before Jetta joined him. Dominic leaned against the back of the chair, his ale mug in his hand. He had actually finished long since, but had stayed, hoping for Jetta to arrive. She almost crept in eventually, hoping in fact that Dominic would already have left. Instead, they faced each other over the table.

"Good morning, my lord," Jetta said, sitting herself opposite. "I was hoping to see you," which was a lie, "and ask what you now expect – from the new king – if you prefer not to talk about this yet, then I'll understand of course. But the fact is, I don't see how we can have lost. I don't know who this foreigner is or how he can be king in our land. And," she exhaled, "I don't understand you."

"There's something else you don't seem to understand," Dominic said, unblinking, "and that's your unpleasant and insane previous employer. I do not claim to understand him either, nor wish to. Percival Maddock came here a couple of hours ago and seemed to think he was coming to collect you. Are you in any manner contracted to him?"

She shook her head and spoke in a whisper. "It's embarrassing, but years ago, I was begging at back doors. You know why. It didn't feel right to live with Ned as I got older. He was my father-figure, but he barely lived off the land and I felt guilty, so I became a beggar. Which wasn't as bad as it sounds. Until I went to the Maddock house that is. Their steward pulled me inside and said I could work there as a cleaner. I wasn't given much choice. But I signed nothing. Absolutely nothing. They just took me in."

"And the son raped you?"

With scarlet blushes, Jetta looked away. "No. He did other things, or at least, he tried to. When I fought him off, he had me whipped."

"Other things which you don't want to tell me?"

"Of course not." Jetta gulped her ale and cut the ham on the platter. I ran away because of him. The father wasn't much better and knew what his son was doing. His mother was disgusting too. Well, you've met them so you know it all. She worked me like an ox, and told Percival he could do what he liked with me."

The small tuck at the side of Dominic's mouth remained. "That sounds both disgusting and remarkably irregular."

"The whole family was odd. And disgusting."

Dominic leaned forwards across the table and reached for her hand. Jetta pulled it away. "You had no part in killing my farrier," Dominic said softly. "I know that. And sadly, the man who protected you while in goal has died. Gimlett was killed during the battle. I found him beside Fen Lane and was deeply saddened. The battle of dynasties has happened many times throughout England's past and perhaps we'll adjust to this change in time. Henry Tudor has no right to the throne except by conquest, but for all I can say, he may make a good and studious monarch. I've never met the man."

"But you sent me to Margaret Beaufort's home, and I met her. I heard her saying that her husband had no intention of fighting."

"But his brother," sighed Dominic, "has fought for anyone and everyone in the past, waiting until he was sure which side was winning."

"And nobody killed any of the Maddock family?"

"I have no idea concerning the father. The son lives and probably never fought." The tuck beside Dominic's mouth turned to a faint smile. "I assume only the father joined the battle and I have no knowledge or interest in him. It's the king's death that will change my life. Indeed, the life of every person living in England. But he was also a friend, a very close friend. As for how Tudor will rule our country, I don't know. Only arrogance could have inspired him to invade."

Finally, Jetta looked up. "I disliked his mother. But I sympathised with her too." Waiting for him to say something more personal, Jetta munched bread and cheese and stared carefully downwards. As she felt the heat of his steady gaze, the silence grew increasingly uncomfortable.

It was some time before Dominic spoke again. He had watched Jetta chewing, drinking and swallowing, all while absolutely determined not to look up or catch his stare.

Then, moving from the bench and standing directly over her, he suddenly slid one finger very gently beneath her chin, lifting her face to his. She stared back now, spluttering crumbs. "You have nothing to say then," he asked so softly it was almost a whisper, "neither to complain, nor any other remark, good or bad, concerning the event – my intrusion. Let us say, – of yesterday."

Without a clear explanation, and following his lead, she could not even be sure what to say. "It was the funeral," she murmured. "I'll miss your grandmother. But I was here. She died peacefully."

"I am, entirely and utterly selfishly," he told her, "thinking of my own behaviour. I don't always behave as others might prefer. But I don't mean to attack. Did it seem that way to you, little one?"

She shook her head although in fact it had. "Perhaps. I don't know."

He paused, then smiled, again a tuck at the corner of his mouth. "And now, have you nothing to say? Tell me what you hope for. Tell me what you hope to escape."

Jetta's courage oozed away like rain in the gutters. She knew exactly what she wanted yet could not say it. She knew exactly what she wished to escape, but neither could she speak of it.

Embarrassment. Cowardice. And equally as mighty as Dominic seemed as he stood over her, was her confusion. She gulped and said nothing at all.

Whether he was cross, or believed he was being helpful, she didn't know. Yet she hated what he eventually said, "perhaps I should arrange a move for you, back to Ned for instance," he told her softly. "In the forest you'll stay hidden from the Maddock family – and to some extent from me. But also from the new king and whatever laws he wants to bring in. I believe Ned would be delighted to have company. After that battle of loss and misery, I imagine all of us yearn for company." As he walked to the doorway he turned briefly, saying, "And perhaps I might visit, as now I consider Ned a friend."

Jetta was stuttering something, not even sure herself of what she wanted to say, and when Dominic left so abruptly, she had no opportunity to think except to blame herself. There had been time before. Now she wanted to slap her own face. She hadn't encouraged – but then, she hadn't expected the nonsense regarding Ned. There was no space for her there even if both of them had wanted such a move. Did Dominic imagine she could cheerfully share a bed with Ned, or sleep on the roof.

She felt like thumping the table. Actually, she wanted to thump Dominic.

Jetta addressed the uneaten bread sitting on her napkin. *"I'm a good person even if I'm a bit stupid sometimes. I should have said something to Dominic. But I can't tell him I think I love him when I know he doesn't love me."*

For a brief moment she sniggered under her breath, then flung out her arms. *"Oh Dominic, you're quite an obnoxious person, but I love you passionately. I want to be your mistress even though I'm an idiot kitchen girl."*

Laughing at first, she stopped abruptly and knew herself on the edge of tears.

"He just wants me in bed every now and again and that might mean those horrible things Percival tried to do. Why didn't Percival get killed in the battle instead of Gimlett? I suppose he didn't even go – vile coward."

Neither the napkin nor the bread seemed in the least interested. Jetta tidied up the table and the remains of both meals, then headed down to the kitchen.

It was Ilda she bumped into first, spilling ale from the jug.

"Mercy me," Ilda said, "mistress, forgive me. I'll clean it up."

"I hoped to talk." Jetta quickly rubbed away the beginning of her tears. "Just, you know, like friends."

"I'll come outside at once," the woman said. "Both my boys are safe, thank the Lord in Heaven. So if we sit at the back of the stables you can tell me what I can do to help."

The warm weather had continued. The sunshine sank into the thatch and the treetops, and as they sat, they found the wooden bench almost uncomfortable with the scalding heat. The day was golden instead of the dark day of mourning that it was.

"It's not as if I really know what to ask you," Jetta told Ilda. "I'm just so confused. And there's things I ought to know. About the battle and this new king – and about things far more personal."

Chapter Thirty

The night before, Dominic had drunk too much. Not too much in his opinion in fact, he had considered it perfectly sufficient. Blurring the tumbling thoughts that filled, then blocked, then drowned his mind, had been his purpose and was successful. He slept the sleep of the almost unconscious.

He awoke without headache or memory.

As the following night clouded in, Dominic lay back on the settle with no desire for sleeping, drifting through all the thoughts he had avoided the previous night. It was early and only a tipsy shaft of wandering shadow announced night's approach. Yet having returned home from his evening at Andrew's, speaking with Andrew and Tyballis, he was troubled and had no desire to face anyone else.

The endless questions remained concerning the new king. It was said that Henry Tudor was instigating a peaceful transition by setting out written requests for the lords to appear at the palace, and pledge their allegiance to him, in return he would agree to leave them in peace with their property safe.

To be left in peace, lands and entitlements intact, was what Dominic and every other lord wished for. To swear loyalty to the new king, however, seemed entirely hypocritical at this stage. He had no idea what the new king might do, want, or intend. To have invaded a country already prospering at peace did not make a bright beginning. Yet now that Richard was gone, Dominic thought, perhaps hypocrisy was better than yet another war.

Andrew had advised it. "I won't work for him. I won't kneel to him unless I have to. But nor will I shove my sword in his back. Let's see what happens first."

"Bending the knee to a man you despise may be vile," Dominic murmured. "But better than another battle. We need a king. Who else might claim the throne now?"

"Since Tudor has announced the legitimacy of King Edward's children, then it must be his son Edward. But I'd not fight for him unless Tudor proves himself a tyrant."

"They say our Tudor usurper will send out requests for each lord to join him at court." Dominic nodded. "When I receive such a request, I'll curse, but I'll also comply. This country needs peace."

For some hours they had discussed the politics, their own hopes for the country, and their lack of trust in the new king. "It is always difficult to trust a usurper, but even William the first had done good as well as evil."

Andrew said, "I thank the Lord above that I didn't live back then."

"He slaughtered half the people of England and replaced them with solitary misery." Dominic spoke quietly, and to the ceiling. "He brought in the French arrogance of feudalism, and he destroyed the north when they dared to disagree with him. He ransacked the lords, good men and working men, putting his own French despots in their place. But we are their descendants. We cannot hate our own fathers."

"I can," Andrew said. "And so do many others."

"I have little memory of mine," Dominic added. "I thought I loved him, but I was too young. Later I hated him for dying."

Dominic had ridden home with the sun on his back and his

thoughts dishevelled. The long summer day did not yet fall into the evening gloom, but it was gloom that Dominic felt. From the memory of the blood ridden battlefield, he sank back into the perplexity of Jetta. It was always now Jetta who crept into his mind whether invited or not.

Once again alone, stretched on the settle in the principal hall, Dominic was draining his second cup of wine when a very small voice murmured from the doorway. Deep in thought and deep in wine, he had not heard the door open.

The whisper drifted a little, as though unsure of its welcome. He turned and gazed. The small figure peeped through the tiny opening crack from the outside corridor. She wore a large wrapped bedrobe and her hair looked as though she had desperately run her fingers through it several times.

"I was wondering – about what you called an intrusion – when you saw me before the funeral. Not the word I was expecting, but now I understand. So thinking back – I was wondering – sorry, I'm repeating myself. But," and she paused while Dominic gazed at her in silence, "then you kissed me. I know I'm talking rubbish and I apologise, but I always do when I'm stressed. So please don't shout at me if you hate the idea, but do you want me to be your mistress?"

As her tentative and barely audible whisper faded, she was already between his arms. Before she had finished speaking, he had taken her in a close embrace. She felt the force of his muscles, the pressure of his hands at her back and the rise of his chest crushing against her own. Her mouth was muffled on his velvet shoulder and she clung there, trying to catch her breath without pulling away.

He spoke down into her hair, and she was surprised. "No, little one. Though perhaps yes. Yet what I want is only a dream, and I won't do what might hurt you. I prefer to make you my friend, and see you happy."

Jetta gulped. "It's only Teresa you want that way?"

He moved back half a step, then led her gently to the great cushioned settle behind him, but only to sit, her hand in his and his other arm around her waist. "I dream of little else but you, little one. But you seemed to think nothing of me in return."

Gulping again, Jetta still whispered. "I thought it was me who cared and not you at all."

"And when I kissed you?"

"But you rushed away."

"My dear, despite the feelings we seem to have for each other, we both continue to misunderstand. I never felt for Teresa the way I feel for you. And for me, Teresa simply served a purpose and no longer exists. She was jealous, treacherous and absurd. I now have no woman in my bed."

Snuggling close, she adored the warmth of his body behind her, next to her, almost around her. Her voice remained muffled against him. "And you don't want me because you don't want to hurt me." She paused. Eventually, "Does it have to hurt?"

He sighed. "I didn't mean in that way, my dear. But it seems we can hurt without intention."

Not love perhaps, but the deep affection was so palpable, so Jetta cuddled tighter, one arm encircling his waist.

It seemed so adorable, when suddenly an abrupt noise interrupted, a clash and then shouting from outside. Both Jetta and Dominic sat up very straight. Jetta clambered back, pulling her bedrobe tight. Dominic strode to the hall's doorway, pulled it wide and looked out to the closed front doors, locked and unattended from within. Late evening, the shadows clung. One solitary candle had been left burning in the hall.

Attack seemed almost expected, the Maddock boy again, the wretched sheriff, or even the Earl of Plymouth. He could hear the commotion, but making little sense of it, Dominic turned quickly back to Jetta. "Stay here. Don't move," he said, pulling the great hall's doors shut behind him.

Jumping up, Jetta listened at the doorway. There was a great deal to hear but she recognised none of the voices, imperious and loud.

Then she heard the unlocking of the outer doorway, the great carved wood swinging open.

"Open in the name of the king."

Dominic stared at the small push of guards and recognised the royal livery. "You may notice, sir, this door's stands already open. What the devil do you want?"

"You, I believe, my lord," one of the guards stepped forwards, his lance upheld but not yet threatening. "I have an arrest warrant signed by his royal majesty the king, for Lord Dominic Stark, Earl of Desford, who is to be taken into custody at the Tower, awaiting further instructions from his majesty."

Surprised, Dominic frowned. "I'm perfectly prepared to speak with the king and have been waiting to do so." He realised that he was now half surrounded by the royal guards but behind him also stood Benson and a large number of his household, unarmed but frightened and also furious.

The principal guard held a lance, and the others were armed with short, hand swords. Their metal reflected only shadows.

"My lord, I have my orders."

"I fought with loyalty for my king and country, considered loyalty at the time." Dominic hesitated. Defying the new king was unlikely to be wise, yet his anger was now equal to his confusion. He spoke with a confidence he no longer felt. "There is a new king now, but I have not yet met his majesty. Nor have I done anything which might be considered treasonous."

"What you did, sir," the guard replied without emotion, "is for his majesty to decide."

Laughing suddenly, Dominic leaned back against the door jam. "I eat my breakfast, my dinner, my supper, and go to bed. Is that a suspicious range of activities? Since returning exhausted from the battlefield, I do little else and have no intention of insurrection or revolt."

The guard remained patient. "That's not my concern, my lord. I merely follow orders, and I hold a signed warrant for your arrest. If your lordship would call for his horse, we will escort you to the Tower. You will be well housed, I assure you, until this situation is more thoroughly examined."

Turning to Benson, Dominic smiled slightly. "What wondrous surprises can happen so close one to the other," he said. "One so utterly delightful, and the next so entirely – let us say –unattractive. So in my absence, Benson, please manage the household as usual, and in particular will you please help Mistress Jetta in whatever she requires. I hope to return soon."

One of the pages had already run for his horse, and now Dominic mounted, nodded to the guards, and in minutes was no longer visible from the house.

Benson sank down on the lowest stair, head in his hands, appalled and distraught. He did not hear that within the hall, Jetta was sobbing loudly into the collar of her bedrobe as she curled on the cushions of the settle.

It was a long ride from the Chiswick mansion to the great Tower of London, but they rode fast along the banks of the Thames, the guardsmen keeping Dominic tight within their group.

Beneath the vast shadows of the Tower, night at past eleven of the clock, the sky was darkening further, the stars more insistent, the ravens were cawing their final wails for the night and the guards were marching from gates to Keep, from bailey to bridge, past the moat and the mixed zoological collection kept there. The caged lion, unhappy at his imprisonment, roared to the river, and the ravens fell silent.

Dominic was taken directly to the Keep and up the old curving stone steps to the two conjoined rooms above the old royal apartments. Outside had been warm with a fresh evening breeze. Here it was chilly with a draught from the arrow slit windows without covering, and the wide gap beneath the heavy wooden door.

Entering and looking around, Dominic sighed, yet at least this was no cell nor dungeon. He was neither chained nor roped but the door was securely locked behind him.

This was no underground cave and moonlight oozed through the

VESPERS

window slit. But at a moment he had treasured, everything had changed, and his sweet contentment was lost. Lying on the bed, he closed his eyes, did not bother to undress, and simply slept where he was. Exhausted by what was both inside and outside him, Dominic did not hear when the lion's final roar announced night's pitch, nor the stamp of boots on stone as the guards marched their Watch.

It was the next morning when the ravens woke, stretched their wings, and called to the rising sun. Over the menagerie the sky turned lemon tinted peach, then splayed into azure. The solitary lion began his frustrated march across his limited domain, and the Tower guards, standing to attention, waited for their night duty to end and be dismissed, replaced by those guards of the day shift. In a blue haze, the warmth increased and in a troubled discomfort, Dominic awakened to a day he dreaded.

He was brought breakfast, both suitable and sufficient, and the guard who served him announced a meeting later in the day.

"The guards'll be coming for you later, my lord. A chat, you might say, about being here and what happens next."

Dominic ate little. It was the interview with Sir John Digby, the new Lieutenant of the Tower which interested him. With no guesses at the reason for his arrest, he sat impatient and irritated. He found the absurd repetition of what he now felt he should have said to Jetta rumbling itself through his thoughts. Other thoughts were as pointless. After midday dinner, which was only one course, he found the silence increasingly distasteful and eventually dozed.

Outside the sky dazzled with sunshine. Once awake, Dominic knew he would have trouble sleeping comfortably throughout the night. He paced, so few steps possible in each direction. He rubbed one finger across the flaking plaster, and blanked his thoughts.

It was a small room with heavy walls, and although the narrow window openings held neither glass nor wooden shutters, sound was blocked. The roars of the lion and the bird song occasionally intruded, but silence became the more common companion.

"Very sorry," said the guard who brought his supper, cheap wine and half a chicken pie, "but Sir John was mighty busy. Says as he'll try and come on the morrow."

He did not. After a stiff and almost sleepless night, Dominic passed a ragged day of absurd thoughts once more, and no visitors.

"Still too busy, my lord. Wishes to send apologies, does his lordship. There were a young lady too, rather small and mighty pretty. But I couldn't let her in. Not allowed. Not till after Sir John sees you, my lord."

The mention of Jetta changed many things. Dominic remained where he was, the Lieutenant of the Tower failed to turn up, the food was sometimes acceptable and sometimes limited and shoddy, and the bed, a straw pallet beneath linen sheets, was excessively uncomfortable. But the knowledge that Jetta had come all this way, presumably on foot, to see him, altered everything.

Settling to the inevitable, Dominic asked for paper and pen and for a messenger to visit his own home, requesting someone to pack a bag of his own clothes and books, then to ask Mistress Jetta to bring this to him within the next two days, riding what might be called her own mare Felicia.

The guard made no objection and Dominic therefore hoped he would soon have a change of clothes, and see the woman he most wanted to see. From the previous description he knew that Jetta had attempted to visit. He lay back, caressed by the news, yet dulled by the knowledge of the guard's refusal.

It was Benson who came. That was still a pleasure.

"But, with deepest apologies Benson, I had hoped for a different messenger."

"It was not permitted, my lord. The guard insisted that your steward play messenger, and Mistress Jetta sent her prayers. And, forgive me, my lord, but Mistress Jetta has certain plans mapped out which she made me swear not to reveal. Therefore, I cannot tell you, my lord, that she and Lord Leays, have made an appointment to meet with the Constable, Sir John de Vere, Earl of Oxford."

After a prolonged silence, Dominic took the parcel Benson had brought, and sitting at the tiny table, asked Benson to sit opposite. "She's been to see Andrew to tell him my delightful news? And they intend speaking with the most powerful man in the kingdom after the king himself?"

"So it would seem, my lord, although of course I cannot say."

"Can you say when, Benson?"

"I cannot, my lord. I promised secrecy. Nor can I tell you that the meeting has been confirmed by the Earl of Oxford at the principal office of Westminster Palace in two days' time. And since I have sworn to divulge none of this, I cannot possibly add that this will be the day of September the fifth at ten of the morning. And since I cannot divulge this or anything else, I must simply ask you to wait, my lord, and after the meeting I imagine that Lord Leays himself will come to tell you what was discussed and what was the final result."

"Such as my immediate execution?"

"I imagine that would be less of a secret, sir."

Dominic laughed. "And Oxford has actually agreed to meet Jetta? That sounds thoroughly scandalous. Does he know who she is? Or perhaps, who she isn't?"

"Sadly these are matters I have sworn not to reveal, my lord," Benson sighed. "So I cannot explain that Lord Leays simply requested a meeting and the added necessity of bringing with him another person who was intimately aware of further details."

"Fascinating. A shame you can't tell me, Benson, especially what these relevant details might be."

Benson grinned. "Strangely enough, my lord, those are details which I must honestly say I do not know." He laughed, then smothered it. "But I hope you will be released at the earliest possibility, sir. There appears to be no motive for this arrest. If you are not immediately released, I shall endeavour to visit again with further information, even if sworn to secrecy."

"I look forward to both," Dominic told him.

Except for the ragged straw filled bed, the two rooms were not badly or uncomfortably furnished. The little bedchamber held chairs, a chest for clothes and a small box for papers or other matters. There was a long, embroidered banner hanging along one wall to add greater warmth to the stone, and the door between the two rooms could be closed. Although the mattress was inadequate, the bed itself was well swathed with pillows, blankets and an eiderdown in heavy down-filled fleece. The other room held a cushioned settle, a larger table two chairs, two stools, and several rugs on the floor. There was a chamber pot, pegs to hang clothes, and a central slate for fire. Now with paper and gall ink as well, Dominic settled to write to the king, to the Earl of Oxford, and to the invisible Sir John Digby. The letter he wrote to Jetta remained in his thoughts.

Without replies to any of his letters, leaving Dominic to wonder if his guards had ever bothered to deliver them, the Tower Lieutenant finally kept his promise of a meeting.

He marched in one afternoon as the bright sunshine was waning, and sat himself on the settle, crossed his legs, and smiled as though Dominic was his honoured guest.

"I am delighted to see you, sir." He tapped his fingers on the uppermost knee. "I see you failed to visit his majesty to pledge your loyalty for the future."

"I did not interrupt his highness, since I was not formally invited."

"Ah, no sweet invitation?" smiled the thin bearded man. "Perhaps his majesty did not know of your existence?"

"Well, it seems he does now," Dominic smiled back.

"And so, my lord, pledging your allegiance will soon be required of you. However, for the moment, it is irrelevant." Sir John uncrossed his legs and leaned forwards. "It is the information gleaned from others that has brought you here, my lord. Important and unexpected information. Let us see what you wish to tell me about it."

"I have not the slightest idea what you are talking about," Dominic replied. "You will have to explain considerably more than that."

And then he knew it all. Sir John, still eyes alight as he leaned forwards, crossed his legs again, crossed his arms over his chest, and said, "There is a certain sheriff of the Chiswick Ward, name of John Kettering, who has accused you of shocking criminal activities, and of improperly helping the escape of a murderer from the cells. The accusation has been verified by the great Earl of Plymouth, and since both he and John Kettering have fought with great loyalty for his royal majesty and sworn absolute allegiance, this matter has not only been brought to the king's notice, but seems to be a matter of shocking illegality both during the previous king's reign, and now."

"Shit," sighed Dominic, leaning back. "What nonsense, and what ridiculous lies. Must I explain the truth to yourself, sir? Or to another?"

"First to me, my lord. I shall be most interested."

"And I shall be monstrously bored," added Dominic. "But the story's simple enough. Some months past, the body of my farrier was discovered dead under a tree in my grounds. At the same time, a young woman was seen asleep in a wherry tied to the bank of the river."

Dominic saw no interest in the other man's eyes. Sir John looked as tired, as bored, and as irritated as Dominic felt.

Sir John coughed. "So finish your story, my lord."

And so he continued. "Some assumed that she must be the killer of the man nearby, even though she was a thin child without a muscle to be seen, whereas my farrier was a large and muscular man. However, I locked the girl in my house until I had the time to bury my farrier and investigate the crime. It was quickly obvious that the girl was innocent, but during my absence one day, the local sheriff turned up and arrested both this girl and the farrier's wife. This was absurd, there was not only no proof, but not even the slightest possibility that he had properly investigated the crime or found the genuine culprits. I therefore, when I discovered what had occurred, went to see the sheriff and demanded the prisoners' release." Dominic yawned. "That's the entire story, sir, and one that I myself can prove. As for the Earl of Plymouth, he was neither present, nor has any possibility of knowing the truth. Indeed, Plymouth was doubtless in France."

"It sounds genuine enough. That doesn't mean it's true," smiled Sir John.

Dominic smiled back. The smile was cold, more menacing than contented. "Only if, Sir John, you prefer to take the wild fantasies of a corrupt sheriff to the word of an earl who has always been loyal to – the crown!"

Chapter Thirty One

Lord Andrew smile down at the girl. "My wife tells me that you have a great deal in common. And I always take my wife's word. It would be dangerous not to." He smiled, "I also invariably agree with Dominic. So although I hardly know you, my dear, I certainly believe your story. Let's see what we can accomplish."

The appointment had been made, verified, and followed by a promise of no cancellations. Whatever the importance of The Earl of Oxford, being the most trusted member of the elite now beneath Henry Tudor, it could not be denied that Andrew Lord Leays was also a significant power, or had been under the previous king. Therefore, a meeting was not to be ignored.

The Earl of Oxford, however, chose not to believe what he would prefer not to be told. A well-muscled man, his neck as thick as his jaw, he neither sat nor rested, but marched the floor from door to windows and back again, his hands tightly clasped behind his back. He spoke to Andrew, though rarely looked at him, and tended to ignore Jetta. She sat obediently and spoke only when Andrew managed to invite her into the discussion.

"The sheriff," Oxford said to the air, "is a trusted man of the law. I cannot disbelieve you, my Lord Leays, and am delighted to make your acquaintance, but you are only passing on the details you have heard from others. You were not present. The female tells you this story and you choose to believe her. But I prefer to believe a solid trustworthy member of those upholding the law."

Andrew was spread, his legs purposefully stretched, arms across the back of the large chair. Marching across the room, Oxford repeatedly avoided Andrew's unmoving ankles.

"Lord Stark, Earl of Desford, is also a lord of known loyalty, honesty and intelligence," Andrew said. "Yet you imprison him without investigating either story in order to confirm which is the truth. And the young woman originally arrested by Sheriff Kettering, who is at the kernel of this entire situation, and who has willingly come here to answer whatever you might wish to know, is being ignored."

With an abrupt twist of the head, Oxford glared down at Andrew. "So you have brought her here for me to arrest her?"

"I have not." Andrew stood, slowly stretching each leg, brushing down his cote and smiling without rancour at the Earl of Oxford. "I came here, accompanied by the very heart of the situation, in order to bring relief to all those who have misunderstood the story. But if those in authority prefer not to understand anything, my visit would appear to be pointless."

"Not in the least, my lord," Oxford continued the march. "But I have spoken to the sheriff, who has made his loyalties clear. He fought bravely at Fen Lane, and risked his life for his majesty, King Henry VII. You, my lord, did not. You fought for the usurper, Richard Plantagenet. But since then, you have pledged your loyalty to our rightful king. The Earl of Desford, however, not only fought for the usurper Richard, but has made no pledge since, and has not even asked to see our king."

Andrew shook his head. "The usual twist of weasel-wallop," he sighed. "You want Dominic under lock and key. The given motive is pure twaddle. The sheriff was, and presumably still is, corrupt. Try checking his collection of taxes."

"Is Sheriff Kettering still a sheriff?" asked Jetta suddenly.

Oxford regarded her with contempt. "He is. And will continue to be so. And if you attempt to cause any trouble, girl, you will go to Newgate."

Jetta quickly shut up, but Andrew did not. "Then I will have the greatest pleasure in meeting with him, with the Earl of Desford within the Tower, and afterwards with his majesty."

With sudden determination, Jetta changed her mind. "You've chosen Lord Stark as an example, haven't you," she accused, staring at the tall man in front of her. "His tussle with the sheriff, and the sheriff arresting me without proof, that doesn't matter in the least. It's just a useful story to make the earl's arrest look legal. He was never sent any order – not even an invitation – to attend his majesty. Also on purpose, so that he could be accused of not complying. But it's by your design – not his. Your king wants to make an example of one lord – someone not on any councils and without important positions – but with masses of property that can be claimed by the king."

Oxford glared, twisting to face her, his hands fisted. It seemed as though he longed to punch her, strangle her, arrest her. But all he said between pursed lips, was, "You are out of place, girl, and had better leave now. Otherwise, you'll find yourself hanging from the gibbet."

Then it was Andrew who stepped forward, pulling Jetta behind him. "But the girl speaks the truth. You know this, my lord, and no doubt planned the situation yourself in accord with the wishes of the Earl of Plymouth. Having made peace, your king now wishes for one solitary example as a serious warning to keep other lords in order. Henry will gain both from beheading one powerful man as an example to others planning rebellion, and he also gains from claiming Desford's property, which is considerable. Will you deny this?"

"Naturally," Oxford told him, clasping his hands once more behind his back. "I completely deny the nonsense you claim. Nor is it any of your business, my lord. So take the servant brat with you, and be very careful to make no more accusations. Otherwise, you may discover yourself in the same position."

Once they had left the palace and the meeting which they had both found irritatingly useless, Andrew rode back to Chiswick with Jetta, seeing her safely home, his own entourage, although now essential as the new king made himself known, kept its distance. "I expected little else," Andrew told her. "But perhaps it was even more obvious than I'd expected. The warning, the example to anyone planning revolt, was clear, but I also believe Henry Tudor wants Dominic at his fingertips for some reason I don't yet know. The excuse of the sheriff is – quite simply – an excuse. We both know that Plymouth is at the back of it. Go in and rest, but be prepared if I need you."

"But what," Jetta spluttered, "does this Plymouth earl want? Dominic says he doesn't even know him. But Plymouth hates Dominic and there has to be a reason. But it's all so sudden."

As Jetta dismounted, Andrew smiled down at her. "How long the man may have waited to put his hatred into action, I've no idea. But now there's a new king and a king that Plymouth supports. It finally gives him backing. And the king also gets his example of what comes if loyalty does not."

He was still thinking around the problem as he rode northeast, but Jetta hurried indoors, and was crying again.

Beneath the sweetness of a continuing summer, beneath the bird song and the hazy warmth, beneath the newly opened markets and the calls of the bakers, the butchers, the pie-makers, the cobblers and the tailors, hovered an atmosphere of careful watchfulness. Few yet trusted the new king. They disliked the armed guards who strode the streets, the sudden gallop of horses pushing all pedestrians to the walls, and the strange stories which spread.

King Richard had purposefully spoken in English, even during sworn oaths, coronation pledges and the announcement of law and order. This had never happened before, and was much loved by a nation of English speakers who neither liked nor understood the French language. Yet the new king was uncomfortable with English and half his words along with his accent, remained Breton.

Few, however, met the new king nor heard him speak. It was fear of the unknown which crept into the shadows. Kings could demand many things. The previous usurper, King William the first, also from France, had altered the way of living that had been acceptable for so many years. Feudalism had bombarded the entire land and a new hierarchy of lords had swept away the comfort of peace.

That had occurred long, long ago, and even feudalism had eventually died out a hundred years gone. Yet stories around campfires, over the dinner table, and in bed when wishing goodnight to the children, still left their echoes.

Now, however, the changes seemed more lenient, and the new usurper more tolerant. Nothing monstrous had yet been brought back by Henry Tudor. There was resentment but there was also hope.

Yet strange contradictions began to appear. The payment of taxes changed remarkably and those who collected them could be both violent and corrupt. It would not take long for families to fall into poverty, yet the prosperity of the middle class which had grown under Edward IV and Richard III continued, overtaking those of the elite who refused to follow the Tudor rule, also the spaces left by the noblemen who had been killed during the battle. But the new king did not rush the changes, calling his coronation for October, and calling no parliament until then.

What he did begin, with advice from Morton, Oxford, his mother and others, was the outpouring of information contradicting and insulting most of the events which had taken place during Richard III's reign.

The Earl of Plymouth announced that King Richard had been a cruel and terrible man who had murdered his own brother by drowning, had slaughtered his two nephews who by right should have inherited their father's crown, and had probably also poisoned his own wife. Henry Tudor enjoyed himself. He denied, with bugles and aplomb, almost anything that Richard III had done, or claimed. He cancelled the validity of Titulus Regious, therefore making Richard the supposed usurper, and so announced his own future wife legitimate.

Yet the young Edward, son of the Duke of Clarence, Richard III's brother who had been executed for rebelling against King Edward IV, might now have the right to proclaim himself king, or at least to deny much of the important Tudor propaganda. Therefore, as soon as the battle at Fen Lane was won, Henry Tudor sent word to London for the young prince to be locked in the Tower.

Hearing the commotion as the Earl of Desford was brought to the small rooms above, Edward Earl of Warwick, son of Clarence was interested in his new neighbour. He had not been long imprisoned himself, but at ten years old, he was desperate to break the threat from the new king. He had been kept in dismal silence for some years already since the death of his father, but he had been released from boredom when Richard III came to the throne, had been knighted, and sent to live in comfortable grandeur with his mother.

Now back in the Tower, the child was desperate for communication. He thumped both feet on the stone floor, then climbed on a stool to see if he could call up through the ceiling gaps. Unlike almost everything else he had attempted during his life, it worked.

"Who are you? I'm Edward. I haven't even met this new king but he sent an order to lock me up. I'm not eleven yet. Can you tell me who you are?"

As the unexpected words floated upwards, Dominic smiled at nobody. "My luck means I am old enough to plan my own salvation. At twenty-seven, I can imagine the pleasure of slaughtering those who put me here."

"I wish I could too," said the boy. "They killed my father too. Different people. They keep changing kings. Evidently my father's death was his own fault. Besides, I hardly knew him, so I have little interest in the rights and wrongs. But I care for my mother. I hope –

very, very much – they let her come here to see me. Well, better than that – I hope they just let me out."

Dominic pulled one of the blankets around his shoulders and stretched back on the larger chair. "I know exactly who you are, Edward, and you have a better claim to the throne than our new king. So don't expect freedom too soon. You need to discover some particular pleasure to pass time. Reading – writing – drawing – make friends with one of the guards who can sit and talk with you. Tell the guard you want to adopt a puppy for loving company. And tell him you'll never tell a soul if only he agrees to help you."

"I've only been here a few days. It's horrible already."

"I doubt prison brings joy to anyone. But there are a hundred ways of shortening every day."

"My mother liked tapestry. She taught me how to do it. I made her a kerchief."

"Then," said Dominic, "ask the guards for the needles and cottons you need, and I shall talk nonsense to you while you work."

"But tapestry is for girls, and boys would be called rude names for doing a girl's thing."

"Not only," said Dominic, "will no one know except myself and your guard, but your own skill will bring compliments."

"At least," said the boy, "now I know I can talk to anyone in the rooms above. That's wonderful."

"Ask the guards for pens and papers, needles and thread, linen fabric, and remind them you're a prince. You must refuse to accept problems – never to be cold – never to be hungry. Is the accommodation acceptable?"

"It's a fair bed and a fair space for living," the young Edward sighed. "But I'm not a villain, truly I'm not. And I'd hate to be king. They have such difficult lives. But living here is going to be difficult too."

At the same time, and also at some distance, Jetta lay on her bed and stared up at the swaying cloth that covered the posts. What had brought such absurdly vicious decisions to the Tudor king, she couldn't imagine. But the world was turning unbelievable circles.

"What difference does a king make?"

Jetta stared at Ilda. "A new king can change everything."

Ilda shook her head, the small crisp white bonnet hiding her greying hair. "I never saw the last one. I surely won't see this one. And I'll never see the next one either. Nor don't want to. He'll do his business and I'll do mine. The battle, well, it frightened me since my boys went marching off and could have been killed. And they tell me the wrong side lost and the wrong side won. But how can anyone tell what's right or wrong? All those grand folk sit in their palaces counting their money. So what? The thing that mattered to me was the death of my husband. He beat me, he shouted and screamed at me, he spilled his piss on the floor and made me wipe it up. And he took his own wages and mine, and spent every ha'penny on ale and pies down the tavern, staggering home at night all ready to beat me again. Him dying made a huge difference. Changed my whole life. But the king? I'm sorry, miss, but us normal folks don't give a damn."

"You might," Jetta whispered, "depending on what happens. He's going to put taxes up for a start."

"I don't pay none," Ilda said. "So from one little naught to another naught won't bother me neither. Can be a far bigger naught. I shan't cry."

She had heard these remarks before, but now, for the first time, Jetta asked, "Hilda dear, have you any idea who killed your husband?"

Ilda had smiled, then looked down at her boots. "I can reckon you'll rightly guess," she murmured. "But if I don't say it aloud, then you can't tell no one else."

"I never would." And Jetta meant it.

"It don't matter," Ilda sniffed. "I reckon you've guessed and I'm proper happy now, Miss Jetta, and I really hope you will be mighty soon."

Jetta had disliked the Earl of Oxford, and she had disliked the sound of the new order. But the only thing that made her cry was Dominic's arrest, particularly at the moment of his sweet explanations, his arm around her and his hand on hers, his voice soft and delicious. He'd said – 'No,' but now she was left unsure what the no had meant, nor what he might have said next. And she cried not for herself but for him.

Locked up, friendless, awaiting something terrible. An example of what the new king had the power to do to anyone who did not cower to him – and that surely meant certain death.

Ilda and her boys continued their work for an absent master, as did everyone else on the estate, and some started treating either Benson or herself as the new authority.

"Ma'am, shall I order the hedges trimmed? 'Tis some weeks since it was done."

"What? Oh, well yes. I suppose so." Jetta knew nothing of hedges, except that they marked boundaries and created lanes and walkways outside the house, then were sometimes used for birds nesting in the spring.

"Will you give me a list of menus for the week, mistress? For both dinner and supper, if you please."

Jetta stared at the chief chef and shook her head. She assumed that previously this had been done by the countess. "Follow the usual sort of thing for dinner. But there's only me. Don't do anything special or difficult or expensive and I only want one course. And nothing at all for supper."

The chef gazed with stupefaction. "Not a single thing, my lady?"

"Just wine." Jetta sighed. She wondered what Dominic would be served for both dinner and supper, and if there would be any wine at all.

It was indeed the wine she was drinking when there was thunderous knocking on the front door, and she could hear Benson marching to answer it. The wild possibility of Dominic coming, suddenly released, or even Andrew and Tyballis, was a wild delight.

Instead it was those she dreaded. The temptation was to run

upstairs and lock herself, with the wine jug, in her bedchamber. Instead, she followed Benson to the doorway.

The group was pushing to enter. Benson barred the way. He had also called two of the scullions up from the kitchen, and sent another to call for the five elder grooms. Ilda peeped beneath Benson's arm and her two sons stamped their way behind the unwanted visitors.

The arrival of Sheriff Kettering and six of his assistants did not surprise Jetta. He was bound to reappear. But Percival Maddock stood at the front, which surprised her. He also appeared to be backed by three guards of his own.

Keeping in the shadows of the great hall, at first Jetta simply listened. There was a good deal to hear, although it was difficult to see, since the mill of furious men with one woman in their midst, constantly moved, turned, shouted, and attempted to burst into the house.

"Where is the whore?" Percival demanded. "She belongs to me. It's not much more than two weeks past when I paid a high price for the slut. As a criminal escaping justice, the sheriff will arrest and whip her. Then she'll be passed over to me."

Amongst the scrum, Jetta could vaguely see weapons, but she had none herself. The smash of steel swung against stone and the shouts of both sides invented pictures, even when she couldn't yet see them.

Then she made two adaptations. A small knife, little more than a dagger, lay on the table beside a large empty platter. This had been set for breakfast the next day. She grabbed it, looking around, wondering if the platter could also be helpful. Then instead she grabbed the wine jug, drank the last few dregs, and smashed it down against the table. It broke into several pieces, and she chose the longest one, its end pointed and excessively sharp.

She then, with the knife in one hand and the long splinter of porcelain in the other, gripping tightly while taking one very deep breath, marched out to the corridor and the yelling huddle at the front door.

VESPERS

It was Percival Maddock who noticed Jetta first, managed to push past Benson, and literally jumped onto her.

With an immediate reaction of fury combined with fear, she pressed outwards with the long sharp splinter of earthenware, and it disappeared into Percival's chest.

Chapter Thirty Two

As Percival fell, he tripped up one of the estate's serving boys, and Ilda grabbed the boy to save him while Jetta grabbed Percival to stab him. She stabbed again, but he caught her arm and forced it behind her. With her other arm, she once again fisted the shaft of the wine jug. It snapped, the larger part remaining in her hand, the tiny end stuck into Percival's neck. He roared, releasing her and grabbing at the small wound.

Beneath them were the scarlet colours of a thick Turkey rug. Now blood splattered scarlet onto scarlet.

Percival was not badly wounded but was yelling in pain and fury. He raced at Jetta and reached out with his long shining metal, but met Benson who had stepped between them. The sheriff dodged and came behind Jetta, lassoing her with a heavy steel chain. She felt it grip around her neck, choking her but she managed to force her fingers up into the links, loosening it.

One of the sheriff's men leapt over, grabbing Jetta to drag her from the house. Two of the grooms stepped into the fury, slashing out at both sheriff and his assistant, stabbing one and kicking out at the other. All five fell entangled, Jetta fighting with the sheriff and the grooms with the others, a squirming swearing mass, now sitting in blood and vomit.

Benson's sword was uncomfortable for a man who had never used one, but one of the grooms grabbed it as Benson waved it, missing everybody. The groom slashed the blade into the face of one of the sheriff's assistants, and the man doubled over, screaming. He had lost just one ear, and the sheriff roared, "That's no loss you pathetic fool. Get up and fight. And never mind about the others, I want that wench dead or captured."

The mill was difficult while men hurtled one onto the other, and only livery helped distinguish them, for the sheriff's men wore plain clothes, belted tunics over knitted hose, while Percival's men were in red and blue livery, smart until stabbed. Those of the estate wore the Desford livery of dark green and silver, with those from the kitchens flapping aprons.

One man fell, then clambered up, knocking down another. Now livery entwined with livery, and Benson, releasing his sword to one of his men, grabbed a smaller knife, offered by Ilda, and stabbed at the sheriff. The sheriff kicked. Benson fell back into the hall, the door swinging open behind him.

The struggle immediately tumbled into the increased space and from doorway to the great hall, the house was a spreading echo of battle.

Someone fell backwards down the stairs and tripped on those fighting below. Benson grabbed the fallen man's elbow. "You'll take no one upstairs."

The man couldn't get back to his feet, his back sprained. "I were going to jump on that bastard from the first landing." But he had misjudged his own strength and now lay gasping. The sheriff kicked him in the groin and left him doubling over. Then standing on the bottom stair, Kettering raised his sword and yelled, "I'm the law around here, you fools. You'll do as I say or I'll arrest the lot of you."

That reminded Jetta of Gimlett and she wished he was there, with his muscled determination and his hatred of the sheriff. Her own hatred of the sheriff was perhaps as vibrant, but she discovered streams of tears flooding her eyes, turning her half blind, a mixture of swallowing Gimlett's fate, the renewed loss of Dominic after being terrified of losing him permanently to the great battle, and now she was under attack herself and both fear and determination grabbed, twisted, making her dizzy.

The sudden blindness and dizzy confusion turned fear into anger, magnified when she realised Percival's arms wrapped her in a shuddering paralysis, his sword across her throat. But one hand was free, She felt the sting of the blade at her neck, and immediately she stabbed back, her earthenware dagger to his elbow. The broken piece of the wine jug was now blunt, but its edges were rough with a dozen tiny points. Percival dropped the sword. Already in pain and bleeding badly, Jetta ran back. Percival's elbow also bled, but she doubted it would kill him.

Benson stood behind Percival, and stabbed at the same minute, his knife to the back of Percival's neck, caught him as he staggered, and threw him to the doorway leading outside.

Ignoring both pain and fear, Jetta thrust out both hands, a kitchen knife and the broken splinter at the sheriff. Seeing her, Ilda jumped into the tussle, pulling at the sheriff's face from behind, her fingers in his eyes as she bit at the back of his neck. Jetta held both her small weapons in one hand now and with the other she grabbed the sheriff's hair, and in minutes realised she had great tufts of unwashed and knotted grease stuck between her fingers.

The fight was somehow growing although too massed for counting either side. But Percival Maddock's assistants seemed to have doubled, while every man from the Desford Estate was now rushing to defend their property and everyone on it. When Jetta whirled around again, she was held not in the cruel grip of the enemy, but in the strong grasp of a friend.

Then it was the head groom who jumped up to the stairs, just the

VESPERS

third step which allowed him to yell over everyone's heads, and shouted, "Desford men, take battle lines. Find your places. At least five of you to the left, the rest to the right. Then march, getting those bastards locked between you."

These were battle orders, but heard by both sides. Yet every man pulled, pushed, roared and cursed, and raged on until attacked himself, then lying, twisted and bleeding, on the ground.

Formidable, since there were more men now and some women too. There had been eleven of the staff but now there were twenty at least, and Jetta, accepting orders, joined the left side, still gripping both the porcelain splinter and the small knife. Ilda and her boys ran to the right, while Benson stood close beside Jetta. Both sides were strong and now well armed. Some carried swords yet most carried kitchen knives or gardening forks, clubs and axes.

Percival's and the sheriff's men were also more numerous, screaming as they rushed forwards, swords and clubs raised.

The head groom was copying Fen Lane tactics, and now both the right and left lines immediately closed, trapping their opposition between them, two bodies, four arms and two weapons to each they grabbed.

Jetta stared at Percival. She had never killed anyone in her life, though a hundred times had wanted to with this man. Pip stood on the opposite side, Percival between them. Pip grabbed the man's neck, strangling, squeezing fingers and thumbs, and shouted, "Now."

It was Jetta he was shouting at. It sounded like King Richard shouting at his men to charge. Percival was flailing, almost fainting, his neck was bright red, the pressure of thumbs blooming at the front with huge purple bruises. His hands stiffened and then were limp, his sword dropping to the ground and bouncing from one boot. Unable to speak now, Percival croaked, wheezing, and then there was no sound at all as Jetta stabbed him with both her weapons, the dagger to the front of his neck between the thumb marks, and the jagged splinter hard into his belly.

Immediately Percival staggered and fell. He pumped blood and only his feet twitched. Both wounds were weeping scarlet. Jetta panted and was out of breath, whispering, "You wanted to hurt me so often. Now you can't, not anymore."

Pip grabbed Jetta, pulling her away. Writhing at their feet, Percival choked, gulped, tried to rise but toppled back. Now the blood was a fountain from his neck although it seemed the seeping wound at his belly was the pain he tried to stifle. His silence was sudden. The writhing stopped. He no longer moved at all.

The fighting was slowing. Seeing their master dead at their feet, the liveried Maddocks staff backed off, slashing their way out of the house and over the stone steps into the pathway outside, then running to the street beyond as if the hounds were chasing.

For a moment Jetta stared around. Percival was a puddle, almost a lake of blood between front door and the opening to the great hall. More blood streamed and splattered, flecking walls and spotting as high as the two portraits hanging on the walls. The first step of the staircase was thick with vomit, and running from there to the front doorway, wide open, were slides and slips of feet in blood, blood on rugs, floors, doors and every man himself who fought.

Jetta, exhausted but only slightly injured, dropped down but avoided Percival's body. Many others were more badly injured. Benson sank to the floorboards, a deep cut to his arm which bled like water from a pump. Then Pip yelled and Jetta could hear his weeping. She crawled over to where he knelt with Sammy beside him, blubbering and sobbing.

Ilda had been stabbed through the ear and lay almost smiling, eyes open though glazed, the blood from her brain spreading over her neck and down her soft round cheek. A tiny scarlet trickle sank towards the corner of her mouth

With a jolt, Jetta sat there and began to cry as well, not just for Ilda and her boys but for everything that seemed unjust, painful and impossible to understand. Clutching at Ilda's hand, she couldn't feel the sting of the cut at her neck, the grazes on both hand and knuckles which bled from her own hand onto Ilda's, nor the deeper slice across her shoulder, cutting into her dress, her shift beneath, the skin, the flesh and muscle down to her elbow.

So she sobbed for Ilda and for Dominic, even for the dead king, and for everyone else who had died in the greater battle. Loyalty was the beauty in amongst the wickedness, and now Ilda had died for her, while dead by the hand of those who didn't even know her. She and her sons had killed their father, who was brutal and cruel and deserved to die. But no one, apart from herself, could know the utter truth of that.

Leaving Ilda in the arms of her sons, Jetta crawled away, finding a stripe of the outer sunshine where she might crouch, catch her breath, and throw off the misery. Then abruptly she was hauled upright by two thickset arms beneath her shoulders. She faced Sheriff Kettering.

"So not just a whore and killer of one innocent man, you've cooked up more trouble than a thief just out of Newgate. But you'll shortly be thrown into Newgate, not out of it."

"It's true. I helped kill Percival Maddock." The tears still streaked Jetta's face and once again she was half blind with weeping. "But that was self-defence. Do you blame anyone from the Fen Lane battle? If you have to kill or you'll be killed yourself, then you do it."

"And this poor old soul here?" demanded the sheriff, prodding at Ilda.

"You're mad, just horrid and mad," Jetta mumbled between sobs. "She's my friend, and that's why I'm crying. It's your wicked people who killed my lovely friend."

Both Pip and Sam stood, protecting their mother's body. "The lady's right. Mistress Jetta was our mum's good friend. She never hurt her."

Backing off a little, the sheriff still grinned, satisfied. "You killed the son of a lord. First the farrier, poor innocent man working hard for his master. But now you slaughter the master himself. This is appalling, and I hereby arrest you for crimes beyond imagination. You'll stand trial, and once found guilty you'll hang. Tis a shame I can't arrange to hang you twice."

"This is Mistress Jetta's home," Benson shouted over the din. "The dead man may be of a higher entitlement, but it was him came here uninvited and unwanted, pushing into an even greater lord's territory, trespassing for his own wicked intentions. He came to fight and kill. Therefore, his death, sheriff, is utterly justified and you damn well know it. I aided Mistress Jetta, and we acted together, forced to kill a man attempting to attack us. He's the one uninvited. We protected our own home. Deny that if you can."

"That might apply to you, sir," the sheriff shouted back, "but not to the strumpet who has no business here. And with your master the earl imprisoned as well, you'd best be mighty careful with your accusations."

"Nothing can get any worse for me though, can it?' Jetta shouted, the tears still clouding her eyes. "You've got the earl in the Tower and you want me in Newgate. And just how is that going to make you so happy? With Percival the scoundrel dead, he can't pay you for passing me over to him, or anyone else since I'm sure no one else wants me. So when I write to the judges and tell them how corrupt you are, there's a good chance of them finding out how true that is."

"You'll not say vile things like that, whore, and get away with it." He grabbed her arm. "And I'd swear you're a penniless doxy. You'll get no judge to listen to your lies."

Other sounds were almost obliterated beneath the shouting, but abruptly a different voice yelled out and everyone paused, startled.

The front doors still swung wide and fully open to the grounds, Now, through the doors marched someone else, shouting imperiously, and just behind him, a small crowd of his retinue dismounted and drew their swords.

"What the devil is going on?" raged a rather handsome and colourfully dressed gentleman.

Some of the sheriff's men stood stout but most were badly

wounded and one lay dead. Behind Jetta came the crowd of the entire household. They were staring at the newcomer, and Kettering backed.

It was only Benson, clutching his injured arm, who appeared to know the newcomer's identity. "My Lord Avery. You have come, I'm afraid, at a most inauspicious moment. I am also deeply sorry to tell you sir, that Lord Dominic is – absent."

Sir Avery Peasop gazed first at Benson, turned to stare at Jetta, and then glared at the sheriff. Sheriff Kettering already appeared somewhat intimidated. Evidently, he also recognised the visitor.

Stepping forwards reluctantly, Kettering bowed, saying, "Sir, this is a private matter concerning this wicked harlot," he pointed. "His lordship has been absent for some days, and this female has no right to be here. Indeed, she should be in gaol, and I have come to arrest her."

Pip shouted, "You and your bastards killed my mother. A mighty good woman, and she worked here in the kitchens. Her home too, it is. Get out now, and your filthy scum with you. Otherwise I'll call every man here to kill every man of yours, and don't you touch Mistress Jetta ever again. She may not be no duchess but she's well liked here and she's done no wrong. I can swear to that."

The clouds were darkening outside. The bright day of peaceful sunshine was threatening rain as evening approached.

"You leave us a house smeared with blood and filth," the head groom shouted. "And I'll complain to the sheriff of the next ward. He's a good man. Sheriff Plast, and I'll bet he already knows how corrupt you are."

"Had I known," Sir Avery interrupted, "what was happening here, I would also have brought Sheriff Plast with me, and fully armed. My entourage is also well armed, and I know my friend Dominic's present misfortune, and came here to discuss how to arrange his release. And I know damned well what you are capable of, Kettering. Did you have anything to do with his absurd arrest?"

"Plast has no jurisdiction here," the sheriff shouted back. "And nor do you, my lord. I had absolutely nothing to do with the earl's arrest, but I certainly intend arresting this whore."

Standing close, his arm cradled as he tried to stop the bleeding, Benson stamped, shouting at the sheriff, "Out, out, before we start the fight again while you know how outnumbered you are."

"Hush, Benson," Sir Avery shook his head. "I have a somewhat different idea." He looked again at Jetta. "Although we've never met, mistress, being a friend of Dominic's, I know exactly who you are. He spoke of you without the slightest animosity, and said that he had, let us say, invited, almost insisted, that you stay here." He was smiling, but then turned back to the sheriff. "I also know you, Kettering. I intend travelling immediately to court, and demanding that our new king hurls you into Newgate."

As one of the few whose injuries were very mild, the sheriff knew himself as an obvious culprit. The palm of one hand was bleeding, but otherwise the blood drips were from his companions or his own attacks on others. He turned stiffly and indicated to his assistants. But before leaving he turned to Jetta.

"I'll get a legal warrant," he spat. "You'll not get away with this. The king's going to have your master under attainder, confiscate every piece of property, and have him beheaded for treason. I reckon I should bring you in chains to see the execution before I order you hanged." He turned again to Avery, shouting, "I have superior backing already, sir, and I assure you my cousin won't see me arrested. He may speak to King Henry of you, and it will not be me in trouble, but yourself.".

One of his assistants sniggered, "The whore fancies the earl, do she? Not rare, I s'pose. Stoopid slut. As if an earl wants a cheap doxy."

"They can hitch up in Purgatory," spat another. "That's where both will be before the end of the month."

Sir Avery blocked the sheriff's departure, and now the Peasop retinue, swords raised, stood behind him. "So," he said, one step towards the sheriff, "it's your vile cousin Howard who has arranged Desford's imprisonment in the Tower. You make it remarkably clear, fool, which will please neither your cousin nor the king. And it opens a new path for me to arrange my friend's release. Your cousin will not thank you."

Jetta stared back. Pip strode to the sheriff, both hands fisted, but Benson pulled him aside. Attacking the man wouldn't help. Addressing the sheriff again, Benson pointed down at Percival's bloody corpse and said, "You need to inform this creature's parents of his death, and have him removed for burial. He lives in Cripplegate, I believe."

"Not my business," the sheriff retorted. "I never brought him along nor asked for his company. Neither his life nor his death are my business, and he's not resident in my ward. Besides, I understand his father was killed in the battle last month. Not much of the family left, then."

She hadn't known, and for a moment Jetta felt a sense of sweeping guilt. She had worsened the situation of a family already in mourning. They had supported the Lancastrian cause, but although Tudor had won, that family had lost. The remaining mother and wife could now cry for both the men of her family.

Yet that woman had been cruel as well, working her twice as hard as any other servant, and promising to give her as a slave to her son

"I didn't know the lord was dead too," Jetta said. "And I think Percival is only about seventeen, so perhaps I shouldn't have – but he attacked me. I could have died."

Sir Avery held up a warning hand to his men who were pushing forwards. He said, "Any woman is entitled to protect herself and you have plenty of injuries to prove your case." He nodded, then turned again to Kettering. "But it's your appalling behaviour," he told the sheriff, "that disgusts me. I know your cousin. We are not friends and now he has the king's ear. But I will speak with him. He won't want to be shamed by some blatant corruption, a petty cousin he rarely sees. And I'll certainly be discussing – without swords – the wrongful imprisonment of Desford."

"Why would you help this slut?" the sheriff demanded. "What has she to do with the titled and powerful lords of this land, especially now? And once she's tossed into Newgate, she can cry all day and all night as she pisses in the gutter and sleeps on the stone."

"Your cousin and your usurper king may also be corrupt for all I know, but it will be you in Newgate, Kettering, and not this innocent girl." Avery glared, stepping very closely to the sheriff, and staring down into his small squinting eyes. "Now, will you leave with a promise to make no further trouble for anyone in this household, or shall I order my men to send all of you straight to Purgatory immediately?"

Holding up both stubby hands, the sheriff lowered his head. "I'll not fight a lord of the land, but I'll be telling my cousin exactly what happened here." He beckoned his assistants and pushed towards the doorway.

"You can say whatever you wish concerning me," Avery said, "but you'll swear, before leaving, not to come after this girl again."

"Humph," said the sheriff, trying to force his way out. But now blocked by those better armed and eager to prove their skills, he nodded. "The girl can rest." He muttered with considerable reluctance. "But it's you, sir, I shall soon see alongside your friend's cell in the Tower."

Sir Avery permitted his departure, with a push and a curse. "Fool," he called. "I'll not be forgetting your stupidity, nor your vile behaviour."

The wind swept in, and Avery shut the door behind the sheriff, calling for his men to make sure and see them away off the grounds. Then he turned to Jetta. "You've done no wrong, mistress, and I'll not permit imprisonment in Newgate for someone so obviously innocent."

"Thank you so very much," Jetta whispered. "I've slept on stone before – in the kitchen of this dead boy and his dead father. But Newgate, that would be – terrifying."

Laughing slightly, Avery nodded. "Never been there. Never will. And don't worry. Nor will you. But first we need to remove that damned corpse."

"Into the river," Benson suggested, curling his lip. "My lord, I thank you with all my heart, but I can handle this."

"Should the Maddock mother be left in ignorance?" Avery now shook his head. "I'll arrange for my men to take the boy back to his mother. In the meantime, I believe you need to send for a doctor – even two of them if possible – and arrange the funeral of this poor woman."

Ilda's body also lay in its own blood. And Jetta knelt beside the glazed and empty face of the woman she had grown to care for and admire. She bent, kissing her forehead while holding back the tears. "I've cried so much for three weeks and more," she mumbled. "Now, Sir Avery, I want to be strong again and you've given me back my courage."

"It has been my pleasure," the man said, and meant it. "I loathe that vile sheriff, and I loathe the Earl of Plymouth. I want Dominic free, and I want that wretched king learning justice and kind decency."

She watched him leave, then Jetta turned immediately and walked to the stairs, avoiding the puddled blood, and began to climb up to her bedchamber. She didn't look back though she heard Benson send another of the grooms to fetch the doctor, while Pip and Sam prepared their mother for the local priest. It was Benson himself, with great reluctance, who arranged to ride to Cripplegate with Avery's men concerning the death of Percival Maddocks.

As all sounds floated into the silence that calmed her, Jetta climbed the stairs and allowed the tears. She sobbed for loss and misery, for the past and for the future. She was still crying as she stopped outside her bedchamber, and then turned. Now she walked the corridor leading to Dominic's room, and pressed her fingers to the door, pushing it open.

The shadows encompassed her. The bedchamber seemed to whisper of him, even sing of him. She tumbled to his bed, curled, wiped her tears, and fell asleep.

Chapter Thirty Three

"I'm leaving," she told Benson. He swirled around in surprise. "Well," she continued, "I'm not a slut nor a whore but I'm not a lady either. I can't just live here adding to the estate's expenses while poor Dominic, I mean his lordship, is locked in the Tower."

Benson lowered his voice. "I've sent a request to his lordship, the Earl of Oxford, begging for our lord's release. I know it's not my place to do so, but I simply knew it had to be done."

She almost wanted to kiss him. "I accompanied Lord Leays and we gained an appointment to see the earl," she said. "But he just twisted everything. Now I'm going to do something else."

Raising both eyebrows, Benson leaned forwards, his voice softer still. "Be very careful Madam. This is a dangerous time. We cannot be sure of the new king's sudden decisions. He isn't bound by Plantagenet tradition I'm sad to say. And respectable women now widowed after the great battle, whatever side their husbands supported, are forced to walk the streets begging, or earn the crusts they need in some other manner, even worse and more shameful."

"I know." Jetta sniffed. "I've done the begging but never the other. Now it's a lot worse. There's widows trying to feed their babies and little children without a penny of help from anywhere." Already she carried a large rattan shopping basket, handles over her shoulder. "I'm taking just a little of the clothes I was given here, but not everything." She paused, then said with a loud sniff, "And if his lordship returns, could you please tell him, just in case he wants to know, that I've gone to Ned."

"Ned?"

"Yes, the forester Ned." Jetta sighed and sniffed again. "But I'm not running away. I've got plans. So if that horrid sheriff has the gall to turn up again, don't tell him a thing about me, just that I've disappeared."

"Should you ever need my help, Mistress Jetta," Benson said softly, "just let me know. There are many here who would gladly do whatever you ask."

Now she was crying again, but her tears were hidden as she slipped outside, for it had rained most of the night and now it was threatening thunder.

"I appreciate that, Benson," she sniffed. "You are so very loyal and very kind. I know you didn't like me at first. No one did. But now I think we're friends."

"Madam, I agree," Benson mumbled. "And with great admiration, I assure you. But Sir Avery may have a better chance of helping his lordship.",

"You're probably right," Jetta nodded. "But I'm going to try too. I won't stop until he's free."

Felicia was waiting ready saddled, Pip and Sam ready with the mounting block.

"You look after yourself, lady."

"You know I'm not a lady, Sam," Jetta smiled.

"I reckon you ought to be," Pip said. "We lost our mother, but it was you she fought for, and we knows why. You kept our secret, even when the danger came to you instead. That was brave and mighty kind. Or we'd be in Newgate ourselves."

"I'm so sorry about your mother." Jetta had mounted, but settled herself in the saddle and looked down sadly on both boys. "She was a lovely person. I don't have friends, not many anyway. But she was a real friend and so are both of you. Benson too. But not many others."

"Perhaps what she did for you," Pip said, half whisper, "will get her sins pardoned. We know our father's in purgatory and he'll be going to hell. Maybe we'll go there too, for what we did to him. But Mum's gone to a better place, we know it."

The rain pelted from clouds to trees, streaming from every leaf as Jetta entered the remains of the old forest. The mare unamused, walked head down and shook its mane in Jetta's face. But she was once again feeling free, and laughed. The tears had stopped. Now it was just rainwater that she wiped away.

She rode for some hours, stopping to speak softly to Felicia and calm her as the thunder followed the lightening. Drenched herself, she was more concerned for the horse becoming stuck in bogs, and already the mud splashed them both.

Such a ride would always have taken some hours, and the pelting rain now slowed everything. The discomfort became monotonous, plodding through rain so heavy it curtained the road ahead, Jetta's back began to shriek and she wondered if poor Felicia felt the same. Sudden forked lightening sizzled right through her path and the horse shrank back in fear, then bolted. Gripping tightly to both the reins and the frantic muscled neck in front of her, she tried desperately to calm the mare, but the thunder which followed, fired greater panic.

It was some time before Felicia calmed, but they were still in the right direction, and it seemed the terrifying gallop had saved them time. But now both woman and horse were in greater pain.

Arriving at Ned's cottage beneath the trees, she almost fell from the mount, and it was Ned's arms she virtually fell into. He was, she silently thanked the magnanimity of the Lord, delighted to see her, lifted her bodily, and carried her indoors. Having plonked her hurriedly on the settle, he ran back into the rain, tethered the horse under the awning, tossed Felicia a handful of hay and appreciated carrots, and strode back to Jetta.

"You are, my little one, the person I'm most glad to see. Indeed, the *only* one I'm glad to see, for I'd be no way pleased to see any of these new guards in their fancy hats."

Not quite sure whether it was the hats that mattered most, Jetta asked, "And I can stay? On the floor and I won't take your bed and you can't make me have it while you sleep on the floor because I know you. That's what you'll think. But a few dead leaves, dry ones if possible, would make a good pillow and the weather's been hot until now anyway."

He was watching her closely and for a moment she wondered what on earth he was thinking. He interrupted her thoughts, "Well, my sweet cherry-blossom, there's a few questions I have. Why here? Why not Lord Andrew? "

"This might sound like me being bad coming here,: she mumbled back. "But I'm wanted by that horrid Chiswick sheriff and I think if he found I'd been welcomed at Andrew's estate, they'd accuse Andrew as they have Dominic. Now you might ask if the same might put you in trouble, and it's sort of true, but no one ever knows about you or who you are or where you live. And if the sheriff ever turned up, I'd just run."

"No need to run with me here, little snow drop," he insisted.

She thought a moment and then spoke so quickly, the words tripped over each other. "When I was little the nuns beat any courage out of me. But you taught me courage all over again, dearest Ned." She blinked back the threat of tears. "The Maddox made me scared again. I kept some courage but not a lot. And always running away – then I met Dominic. It's more panic now. I learned courage but lost it all over and over again."

"Interesting," said Ned, nodding vigorously. "And I've got a story to tell as well, for yesterday, not happy at knowing naught about naught, I went very quiet when up come Lord Andrew of Leays. That was mighty interesting too."

VESPERS

She found herself clutching a cup of wine. "Tell me," she said over the rim of the cup.

"Oh yes, tell you I will, for it's as much your story, my dear," Ned said. "Having fought with him for King Richard, he came to see me yesterday. Just turned up, no fancy retinue. He said as how he was mighty sorry for Gimlett's death, since he used to live in his old house years back, when his lordship worked for many years for the Duke of Gloucester before ever he was king, and was his top spy. An interesting job, but maybe risky. Anyway, that's not really the story. Instead we talked for hours, and mostly how to get your friend released. Lord Andrew's friend as well, it seems."

She almost dropped her cup. "How?"

"His lordship," Ned said with a smirk, "first of all and with my help, reckons he can get you into the Tower, though only for a few moments. Then a few days later, if Dominic is still locked in, Lord Leays is going to get you into the palace, and see the king."

"Oh dear," sighed Jetta. "I'm sorry and here's the cowardice again, but that sound so absolutely impossible. Do I jump in the window? Or down the chimney? It's crazy, Ned – too ambitious. Can you really believe it?"

"Seems you're a disbelieving young snapper," grinned Ned. "I'd not say it if it was so impossible, but as for Lord Andrew – do you think he's more daft than I am? He's worked for kings and been a spy but never caught. So now, listen to me. It won't be quick."

"Anything. Except climb into some guard's bed. Actually, for Dominic, I'd probably try that too."

"No forced bedding required," Ned frowned. "But it's the Tower first, so let me explain. The first thing to say, is a have a very old friend amongst the Tower guards. He might not remember me, he might not even work there anymore, but I have to hope for the best. He's James, and was married to the sister of my father's neighbour, years ago. I was fifteen, and he was eighteen. I never saw him again."

"So it's a small chance?"

"Folk getting mighty good jobs like that," Ned insisted, "trust, meeting kings and lords, good earnings and good sleeping quarters, no way they leave that job unless they get chucked out. So I'm going to find him. Getting to meet the guards won't be easy to start with, but reckon I'll make it in a couple of days."

"And if you find him, he'll let me in?" Jetta didn't believe it. "That would be risking his wonderful job you've been telling me about."

"Just a brief few minutes to deliver something proper – a meal – or a book – even a message. If you dress up, the lady's finest, and Lord Andrew comes with us, we'd not be stopped at the gates. And just to ask to see a guard – not a prisoner, makes it seem innocent. We ask for James Harringford. Important. And easy enough."

The rain stopped, the sun came out, and the world turned cheerful. Those who had feared the new monarchy now settled, their trust growing. Where the taxes demanded were far greater than previously, the richer swore but paid.

Widows whose husbands had been killed during the great battle, now dragged from slum to village and made quick pennies from the only work available to them, but the privileged remained safe, although they paid for that safety. Situations once only held by the titled, either because the titled had been killed, or because the more successful masses fostered the ambition to be greater still, were now taken by the common man. Such success rebounded. After all, many said, the king himself was no genuine royalty. Even his previous title, being Earl of Richmond, had been attaindered by Edward IV, and so King Henry, whatever mythical Welsh history he claimed, was as common a man as the one selling cabbages, onions and garlic in the market.

If an ordinary gentleman could become king, then an ordinary trader could become as rich as he might dream.

In company with Ned, Jetta visited the Leays mansion and was greeted, as she had hoped, by Tyballis. Immediately she was almost dragged up the stairs to a huge bedchamber on the first floor, and ordered to sit on the massive bed. Jetta had an idea, although naturally didn't ask, that here the normal practise of a lord and his lady keeping separate quarters, might not apply.

Jetta sat, and breathed in deeply. There was a scent of wild-flowers and sweet soap. The colours were pale except for murals of fields sweeping down to rivers, and the birds flying down to drink and feed.

"I love your room."

"Thank you," Tyballis smiled. "Now let's see if you love any of my clothes. Most will be a little too big, since you're more of a nymph than a woman, my dear. But we'll find something to make you grand and look like a duchess at first glance."

And so it was between the Earl of Leays and Ned, the forester, that Jetta rode to the Tower, dressed in immaculate green silk grandeur and so felt entirely out of character.

At the gates beneath the great stone arch, they were stopped, and Andrew removed his hat, stared down at the two guards, and announced himself. "I have personal and private business with one of your official attendants," he said. "I am prepared to wait at the Wakefield Tower, but I assume that I will not be required to wait for long."

"Indeed, my lord," the guard bowed. "Captain Harringford is on duty and therefore can be informed immediately of your presence."

The Wakefield Tower had once housed kings. Jetta stared impressed at the faded beauty and the continuing comfort of the seating and curtains, but it was not her surroundings that flooded her thoughts. She wondered with suffocating excitement if she'd succeed in the one desire she held as important as her own life. Now she sat silent. They had waited a short few minutes, and then one of the highly liveried Tower guards strode in, looking utterly mystified. But then he looked around and saw Ned as Ned almost jumped on him with a bellow of satisfaction

"It's you, Jamie. Scumbag you are, not to keep in touch all these years."

"And where do I write? To Ned probably living somewhere in England? And no doubt up in a tree."

"You and me, Jamie, down the Barrel and Joker this evening, and I drink the ale you buy me, and you drink the ale I buy you."

The man was beaming within his scarlet dazzle. "You came for that? Well, I'm grateful, Ned, truly grateful. But I'm not off duty until five of the clock."

Smiling, Andrew stepped forwards. "Your friend Ned comes for you, longing to discover you after so long. But my lady friend and I myself have come for a different reason, and It's a reason you are going to dislike."

Shaking his head, the guard stared at Ned, then Andrew. Finally he gazed at Jetta, and bowed again. "My Lady, if I can help? But I must warn you all that I'm a captain now and must fulfil my duty. I'll not risk actions against the strict rules here, nor against my own conscience."

"If what I ask is against your conscience, then I shall apologise and leave you in peace, sir," Jetta said, sitting very still. "And the details of what I need may well be against your rules. However, there is neither any need nor any possibility of me causing a troublesome situation. I shall dress in the simple clothes I carry in my basket, and quickly deliver something small to one of your important prisoners. Then I shall leave without another word."

The captain of the guard sighed. "I knew it. Oh Ned, you want to lose me my job."

"Not a crumb of it," Ned said, keeping his voice low. "You have Lord Stark, the Earl of Desford locked up here, as you must clearly know."

"The earl is not allowed visitors. Visiting is what you hope for, isn't it?" Jamie frowned. "I'm sorry. I won't do it. Indeed, I can't do it."

"Quite right, my friend," Ned grinned. "I've always known you as a man of honour, and honour it is, true and clean. The earl has asked for deliveries from time to time, and I know it. He asked for paper and gall and quills. He got them, and managed to send out a short letter. No trouble. He asked for books, and got them. No one complained. Did you deliver any of that?"

"No." James shook his head. "But I sanctioned the deliveries."

"Now, what a sweet coincidence. So now you can sanction this one. It's only a kitchen girl will deliver, and she'll hand over something you'll see beforehand. No knives, no poisons, no ropes or bricks. What's wrong with that?"

"If you wish it," Andrew said, soft voiced, "I will stand as assurance. Meaning that if you are discovered as the perpetrator behind the delivery, you may say I ordered you. As an earl of the land, you found it difficult to disobey."

"And do you order me, my lord?" The guard stared back.

Andrew was smiling again. "Let us say that the word is a little loose around the corners. I order, I ask – I plead, I beg. Take your pick. And in the meantime, enjoy meeting your friend from the past. Ned is in charge of the old forest near St. John's, working for king and country, and thus a gentleman of respectable importance. My own position is untenable, and I have now sworn allegiance, regretfully, to his majesty. We are not, I assure you, asking for some appalling act of irreparable illegality."

Jetta was pulling off Tyballis' clothes, then folding them carefully on the chair in the tiny vestibule. Beneath she wore the simple kitchen tunic and apron, her hair tucked up into a starched white cap. When she scurried back into the waiting-office beyond the vestibule, she saw Andrew showing the guard the items that she intended delivering to Dominic.

"Not that any of these are important," Andrew said, passing the small basket to Jetta, "It is the chance to see him and quickly discuss how to approach the king for his release, that matters."

"I accept it. Considering what is expected – considering what is allowed – I am behaving badly. But not badly enough to be hanged, I hope. But, madam, you must be quick. One minute – three minutes – hand over the package. Then it's time to go. And of course, I'll be with you to unlock the door and lock it again behind you. Then, on the way out, I shall dismiss you as a kitchen girl delivering something of no consequence. I must apologise but I'll have no choice."

Jetta heard Ned and Andrew talking as she walked off, scuttling like the kitchen maid she had always been, just a little behind the Captain of the Guard. No one took the slightest notice of them as James Hollingford led Jetta to the Keep, and up the short stone staircase on the outside of the great central building, open to the guards who constantly marched the grounds night and day. It was the only entrance and therefore ensured great security.

There Jetta waited as Jamie took the dark steps leading to the floor above, and he stopped at one heavily barred doorway. Here he knocked and as he loudly unlocked both the padlock and the inverted key, he called out, "Your lordship, if you are prepared to accept, I have here a quick delivery. Are you ready, my lord?"

And Dominic's voice from across the room, "I'm ready for anything which might break the monotony."

His voice was faintly contemptuous, but it was him. So recognisably him, that, in spite of her earlier determination, Jetta abruptly burst into sobs.

Chapter Thirty Four

The basket dropped to the stone floor, and Dominic pulled her immediately between his arms.

Jetta flung her arms around his waist, while his tightened around her shoulders, and for some moments neither of them seemed able to move. She whispered, "I'm not allowed to stay. I wish I could."

"This is an amazing and unexpected surprise. Possibly a miracle." His own whisper tickled her ear. "At least now I can tell you the truth. I couldn't before. Now I feel that nothing matters. So I'm free to tell you how much I've missed you."

Gazing up at him, Jetta saw the weariness, the lines from nose to mouth and the faded sadness in his eyes. He had lost muscle weight, and she wanted to kiss him as he had once kissed her.

"And am I free to tell you I adore you?" She peeped up, looking into his eyes again, and was startled. For so long she'd seen his expression as cold, drowning in ice, his brows low, the lids heavy. She'd sometimes seen him smile, even seen him laugh. Yet sometimes even that could be cold.

Now, just moments past, she had seen the weary sadness.

Yet instantly he simmered and his eyes burned against her forehead. "Love?" he whispered back. "Do I know what that is? But wanting you, missing you – dreaming of you. I've been doing that. Holding you like this is what I've longed for every day."

She gasped, this was what she could never have expected. "And I'm going to get you out," Jetta said, no longer bothering to whisper. "Andrew's downstairs. He has ideas. Ned's there too. He's a friend of this nice guard who let me in."

"But you can't stay any longer, miss," the guard interrupted. "Leave whatever's in your basket. Tip it out and bring it empty. Now, goodbyes, it has to be I'm afraid. If anyone notices a longer stay, it'll be a disaster for all three of us."

Gabbling over the demand to leave, Jetta spoke almost too fast for anyone to understand. "Andrew says the king has you here to make an example. But I'm going to prove you're not the right one for that."

"There are already examples of ruthlessness – even cruelty. Clarence's poor son is locked downstairs."

"But the child's what? Ten? Eleven? What terrible crime could be committed so soon after the battle. We've not even had the coronation yet."

"The boy has committed the terrible crime of having more right to the throne than the invader," Dominic told her, ignoring the guard.

Jetta struggled to speak clearly. "But it's not just the king who put you here, Dominic. It's that ugly Howard, Earl of Plymouth. I can't understand why but he's to blame.."

The guard sympathised. "But I have to insist, mistress, whether it seems like another cruelty or not. Tis always watched here – times in – times out. Too long is mighty dangerous."

Dominic leaned forwards to kiss her, but as their faces touched, he murmured, "I can't. Not here. But thank my dear friends for me, and look after yourself, little one."

She was in tears again when she left and hurried back to Ned and Lord Leays.

VESPERS

They rode through the length of the city from the Tower to Ludgate, passing the cheaps, St. Paul's, Watling Street and the closed shutters in the shadows. They saw that most streets were still half empty but now a few were half full. Many of the city's inhabitants were discovering courage, even trust.

As Jetta, Ned and Andrew rode out beneath the high arch of Ludgate, back in the Tower Dominic was sitting, legs stretched, beneath the long streaks of sunshine gleaming through the high arrow slit.

He had felt the delicious tingle in his fingers as he had clasped her so tightly to him, also feeling her warmth and the push of her small breasts against his ribs. Jetta's breath on his face had been sweet and his entire body had felt loved, while his mind lost any other direction, nor retained any other memory.

Dominic had assumed there would be little of interest in the emptied contents of Jetta's basket. It had simply been the method by which she had gained entry. And so at first he had not looked. When he did, it was different to his expectations.

Some items were extremely welcome. There was food, the first of the autumn fruit and new baked bread with a thick layer of beef dripping. There was his own bedrobe, deep blue and woollen lined so that climbing naked from his bed, he could immediately be warm. This was a great convenience. There was also, wrapped in the folds of the bedrobe, a small and beautifully scribed prayer book, partially in English and partially in Latin as was normal, but this was not something Dominic felt he needed. The assumption was that either Jetta wished to fill the basket, or make a good impression. He appreciated the illuminated letters. And then, fleetingly regarding the pages, he noticed the end of the small book was empty of either words or illustrations.

The boy in the rooms beneath, was calling to him. "Dominic, you had a delivery. What a lucky soul you are. Is there good food?"

"I wish I could pass you some." Then Dominic paused. There was ribbon wrapped around the prayer book. Untying this, he tied it around one roll of bread and dripping, pulled it tight, and slipped it up through the arrow slit, dropping it slowly outside. "Put your hand through the window. Can you grab what I'm sending? But untie it and let me pull back the ribbon or I'll never be able to pass you anything again."

At first it swung away, and Edward thought he had lost it. Then the breeze blew it into his hand, he grabbed, untied the ribbon, and shouted about the success. Dominic pulled up the ribbon. "It works," Edward squeaked. "We can do magical things every day. I'll send to you and you can send to me."

Dominic grinned. There was not going to be so much to send either way, since neither had such treasures in their prisons.

But one thing suddenly made unexpected sense. Tying the silk ribbon back around the prayer book to keep it safe, he realised that something had slipped from the spine. Where the small cuts of decorated parchment were knotted together, they were then attached to a stiff cover. But within the spine had been something with very little to do with prayer.

A short narrow piece of sharp steel had been hidden there. Now it lay on the palm of Dominic's hand. A blade so small it would surely neither kill nor even wound. But Dominic understood entirely, remembering exactly what Jetta had once done with the breakfast knife in his own home.

Without a handle it might be harder to manipulate, but with a wrapping of some material or even parchment, he could try as he wished. The padlock, of course, hung outside his door. But an extremely sharp blade was a sublime addition to his small collection of belongings. It might well prove utterly unhelpful, but he adored Jetta for her ingenuity and courage.

And, as he looked through the book, the tiny weapon now in his hand, he saw something else. On one of the blank pages was a message from Andrew. Dominic read it at once.

"You will be free soon, my dear friend. You have Howard Earl of

VESPERS

Plymouth to thank for this imprisonment. He convinced Tudor to use you as a warning to others. I intend killing the man, unless you manage to do so first."

Smiling, he closed the book and tucked it safely away.

Later, calling down to Edward, Dominic discussed the routines and general practise of the Tower prisons, something the boy knew better.

"Used to be rooms for other reasons," Edward said. "They didn't have many prisoners when the last two kings ruled. There was my father. He was killed here, in private they said, but they didn't tell me till I was older. Poor man. He always wanted more power than he got."

"It seems most do, even the cobblers and the armourers, smiths and butchers. Do we all dream of more?"

"I don't," the boy sighed. "I never did a wrong thing to anybody far as I know, especially this new king since I never met him. But here I am locked up and likely to stay that way. I sleep. I walk in circles. I'm too hot or I'm too cold."

"Can you read?"

"Oh yes. I've had a good education. My tutor was Duncan Ray, one of the best. Do you have books?"

"I'll send some down," Dominic said. From the delight of seeing Jetta, and the need of a decision for what he might do with the knife blade, now he felt suddenly bilious. The boy he spoke too, a royal son of a royal prince, was being sent mad by inactivity without cause. If this could be done to an innocent child, why should he expect better.

Clarence, brother of both Edward IV and Richard III, had rebelled violently and more than once. He had earned prison and death. His son had not.

"Oh please," young Edward begged. "A precious thought , my lord, something to do. Something to read. And at least as yet – no torture. It was never done, never discussed, against the laws of God and man as you know. But now they say King Henry is going to bring it back. The guards say there's a rack in the dungeon. It'll be used. Can you imagine?"

"I've no desire to imagine," Dominic said. "This new king, I believe, is not a good man. But without meeting him, not even to plead for my life, I can't be sure."

"If you meet him to plead for your life, plead for mine too," called Edward.

"I'm not quite ready to beg," Dominic smiled. "I'm more inclined to imagine killing. Secondly, bribing. Pleading comes last."

The boy laughed, "You're already helping so much. Just to have someone to talk with, and real books to read. This one is Chaucer?"

"Should I ever manage to leave," Dominic sighed, "I shall pass you every book I have. Perhaps I should write one. Or perhaps you should, proclaiming the sweetness of life locked in the Tower for no crime whatsoever."

"Humph," Edward half sniggered. "I'd have to be clever for that. But maybe I'll do it in my head."

Nearly three miles distant as the sky clouded once more and the rain threatened, Ned's small home welcomed its owner and the two visitors. Each of them clutched a cup of wine, poured from an enormous casket delivered on the orders of Lord Leays.

"That should last a couple of years," Ned said, staring at the barrel with awe.

"Not if I keep visiting, and especially after we get Dominic released and he visits here as well. You'll be lucky to keep it going for a month."

Jetta, drinking less, seemed to be floating in a daze of both misery and delight. Ned understood her problem. "Don't you worry, little rose bud. We'll be getting him out, and it's for all of us. No innocent man should be treated in such a way."

"It's even more unfair, if that's possible, for the boy locked up below. Remember poor young Edward, son of Clarence. The child's still only ten, but the new king has him incarcerated because when he gets older he just might – and might not – claim the right to the crown since it's more his than this usurpers."

"Sadly predictable," Andrew sighed. "It seems our new king has no sympathy for anyone except himself."

"And his mother," Ned added.

Jetta sat up straight, drained her cup, and smiled. "I've had an idea. You said you might be able to get me into the palace. Can you really? And can you do it within the week?"

"Every honest soul in England who calls this man king," Andrew sighed, "has the right to meet with the monarch to make his request. This usually requires a bribe. In the past with Edward IV, bribing Hastings was the usual entrance fee. I have no idea if Oxford now takes that place or not. But I shall discover the truth and pay if necessary. Keep in touch, my dear."

"And I wear my grandeur, or my peasant's shift?" Jetta had already packed the clothes she needed to return to Tyballis, and handed over the neat parcel to Andrew.

"I shall think this over," Andrew decided. He left within the hour, offering hospitality to Jetta, but understanding her refusal.

Indeed, the initial reason was simply to relax, to wander the forest when the rain leaked away and the sunshine reasserted itself. She sat on the doorstep watching the birds and the small animals, the wandering herds of deer and the skuttle of weasels and badgers. Daily she gazed at the glory of both sunrise and sunset, and then the silver sweep of the moon.

But there was more. Although she thought Andrew a magnificent man of incredible magnanimity, he was an earl and she was too embarrassed, impressed and ridiculously awed to speak of anything personal while he was present. He seemed already well aware of her feelings for Dominic, but it was only with Ned she could admit this openly.

He accompanied her on one more visit, arranged on the following day. The sheriff whose wardship covered the forest, even the Chapel of St, John's and the convent of Saint Alkeld, was neither Sheriff Kettering, Nor Sheriff Plast. He was an elderly man who tended to shuffle and invariably refused to attend meetings, requiring everyone to come to him.

Jetta and Ned rode to his office by the road where the woods almost bordered the river in the south. Sheriff Manfield was contemplating his generous breakfast.

"Ah," with his mouth full as he looked up, spoon hovering, "it's you, Ned. And a new young friend I've not seen before. Don't tell me you've decided to wed at last?"

"By no means," Ned smiled, telling Jetta to sit as he sat himself, both stools drawn up to the little table. "It's something perhaps even more unexpected, sir. But I'll wait till you've wiped the platter clean of your crumbs."

"Now you have me interested." He mopped the drips of ale from his beard. "You have a most valuable position and were a trusted servant to the king. Now a few things have altered, but hopefully the important things won't alter too much. So let's have a confidential discussion, my friend."

"It's simple." Ned nodded. "First meet my young friend Jetta Lawson. Neither lady nor whore, and I can swear on our friendship that she's a girl of respectable honesty and kindness. Now, the previous king was working towards stopping corruption in a number of ways. Any idea what our new king has to say about it?"

"Not the faintest,"

"Then I'll have to confess, I'm about to find out. Two wards away where Jetta Lawson used to live on the Desford estate, there's a sheriff I'd call a bastard of absolute corruption and greed. You may know him but I hope he's no friend."

"Sheriff John Kettering. I know him indeed. And I've threatened him more than once." Sheriff Mansfield didn't bother to stand, but he nodded, and waited.

"He's accused this young woman of crimes she has never committed. There's a dozen witnesses, including a grand lord, who swear she's innocent, and have said so more than once. But the sheriff thinks he's been made to look a fool, and he's thought up some noise to blame on the grand lord. Now that lord is in the Tower, and my young friend here is in danger of imminent arrest. You've no power over any of that, and I know it, shame that it is. But the sheriff is a troublemaker, and there's no one to complain to, but the king himself. Lord Oxford is reckoned honest, though I've no way of knowing it. Will you help me accuse Sheriff Kettering of all the wickedness I know he's done and is still doing? It bubbles out of the bastard unless you fill his grubby hand with coins."

The sheriff smiled, finished his breakfast, and leaned back in his chair. "I'll do it," he said. "I'll benefit, I reckon, by getting to know something of this new king of ours. So there's undoubtedly an appointment for a day soon enough. And you'll come with me, Ned. We both hold respectable positions, and both get our pay through official channels. Come back in two days, and I'll have the date by then. If you wish to come, young lady," he turned to Jetta, "I see no reason why not."

"I have a reason," Jetta said. "I'm not official and I'm not paid by the crown. I'm not paid by anyone. I could be seen as – well – not even respectable. That's happened before. I might spoil your mission."

The sunshine was bright again as they rode back through the forest.

It was almost a dream again, and that night when she dreamed indeed, she dreamed of the dream. Twice she had stolen Dominic's bedchamber, and that space had been so beautiful that now she thought of sleeping there again, but not alone.

Three walls facing the bed were painted with a wistful mural of mountains and the deer scrambling the heights. The huge hearth, mantled in dark streaked marble, she had only seen empty but had imagined it lit, a roaring fire of perfumed logs, herself in Dominic's arms as she gazed at the brilliance of the flames. The bed itself was luxury, paintings were hanging on the wall behind, partially hidden by thick velvet curtains. There were chests, small tables, large chairs, and a door to the garderobe. The dream was to share it with its true owner, and so she slept smiling, and believing.

Chapter Thirty Five

Without visits from any person except those delivering his meals, and another bringing the books, quill, gall and parchment he had asked for several times, there was no person for Dominic to talk with except the young Earl of Warwick, imprisoned in the rooms below. They laughed together, chatted together, discussed politics together.

But Dominic's only companion being a ten-year-old boy was not what he yearned for.

His thoughts of Jetta increased. He found himself unable to sleep until he thought of her, imagining her beside him, and his arms around her. Then, calm, deeply breathing and not alone, he slept and dreamed of the woman he now knew he loved. For an earl to marry a kitchen girl would be a scandal. It would be accepted only if he aligned himself with someone of his own class, and kept the kitchen girl as his mistress. That was common enough. Yet, since he might never emerge from the Tower except to face the execution block, it was a decision he might never need to make.

Dominic kept Jetta's knife blade safe, but could not yet see a use for it. He had attempted every keyhole and had passed many dull hours considering escape. The possibility did not seem in the least possible.

"So if you find a way out, please tell me," Edward of Warwick sighed.

Dominic had lowered more books. "Ask for them yourself," he advised. "Being trapped here doesn't mean you can't have any relief. Visitors seem forbidden unless it's for legal reasons. But books and pens seem to be on offer. At least that's something I assume you can afford."

"Yes, thank the Lord, if He remembers me at all," the boys said. "Everything here has to be paid for, even food. Of course I can pay – but what about those who can't? Though I guess it's only the rich and titled that end up in these rooms."

"Not having visited Newgate," Dominic answered, "I can't be sure of the difference. But paying for anything better than scraps of black bread and dirty water seem to be all they'll get unless they have money. Those locked up for theft can presumably use those stolen coins to feed themselves. I've heard that more die of starvation and disease in there, than by execution. So, in one sense although hardly sensible, we are the lucky ones."

"At least starvation doesn't happen here."

"Only because we can pay."

Enjoying the only thing she could think of to do in Ned's absence, Jetta tidied, cleaned, rearranged, and added anything she considered both attractive and accessible. She sang while dancing in the large shadows of the ground floor. Small clumps of grass pushed up between the floorboards, but Jetta couldn't guess whether Ned welcomed such things or not. She left the little green intruders, but yanked out the claws of the ivy which threatened to enter through the roof and collapse the walls.

Upstairs was a slight struggle since half the steps were missing but there wasn't much she could do about that. Indeed, there was very little there except a tiny pile of clothes. She was making up the bed when Ned and Sheriff Manfield returned, both looking surprisingly pleased with themselves.

"It went well then?" Jetta scuttled down the stairs, jumping over the broken parts.

Ned caught her. "Very well, little duckling. Let's celebrate with some wine, and I'll tell you all about it."

The one chair went to the sheriff, and Jetta and Ned sat on the stools, cups cradled. It was a warm day, and no rain threatened.

"I admit it," the sheriff said, enjoying the wine. "Perhaps not perfect in the sense of having your friend released from the Tower though."

Jetta's expression dropped. She drained her cup and placed it back on the table. "I never expected anything that good," she said, which was true. But she had spent that entire night just hoping and praying.

"Our turn came, and in we marched to the throne room," the sheriff smiled. "Bigger and grander than anything I've ever seen. Gold this and gold that. Amazing."

"I prefer the forest," Ned muttered, but was patiently ignored.

"We introduced ourselves, and the king did a fairly good job of greeting us, asking about our work, and treating us as important members of his own staff. Then Ned started talking about the corruption."

"He seemed a little defensive at first," Ned grinned. "Maybe he thought we'd seen through some of his own."

"He's definitely not honest," Jetta sniffed. "But I'm not sure if you call that corruption. I mean, he has Dominic in the Tower for no reason, no treason, and no other accusation. Dominic's his warning to others."

"But he's used that damned corrupt sheriff's accusations as his excuse. So now we've booted those accusations and everything else that sheriff says, straight down the well." Ned crossed his arms. Looking smug.

Mansfield took over. "He didn't seem a bad man. He listened. He sounded shocked at the lies the sheriff was shouting, and especially slinging two innocent females into his cell without a whisper of evidence, let alone proof."

"He's promised to bring Kettering to court," Ned continued. "And this king will question the bastard himself. If he suspects corruption, then Kettering'll be sacked. Perhaps even slung into his own cells."

"Or Newgate."

"Then brought to trial and if he's found guilty – which he will be if it's the king who sent him there, he'll be hung."

A fleeting and momentary sniff of guilt made Jetta pause. She had always thought hanging was a foul way to die. "At least I won't have to watch, though he deserves it," she said. "He would have hung me and poor Ilda. Or had us pressed, that's a favourite for women. But it sounds even slower and more brutal. And anyway, perhaps they won't kill him off, just sack him and send him away."

"In which case," Mansfield shook his head, "he'll just find another method of theft and corruption so he can live a comfortable life."

Jetta turned away. "And you didn't mention Dominic?"

"Ah, we did indeed, little sparrow," Ned insisted. "But we met with a blank. The honest sheriff here went into some detail, saying how Dominic had been accused by Sheriff Kettering, and no one else. There was no other reason to lock him up and no other possible accusations."

"It would seem," the sheriff said, "and I promise this is exactly what I told the king, that the Earl of Desford rescued the young woman – you, my dear – who was locked in gaol, accused of a nonsense crime she could never have committed, simply because she'd not paid up the bribe. And that sheriff came again, accusing this and that. But afterwards it was discovered that this time the accusations were even more corrupt, coming from a pretty whore that the

VESPERS

earl had not wanted and chucked her out – who got her revenge by telling lies to the sheriff, and handing over a heavy purse."

"Teresa?"

"The king cleared his throat and coughed a bit," added Ned. "This was too much for him. It proved Dominic innocent of everything, and Tudor doesn't want that. He stared at us through that squinty eye of his and promised he'd have his men look into the matter."

"That's something," Jetta sighed.

"It might not be anything," Ned said sorrowfully. "He's gone this far, and I don't reckon he'll be letting Dominic out so easily. He'll think up another accusation. Just remember all the strange lies, some of them absurd, he's making public concerning the last king. I know they're lies. So does most of London. But there's plenty who won't. That way Tudor makes himself look almost justified for the invasion."

"No one could believe that."

"He's banned the Titulus Regus so now the two boys King Richard sent abroad to his sister would be the legal king and prince. Let's hope they sail back before too long and prove themselves alive."

"That still doesn't help Dominic," Jetta said with another sniff. It had been good news. It seemed that her own innocence had been proved. But Dominic's imprisonment in the Tower was being ignored – proved innocent or not.

"That's what you're going to do, young woman," the sheriff said. "You refer to me, you refer to your friend here, and I'll help you make the appointment. Ned may chaperone you. But you need to go in on your own. That's important. You have to be respectable and vulnerable. Dress smartly but plain. Extremely plain. Even though unmarried, I suggest you pile your hair up at the back to look more sedate."

It was a constant conversation throughout that evening. The sheriff rode home, while Jetta cooked for Ned and continued to talk nonstop.

"The king can have Sheriff Kettering as an example instead."

"Not important enough." Ned refilled his cup. He knew this was going to last all evening. "Plymouth would be important enough but he's a Tudor supporter, so he can't count as an example."

It was just four days later when the sheriff managed to secure the next appointment for Jetta.

Mistress Jetta Lawson, you are expected at the Royal Palace of Westminster at eight of the clock on the morning of October 18th. You will not be admitted if you arrive late or fail to bring this sealed document as evidence of the meeting.

It was signed by someone with a highly exaggerated signature, certainly neither the king himself, neither the Earl of Oxford.

"Some underling," said Ned, dutifully pouring the wine. "Unimportant. Tis the day after tomorrow, lass, and you'll be there bright and early, pretty as a picture, but plain as a willow leaf in one dark colour and all that rich silk hair of yours tied up in a dark ribbon without bows. Just a little ribbon tag-tail hanging down. I shall do that for you, and we'll both ride to the palace, where I, of course, will wait outside like a good boy."

"I have the very dark blue gown I borrowed for the countess's funeral."

"Excellent," Ned grinned. "And no diamonds or golden flowers around your neck or wrists or fingers."

"You mean I can't wear any of my gorgeous jewellery?"

And while trying to laugh, Jetta was wondering if she might ever own such a thing.

Chapter Thirty Six

Unable to sleep the night before her royal appointment, Jetta wondered if turning up with red rimmed eyes and a face flat and pale with exhaustion, might actually bring more passion to her cause.

She had not been frightened before, but now she was.

"This Tudor may not be a great man," Ned told her. "But I doubt he'll eat you for dinner."

"Very funny. I'm not scared."

"Yes you are," Ned told her. "I can see it written all over you. Beautifully scribed – *I am terrified. I'm shivering with fear.* And did you sleep a blink last night?"

Jetta shook her head. It was early but she was already dressed like a little child's tutor in neat restraint without a bow or flounce to be seen. Only the tight inner sleeve came over her wrists and no embroidered outer sleeve covered it. High waisted, high necked, and low to her ankles. Ned had managed an excellent job of her long hair.

Ned grinned. "Now look, my little heroine, kings meeting their subjects and listening to the varied complaints and pleadings, well it happens day after day – king after king. You'll get it right – or you won't. If you don't, it won't be your fault, and we'll try something else."

She rode a little behind Ned. He took both horses to the royal stables, and waited there as Jetta looked regretfully at him, and then obediently joined the solitary guard who escorted her to the palace assembly. On his throne, Henry Tudor seemed just a little uncomfortable. The lines of those waiting to be brought forward, to bow or curtsey and then to explain why they had come, trailed around the great hall in double circles.

It would be several hours, she thought, before it would be her place to speak. By then the bored king might give up and send the last few away.

Another step. Two steps. Then a longer wait before a third step.

Jetta waited, waited, and continued waiting. One step forward, another step forwards. Sometimes, not often, she rounded an entire corner and felt she was an entire row closer. Then just another step, and another hour to wait. She could hear much of what was said as she drew nearer to the throne, but would then fall back into silence as the shuffling queue moved along into the shadows.

Some of the meetings were brief. Men had waited two hours or more simply to thank his majesty, or relate the success of some project, much appreciated. Jetta was fairly sure she wouldn't repeat such a waste of an entire day simply to thank a man for what he had surely forgotten.

Another step. Then two.

The guard who had brought her into the hall, was now one of the many standing rigid against the wall. They were armed, but there was no disturbance requiring discipline. The dreary shuffle continued without complaint. Jetta imagined the boredom like a thin trickle of dirty water winding throughout the hall, and finishing in a puddle at the king's feet. He made little attempt to seem interested. His voice echoed monotony.

Now exhausted, it was becoming difficult to stand upright, to hold up her head, and to continue seeming eager. Almost the entire queue was male. Jetta saw only three other women, one with a child clasping its mother's hand, another with a baby in her arms. The third was elderly and looked half starved.

Another step.

Finally, after what had seemed days, ahead of Jetta, there were just five men. The first was slow, and his words were soft, respectful and endlessly apologetic. But the king made no attempt to hurry him, and eventually granted what he had asked.

Another step forwards.

The fourth man complained about his neighbour, claiming that the family next door kept too many pigs and they constantly roamed the lanes, defecating and scavenging. He was told to offer the family an iron pen to be set up at the back of the house and at his own expense. But then, if the pigs were not kept in that pen, he could obtain both compensation and one of the pigs either to keep within his own home, or to eat.

Jetta was not particularly impressed by this decision, but she was no expert on pigs. Another step forward, and now only three men stood before her. The third spoke of his son who was training as an apprentice smith, but had been left without work when his master the smith was killed during the battle, and so the apprentice was left abandoned. Henry Tudor passed him over to one of the guards, ordering him to escort the boy to the guild where he would by right discover another position for the apprentice.

Another step.

Six men stood behind her and two in front. The morning's endless drudgery was finishing. Jetta prayed that the king would not dismiss those final few. The next supplicant stated loudly that he had married his wife less than a year back, not at the church porch admittedly, but a handfast with two witnesses, being his own mother and father. Yet now his wife had walked out on him and taken all her money with her. What was worse, she now denied they were ever married.

He was dismissed. A handfasting could not be proved, said the king, unless there were unbiased witnesses.

Jetta smiled. It was two kings past, Edward IV, whose second bigamous handfasting had blocked his own son's inheritance of the crown, and true to his previous contention, Henry Tudor was denying this new story of a city man's wife.

One more supplicant stood before Jetta. She breathed deep. The man was begging for an annulment, since his wife had not given birth to a single child. He had already, he explained, taken his cause to the local priest and then to the bishop, but his annulment had been denied.

The king was impatient. He had no authorisation nor interest in granting divorce nor annulments, and if the great wisdom of the church leaders had denied him, then there must be some other difficulty involved which the husband was not now admitting.

"Only cos I couldn't afford it," he said, raising his voice. "The wretched priest wanted donations I couldn't afford, then the wretched bishop wanted even more. It ain't right and I curse them both."

Henry Tudor turned away. One of the guards immediately came to his side. "Take this man from my sight," murmured the king. "And warn him never to speak those words again or I shall have him arrested."

That next step brought Jetta before the king. She curtsied as low as her lack of practise permitted and addressed her monarch with the deepest words of respect, taught by Ned.

"My sovereign lord, your majesty my beloved king, I have for a short period of time, worked as the housekeeper at the Desford Estate. For long years this mansion has been a peaceful home to several generations and the Earl of Desford has always been a kind master and utterly loyal to each and every monarch. Quite recently, your gracious highness, our local sheriff, John Kettering, accused his lordship of improper behaviour related to the sheriff's accusation that I myself brutally murdered the estate's farrier."

VESPERS

She took a deep breath, watching the king's expression. For almost the first time, he was listening, having no intention of releasing the earl who was an important part of his plans.

"Continue, girl."

"But now, your majesty, the sheriff has been removed from his position by yourself, sire, and cast out of his ward. He was utterly corrupt, and every arrest he made was equally corrupt. Now that his wickedness has been declared by your majesty, there would seem to be no proof of any kind against the Earl of Desford."

"Nonsense, girl. I myself ordered his arrest and he remains in the Tower." The king was leaning forwards, almost as though tempted to reach out and slap her.

Very quickly, Jetta again curtsied. "With great and patient judgement, sire. However, now that the sheriff who brought the original and only complaint against my Lord of Desford, has been accepted as a corrupt liar, there remains no further crime of which his lordship can be accused. Therefore, the entire household at the estate has combined to beg for his release. His lordship is a just and dutiful master, your majesty, and would never commit any crime or disloyalty towards your almighty self. I can swear on the Holy Book that he never received the command to attend your majesty for the purpose of kneeling and swearing loyalty. I know that he was waiting patiently for such an invitation. If now asked, I know he would be delighted to come at your magnanimous request."

And with her prayers whispered unheard, Jetta stepped back.

The king was frowning. Jetta thought him strangely self-absorbed, almost hooded and seemed far older than she knew. The man, in his late twenties, could easily be assumed as a forty-year-old, or more. The unrelenting squint in his eye and the prominence of both nose and chin seemed disproportionate, whilst the other features, lips, eyes and cheeks, sank almost without trace. One eye seemed unbalanced, as though looking in a different direction.

As the thought swirled while waiting for the king to answer, Jetta lost confidence. He had not smiled. Perhaps he did not know how to smile. But there was neither warmth nor sympathy in his face, nor any place for it.

She loved a man who had seemed fashioned of ice. A man with a virtually permanent expression of disinterest or dislike. More often of cold ambiguity. And yet she had discovered that Dominic's emotions were a tumult enclosed within. Jetta hoped this man might be the same.

His expression had not changed but Jetta quickly realised that his voice had deepened. The Breton accent became more noticeable, and the voice became a growl. "My decision was made without the interference of your sheriff, for whom I have no trust neither then nor now. Every decision in this land, Mistress Lawson, is mine. His lordship the Earl of Desford remains where he is awaiting my final verdict whether to send him to trial, or otherwise. You, will not interfere."

Quickly stepping back, feeling almost whipped, Jetta shrank, unsteady. With her brain whirling, she thought of yet another argument but realised in time that she must not say another word. The guard who had led her in, now took her arm and began to usher her back to the wide partially open doorway.

When the king roared for her to stop, Jetta almost fainted. Forcing herself to turn, when she would have preferred to run, she again faced the throne. Having almost tripped over her own feet, now she stood quiet and still. But when she dared look up, she was surprised. Standing behind the king on his throne, and bending over him, was his mother Margaret Beaufort. Jetta had no idea what might be said, but a vague sense of hope reasserted.

"Come here," ordered the king, his expression unchanging.

Somewhat ashamed of her own trembling knees and fear of rejection, Jetta walked firmly forwards. She didn't trouble herself to apologise to the six more supplicants waiting behind her in the queue. They might benefit anyway if she was beheaded on the spot.

It was Margaret Beaufort, now probably considered the most

VESPERS

important woman in the country, who spoke first. She came forwards, her nun's outfit as plain as Jetta's funeral clothes.

"It's Miss Lawson, I remember you," she said quietly. "I'm aware of the good work you did at my property, and I appreciated your respectful behaviour. I considered you helpful, respectable and unusually intelligent. I am entirely unacquainted with the Lord of Desford, but I have heard a little of this particular situation. I am interested. I am now prepared to speak with you in private concerning this."

Her son looked away, sour mouthed.

Jetta curtsied to the lady, and followed her back to the corridor and to a small annexe. Two guards stood either side of the doorway, but they did not enter as the door was opened. Margaret Beaufort sat, and Jetta did not, instead standing before the lady.

"Your disappearance from my employment was a little brusque, mistress," she said, her voice quietly gruff as always. "I know that the son of my brief visitor was shockingly unkind to you."

Jetta bowed her head. "But you were so wonderfully kind, my lady."

"I know exactly what happened, but that is no longer relevant," she said. "But now I want to hear about this Earl of Desford whom you choose to defend. A housekeeper defends her master? This is somewhat unusual. Forgive me, child, but do you love him? Does he bed you?"

Jetta blanched, felt sick, and went white. "Good gracious no, my lady. Never. It has been the entire staff uniting to help our master, since we admire him and feel his imprisonment is an injustice."

"You cannot possibly argue with a monarch's words," she said.

"Yes indeed, my lady. That would be a wicked presumption," Jetta answered carefully. "But I can argue with the accusations of Sheriff Kettering who was corrupt. Only he and no one else has made such accusations against my master, and every one of those can be disproved. A loyal and honest man, my lady, whose grandmother, the countess of Desford, who brought him up after both his parents died, also died less than a month past. He is therefore already a man distraught. And I can swear, being the housekeeper, that no request for the earl to attend his majesty was ever received. It would never have been ignored."

It was a tussle of a conversation but neither woman raised her voice. Jetta remained standing and kept her eyes lowered. She was given no promises however, when she was dismissed.

"I shall look into it," said the king's mother." Eventually you will hear my decision."

"Bless you, my lady," Jetta said quickly, "I trust your decisions more than I can any other living soul. I know you to be a lady of tremendous justice."

The words had written themselves in her mind. This was a woman who could lie and deal in conspiracies as well as any sheriff, but her corruption had nothing to do with coin since she was dramatically wealthy, and she adored being treated as a woman of outstanding piety. She relished the words, and smiled, which was rare.

"I'll see," she said. "Now you must leave. Both my son and I have other duties, of far more import."

Nothing, Jetta thought, was more important than Dominic's release.

As she rode home with Ned at her side, Jetta felt neither despondent nor joyful. Lady Margaret Beaufort was consistently unemotional but consistently followed the path of obvious justice, unless she could hide her own less just opinions. Whether or not she experienced genuine happiness could rarely be guessed. Jetta could easily imagine what the lady had felt when the result of the Fen Lane battle had been announced and she once again, after so long, was able to see her son. Yet in public, such pleasure could never be shown.

Jetta was thinking of this as she followed Ned, their horses trotting slowly along the bank of the great river. Both were quiet. What had happened was difficult to judge. And then Jetta turned, seeing the sweep of bright blue skirts. It wasn't the gown she recognised. A swirl of bright blue was common enough for those who could afford it.

It was the swing of the hips, the method of turning, and the manner of the twist that she recognised. From the high saddle, Jetta looked down silently on Teresa. Without the anger she tried not to feel, Jetta saw that Teresa was walking the streets, her hair pretty, rouge on her cheeks, a touch of charcoal over her eyelids, and a slick of oil over her lips. But the grand dress was a little torn at the hem and badly soiled at the back. She had pulled down the neckline, revealing as much as possible of her cleavage almost down to the blush of her nipples. There was a faint bruise on one side of her jaw as though one of her clients had punched her.

As Jetta stared down, Teresa caught the sleeve of a middle-aged gentleman walking past. But he shook his head and pushed her off. She did not look up nor did she see Jetta. She looked down, disappointed, kicked at a stray dog wandering past, and carried on in the opposite direction.

Another very deep breath, and Jetta also continued on her way, the horses now making an abrupt left turn away from the river and up towards the forest.

In the distance, before the thick greenery obscured every other thing except the sky, Jetta saw the chapel of St. John of Jerusalem, the late rays of sunshine striking the large copper bell which hung from the spire. But she turned away and followed Ned into the woods, the thick perfume of the trees, the lush aroma of the undergrowth, and the road to her new home. In truth, her old home. First in the convent, and then with Ned, she had lived most of her life before the horrendous mistake of being captured by the Maddock family.

Which gave her something else to wonder. Now the family she had hated so much was almost gone, and she'd had a large part herself in the annihilation. The mother had also been a tyrant, but was now alone and perhaps deeply miserable having lost her only son and her husband too. Whether wealth remained, and perhaps large groups of friends, Jetta neither knew nor cared.

Revenge, unintentional, had blown to her lap. Jetta had never considered revenge, only self-protection. Yet the family which had so persistently abused her was dead, with one bereft survivor, meanwhile Teresa was reduced to walking the streets, and Sheriff Kettering was no longer a sheriff, no longer considered important, and no longer highly paid.

Now there was a far larger question unanswered floating just above her.

His first consideration as soon as the horses were settled and one candle lit, "Wine?" offered Ned.

Jetta laughed. "What a beautiful offer – every time I'm about to cry – or faint – or fall asleep. Wine is truly a magnificent medicine."

"It does shocking violence too, they says, little blossom. I've heard of a working man beating his poor lady wife to death after downing too much ale and wine. But there's no way you drink that much, little honeybee. Nor myself. Can't afford it."

"You've got no wife to beat," Jetta grinned.

"Reckon I've seen plenty of husbands deserving it," Ned cackled, "far more than them poor wives."

Staring a moment, Jetta muttered, "Killing anyone must be the worst possible – too terrible – but so many were killed in this last battle. You may have – but that's not for me to think of – it was me that did what I never thought possible. I killed a man I hated. Only a boy really. Is that wicked?"

"Listen, my little apple blossom," Ned pressed his hand to her shoulder, "what you did was self-protection and that means courage and helping any other lass the boy might have killed in the future. What you did was good and right, and the Lord God helped you do it. As for me and that battle, it was Henry Tudor responsible for every wound and every death. What I did, I had to do. And what your Lord Stark did, he had no grain of fault. Now I serve a new king, but I feel no love for him and never will."

Chapter Thirty Seven

The rickety door flew open, Jetta blinked and woke with the wind in her face, peeped up from her straw bed on the floor, and buried her head again beneath her blanket, glimpsing the threat of rushing shadows. The door slammed. The entire shack's walls vibrated.

"Humph," she could hear Ned's muttered disturbance from upstairs. Then the deep rumble of his snoring continued.

This was no creeping shadow, no secretive ghost-like flitter. It was an abrupt and crashing chaos that woke her from sleep. From beneath the blankets she hoped, perhaps, it was just a fallen tree.

But then Jetta opened her eyes to the weight of something directly on top of her. She wore only her shift so wanted neither branches, badgers, nor Ned falling through the ceiling.

Then there was an incredible warmth and lips pressed down onto her, pushing open her mouth, a hot tongue slipping over her own, and someone else's breath warming her throat.

All confusion evaporated. She opened her eyes to his, seeing them shining like beacons, the ice cold quickly melted into adoration, his affection stronger than she'd ever thought possible, and her own reflected back to her from his pupils.

"You're out."

"You noticed." His fingers traced down from her cheek to neck to shoulder, but when he realised her shoulder was practically bare, he stopped, rolling off her and back to the floorboards. "That's something for another day," he murmured. "I've dreamed of seeing you a thousand times. During those long bleak days in the Tower, I've treated you so wickedly, little one, undressing you daily. But on Ned's floor is definitely not – the best place,"

Thunderous echoes followed each step and Ned burst into his downstairs room with a cry of ecstasy, both arms outstretched. "Tis the man I been thinking of, back to the girl I care for most. Tis our little parsnip root that got you free – did you know?"

"I did." Dominic remained sitting on the floor. "My release was just before dawn although without any explanation, and I immediately travelled home. There Benson told me the details, including where you are."

He smiled up at Ned, but one arm remained tucked around Jetta's shoulders. She had the blanket gripped up tight beneath her own arms.

Ned's grin was wide enough for a cabbage to pop in. "It's been the only damned thing we've thought of, dreamed of and spoken of," he said. "So damned unfair. I don't think much of our new king."

"A good man wouldn't have invaded, nor usurped in the first place. He has another prisoner in the Tower even more reprehensively imprisoned than I was myself, a ten-year-old child he's never met. But now, thanks to you my angel, I am free. Indeed, I shall call you both angels."

Jetta told her own story of meeting the king. "I was such a fool, quaking and trembling. I just couldn't get accustomed to the idea of meeting a king and talking to him and hopefully having him listen to me. It was all so grand. The room, the clothes, the livery and a thousand candles. They do it on purpose to frighten their subjects? Or they actually like it that way?"

"Both."

"Of course, I tried reminding myself that he really wasn't a proper king – and I shouldn't be nervous. But he didn't help. He refused me first. I didn't like him, and I don't think he liked me. He dismissed me as if I was a scraping of oak gall. And then his mother walked over. I'm really sure she doesn't like me either, but she has this thing about doing what she thinks she should. That nun's costume she hides in – it says *Look at me. I'm perfect*. But you told me once that she had a vile childhood so perhaps, I can't blame her for anything. Anyway, it was her recognising me that got you out."

"I tried. Andrew tried. Even Benson tried. And I heard that Avery Peasop tried. But it was our little pigeon that found the right magic."

Jetta giggled slightly. "It's hard to believe. It must have been monstrous inside the Tower for so long."

"Monstrous? Perhaps. It's not an experience I'd choose to repeat. But," and he leaned back, "others have it worse."

"Whatever happens," Jetta nodded, "there's someone will have it worse." The wood pigeons were cooing outside. "I suppose I should thank Lady Beaufort, but I don't want to wait in that hideous queue again."

"I shall write to her," Dominic said. "That's sufficient. I want very little involvement with this royal family."

"And do you know, my friend," Ned asked, "did our blessed monarch simply want an example to make the rest of the population behave itself?"

"I believe so." Still on the floor, Dominic leaned back against the wall. There was no hearth, and should it grow too cold, a slightly raised slab in the middle of the room could be used to light a fire. There was no chimney and as usual the smoke would swirl inside the room and eventually find its way through the thatch above. Jetta sat there, a few ancient ashes marking the back of the blanket she'd wrapped around herself. "He needed someone with a title," Dominic continued, "so the news would spread, and the entire population would learn that the new king accepted no petty treason. The story was created with the idea that I'd never answered his invitation to go and swear allegiance, not mentioning, naturally, that he'd never sent the invitation. There was also the absurd accusation of our friend Sheriff Kettering."

"He's a sheriff again? He shouldn't be."

Laughing suddenly, Dominic pulled Jetta even more tightly between his arms. "And all because of my wretched farrier. The poor man's death sparked an entirely new life and yet I still have little idea of how he died."

Jetta sniffed but without laughter. "I thought you'd guessed. Well, poor Ilda's dead too now, so I can tell you it was her. Her husband was a brute. He attacked her again, drunk and angry, so she killed him for self-protection. The two boys helped. But you won't blame them now, will you?"

He had stopped laughing, burying his head against her hair. "I blame nobody. Yes, I'd guessed but knew nothing for sure. And now I don't care. It's not why I was arrested and I'm selfish enough to be more interested in my own imprisonment, and my own escape."

"And if it wasn't for the king's own mother!"

"No, not her. If it wasn't for you, my little one."

"It's funny the way things work," Jetta sighed. "Dominic, you sent me to Margaret Beaufort to find out about Henry Tudor. But she never knew I was spying. She just thought I was a dutiful cleaner. And now – well, that's crazy."

"I like crazy," said Ned.

Dominic lay back, stretching his legs. "Being confined is grim," he murmured, now stretching his arms upwards as if searching for space. "I've a sense of outright fatigue, yet I've done nothing for many, many days. I've not left those two tiny rooms, though having a window, even though that was minute too, being without a covering except two iron bars, at least I had constant fresh air. Strangely enough, it helped."

"And it has been a warm summer," Ned nodded. "Still is."

"I almost want it cold," Dominic smiled. "Too small rooms leave the average man yearning for space. Boiled during the day and frozen at night." He paused, then smiled directly at Jetta. "But what I yearned for, little one, was you. Night and day, it was you that filled my dreams."

Blushing, Jetta shrank into her blanket. "It's almost too much to think about. Except of course I thought – well, exactly the same about you, and it's marvellous, truly unexpected and glorious, having you back so suddenly. I suppose," she laughed, "I ought to get dressed."

"Get dressed? It seems a shame," Dominic smiled, but stood, beckoned to Ned, and added, "Tell us when we're permitted back indoors."

Since it took just three minutes to dress in the old shift and then the old gown, slipping on the shoes and tying back her hair without bothering to brush it, she was able to open the door two cracks, and call. The two men bustled back indoors, smiles large.

"We need plans," Ned rediscovered his stool. "We do – what? Kill a few Lancastrians? Pop over to the Beaufort Mansion? Or back to the Dominic estate?"

"Yes, Dominic's home," Jetta said, "but perhaps visit Andrew and Tyballis on the way. They did such a lot to help. And I haven't seen the new baby yet. He must be nearly six months old."

"And it also seems that long I've been stuck in the Tower, although I know it isn't." Dominic sighed. "Being an idle man accustomed to a house large enough house an army, suddenly being confined to a small corner the size of a beer barrel was a difficult adaptation.

"So? Rest – or move?"

At Andrew's estate, although it was the steward who politely answered the door, it was Tyballis who flew into Dominic's arms, and then embraced Jetta, while Ned complained that he was being left out.

They talked for several hours, Andrew leaning back on the settle and the others all watching him. Although the baby's nurse hovered in the background, as though fearing that the actual mother wouldn't know how to look after her growing baby, Tyballis had the somewhat robust child on her lap, hanging on to him even though he wriggled and bounced with an obvious desire to explore more than just the two small knees beneath him.

"You're getting on with the new monarch?"

"Don't be ridiculous."

"We are invited to the coronation, though I'm not sure we intend accepting." Andrew sighed. "I miss Richard. But everyone dies sooner or later."

"He was only thirty-two," Dominic interrupted. "That's not a sensible dying age."

"The same age as Jesus Christ, though perhaps that's not an appropriate analogy."

Ned was muttering. "I'll be working for the bugger, looking after the forest, chopping and pruning. He'll want the charcoal. But hopefully the bastard himself won't ever come. I'll get orders from some grounds manager."

Once again Andrew sighed. "I worry about another war, and you worry about a tree trunk."

"Lovell may start a new rebellion," Dominic said, "but if this king marries Edward IV's eldest daughter as he's promised, then he's combined Lancaster and York. We may have peace."

"I doubt it." Andrew shook his head, which made the wine in his cup slurp over the edge. "Richard sent both Edward's boys north, and then to his sister. They're now the legal heirs, thanks to the Tudor idiot himself."

"Not to mention that poor wretched boy in the Tower."

"Richard's sister will probably encourage both boys to gallop back over here to claim the throne," Tyballis said, her hand clamped over her baby's mouth as he fisted both hands and complained regarding the restraint. "They'll bring more battles, wait and see."

The discussion continued, baby Dickon finally fought his way to the ground and proved his ability to crawl, especially wriggling forwards and in circles on his padded bottom while the nurse, still hovering beneath her frown, watched in case he did something worse than usual. He was too old now for swaddling, but she would have eagerly wrapped him tight had she been given the chance.

As Dickon attempted to demolish the patterned tiles across the hearth, the discussions continued until eventually Ned announced that he wished to return home, and Dominic took Jetta's hand.

"I need to rediscover my own home and remember where the stairs go," Dominic said. "Since I've had no coronation invitation, nor want one, I won't be seeing you at the high table. But I shall see you soon, or perhaps sooner."

It was a slow ride in the weakening sunbeams, down to the river and past the palace, from Westminster to Chiswick and finally the late afternoon gloaming over the dark and massive house, its ivy vines and the late summer growth of the hedges ready for next year's nesting.

Benson opened the door.

"My lord, you cannot guess how delighted every member of staff has been over the news of your release and return. And naturally to Mistress Lawson also. I shall order the best wine, and if you will both accompany me to the great hall, I will ensure that supper will be served within the shortest possible time."

"That," smiled Dominic, "will be the most welcome."

They ate, they drank, and quite exhausted, both climbed the stairs for sleep. But it was at the door to Jetta's bedchamber that Dominic stopped her in the darkest shadows, placed the candle on the floor, and took Jetta in his arms.

She could smell the wine on his breath, but the same was on hers. She could smell the guttering candle but didn't care. She leaned up and kissed Dominic, first finding his cheek and then his lips. His cheek, faint with stubble, was deliciously warm, but his mouth was fire. He took over her initiative and explored her tongue and throat.

Stopping to breathe, she whispered, "Come with me. Come to bed. Show me."

And to her disappointment, he murmured, "Not tonight, my little sweetness. I am a drunken fool, slaked on exhaustion. I could show you very little. You'd think me a foul-smelling disappointment. But forgive me, tonight I shall dream and tomorrow I promise to fulfil that dream."

Chapter Thirty Eight

Waking alone suddenly seemed a cold and lonely mistake. Jetta sat up beneath the eiderdown and hugged her knees. A cloud of dark confusion surrounded her, even though she saw a golden blazing happiness dawning behind. Dominic was free and Dominic said he wanted her and that was the greatest happiness she had dreamed about. Yet there she sat alone and shivering, reminding herself that the life of a mistress was not joyful for it contained the constant risk of collapse. One day Dominic must marry and then she would become the discarded memory.

She dressed, went to the dining table for a solitary breakfast, and then wandered outside. The day was cool, and clouds edged up from the horizon.

The warm hands came suddenly from behind. Dominic held up Jetta's cape and wrapped it around her shoulders.

"Walk with me," he said softly, and again took her hand, leading her down towards the river. The freshness of the breeze followed the current as the Thames swept downstream. The trail of willow trees marked the bank, sweeping the magic of leaves over the thick grass, the pearlised clumps of clover and the smother of daisies. The water was a lullaby and beneath the trees, the cold sky was almost invisible.

Dominic avoided the place where his farrier had been discovered dead, and where long past, Jetta had tied her stolen boat and slept into the beginning of a whole new life.

He walked further upstream and led Jetta to a small slope where the falling leaves were thicker, almost creating a curtain of privacy. He laid his own cloak here, and pulled her down to sit with him.

Taking her between his arms, he kissed her ear, pulling her close.

She whispered, "Dominic, I think I love you. Will you take me for your mistress?" She had practised the words and for endless weeks, she had longed to say them. Teresa had suffered, but principally because of her own jealous spite. Jetta knew that her own behaviour would never echo Teresa's.

His eyes closed and Jetta heard his sudden intake of breath. When he then whispered, his word was part of that breath. His eyes seemed to light, and he pulled her closer and whispered, "No, my beloved."

The denial fell like stone in her throat. She closed her eyes and buried her head at his shoulder. "You say no, Dominic, and I have to accept it. But it's what I want, even just for a little while. I promise, when you think it's over, I'll just go. I'll never act the way Teresa did. You've called me your beloved. You said you wanted me. Couldn't it be more than once? Perhaps more than twice? For a week? For a month?"

Whilst he was pulling her closer, crushing her against him, while his mouth was so close and wrapped in her hair, she almost didn't hear him. But he whispered again, saying, "Not simply a month, not simply a year, my little one. I want you forever. I need you as my wife."

She sat up with a lurch and stared down at him. "You don't mean it. Don't tease me, Dominic. It hurts."

"Untrusting child." He sat, taking her back into his arms. "To lie or tease on such a subject would be strange indeed. I'm not such a fool to speak of marriage as a joke, and I've spoken these words to no other woman in my life. Perhaps you dislike looking so far ahead. Or do you suppose that living with me for so long would lapse into nightmare?"

Still staring, Jetta attempted the impossible. "I can't believe you. Nobody knows who I am. I don't know myself. I don't even know how old I am. I think Jetta might be my real name, but I can't even be sure of that. I think Lawson was made up by the nuns." She shook her head and the ribbon disentangled, her hair tumbling over her face. When she pushed it from her eyes, Dominic saw the tears. "You're a lord," she mumbled, "I'm a servant. You fight battles. I scrub floors."

"You'll scrub no more floors," he answered softly. "And you're no longer any one's servant." His fingers stroked her cheek, wiping back both tears and curls. "You're a remarkable woman," he murmured, "and I have never considered myself remarkable. A king is simply another man, good or bad, and a lord is simply a man who inherited a title."

"It can't be –," her voice disappeared into his cote.

"Am I arrogant? It's simply the way I was brought up by a man more arrogant still. Listen, little one, and believe me." There was no arrogance in his voice, just the gentle tickle of his breath against her cheek. "I'm as much the fool as most men. Is that the action of a mighty warrior? I drink too much to overcome the bland existence of a man without ambition. I was once so drunk I fell down those stairs, broke two ribs and knocked my head on the balustrade. When Benson trotted to the rescue, I told him I didn't wish to be moved, simply to bring me a cup of wine. "

With faint reluctance, Jetta smiled, burying her head against his shoulder. "That's sweet."

"Entirely stupid, my love. Once my parents died, the only soul I loved was my grandmother. I never loved that woman whose name I've now forgotten. Also the actions of a fool with more wealth than sense. When too pissed to remember my name, I once attempted to cut my own toenails, and nearly severed the entire bone. That toe remains crooked."

Jetta giggled. "It doesn't stop you being a lord."

"That title was passed down to me, not made by me. Titles mean nothing when inherited." Dominic smiled. "And you are no kitchen maid. I know who you are."

She was puzzled and sat up straighter. "I'm me."

"Yes, you who I've learned to love. I had a great deal to explain to you," Dominic now told her quietly, "but was somewhat interrupted when arrested and imprisoned in the Tower. I'd have written before facing the block, yet hoped to tell you myself."

Jetta looked away. "Then tell me. I already know I'm a kitchen girl, a cleaner and sweeper. I was a beggar for many years, and at one time a prisoner, arrested for murder. What a good wife I'd make! You'd be shunned by the royal court. You'd never be accepted by the elite. The king might even banish you. We'd have to go to some distant island. People would spit at a man who took a slum brat for wife."

Turning to face her, Dominic took Jetta's arms, holding her opposite him, forcing her to watch him. "Listen and believe," he told her, his voice soft but no longer a whisper. "Your false opinion of yourself is so wrong, that you lack confidence. But I know your courage is huge, when you dare express it. Even if I knew no more of you than the story of a kitchen girl, I'd take you as the woman I want, and pray for your acceptance. I have plans, and they include leaving England. I don't love this king and distrust his rule. And my plans include you, little one."

"So what do you know about me, Dominic?" Now it was Jetta who whispered.

He cuddled her against him once again as the wind bounced the willow leaves and a faint patter of old raindrops drifted through.

"One of your convent friends had overheard the Abbot Francis speak of you." His fingers slipped to the back of her neck, soothing and warm. "The abbot is clearly Venetian, not Francis but Francesco, and his accent has outlasted his arrival in this country. It was an Italian woman, I believe, who was your mother. Nameless perhaps, but no kitchen girl. The abbot took the child as deserving of a careful and, let us say, respectable upbringing."

"And virtuous, I suppose. Expected to be a nun."

"I imagine any abbot would believe virtue important."

They sat together in silence, loving the closeness. It was sometime before Jetta asked, "An Italian mother? I never imagined such a thing. And no father? Is Jetta an Italian name?"

Dominic smiled into her ear, pulling her back down to the soft grassy slope where his cape lay as a mattress, and now hers as a blanket.

"Yes, an Italian mother. Perhaps an Italian father, but I have no knowledge of him. Nor do I know the name Jetta, but I assume it comes from somewhere and Italy seems the most probable. Lawson perhaps not, likely invented by nun or monk. So will you travel to Italy with me, and discover more? Or perhaps, simply to live as we wish without heartbreak or Tudor kings?"

It almost sounded real. It had begun to light stars in her eyes.

"I don't care about the parents who abandoned me. But living with you, oh Dominic. That would be bliss. And in Italy no one would know you married an orphaned brat. And a bastard, no doubt. You need never marry me, Dominic. Foreigners wouldn't ever need to know."

"I have neither parents nor interesting relatives," Dominic told her. "Do I diminish in miserable loneliness? My parents did not abandon me, but perhaps my God did. Both parents died when I was a child. My father, the original earl, died of the pox when I was eleven, and so I inherited a title I didn't really understand. My mother had died in childbirth, poor soul, which is why I have no siblings. My grandfather died when I was one or two, and my grandmother died holding your hand. Does this make our misfortunes equal?"

She laughed, but stopped and shook her head. "It's horrible to laugh because of such a sad story. But I don't even know when I was born. Perhaps, just perhaps, now I know where."

He kissed her mouth, his breath burning her throat, his eyes large as they came close to hers. And then, his fingers dancing across her neck, he began to undress her. He moved slowly. Her own eyes, squeezed tight, didn't dare open but the warmth of his caresses excited her beyond anything she had ever known before. The sun on her skin mattered far less than the heat of Dominic's kisses.

It was an hour later that Dominic wrapped Jetta in both their cloaks, and carried her back into the house. "You weigh as little as a puppy," he smiled down at her, as she laid her head on his shoulder. He took her to his bedroom, laid her naked on his pillows, and covered her with the eiderdown, sitting at her side, watching her.

She whispered, "I thought it would hurt. It didn't. That was wonderful."

"I always wanted to see you naked," he smiled back at her. "Touching you naked was even more glorious, and no, little one. I would never hurt you. But if you agree, you'll share my bedroom and consider it yours."

"Oh, Dominic, yes please."

Kissing her forehead, Dominic stood and walked quickly to the door. She pulled the eiderdown up to cover her breasts, watching him in slight alarm, assuming he was about to leave her. But he simply opened the door, and called. Benson came at once, clearly not having expected the event. He seemed even more confused than Jetta, for he was not accustomed to his master's bedchamber, but he stood at the far wall, hands clasped, and his head slightly bowed.

"I am ready my lord."

"Excellent," Dominic said, turning back to Jetta. "Benson is our witness, my love."

They had made love beneath the willow trees. Now worried,

VESPERS

Jetta wondered what he wished to repeat with a witness. But he took her hand gently between both his own.

"Take my hand," Dominic told her, "and speak the words after me. Say, as I say. *I willingly take you, Dominic, Earl of Desford, as my legal husband.*"

With her heart beating loud enough to hear and fast enough to feel like ecstasy or death, Jetta's hand trembled as she repeated Dominic's words.

"And I take you, my beloved, known as Jetta Lawson, as my legal wife, and will love you and protect you for the rest of my life, whatever may happen."

Benson bowed. "I stand witness, my lord. I now accept that the Earl of Desford and his lady, the Countess of Desford, are the legal married inhabitants of the Desford Estate, and will swear to this as witness should it ever be questioned."

Benson bowed, grinned, and quickly departed, pattering back down the stairs, sounding as delighted as those he had left in the bedchamber, and was soon calling, "Come now, all of you, for we have a celebration to arrange. The earl has his beautiful countess, and we will celebrate with a feast, some music perhaps, and drink to their health and happiness for ever more."

Upstairs Jetta continued to lie with Dominic, whispering together as Dominic caressed her and promised their life together. He could not take his eyes from her smile, her own eyes, and her body.

"You really meant it then." Her voice was more gasp than statement.

Smothering the chuckle, he kissed her forehead. "Can you never believe me, my sweet new countess?"

"Perhaps," Jetta suggested, "I'm too little for you. Dominic, you're tall and handsome and muscled, while I'm just a scraggy little thing."

He laughed dutifully. "Fairy bride," he called her. "Tiny but beautiful. And now my legal wife, Jetta, my love, remember that. You are my countess, and if we do go to live in some other country, you are still my legal wife, and a countess just the same."

"You still want to go to Italy?"

"Why not? From what I know of this new king, I've no wish to stay in England. France likes to call itself our enemy, and backed the Tudor invasion. Spain perhaps and the glory of their power. But they have turned the love of the church into the hatred of independence, and the laws are becoming cruel. Flanders maybe. I know nothing of Richard's sister who helps to rule there, but I've no desire to become embroiled in the inevitable wars to come, where Edward's two boys will begin to claim the English throne. There are many countries in the world, but most are too distant, or too dismal. Too unknown and dangerous. In Italy, my love, perhaps we can discover your mother if she still lives."

Jetta nodded with sudden excitement. "Even my father."

"Yes, even him. A king, perhaps. Or a duke."

"Or a butcher's son without a penny but with a terrible temper."

"I am sometimes," Dominic grinned, "just a little surprised at your prevailing and positive optimism."

And she laughed back at him. "But a strong and loving man surely wouldn't let his daughter be snatched away, even taken to another country. I'm illegitimate, my love. Perhaps it was Abbot Francis himself who was my father, and that's why he brought me to the convent. After all, for an abbot to have a child would be heretically shocking."

He helped her dress and brought out clothes that had belonged to the countess when younger and slimmer. They were all too long. "I shall have a thousand ordered, fitted perfectly, designed to your choice, and delivered within the month."

"Delivered to Italy?"

"Sadly, we'll still be here, since first I must sell as much of my property as I can. I'll not carry you into a new world in poverty. I have no heir, and no constraint on sale, except our sweet natured king if he decides to claim it for himself."

VESPERS

It was a feast, however quickly prepared. They had no guests, but insisted that the staff join them in the celebration they had prepared themselves. The venison had already been hanging in the pantry, and was now roasted over the fire, turning on the spit. A pie of brains and liver in wine and suet crust sat mid table, and a huge dish of flounder, baked in honey. The wine, unearthed from the cellar, was share by all and very much appreciated by the pages.

Unaccustomed to large quantities of alcohol except for light ale, some of the staff became especially jovial, and two began to sing, which didn't upset anyone. Dominic lay back in the grand chair and watched beneath lowered lids, enjoying everything yet nothing more than the closeness of his wife, who ate and drank and kept laughing. Dominic had never known her to laugh so often or so sweetly, and sometimes leaned across the small space between their chairs, kissing her cheek, her forehead, or even the tip of her nose.

Pip and Sam, the two young grooms, sons of the dead farrier, their mother killed during the attempt to protect her mistress, both sat near Dominic and Jetta, and raised their cups so frequently to the newlyweds, they soon became sozzled themselves and fell off their stools.

Benson refused to drink too much, but grinned throughout the feast, eventually aching from the stretch of his mouth in such unusual width and such unusual circumstances. Later, when he locked up the house, he fell asleep on the cushioned settle, and dreamed through the night of all the food he had eaten, which still smelled rich and tempting against the dining table, even once cleared.

Once again Jetta lay in bed with Dominic, making love very slowly with soft touches and whispered adoration.

Later as they lay entwined, Jetta said, "I wish we'd been able to invite Andrew and Tyballis to such a gorgeous party. Ned too. And your nice friend Avery. I'm longing to tell the world that we're truly married."

"Perhaps," smiled Dominic, "we can arrange a somewhat more orthodox feast for next week and invite our friends. I've a few friends

I should enjoy meeting again. They'll not approve of who you are, my dear, but they'll have no idea until later when they go home and start fussing through their documents and lists of those unknown daughters from further north. But I'll need to explore the possibility of those who might buy what I wish to sell."

"But not Margaret Beaufort or her son?"

He laughed, eyes now permanently alight. "I think not. They will be far too busy preparing for the coronation, so I shall leave them in peace."

And so, when the thirtieth of October dawned, Dominic and his wife did not leave their home, spending the day on horseback, and collecting the great stitched and embroidered pile of silks, satins, taffeta, brocades, velvet and damask, more clothes than Jetta thought she could ever wear.

She was wearing linen and wool. Too cold for silk, and it threatened rain. The fur lined cloak was patterned and matched her eyes. "Now," she said, climbing back into the saddle, "I have so many clothes, we'll sink the boat."

"Then I shall swim ashore," Dominic told her, "with you sitting on my back."

Chapter Thirty Nine

The coronation, people said, had been a success. Yet on his journey from the Tower to the abbey, the new king had carefully surrounded himself with his newly employed guard, brilliant in scarlet, and marching so closely that his majesty was virtually invisible. He was conscious of the risk, and clearly feared those he called his own people.

Although his promised marriage was not scheduled until the following year, and those close to him understood why, Henry Tudor was gaining support from the Yorkists who approved the future union of the two rival powers. It would, folk hoped beyond all else, mean a peaceful reign in a peaceful country.

Some remained, who might have preferred the excitement of battle, being a vengeful excuse to vent their hatreds. But prosperity was still growing amongst the middle classes, while war destroyed prosperity too often.

With Tudor only two months on the throne and less than two weeks since the coronation, no one was yet sure what manner of king he might be, but except for Clarence's poor son and the Earl of Desford himself, few had suffered so far, his pious mother appeared to guide him with as much power as he had himself, and confiscation of others' property had not happened as frequently as expected.

At first, never having met his future wife, Henry resented her. He disliked the need to place a royal Yorkist as his partner, thus allowing his own Lancastrian heritage to become a mixed power, submitting to an equal footing with his enemies. But he needed an heir and hoped that once there were children, he might learn a fondness for the woman who had supplied them.

Henry VII's court stumbled into the patterns of previous kings, though clung to some differences which pleased some and not others. Many of the titled lords had been killed in the great battle when they had supported their king against the invader. Other lords refused to obey the new king at first, so Henry Tudor found it easier to collect advisors and councils from amongst the middle classes and those making money from new trade and their Lancastrian roots. This created a new sense of rule, which benefitted some and dismayed others. It was hoped that the new queen, once she and Henry married in the following year, would gain friends more easily, being accustomed to privilege.

Yet the new court fell into its usual conspiracies, rivalries and spiteful word battles. Gossip recommenced, hatreds although quietly fostered, were kept partially underground, and those eventually promoted quickly learned to treat their inferiors with brutality and deviousness. With those unused to power, striving for it became more important, and more ruthless.

King Henry had not always known the benefit of riches. Now he relished money above all else and discovered the joy of gaining more from every small diversion, every tiny plot and plan, every trade, every tax, and every small endeavour he could invent.

Keeping a tally of all such income was his favourite pastime, and so his counting house gained notoriety. Bishop Morton was his ally who devised more methods of enriching the crown, and leaving the poor begging, whoring, and thieving. Tactical manoeuvre within the court became the only possible practise. Some fell. Some gained.

Andrew, Lord Leays, was offered a seat on the royal council, and he accepted

The Earl of Desford was offered no such temptation.

The lack of importance connected to his wife was considered strange, even disgraceful, and therefore very few of the growing elite, who were quickly becoming far more critical than their titled predecessors, would consider counting the Earl of Desford as a friend. Naturally this didn't bother him at all. But, with new property taking time to build, Dominic sold the grounds, farms, country establishments and small buildings on the city edges that had once supplied his income.

It was during the signing of contracts, when the lawyer looked up and frowned.

A mild but cloudy day was pleasant for the time of the year, and Dominic was comfortable. Selling his property for a high price sang to him of an even more comfortable future. His lawyer had spread the relevant papers across his scrivener, and signed the very last contract as witness to his client's business.

Underlining his signature with the quill, Lawyer Graston looked up, frowning. "My lord, there's some sort of confabulation milling out there. I presume you haven't brought bad tempered followers as an entourage. I can't sign documents and check legality with that bombardment outside."

Dominic was laughing at first, then also frowned. His lawyer's words were no exaggeration. He stood. "I'll go and see." He nodded to Jetta. "Stay here, my love. I'll be back in a moment or two."

Beneath the lowering grey sky, a gentleman stood outside, elegantly dressed. His face appeared twisted in fury. He stood, legs wide, and leaned on the hilt of his sword. Beside him stood Bishop Morton, and at his other side stood Sheriff Kettering.

The Earl of Plymouth was tall. The sheriff came only to his shoulder, and this only by virtue of his hat. Morton, medium height, was armed, yet wore his bishop's robes.

The three men, so differently attired and so obviously intending attack, now drew the interest of others. The lawyer's office sat, as most did, north of the East Minster, St. Paul's Cathedral. The chant of the clergy was a soft echo from those vast and decorated windows and the spire reaching between the clouds. Yet Holy devotion, it seemed, attracted less interest. The courtyard, surrounded by those same busy offices, was as usual partially crowded. Now the folk, whether aiming for Holy Mass or their solicitor's demands for payment, stopped, watching.

Someone called. "Hey, bishop, you singing hymns or shouting for battle."

The Earl of Plymouth wore satin over scarlet silken hose, and carried his cape over the arm which now half lifted his sword. His grimace was ugly, but the narrow streak of sunshine flashed against both satin and steel.

Dominic sighed. "Must it be now?" he said. "I'm not in the mood for cleaning up the shit of this city."

Plymouth smiled, twisting his mouth sideways across the scarred and puckered cheek. Morton glared. Kettering stamped. "You thought to get me sacked, fool. I'll have you know that I've been reinstated, thanks to my cousin."

Dominic lifted one eyebrow and addressed the earl. "You degrade yourself to that extent? Do you know that your cousin is worse than scum?"

Surprising Dominic, the earl nodded. "I know and he knows. I have no interest in such nonsense. The royal court appears to consider corruption a virtue. Personally, I am disinterested, either way. But there exist those whose fate is already sealed for other reasons, and one of those is you, my Lord Stark. Your death is already sealed, sir, and it will not take long to resolve."

"You back your lowly cousin," Dominic said, now only barely surprised. "Yet, although he calls you cousin, I presume he is a more distant relation?"

Nodding, Plymouth smiled. "A lowly sheriff? But he is the grandson of my aunt's sister-in-law, who married well beneath her station, as you clearly have yourself, Desford. And he comes in useful from time to time. I have no intention of disowning him. Now. Will you surrender yourself to me, or do we entertain the law courts by fighting on the steps of St. Paul's?"

Of the solicitors, lawyers and scribes packed into the outer courtyard of St. Paul's, many already peered from their windows, annoyed or intrigued by the shouting outside.

"I'll willingly fight you, all three," Dominic nodded, eyes now iced glass and rich with sarcasm. "Indeed, I could use a diversion. However, I am also curious. Your motives are quite beyond my simple and perhaps tedious honesty. Is this all for your small and vile cousin?"

"Oh, gracious no," the earl answered, lifting his sword and pointing it directly at Dominic, who did not move. "Shall I bother to explain? Perhaps I shall, since you will be dead within minutes. It started with your father, who stole away my lover, and killed her within the year. Do you know you are illegitimate? I cannot nor want to bother with proof. However, as your mother was already my intended bride, promised to me by both word and bed, having been my lover for some weeks, the marriage she then made with your father was illegal. There was neither annulment nor explanation. Whether your father forced her or kidnapped her, I do not know. Once I knew her to have been bedded by another, I no longer wanted her. But you are no earl, nor are you legitimate. You and your father killed her, a vile crime, although one I cannot prove."

At first Dominic was speechless. He stood, interpreting the words which had been hurled as a slap in the face and a knife in the back. For some silent moments he believed, then realised the opposite. He denied this amounted to illegality. The story did not prove nor suggest anything beyond a brief affair and nothing more. Now Plymouth had sunk simply to jealousy and hatred.

Only to himself, he smiled. Jetta believed herself illegitimate. If he was the same, they could laugh together. But Plymouth's malicious accusation proved no bigamous marriage.

Finally, Dominic said, "You speak nonsense, sir. I never knew my mother, and if you wish to accuse anyone of murder, it would be God above, since she died giving birth. As for the rest, I find your claim absurd. Had this been true, there would have been endless gossip and endless accusations long before now. You are twisting the facts. The abduction was probably your own action, followed with her rescue by my father. I have no knowledge of this, however, and never heard my father speak of it. I can only be certain that had it occurred as you say, your own hatred would have spouted like a poisoned fountain long before now. You are slow to seek absurd and improper revenge, my lord."

"You know nothing. Ignorance, nothing more. You are clearly your father's son." The earl sneered, but did not explain.

Dominic shrugged. "You invent nonsense regarding my parents. Your hatreds arise so easily? Or does your precious cousin force your hand?"

"He rightly encourages me," the earl half smiled. "And you yourself have encouraged me. I watched you at Fen Lane. I saw you as you killed my young brother."

It was news to Dominic. "In a battle charge, many die. I took no names. I would not have recognised your brother – not even yourself. In full armour, visors down, the disguise is complete. I doubt you could have recognised me. Neither I nor my king provoked that battle. It was the man you supported who invaded. Whoever died, including the rightful king of this land, is the fault of Henry Tudor And you know it well."

"Treason," roared Plymouth. "You'll not speak that way of our lawful sovereign in such a manner. Kettering is now entitled to arrest you forthwith." Smiling, Dominic nodded. "Speaking the truth can sometimes prove dangerous, sir. But I doubt you've ever tried it."

"And now your words ensure your death." Plymouth walked forward, his sword raised. "You will know, I am sure, my reputation as a great warrior. Ask God to forgive your many sins and raise your sword."

VESPERS

"I am unarmed," Dominic said, shrugging again. "So fight an unarmed man, sir, or wait until I arm myself."

Plymouth nodded. "Quickly, or I take you as you are." Kettering jumped, almost dancing. Morton remained silent and still. Both kept a tight grasp on their own weapons. The earl was impatient and called constantly both towards Dominic and the growing crowd. "Someone, give the fool a sword. A kitchen knife perhaps, or a penknife for stealing purses."

It was the solicitor from his office behind Dominic, who marched out, and thrust a large wooden handle between the waiting fingers. Dominic grasped the hilt and smiled. "I know your reputation. But perhaps you're unaware that I carry some small reputation myself."

"Then we'll test it out here," Plymouth answered quickly, "with a good audience to judge the greater man."

"More illegality?" Dominic murmured. "Does our new king condone armed fighting in the street?"

"He will, once I've killed you," the earl grinned. "And Kettering, sheriff again now, will mop up your blood with pleasure."

A crowd surrounded them, urging on both sides as though they watched a cock fight. Every small office emptied as folk waved their arms in distress or delight. But it was Jetta's voice which Dominic heard more clearly.

"My dearest," she sounded out of breath, "Andrew is coming, and the sheriff of this ward is already pushing through the crowd."

And at the same moment, he felt another small hilt press into his second hand.

Plymouth roared, "You'll not cheat, bastard, bringing your friends in to outnumber me. You bring in Leays, and I'll have him thrown from the royal council, and you beheaded."

"It would be cheating? Even though the sheriff beside you is also armed?"

"He'll keep his distance unless I call him. Besides, he fights like a puppy."

The Earl of Plymouth was still speaking as Dominic abruptly

kicked out, and his riding boot slammed sideways against the earl's knee. Plymouth staggered back. Furious, he regained his balance and rushed onto Dominic, blade flashing directly at his throat. Dominic smashed it away. He held the knife Jetta had passed him, and a huge battle axe, passed by the interested solicitor. The weight of the axe against his sword caused Plymouth to stagger backwards once again.

Stepping away, Dominic watched, slit eyed, as his opponent again pushed forwards, sword swinging. Dominic simply dodged, but as he stepped aside, he heaved the flat blade of the axe against the back of Plymouth's head. The earl fell forwards onto his face, almost unconscious. As he crawled upwards, he was bleeding from nose, lips, and skull. He looked sick, wiping the blood from his face.

Dominic stood still and silent, looking down and waiting. It had taken only a few moments. The crowd held their breath.

Back on his feet but dazed, Plymouth ran crookedly, his blade cutting at an unexpected angle as he ran past. Dominic's wrist dripped blood, but he had twisted away in time and the wound was shallow. He confronted Plymouth as the earl turned, now using the axe with greater force. Marching forwards, Dominic appeared to be attacking head on and Plymouth immediately moved sideways, laughing at his adversary's obvious mistake.

But no mistake, the movement had been intentional since now Dominic spun, the axe gaining speed and force, and slammed into Plymouth's chest. It winded him, but clearly the earl had been prepared and wore chain mail beneath his surcoat. The force of the axe penetrated, cutting through the metal, yet not sufficiently to injure .

Each man bent, intent on the other's intentions. Pausing for breath, then forwards, forced backwards, then forwards again. The crowd cheered and yelled, choosing sides, while the game of cat and mouse steamed before them.

So Plymouth stood a moment, regaining breath and balance. Again, Dominic waited, then moved quickly forwards. The steel of sword and axe clashed mid-air as the sun reflected as though a

VESPERS

weapon itself. For one brief moment out of breath, each circled the other. Without the crushing violence of the crowded battlefield, there was the advantage of thought, and plans made within the blink. To watch while pausing, to sidestep, then slow, then fast.

Walking aside, Plymouth slammed suddenly, the sword edge to Dominic's shoulder. It sliced through his silks, but the cut was shallow. Dominic had already moved, pounding backwards with both axe and knife. Plymouth avoided the attack, laughing, this time bending low to slice his enemy's legs.

In avoidance, although as though dancing, Dominic raised the axe again, hand tight to the hilt, and twisted it high in the air as though proclaiming some victory.

Plymouth followed the sunlit swirl, staring upwards. "What a fool you are, Desford," Plymouth snorted. "Now breathe deep while I slaughter you as you deserve." Yet his gaze remained distorted, half blinded by the golden dazzle of the sun on the axe blade, waiting for its downwards sweep and expected aim. Mouth open in derision, he pointed his sword.

As Dominic swung the axe high, with his other hand he balanced Jetta's small knife blade flat on his palm, and immediately threw it. His aim was known as inevitably perfect. It slammed between Plymouth's open lips, cutting his tongue and shattering a tooth. In shock and horror, the earl collapsed to his knees on the cobbles, tugging the knife from his bleeding mouth. He had dropped his sword, now thick with his own blood. As though paralysed, Plymouth stared, panting, eyes glazed.

Staggering upwards while spitting blood, he grappled Dominic. Within seconds they stood fighting hand to hand. The axe lay on the cobbles, but Desford retained the small knife as the other fist slammed into Plymouth's broken lips, then plunged the knife point into the other man's thick neck. Both spouted blood.

Not seeing his own stream of blood from the deep cut across his forehead, Dominic stood back, looking down. Plymouth lay on his back across the cobbles, gasping for breath.

"It would appear that your reputation as a great fighter is somewhat exaggerated," Dominic said.

With a roar of fury, it was the sheriff who now danced, waving his own sword. But from the crowd, Andrew also stepped forwards, grabbing the small man from behind, wrenching the sword from him.

"One to one, or face arrest," he said mildly, "it is the sheriff of this ward who will deal with this unfortunate situation." He turned as the liveried gentleman marched past the crowd. Andrew ignored the cheering groups, announcing, "Sheriff Mansfield, you are most welcome. We await your decision."

Mansfield marched from shadow to light, a red-haired man, tall and clearly angry. "This is a disgraceful violation of civil liberty," he said. "I am appalled. And just outside the Cathedral."

But Andrew, still holding Kettering, announced in his most imperious voice, "I have been witness to this dreadful situation from the beginning. The Earl of Plymouth abruptly called the Earl of Desford from his business with the lawyer , and challenged him to fight, threatening it would be to the death."

"He's not dead," Dominic pointed down. "Though the fool could do with a doctor."

But Plymouth lay flat on his back, staring up at nothing as he choked on the blood bubbling at his lips.

"He's dying. You slaughtered him," shouted Kettering.

"Self-defence. I also stand witness," Jetta shouted. "Along with the hundred other witnesses here."

The audience still clapped, cheering and shouting.

"And, Master Mansfield," said the lawyer , stepping forwards from his own doorway, "I am also a witness here. The Earl of Desford was discussing business, and the signing of documents with me, as his lawyer. He has been with me for nearly an hour before he was threatened and called out for this unfortunate duel."

"And," Andrew continued, "the so-called Sheriff Kettering, only recently reinstated after having been removed from his post on proof

VESPERS

of corruption, attempted to enter the fight, backing Plymouth after he fell. Corrupt indeed."

Sheriff Mansfield gazed, blotches of scarlet anger beneath his eyes. "As the law in this ward," he announced, "I exonerate the Earl of Desford from any blame. He did not instigate this fight, although it appears that he has been victorious. I herewith accuse the Earl of Plymouth and Sheriff Kettering of all illegal initiation, cause and blame, and hereby arrest Master Kettering, who will immediately be taken to Newgate Gaol by my assistants."

The appearance of the assistants was immediate. Few sheriffs walked alone. They grabbed Kettering from Andrew's grasp and marched him north through the St. Paul's courtyard to Newgate gaol. It was not far. The corrupt sheriff was screaming but his struggles didn't help him. One of the assistants fisted the side of his face, and Kettering flopped into silence.

Bishop Morton had long since slipped away yet Howard Temper, eyes now closed as his breath faded, still lay on the cobbled paving of St. Paul's courtyard. His head was unmoving in a growing puddle of blood, that still leaked from his open mouth, gurgling like the ebbing of the tide. Clearly the small blade had not only sliced lips, gums and tongue, it had then been thrust lower, the minute point now protruding from the neck.

Sheriff Mansfield turned to another of his assistants. "Get a litter at once, and have this gentleman taken to the doctor."

"The fool's more than half dead," one assistant objected. "Not worth paying a doctor to tell me what I know already."

The sheriff turned to Dominic. "My lord, are you injured?"

"One wrist, and barely a graze," Dominic said, wiping blood from his forehead Jetta was now in his arms. "And of no consequence. I thank you for seeing the position correctly, sir, and appreciate your justice." He looked at Andrew. "No doubt someone will inform me in due time whether or not the earl has died or survived."

"You will not be held responsible either way, my lord."

And as Dominic returned to his lawyer's office, the crowd, still laughing and some clapping, slowly dispersed.

"I ain't never seen a fight so good," one man said. "But too quick. I wanted more."

"It seems that earls does it best," said another.

"Sure true," said a third. "Reputations, they was saying at the start. Well, now I reckons we knows."

Dominic sat, Jetta close, staring at the lawyer. He was also out of breath and felt nauseas. "The unexpected," he said softly, "is invariably unpleasant. I admit to being entirely unprepared."

"But didn't spoil your skills, sir," the lawyer beamed.

"We'll be out of the country before Plymouth has any chance of recovering," Jetta whispered.

"I've seen men dying many times," the lawyer said beneath his breath. "I promise you the Earl of Plymouth is as good as dead."

"I hope so. The creature is vile and deserves to die. I rarely welcome the death of others, but perhaps this one I do. Even more, I welcome Kettering slung into Newgate." Dominic nodded. "Fighting so suddenly and without warning is not the most charming way to spend an afternoon." He smiled, quietening the nausea. "Who expects a public fight to the death with a man barely acquainted? The fool hated me for my father's actions. I knew nothing of them, nor of him. Indeed, I still don't. A mystery and a bad one."

"Not the happiest afternoon my love. But achieving long needed results," Jetta added, "makes it a good one. You've no one left to fight."

The lawyer abruptly leaned across the table. "My lord, it seems you're unaware of Plymouth's past."

"Entirely unaware. You know something of him?" Dominic asked.

"A little," the lawyer spoke softly, "and it's no decent tale, sir. Nigh on thirty years past, the earl's father, the first Earl of Plymouth, kidnapped a farm wench for rape and abuse. Once finished with her, he passed her onto his son, the present earl. When the story became known, your father, my lord, challenged the first earl. The farm itself where the stolen girl had worked, belonged to the Desford estate. Therefore, he rescued the poor girl, returned her to her parents, and fought the beast on his own territory."

Dominic stared. "A story I was never told. Tell me now."

"In a battle of hours, it was said, your father killed Plymouth. It had been a fair fight and although King Edward investigated, he announced no fault and no illegality."

"And that infuriated the son. I understand," Dominic murmured.

"Oh, more than that, my lord," continued the lawyer. "It was known that your father was engaged to be wedded to a certain young lady, youngest daughter of a baron. The Plymouth son in utter fury, dragged that same young woman off to his own home. Whether he dishonoured her, I have no idea, but he claimed to have done so. Your father went straight to the king, and Plymouth was arrested. Your father rescued the young woman, your lady mother, and wedded her while Plymouth remained in the Tower for several years."

"But eventually released, swearing he'd one day wreak his vengeance on my father?"

"Exactly, my lord. But once free, Plymouth found that your father had died of natural causes, and your poor mother too. He immediately left the country, changing his allegiance to Lancaster, but shouting that whenever he returned to England, he would find the Desford son and kill him in his father's place."

Very softly, into her cloak's fur collar, Jetta was crying.

Dominic put both arms around her but looked over her shoulder at the lawyer. "I thank you, sir. That was a story I've long needed to know. I'm simply glad now that the family has little chance of continuing."

And Jetta whispered through her tears, "We'll never know all the misery in this world. But at least now we can forget Plymouth. You will, won't you, my darling? We're going to forget all the past and adore the future."

"The earl may live," added the lawyer. "But I shall never tell a soul of your future plans, my lord, nor of where you may be found."

"Otherwise," Dominic said, "I would kill him again."

The lawyer bowed his head, hiding the faint smile. "You'll want no vicious fool following you across the ocean and shouting revenge, sir. It's a foul story, but amongst the old court, many such games have been played out. One man became a lord by capturing and enslaving the local earl's daughter and then wedding her by force."

Jetta sniffed, wiping the tears with her fist. "It seems the elite can be worse than the drunken slum-bred idiots who fall from the tavern and knife each other in the gutters."

"And so many lords gain their titles without honour, as I did," Dominic smiled, "simply because their father supported and fought for his king."

Chapter Forty

"I like the idea," said Andrew.

"I love the idea," said Tyballis. "But sadly, it's not going to happen for us. Though perhaps we can sail over and visit, once you tell us where you are. I've always loved the sound of Italy. But our home's here."

"How's the seat on the council?" Dominic asked.

"After three days, I can hardly be expected to make much of a judgement," Andrew smiled. "But I take no joy in the position. Whether I can discover the faintest authority in such a gathering, I doubt. I would advise the opposite to the other council members, and whether the king would listen to any of us is also doubtful. He listens to his mother. Sometimes he listens to Oxford. I believe he usually listens to Morton. He listens consistently to the relentless fall of coins into his growing wealth. He then trots off, retiring to his study, to count and tally. Whatever I might say will be a faint echo disappearing behind the weight of his purse."

"I shall miss you when we leave," Dominic nodded. "But this is a king I won't miss."

"He's the principal reason for your leaving, I thought?" Andrew said. "And I may feel the same after a few years. I doubt the council will overtake me, and there will certainly be no more espionage. So do I simply play with my children, and grow old peacefully?"

"When have you ever been peaceful, Drew?" Tyballis demanded. "And just how many children are you hoping for? No more than three, I promise you. Perhaps in a couple of years we should go to Flanders and find Edward IV's two boys."

"You plan on starting your own war?" Andrew grinned. "Whatever this Tudor creature has decided, we know those boys to be illegitimate and not lawfully able to inherit the crown."

"More legal than Henry Tudor," muttered Dominic.

Tyballis paused, thinking. "It's hard to accept a new king after loving the previous one," she said. "But this one isn't going to drop dead any day. So unless those two boys turn up, we'll have to get used to this one."

"He's claimed the throne by conquest. Which is legal enough," Dominic sighed. "And if we accept his claim by conquest and forget his title as usurper, then we must also accept his legalisation of Edward's children as being legitimate. Thus the boys are still princes."

"Yet if Henry is now accepted as the true king, any claim from those boys would be as usurpers themselves."

"Or equally – by conquest."

"Which is one of the reasons," Dominic smiled, "I'm leaving Tudor England to her own resources. But not for Flanders. As you already know, Jetta and I are heading for Italy, and she, my silent bride, might explain why."

"But I don't know why," Jetta murmured, "it's as convoluted as the position of this wretched king. I may be Italian. I may not. My mother may be Italian, or perhaps my father, perhaps both and perhaps neither. Does that sound like a valid motive for sailing to Italy?"

"Yes," Tyballis said at once. "I know from my own experience. Finding your own feet is the first step. Then you can put those feet on solid ground and stand firm. But until you find those feet, you're floating and that means you're blown by any insignificant breeze that comes along."

"That's an admirable explanation," Dominic nodded. "I shall try to remember that and use it as my own in the future."

The arrest of Sheriff Kettering and the announcement of his imminent trial aroused little curiosity amongst the people. Only the folk of Chiswick who had hated their sheriff for long years, took enjoyment, and prayed for the right result at trial.

Meanwhile gossip floated with the autumn winds, whispering of the duel almost within the cathedral, two raging earls making little sense as they paraded and flashed their weapons. Many said the Earl of Desford had committed treason by speaking harshly of the new king. Yet he had escaped arrest himself. Others denied that, saying that Dominic had never provoked the attack, was the victor and deserved the win.

Little was said of the Earl of Plymouth. For all the years of Richard III's rule and more, Plymouth had remained abroad. He was little known and not admired.

"Dead and deserves it."

"I heard he's living and planning another fight."

"But I never knowed what he were doing in the first place."

It was shortly after the coronation that Dominic suggested a visit to Abbot Francis. The property of the Desford inheritance had been sold except for the family manor itself, which the earl did not attempt to sell. Only the transfer of funds and the final goodbyes remained before the earl and his countess were ready to leave the country.

The day was cold when Jetta watched Dominic over the breakfast ale jug, swallowed her cheese and bread, and said, "I've been thinking for some time. Now, we haven't any plans today. It's too dismal for staying in but at least it's not raining. How about doing it today?"

Dominic spluttered into his baked eggs. "Sail to Italy?"

"For Abbot Francis. Maybe see Ned on the way back. Perhaps the convent, depending on what the abbot says."

"Tell Benson to call Pip. We'll need the horses saddled within the hour." He smiled. "Unless it rains."

It did not rain.

The small church of St. John of Jerusalem, fronting the tiny monastery, was a dither of flickering candle flames, echoing with the voices of the choir. Five of the monks stood before the alter and sang first in unison and then in turn, first their voices muted but then rich, changing a light religious prayer into the chanting holiness of absolute beauty.

Dominic and Jetta, having brought neither guards nor retinue, did not dismount, but waited alone, listening, outside the church. When the singing eventually sank into silence, they also waited for the bustle of the monks to leave, then tethered their horses and walked quietly into the shimmer of the candles. The abbot sat below the great wooden cross, his eyes closed.

There were no pews and no seats for the church stood as only the glorious front to the monastery, but the blunt spire held a great bronze bell which peeled both at prime and at vespers, and the magical echoes caught in the summer breezes and the winter gales, spilling through windows and doorways, chimneys and treetops.

Once opening his eyes and seeing his visitors, the abbot tottered upwards, smiling widely. Jetta realised perhaps for the first time how elderly her friend had grown, but not too old, she thought, to be her father. A sweet thought perhaps, she decided, however unlikely.

"We have come for information and perhaps advice," Dominic told him, taking the abbot's long fingered and heavily wrinkled hand. "We have questions, sir, and beg for answers."

"It's privacy that's important," Jetta said, squeezing his other hand. "We could sit in the confessional."

Abbot Francesco nodded, "I know why you're here," he said softly. "I understand you are now husband and wife. I would have gladly conducted such a holy union, my friends. But no doubt the desire for privacy also seemed important at such a time. Come with me to my quarters at the back. I shall call for wine."

No candles lit the small room, but two chairs and two stools encircled the centre, and a monk silently brought cups of wine to balance on a small tree stump table.

Dominic lifted his cup. "If you know why we are here," he said, "do you indeed intend answering the questions you've not answered before?"

"Perhaps." The abbot smiled over the rim of his cup. "It was almost twenty-one years ago when a young woman I knew from my church, came to speak secretly with me. I was simply a priest at that time, and sometimes led the prayers in church. This was Rome, just beyond the Vatican State where I knew many of the leading bishops, but I held no power and wanted none. Sadly, the Papacy jostled and fought, much like our new royal court, and it was craft rather than religion which brought holy promotion."

"Our world," smiled Dominic, "has a lot to learn."

"I was born in Firenze," the abbot said. "They claim culture and beauty there, but war is never far."

Jetta leaned forwards, eagerly interrupting. "Where did my mother come from?"

"There are still parts of this story which are forbidden for me to tell," the abbot sighed. "I swore on the holy book and will never break that promise. But there were other parts of the story she told me later when she came the second time to see you while still in Italy, and I am free to tell you that, since I think you should know."

"She was Italian?"

"Your mother was exceedingly young. Her name, Alania Romano, the eldest daughter of a powerful figure in Rome. She had been romanced by a young man with a Spanish background, but who was increasingly important within the Papal State. Your mother was so young, thirteen I believe. When Alania became pregnant, she was cast out by her family and sent to a convent. She was forbidden to return to her home until the child was born and left in the charge of some other house of the Lord."

Jetta whispered, "So I'm the illegitimate daughter of Alania Romano."

"At her request, and generously paid by the family, I brought the young infant to England," the abbot continued. "I can tell you little more except that when your mother came a second time before we left Florence, to pay for my travels across the Middle Sea, she informed me that she had married. She had not married your father, and this new husband knew nothing of her daughter. She knew he would beat her should he ever discover your existence."

"That's a sad story." Dominic took Jetta's arm, kissing her fingers. "Both for you, my little one, and for your mother."

"Anything else I can learn?" Jetta asked. "Does my mother live? If so – where? Could I visit, do you think, just as a friend, to tell her who I am but only in secret of course?"

Dominic nodded to the abbot. "We travel in a month or so," he said, "before the winter storms make sailing uncomfortable. Our aim is to arrive in Italy and to discover more of my wife's past."

"There is a young woman in the convent here," the abbot said, waving his fingers north, "who can tell you more." He grinned suddenly and then laughed, a rare cackle. "I may be an abbot, and one who believes in the truth of my faith. But I like to twist a little sometimes, when I consider it important and no doubt the Lord God's will. I am well aware, my lord, since she confessed it to me, that a good-hearted nun already whispered to you the parts of the story she had once overheard years back."

Dominic nodded, 'She did, sir. But only scraps. Overhearing a tale is rarely an insight to the complete truth."

The abbot smiled, tucking his hands into his opposing sleeves. "Now I can bring you both to meet someone quite different, but who knows more. This noviciate recently travelled from Italy, wishing to escape the rivalries of a particular family known as Borgia, who attempted to marry her off to an elderly gentleman known for his cruelty. But when she first came here, she had many stories to tell. You, my lady, take part in one."

The wine was drunk, a candle was lit, and the darkness of mystery and misery faded.

"We will ride now to the convent," Dominic said, "thank you, from our hearts, for your help."

"It's not a long walk," said the abbot. "I shall come with you."

Dominic gave his mount to the abbot, walking beside him and his wife across the small tufts of countryside and into the great rolling lawns and herb gardens of the convent. The wind whistled through the climbing leaves of beans and peas, the long grass and the short grass, and through the horses' manes.

With their eyes blasted by gales, they dismounted at the convent doors, and rang the bell. As usual, the little barred window slid open.

It was the abbot who stepped forwards. "Open up, my dear," he said as a faintly arrogant demand, "I have business with your young Paoletta, the noviciate, and it is far too cold out here to be kept waiting."

The main doors opened. Inside there was light and warmth, and Jetta, Dominic and the abbot hurried inside. Marching to the main hall, Abbot Francesco waved to his friends to follow him, and quickly found a place by the fire. Candles lit the huge room, but it was the gold and scarlet of the flames that brought back both heat and comfort. They waited only a few moments while watched with curiosity by those also keeping warm, chattering softly.

The noviciate scurried to fetch the girl needed by the abbot. Paoletta was small and dark with big eyes and a cherubic smile.

"Abbot Francesco?"

"Indeed," he told her. "And these are my friends, the Earl of Desford and his countess. She is Jetta Lawson by name, and I believe you know a great deal about her. What I know, I am forbidden to reveal. But what you know, you are free to relate in all its colourful detail. Indeed, by now I presume you know more than I do."

She was staring at Jetta, intrigued. "Perhaps I do, my lord. And am I allowed to tell?"

"That is precisely why we are here," the abbot said softly. "I know half the story and perhaps you know the rest. But I am sworn to secrecy. You are not, for you know the story first-hand. But I doubt we wish to educate the entire convent in such matters. A religious house should, I believe, keep its religion as pure as possible."

"It's too cold to walk the grounds," Paoletta whispered into her starched white headdress.

"You have sheltered places outside?"

Paoletta still whispered, peeping around to make sure she was not overheard. "Only where the gardening tools are kept, but the donkeys live there."

"I have no objection to donkeys," Dominic smiled. "And if there's space enough, I'll bring the horses. At the moment they're tethered outside, expecting to be carried off into the clouds at any moment by these winds."

The small dark noviciate giggled. "Yes. If you don't mind sitting on spades."

"I shall bring one of these stools for my wife," Dominic told her, lifting one under his arm.

The winds were strengthening. The horses, heads down, stood flat against the great stone walls, tails between their legs as they searched for shelter. Dominic took the reins of one and Jetta the other, and they led the frightened animals behind Paoletta as she walked across one of the garden patches, and between a narrow opening in the tall hedge. Immediately there stood a high roofed wooden shed of considerable size, the door shut.

"Here."

She unclipped the door, the horses trotted in swishing their tails with snorted thanks, Dominic set down the stool, and Abbot Francis pushed the door shut behind them.

The wind howled, the walls rattled and shook, the two small donkeys which had been hiding in a corner now shuffled out to rub noses with the horses, and Jetta sat down where she was told. The others found small boxes, tipped them over and sat tenuously. There were smells of donkey faeces, dried herbs in great bunches, sacks of dry earth and others of wet mud, and boxes of picked vegetables trying to ripen. The metal tools were packed in one corner, and these were avoided along with the animals as the wind thumped against the roof and the light ceiling beams threatened to fall.

Jetta murmured, "it's a strange place to hear about who I am."

"Actually," Paoletta shook her head. "It's probably very apt."

"In that case," Dominic said, ignoring certain possibilities, "we should have brought some wine."

Chapter Forty One

"Not an easy story, then?" Jetta shivered.

"It's the people that aren't easy," Paoletta admitted. "The church in Italy and the Vatican in particular are caught up in power games. I came to join a convent in England for this reason, although also because my mother is English."

"But mine isn't?"

"No," Paoletta bent her head to the donkey's soft coat, as though smelling the earthy reality. "Not English. You, my lady, are Italian and Spanish."

"You mentioned wine," the abbot smiled. "I know most of this difficult tale, so I'll miss very little. I shall return to the convent and bring back lubrication."

It was as the abbot left, that Paoletta began to explain. With both her arms around the neck of the smallest donkey, she spoke softly and sometimes with apologies.

"I wasn't born of course, but my father knew the Lady Alania, the eldest daughter of Count Rimasto di Roma, a powerful man of a rich family. Later, as a child, I grew to know the Lady Alania and loved her, and her mother the Contessa Maria di Roma."

"My mother was the daughter, Alania?" Jetta savoured the name. She had never been sure of her own and had certainly never known that of her mother. "And her parents were titled?"

"Yes," the noviciate whispered. "The count was Sebastiano, your grandfather, and Maria was your grandmother. Alania was their eldest daughter and was soon promised as wife to Count Torradino. He was rich and powerful. It would have been known as a good match. But he was fifty-six, while at the time she was thirteen, and he was known to be cruel and had beaten his first wife so often she ran away a hundred times before she died. It was a scandal both regarding the count and his first wife, and then the idea of giving him a wife little more than a child!"

"My mother, – she was thirteen?"

"The scandal simmered throughout Rome, but your grandfather insisted. He needed Torradio's backing for his own ambitions. That was how everything was done and still is. It's why I left and came to my own mother here, and joined this convent."

Dominic leaned back against the moss and mould covered wall, arms crossed over his lap, his legs stretched. He was listening carefully, wishing to remember the details. His horse nudged his knee, but Dominic ignored the interruption. His own plans simmering.

When Abbot Francesco returned with wine and dry biscuits, the story paused, but as they drank, Paoletta continued.

"Your mother was terrified of such a marriage and ran away. Even at that age, she had the money and the intelligence to set herself up as someone else, in a small apartment near the Vatican, and hardly ever went out as she was unaccompanied. She lived some months in fear and isolation."

Almost crying, Jetta tightened her fingers, staring first at Paoletta and then at Dominic. "Is it that horrible in England too? Is that what happens here?"

"It does, amongst the elite," Dominic said. "The royal court is run on superstitions, conspiracies, alliances and hatreds. Richard wasn't in power long enough to eradicate it, most of it being accepted as normal. It was why before he wore the crown, he avoided the court and remained in the north. Those of the south didn't love him for that either."

The young noviciate nodded. "Luckily, I have no entrance to the royal court, nor want one. They certainly wouldn't want me."

"Nor me," Jetta smiled, "even though now I'm a countess. It doesn't feel real at all."

"But you're almost a countess by birth too," Paoletta said. "Although your mother never married your father, and never could have," she added. "I'm sorry to tell you."

"I guessed it and don't care," Jetta said, raising her voice.

Dominic interrupted her. "But I understand that your highly unusual father," he said, still softly, "had other children of unwed mothers, and they have been given titles and marriages of great wealth and importance. And now, my love, whoever your parents were, you are my countess, and my beautiful wife." He kissed her forehead gently.

Paoletta was also smiling. "Even though your mother had only been thirteen, she gave birth without a problem, and she told me that you were born as easily as an almond blossom but far prettier."

Laughing, Dominic reached over and took Jetta's arm, drawing her closer. "Your friend Ned calls you something similar. Such names suit you perfectly, my love."

But Jetta stared at Paoletta. "And my mysterious father?"

"Younger," she answered. "Spanish by birth but came to Italy after negotiations and great work within the church which made him a Cardinal. Now I believe he aims even higher and intends becoming pope. His name is Rodrigo. Rodrigo Borgia."

There was a momentary silence of shock.

"I've heard a great deal of him," murmured Dominic.

But Jetta had not. Too young to understand the whispers of the nuns while living there, nor had the kitchen gossip at the Maddock house enjoyed any direction towards religion. The inner machinations of the church had never touched her. "My father is a cardinal?

VESPERS

My father wants to be pope? How can a man of the church have children? Aren't they all celibate?"

Laughing again, Dominic said, "Some of them manage to stay that way."

For the first time, the abbot spoke loudly. "I can assure you, celibacy has been my constant state. But the twists and turns of the Vatican are also required, you see, to ensure finances and the force of faith. But I was pleased to leave the corruption of Italy and instead travel to England. Still corrupt, but nowhere near that of Rome."

"I shouldn't laugh," Dominic said, although he did. "But I gather that before you left, you'd learned of my wife's past?"

It was the abbot who nodded. "I cannot say much more, as you know. But I can tell you that your mother is a loving and kind woman, who would adore to meet you now, even though your identity should remain a secret between you both. Your father is licentious, craves power and riches, and he's gained all of these over the years. He's known as remarkably intelligent and apart from children, he's capable of great deeds and has already achieved so many in both Spain and Italy. I truly believe he'll make pope at some time."

"My father could be the pope," Jetta was now whispering only to herself.

"I don't know how they met," Paoletta said. "But your mother fell in love with your father, and they had a secret affair. Your father was not a handsome young man, but he's unique and loving. Then when Aliana knew herself with child, she understood her huge problems. She believed that as an important and ambitious member of the clergy, it would be cruel to announce him as the father of her child. Perhaps even more importantly, she feared her own father, and what he would do if he discovered her. So she went into hiding, had the baby, and then passed you to the abbot she had grown to admire as he attended her in the convent hospital."

Nodding cheerfully, Abbot Francesco said, "And it was my idea to increase the protection of both mother and child, by bringing you over here and passing you to another convent."

Jetta didn't add that she had hated the place. "It – it's an amazing story. But sad too. Where's my mother now?"

"Not so sad. The man she was originally supposed to marry had died, luckily just in time," Paoletta said. "And so she was given in marriage to her own second cousin, who is her father's heir since he didn't have sons. He's not dead yet. But when your grandfather dies, your step-father will be Count Rimasto di Roma, and your mother the countess of course. But now you also have a brother, Paolo. Younger than you, of course, my lady."

"But not a full brother."

"No. And your real father has children too, some now becoming extremely powerful. But by different mothers. Or at least, not by yours."

"It seems," Dominic said, "You have both half-sisters and half-brothers, some holding significant power. An interesting situation, my love."

Jetta gulped and turned back to the novice. "And you've met my mother, and you liked her?"

"I loved her."

Jetta turned back to Dominic. "I don't know whether to laugh or cry. And you knew all this already and didn't tell me?"

"I was told a little by one of the nuns," he said, softly again. "She had overheard Abbot Francesco relating this to the abbess at the time, but she heard only a little and remembered less. I certainly didn't know the whole nor any word of your father's identity. And then I was invited to pass a few weeks in the Tower, and could repeat very little, although you, my beloved, had the courage to visit me."

He leaned over the back of a donkey and kissed his wife. "Strange things happen to all of us." The donkey raised its ears and snorted.

"Indeed, all the time," said the abbot. "And now, before she is unfairly disciplined, I must escort this young noviciate back to the convent. She has been of enormous help, and I shall inform the abbess of that, but without explaining why."

One last detail," Jetta stood, taking the young woman's hand. "I've only known myself as Jetta Lawson. Is that my real name?"

Hesitating, Dominic said, "That is something I remember, my dearest, but said nothing. I didn't want to leave you without a name. Your real name is Jetta, given by your mother. But the name Lawson, I believe was invented by the abbot."

And the abbot nodded. "Now I must return this young novice to her proper place," he said, taking her arm.

The larger donkey objected at the departures, rubbing his fur tufted head on the young woman's legs and snorting at Jetta.

Jetta thanked Paoletta, kissing her cheek. "Unlike me, you're going to go through with it. I mean, you'll be a nun soon."

"Yes." She hurried from the shed beside the abbot, waving a last kiss to both Jetta and the donkeys.

"Amazing," Jetta muttered to herself. "I should find a way of thanking that novice."

"She needs no gifts." Dominic laughed. "The Tudor king now knows how the convent supported him in secret, and his mother has donated handsomely. They're becoming the most famous – or infamous depending on your own loyalties in the land. The richest convent as well, I believe. But it's the abbess who gains the most."

"Not Rondella, the one I hated."

"She was less eager to swallow the Tudor politics, and the new abbess got rid of her. At least we know the convent had nothing to do with my incarceration in that damned lime cave, that was purely Plymouth. Some gain. Some lose."

"Not here," Jetta whispered, "but we'll be the ones who gain."

Dominic took Jetta into his arms, gently pressing her head to his shoulder. The warmth of the four animals was also close, but Jetta felt only the strength of her husband's hands on her back. He murmured to her, kissing her cheek, then her fingers, and then back to the other cheek, saying, "My dearest, this cannot be an easy tale to swallow, but it is not so bad. Your father knows nothing of you, though he's a great and powerful man, and has been kind to his other children, accepting them even though not married to their mother. The boy Cesare is already important, I believe, and his daughter Lucrezia too. They carry considerable fame beyond their own country."

"That's intimidating."

'You've no obligation to meet any of them."

She kissed his neck, the only part of him she could reach. "Alright, I'll hide and avoid them all. But you'll call me a coward."

"Then I shall now promise never to do so. But remember, he may become pope. Claiming friendship with a pope would most certainly carry advantages." Dominic's fingers tickled the back of her neck. "Yet even without the knowledge of Borgia being your father, I already knew a good deal concerning him. Borgia himself and those two illegitimate offspring are famous. I have no knowledge of others. And as consolation, we now know your mother is happily married with a son she loves. I believe us happily married, my dearest, and will have children one day if God be willing."

She snuggled tightly to his warmth and caresses. "I'd love to meet her."

"So we travel to Italy while the weather is kind."

"Is November weather so kind?"

He smoothed her hair back from her forehead and kissed her there. "Selling my own properties and keeping the monies safe is already in place as you know." He nibbled the end of her ear, whispering again. "The estate will stay, awaiting our sons. I leave Benson in charge, but the property will be closed and only a fraction of the staff will remain."

"You won't sack the rest? They all fought for us."

Dominic shook his head and kissed both her eyelids. "No. I'll find them positions, or Benson will. Otherwise, they stay. Some will go to Andrew, even Avery. But one day we'll return, my love, and our own home will be waiting for us."

"With half a dozen babies."

He was laughing silently into her hair. "You'd like that many?"

"Perhaps not," Jetta laughed. "I thought just three, but I don't know until the first one. And I promise I won't die in childbirth."

"Forbidden and will never happen. I'm more likely to die of pleasure with my first born in my arms. But I mean to leave this country by mid-November, weather permitting. And that leaves just ten days."

"I can be ready tomorrow."

"I believe I might be a little slower." He was laughing again. "Yet since the Medici family devised a money saving system in Florence, I now have a perfect plan for banking, as they now call it. Ten busy days, little one. And the ship will be waiting at the quay."

It was as the abbot returned that they left, said what was probably a permanent goodbye to Francesco, and rode on to visit Ned.

Ned was working, preparing for winter, bare chested and dripping sweat across the muscles of his upper arms, logs piled beside his cottage. They did not stay long. As they rode down to the river and approached Chiswick, the dusk crept up from the damp grass and down from the misted clouds. A small army of ducks were flying west and squawked from the sky, sharing the gossip as they divided the clouds.

At the same time, Dominic dismounted, stretching out his arms to Jetta. She loved dismounting directly into his embrace. It seemed typical of the type of thing she had imagined being romantic, a positive yearning when she had been locked in the Maddock's house.

They ate supper smiling at each other over the table, half dreaming, half discussing the adventures ahead, the essentials, the possibilities, and the hopeful discovery of Alania, soon to be a countess in her own inherited right.

"I can't stop smiling. I can't breathe slowly. My heartbeat races. Is that usual," she asked, grinning, "during the first months of marriage?"

"They say so." Dominic grinned back over the brim of his wine cup. "But with us, my extremely small cherry blossom, that feeling will be with us for life."

"Glorious." She did not attempt to hide the grin. "A crazy story for a kitchen girl told to scrub the flour from the tiles."

"Forget the past, my little one," Dominic told her, draining his cup. "Your parents are persons of considerable importance, and even though your father has no notion of your existence, who knows – perhaps there will come a time to tell him. But in the meantime, being my wife carries its own title. And I can only hope that being in my arms carries its own sweet thoughts."

"Sweeter than sweet."

"I shall see if I can surpass that compliment tonight."

Jetta blushed, not at Dominic's words but at the thoughts she immediately had herself. "And I'm learning," she whispered.

"Now learn something else, my beloved." He felt her indrawn breath and laughed at her. "You call yourself the scullery maid, and me the lord. Now I trust you've realised how wrong that truly is. You are the daughter of two mighty families."

"But bastard born," she giggled. "You know I don't care about that – but it hardly makes me a princess."

"When I explained how lacking I am in the practises of the elite, did I mention how I fell asleep in church whenever dragged there for early Mass? No one informed me that I snored, but it's possible, I warn you, my love. I may be legitimate, in spite of Plymouth's fabricated stories, but I'm no prince. You'll doubtless overshadow me entirely within the year."

It was the following day when they spoke to Benson at length, rallied the staff and spoke to them all for some time.

"My friend Andrew, Lord Leays, will gladly employ some of you," he told them. "Benson will organise this. Others I hope will remain here. One day I feel sure we'll return. But in the meantime, anyone longing to leave my establishment is certainly free to do so and will be paid a month in advance."

"With a letter of reference," Jetta added.

Dominic also arranged the necessary passage on the comfortable ship bound for Italy by the seventeenth of the month, and organised the transference of their baggage, his own wealth into the Medici Bank, and the payment for a small house in outer Rome, ready for a temporary exploration, love making, and peaceful delight. Never having seen the house, they trusted the word of the agent who bought the property in Dominic's name.

"If we dislike it, we move on," he told Jetta.

"And if we love it, we'll stay."

Dominic was frowning. "I doubt we'll be content as countryside plodders. Moving more directly to Rome may be a better choice. But of course, however grand my estate here, it is in fact a country home. However," and the frown turned to grin, "our Roman dwelling will be considerably smaller. I've no desire to move to the Vatican." He turned frown to grin. "We'll decide our futures once there."

"I don't care. I once lived under a table."

"And once I lived in a cave beside a quarry, and then a cell in the Tower."

"If I mustn't talk of the past," Jetta mumbled, "you mustn't speak of the Tower. We are about to become rich and important."

"We already are, my sweet," he laughed. "But in Italy, it will all be remarkably different."

"Especially getting to know the pope."

"Not the pope yet, but it seems you have interesting brothers and sister."

"Something I never dreamed could happen. Who would ever imagine having a pope as their father?"

"First are the goodbyes," Dominic laughed. "And then the hellos."

"Yes." Jetta's smile dazzled.

Chapter Forty Two

La Bellezza released her moorings and as the wind took her, her sails were unfurled and she left the quay, aiming downstream towards the great Thames estuary.

The Earl of Desford and his countess stood on deck, smiling into the slap of the wind. The crew ran like a maelstrom, rushing to haul in the ropes, reporting to the captain who stood at the raised prow. The triple masted carrack seemed impressive enough to withstand pirates, and stable enough to withstand rough seas with high waves. Even in winter, the Middle Sea was rarely known as a threat except to smaller vessels, but few set sale beyond November.

Leaving the city felt to Jetta as the greatest adventure, and as the waves took hold of the ship's keel, the ship began to heave and roll. At first Jetta lost her footing, clutching at Dominic, who laughed at her, but held her steady as they leaned against the gunwales.

And they saw, briefly, as they left the city docks, the one thing they had not expected. Thumping from the main road behind the docks, marched five royal guards, bright in their scarlet livery, scowling at the departing ship and its passengers. The leader, clutching his hat in the wind, thumped down his staff and banner, shouting, "In the name of his majesty, King Henry, I arrest you, Dominic Stark, second Earl of Desford, for murder and public mayhem and the death of Howard Temper, Earl of Plymouth."

Dominic stared back. The wind had carried those words, even though the ship was ever further from its moorings. He wondered, briefly, if the guards would pull out one of the smaller boats from the shorter quay, and row to *La Bellezza's* towering sides, forcing the arrest of the principal passenger. But, knowing that such a decision would take too long to arrange, he leaned back, removing his identity into the shadows of the main mast and her great double sail.

He looked around at Jetta, who clung to the gunwales, still staring back at the shore. "I didn't know. Thank the heavens above that we left today."

"And are already at sea."

"But did you know? Could you even have guessed?"

Dominic shook his head into the wind, hair in his eyes. "I had no idea. Andrew's goodbye wishes yesterday, were meek enough. So he knew nothing of it either. Indeed, I'd assumed Plymouth was recovering. Damnation, this was never expected, and now I've visions of the prison in the Tower all over again."

"And it's that same damned man getting you in trouble when you're as innocent as a turnip."

"Damned or otherwise," Dominic said softly, watching as the royal guard stood their ground, shouting across the water. "It seems now the creature has died. And it seems as though no one has bothered to check on the witnesses' statements."

"They can't bring us back from Rome?" She moved again into Dominic's protective hold. "The Italians wouldn't let them, surely?"

Dominic was suddenly laughing. "They'd be more likely to arrest the guards for causing riots in their city. I'm safe now, my love. We both are. But we'll delay our return here, perhaps. And while I think of it, I should tell you I feel absolutely nothing like a turnip."

"They'll find the truth by then," Jetta sighed.

"I doubt they'll bother looking," Dominic told her. "But the warrant will fade in a few years. And soon we'll discover whether or not we'll ever want to return."

"Never," Jetta whispered.

The keel had caught the current and the carrack had begun to roll with a greater force. Jetta heaved, never having experienced such a loss of footage before.

"Down we go, my love," Dominic smiled. "We have the cabin below deck where you can lie down and I can kiss you, thinking of my escape from the Tower."

The journey across to the Middle Sea, and onwards to Porto, the port of Rome, took some days and Jetta was permanently on her bed. The cabin was tiny and without window, but the bed was wide enough for two, comfortable and warm. Dominic stayed with her but sometimes climbed on deck, watching the constant work of the crew, on the oars when the wind dropped, furling the sails, climbing the main mast, then pulling back on course as the wind blew up again, veering against their route, each sail adjusted to fill with or against the winds' consistent changes.

They stopped one day at Marseilles on the French coast, collecting more supplies and waiting out the sudden storm. Moored tight to the land, Jetta's nausea lessened. Then, as night came the torrents calmed, Jetta fell back into bed, the crew descended to their ropes and hammocks, the captain to his tiny cabin at the prow, and the three men left awake strode the deck, their turn as lookouts.

The coast of Italy was soft with breezes and the ship sailed on, rocking slowly as her sails flattened. The men once again took to the oars, and Jetta regained her breath.

Then *La Bellezza* was tracking south, following the coast and the sweet smell of leaves still in their autumn colours. An embracing swirl of mild warmth enclosed the ship, blown from the land. It was something Jetta had not expected.

"As we move south," Dominic murmured as he sat on the side of the bed where Jetta still lay, "the weather becomes more gentle. Can you face coming up onto the deck, my love? It may be the last you'll see of a mild blue ocean reflecting a mild blue sky."

The pitch and roll had sunk to a smooth glide as the bow wave tipped and a small flock of gulls sailed over their heads, and beyond the keel a dolphin, and then another, broke the surface of the water as they breached, playing with the ship's rattle and slide.

Clambering up to the sides, clutching the gunwales, Jetta gazed in wonder at the calm waters all around her, the little chatter of the crew as they waited to pull into shore, the ropes already in their hands. The sky sang of sunbeams peeking past the white clouds, avoiding the sea breeze which still gusted from the north, fresh and chilly.

As Porto glided into the far horizon, they saw the spires of churches, the great dark blocks of the warehouses, and the dither and flash of the small boats piloting the great sailing caravels, carracks, and cogs into port, roped to the quay and then the cranes, moving to unload the cargo. The crews had already furled the sails, and were lining up, hoping to disembark into the arms of the groups of waiting women, grand in their low-necked satins, irrelevantly dressed for the possible November gales.

Yet the weather was calm, and Jetta itched to get on shore, to find solid ground beneath her feet, and to see this strange new land and the people shouting in a strange language.

"Bon giorno, piccola," Dominic teased her. "Soon we'll be home. No one waits to arrest us, and our baggage will be delivered directly to our new address. A horse drawn litter will be waiting."

"But I hate litters," mused Jetta. "Your grandmother used to push me onto one and I was nearly as sick as I've been at sea."

"But," Dominic laughed, "since we have no idea where we are going, nor the slightest notion of how to get there, we can hardly ride off alone."

"I wager you'll have a horse," Jetta pulled a face. "You won't come into the litter, you'll just follow it on horseback."

"How did you guess, my sweet? But watch now, we're coming into land."

As the port neared, as though it was the quay which moved rather than themselves, the captain stood tall behind the central mast, shouting in Italian to his crew. Already the pilot was approaching in the little boat, waving up and shouting back, his words equally unintelligible to Jetta.

She stared up at her husband, both of them smiling with the new excitement.

"You understand? But how do you speak Italian?"

"I know Latin, my love. That's the obligatory part of every young gentleman's education. Italian is similar enough to catch the meaning, if not every word. And no doubt, most of the crew speak a dialect."

"I'll learn it all as quickly as possible. At least I can say *yes* and *no*. *Si* and *Non*."

"I wonder," Dominic grinned, "which you'll say most often."

About the Author

My passion is for late English medieval history and this forms the background for my historical fiction. I also have a love of fantasy and the wild freedom of the imagination, with its haunting threads of sadness and the exploration of evil. Although all my books have romantic undertones, I would not class them purely as romances. We all wish to enjoy some romance in our lives, there is also a yearning for adventure, mystery, suspense, friendship and spontaneous experience. My books include all of this and more, but my greatest loves are the beauty of the written word, and the utter fascination of good characterisation. Bringing my characters to life is my principal aim.

For more information on this and other books, or to subscribe for updates, new releases and free downloads, please visit
barbaragaskelldenvil.com

Printed in Great Britain
by Amazon